W9-BGI-096

THE VICAR CHRONICLES

The Mysterious Case
of
Billy's G String

By Punk Sanderson

www.thevicar.com

The Legal Bit.

© TheVicar Ltd 2012,
PO BOX 1533, Salisbury, Wilts, SP5 5ER, UK
The copyright is operated by TheVicar Ltd
on behalf of the writer, with whom it resides.

The writer asserts his moral right (whatever that may be) to
be identified as the author of this work in accordance with
the Copyright, Designs and Patents Act.

First edition
Names, characters, places and incidents featured
in this publication either are the product of the author's
imagination or are used fictitiously.
Any resemblance to actual persons (living or dead) or events,
without satiric intent, is coincidental.

Typesetting by Barry Stock
Thanks to Don, Robert and my family, without whom...
(or 'without who' if we're not being so pedantic)

No part of this publication may be reproduced or
transmitted, in any form or by any means, without
the prior written permission of the copyright owner.
All Rights Reserved

Published by TheVicar Ltd
ISBN 978 1 909019 00 3

You have the author's FULL permission to return this book if it has been made from ANYTHING other than:

1. Recycled used toilet paper.

2. Unsolicited handouts asking you to vote for your favourite soap star.

3. Adverts claiming you can get fit in less than five minutes a day.

4. Books of Paul McCartney's paintings.

5. Old Britney Spears posters.

T HE PUBLISHERS HAVE ASKED ME TO EXPLAIN WHY A SHY and retiring man, like myself, might allow his life to be used as material for a book and TV show. I myself wonder how it could be otherwise. How could a man who pays lip service to lofty notions of Integrity, Justice and Art avoid such a project once it presented itself? There are times when the creative impulse takes us into its confidence and beckons us forward. This is one of those times, and we must trust the process. Or not.

And yet, even as I write this, I realise that these self-same publishers may not like my reasoning. They may prefer to believe in a devious plot, as expounded recently on several websites, that will make me the cruel, heartless, raging venal leader of a Vicarious empire, designed to enhance the sale of Vicar barbie dolls to an unsuspecting public. I reply that, if such a plot involves the flow of unhealthily large sums of money in my direction, I am happy to consider it.

And what of the writing itself. In a post-modern world, there is no one privileged position. I do not always agree with Punk's point of view, but they are his opinions, honourably held, which will, I trust, be received with generosity and goodwill. In over 30 years of jumping in and out of vans, travelling the world, playing and recording music in the most unlikely and inappropriate venues, I have yet to find a book that accurately describes the industry in which I earn my daily crust – an industry which encompasses the very best and very worst of humanity, its excesses, greed, jealousies, capacity for infinite beauty, strange attraction to mind altering substances, big people with big egos and even bigger erections. And that's just the good guys.

Some of Punk's writing may touch on these truths, much of it will not, but I trust it will always be entertaining.

At the time of writing, Punk's simplistic direct prose has yet to be 'moulded' at the hands of an editor. I now realise that this process is to be feared as much as the A & R man at a record label, who loves your album, but suggests you "rework it with different musicians", or that he "cannot promote your album without a single". I therefore have no idea if, when you turn this page, you will be greeted by Punk's six rules, which I love so much, or by a new sanitized beginning. This is a creative process. The outcome is therefore necessarily uncertain. The book, which you hold within your carefully washed and manicured hands, may by now be a bestseller or an abject failure.

That is for the future. We must all begin somewhere, and Punk's initial verbal onslaught awaits you over the page.

The Vicar,

The Vicarage 5th November '10.

The Mysterious Case
of
Billy's G String

God I'm going to hate writing this book! It's hardly very rock'n'roll, is it Punksters? – locked in a tape store by my boss, the legendary (some would say infamous) record producer extraordinaire, The Vicar, to scribble the first of his beloved Chronicles.

Perhaps we'd better set some ground rules before we start:

RULE ONE: *Absolutely* no rewrites. Life's too short.

RULE TWO: *Absolutely* no complaints about my bad grammar and loose tongue. If you want slick, watch TV. If you want real and raw… well you may not get that from me either.

RULE THREE: *Absolutely* some bits of this story are going to be changed and pulled completely out of my arse for legal reasons. There's a difference between telling the truth and spending the rest of your life in jail for libel.

RULE FOUR: *Absolutely* no girly poncey language like in all that chick lit.

Is that enough? OK how about…

RULE FIVE: I don't care if you fart, wipe your nose or spill coffee over yourself while you're reading this, so I reserve the right to do all of them while I'm writing it.

Oh and most importantly

RULE SIX: *Absotively Posilutely* no more tapping away in this Tape Store!

TTFN

☺

PS. Oh yes. In case you missed it, the name's Punk. Punk Sanderson (Or not. Believe what you will).

SIOBHAN
takes a Call

So. CHAPTER ONE. AND OUR STORY BEGINS, AS SO MANY do, with a telephone call. It came at 9.43 pm (my boss, the enigmatic Vicar is very precise about such things) on March the...something (and I'm not). Siobhan, resident angel, dealer in intravenous caffeine and endless cups of Earl Grey tea, looked inquiringly at The Vicar, who shook his head.

"I only take calls from my wife and direct communications from God".

He was growing irritable. I knew the signs. Cigarette burns in the carpet, broken whisky bottles on the floor, cocaine in the sliders on the mixing desk, rubber dolls in the corner of the studio, televisions being thrown out of hotel windows, cars being driven into swimming pools...

No, I jest, Punksters. No such excitement here. Just hard work. And raw nerves. Tempers often get a little frayed at the end of a long recording session. And we were well into the frayed stage.

Siobhan couldn't persuade the person on the phone to go away, and she looked despairingly at The Vicar.

"Will this call make my life richer and better?" he asked,

in that calm, authoritative, slightly teasing manner of his.

"Will it nourish me? Will I look back in years to come and say 'Thank you God' for that call?"

Siobhan knew better than to try to answer such questions. She simply put her hand across the mouthpiece, and waited to see if he would come to the phone.

"And sikerly she hadde a lecherous eye:
 Full small e-pulled were her brows two
 And though were bent and black as any sloo."

"Chaucer. He's in a good mood. He's going to take the call," I whispered under my breath.

Sure enough, he moved over and picked up the phone.

"Hello, Real World Vicarage..."

It was our first time at Real World, the Holy Grail of English recording studios. Peter Gabriel's accountant apparently advised him to spend no more than half a million or so on a studio and he obligingly spent at least ten times that. Well, you know what they say about musicians, "Big Studio, Small ****" (I'm only joking, Peter. Please, don't sue me). There's a great photo of it on their website (the studio, not Peter's ****).

The person on the other end of the phone evidently began by saying "May I disturb you?" or somesuch. Always a mistake.

"It is a little too late for such thoughts now," The Vicar said caustically. "You have, of course, already disturbed me by bringing me to the phone, as you well know."

A pause while the unfortunate victim tried to explain himself.

"Your timing is as impeccable as ever. You could not have chosen a more inconvenient or inopportune time, if it were the result of years of well-focussed practice in the art of making poorly timed phone calls. Which is roughly how you make your living, is it not?"

Another pause as the person presumably wriggled on the other end of the phone.

"I think we know each other well enough to dispense with the formalities. Whoever is paying your bills will thank me for every minute that I save them. What are lawyers charging now. £5 a minute? That means you can probably earn a £1 just by sneezing. "

A longer pause as he listened.

"Well, if you wish to see me in person, you clearly know where my person is to be found. I have been here for," he looked at his watch, "fourteen days, ten hours and," he paused while he did a quick calculation, "three minutes, and expect to be here for a further...7 days and 12 hours. It is a public place. I cannot prevent you from visiting."

Not the answer the caller wanted.

"It is however quite impossible for me to leave and come to London. I have commitments that I must honour. A concept that you would perhaps find difficult to understand..."

"...Come and see me here if you must. I do not even have to consult my diary to know that at two o'clock in the morning, I was planning to be safely tucked up between some fine white starched linen sheets. Another of those little English pleasures gradually being eroded by the contagion of the European Community, with its damn continental *doovetts*."

He loved mispronouncing foreign words.

"Punk and I will simply keep working and await your arrival. I may be a feeble, dribbling wreck by the time you arrive, but that, I fear, is a chance you will have to take."

He handed the phone back to Siobhan, who stood still

as if awaiting her punishment. He enjoyed her discomfort.

So did I. I am not one to derive much pleasure in the pain of others (unless, of course, it's the Welsh Rugby team) but I had not put up with years of tongue lashings from the Vicar, to allow her to get away scot-free with the near mortal sin of allowing someone to disturb him while he was working.

"Ah yes. The lovely Siobhan, who recommended that I take the call. What is to be done with you?" He looked her in the eye, and then slowly bowed, as if greeting a princess.

"In her is great beauty without vanity
Virtue guides her every action."

More Chaucer, I shouldn't wonder. How the hell did she get away with it?! I would have been crucified for interrupting a session like that. Remind me to invest in a pair of big tits.

"Thank you, Siobhan. You were right to insist that I took that call. At one of my seminars, we would describe it as a pointed stick."

She stared blankly back.

"We should be thankful for the interruption from Mr Big," he pretended to spit on the floor, "in the same way we should be thankful for the sound of a baby crying on a sunny afternoon. Even if you have to give it a good poke to get it going! It pisses you off, but it also wakes you up and helps you to concentrate on the task at hand. Just as we shall now concentrate on Diva's backing vocals."

Which is exactly what he did.

You can tell from this somewhat bizarre lecture that The Vicar neither has, nor will ever have, any children. He is inclined to treat them a little like dogs – something to be patted and kept on a leash. Nor has he ever had a real pointed stick shoved up his arse. Although I have often been sorely tempted, especially at moments like this, when he insisted on swatting aside all my attempts to probe him about the phone call, while giving his full concentration to getting the perfect performance from Diva.

Are you interested in The Vicar's production techniques? Probably, but this isn't the time. The main thing is that he is famous (and very well paid) for the speed at which he works – painting in what he calls 'broad brush strokes'. "Impatience is a virtue," as he likes to tell me. Even so, it seemed a long while before he and Diva took a break, and he swivelled his chair round to face me.

"Well, who was it?" I asked, "Come on. Who was on the phone? You are going to tell me, aren't you?"

❝THE MYSTERY CALLER? WHO WAS IT THEN?" I ASKED AGAIN.

"Who was what *then*?" He disapproved of my abuse of his beloved English language.

"The telephone call?" I reminded him.

"Oh yes. The mysterious telephone call." He smiled at me. "It was Richard Branson."

"Richard Branson?!" I gasped. "And he is driving down to meet with you at two o'clock in the morning?!"

"No. Sorry, Richard B-r-e-a-m-o-r-e." He spelled out the surname. "I always get the two confused."

Richard Breamore. (Probably not a name you'd recognize. But then after all, Punksters, how many of you would recognize the names of the managers of Robbie Williams, Michael Jacksick or the fallen Madonna with the big boobies? And they are big, powerful people. Trust me. In my pitiful world, this was a big deal).

"But isn't he the guy…" I tried not to get excited. "Isn't he the manager who created that band with those two girls." I made a pathetic attempt to hide the fact that I had a room full of their CDs, posters and blow up memorabilia. "Oh, you know…TITS 'N' ARSE!"

(Under RULE THREE, you'll remember, I reserve the right to invent names to protect my own sorry arse from being sued by, in this case, a fairly big famous band. So guess what. This is a name I just invented. Welcome to Punk's new R&B act – Tits 'n' Arse).

"And does he want you to produce one of their records?" I asked, trying to hide my excitement. "It's not the sort of thing that you normally handle."

"And what exactly, pray tell, is the sort of thing that I normally handle? I trust you are not trying to pigeonhole me."

I avoided the question completely.

"Well does he?"

"Well does he what?"

"Does he want you to produce them?" I asked again.

"I very much doubt it," he said. "If I did make a record for him, he would almost certainly not like the result and would conspire to prevent its release. Not unlike the album I made for Andy S****. Have I told you that story?"

I found myself shaking my head, no.

Why did I do that? I had heard that story several times before. The Vicar has that effect on you. I knew he wanted to tell the story, and wasn't strong enough to simply nod my head, and tell him that I had heard it already. What a limp dick! I hear you thinking. Is this a man or a mouse? I feel my manhood shrinking even as I write this.

"Fascinating!" I lied as he eventually finished his tale and looked at me to see my reaction. It suddenly occurred to me that he *knew* that I'd heard it already. Was he laughing at me, wondering how many times I would be willing to sit through the same story, before I finally mustered the courage to tell him that I had suffered it before?!

"So. Er. What was the call about then?" I muttered, putting such disturbing thoughts to the back of my mind.

"Just a social visit," he teased, unhelpfully.

"At two o'clock in the morning?!"

"And why should not two old enemies take a night cap together?" He was smiling.

"I didn't know that you knew him."

"There is much that you do not know, my fine fellow. You evidently did not know that I had produced a record for Andy S***. Richard and his R&B management company bought out my infamous former manager Malvolio," he lent over and pretended to spit on the floor, "who I believe you met in Amsterdam some seven years ago, when I handed him over for insurance fraud. Did I ever tell you that Malvolio and I shared a room at Cambridge?"

"Oh come on …" I started.

"But you want to know about Breamore. And I am afraid that I cannot satisfy your rampant curiosity as I have absolutely no idea why he is so anxious to see me. Unless to pay me my overdue publishing royalties. Apparently something happened tonight when Billy G was on the television. That is all I know. All will no doubt be revealed at the right time."

And with that he got up and stretched himself out on the studio floor to meditate.

You'll get used to The Vicar's various obsessions – such as the fact that he never wastes time.

I, of course, could waste time for England – playing pocket billiards, admiring my face being distorted in the windows on the tube, staring at the porn magazines on the top shelf of the newsagents while pretending to look at the music magazines, watching the other people who are also assessing the same porn magazines while pretending to look at the same music magazines, and any number of mediocre witticisms which I can't think of right now.

But even I couldn't manage the next hour or so without some support.

Fortunately, Siobhan offered the perfect, rounded, curvaceous solution.

And when the studio door opened and in walked Mr Richard Breamore, he disturbed nothing less than the last throes of my mad passionate fucktacular lovemaking with such a solution.

A bottle of brandy.

"Is David here?" he bellowed, with a look that reduced me instantly to the role of talking doormat.

I pointed over my shoulder to the space behind the FX racks, where The Vicar was stretched out. He rose from behind them almost like a magician appearing out of thin air.

"Richard the B. It has been a long while. A pity it could not have been a bit longer.

I told Punk that you were coming for a nightcap. He would seem to have started without you. I think he had designs on both that expensive brandy bottle, and also the adorable, divine, sensual but even more expensive form of Siobhan. Between you and me, I think that he has only been fifty percent successful."

"I don't have time, David. Did you see the National lottery tonight?" Breamore was all business.

"No, I cannot say that I find the lottery very enthralling. Not much chance of winning, you see. Even with God on my side. Small problem of not buying a ticket. And I do not entirely approve of that presenter, Anthea Whoever. Call me old fashioned, but I do feel that celebrities should set a moral example".

"You were always high on your morality. And low on your wealth," he bragged. "And I am afraid you are years out of date. Anthea Turner resigned long ago. But let's skip the discussion on the poor man's stock exchange. Billy G performed live on the show tonight".

Billy G, for those who don't have my extensive background knowledge, had recently left Tits 'N' Arse, to pursue a solo career.

"Billy G?" The Vicar raised his eyebrows. "It surprises me that she would appear on the lottery. Is she not the self same lady who has been filling the tabloids with campaigns to bring back live music and to ban lip syncing on television. A most worthy cause."

"Yes," Breamore nodded wearily.

"And is not the National Lottery *mimed*?" The Vicar made it sound like a mock swear word.

"Yes," Breamore continued patiently. "This slot became free at the last minute, and I persuaded her that it was critical to her solo career that she should appear on it. It's prime time TV. Millions of viewers,"

"So you gave her millions of reasons to swallow her scruples, and she did."

"Always the philosopher. I must get on. I need to get back to London shortly. I have a video of the show here. Have you a player somewhere?"

We watched it in The Vicar's room.

What could have troubled Breamore so much as to bring him to Real World at two o'clock in the morning? The performance was bound to be note perfect, as she was just miming on top of the CD. The camera angles chopped and changed and swirled around in what seemed a pretty standard British Broadcorping Castration sort of way. Made her look pretty lick-a licious. I wouldn't mind the chance to work on her, if you know what I mean. Great song. Great performance.

Until it all went wrong.

THE *Vicar*
LicensED to Thrill

THE VICAR, BREAMORE AND I WERE WATCHING BILLY G's performance at the lottery in The Vicar's bedroom. And we soon discovered why Breamore was so distressed. The first two verses were perfect (they had to be. After all she was miming). But at the beginning of the third verse she got the words muddled. It looked ridiculous. Her lips were saying one thing, while the sound did something different. There was a short instrumental break, during which she whirled and twirled, and then she sang again. It was unbelievable. She still hadn't remembered the words. In fact, her body movements were now completely out of time with the track. It was like a comedy of errors. How to make a complete idiot of yourself live in front of 10 million viewers. Breamore paused the video.

The Vicar spoke first.

"A complete public relations success I should say. Congratulations. That will certainly bring the question of lip syncing to the public attention. I am not sure, however, that it will be exactly good publicity for her. A selfless act of professional suicide."

"You're not suggesting that she did it on purpose?"

Breamore was appalled at the idea.

"No professional singer can get a song they have rehearsed that wrong. She must have done it on purpose".

"As usual you have not entirely grasped the point. She did not forget the song. It was the backing track that was wrong, not her. Someone altered the backing track."

"Are you suggesting that while la prima donna was singing, the track veered off into previously uncharted territories?"

The thought was appalling. Imagine singing live in front of 10 million people, when suddenly someone alters the music you are singing to. It would be enough to give you stage fright for the rest of your life.

"Was she singing to a CD or a DAT?" The Vicar asked.

A DAT, for those unfamiliar with recording technology, is a Digital Audio Tape, once popular with studios for storing their musical masterpieces.

"A CD," Breamore wheezed.

He pulled the offending item out of his briefcase and handed it to him.

"I am not quite sure that we should be handling this." The Vicar chuckled. "If you are suggesting that there has been some sort of deliberate crime, then presumably this is a matter for the police. I am not sure what the crime would be. Something like making the National Lottery almost watchable?"

"I am pleased that you find things so amusing!" Breamore puffed his nostrils, and snorted like a thoroughbred race-horse. "I regard it with the utmost seriousness. As Billy G's manager I have a duty to protect her from anything like this".

"Not to mention the fact that it was you that encouraged her to appear on the show in the first place, and that if her sales drop, you may not be able to afford that chauffeur. Or your golden reputation might be tarnished. It might even damage your chances of getting a knighthood."

Breamore stared at The Vicar. He was clearly not accustomed to being spoken to in this manner. I couldn't take my eyes from them as they stared each other down. It was better than watching a boxing match. Some cable channel should have Breamore versus The Vicar on pay per view.

"I came here in the hope that you might be willing to help me."

The moment of surrender. This was probably as close to pleading as a man like Breamore ever gets. Hey, if this was WWE wrestling, by my reckoning, Breamore had now been choke slammed and was banging on the mat.

The Vicar played the merciful conqueror. He drew up a chair and offered one to Breamore.

"I am intrigued. Given our previous history, why on earth would you suppose that I would help you? And what exactly do you think that I can do for you? Always supposing that I am willing."

"You have something of a reputation." Breamore shuffled in his seat. "As I should know having been on the receiving end of your skills in the past."

He laughed nervously at his own joke.

"I hope, as two gentlemen, we can set that aside. I am sure you will agree that I have eaten my fair share of humble pie by being here at all."

This comment seemed to invite a friendly reply from The Vicar, but none was forthcoming, so Breamore continued. "I can recall reading in Music Week of several other cases where you have triumphed. There was one only recently, about that Argentinian band you were producing, whose record label was deliberately trying to bury their releases."

He looked up at the Vicar, who still sat there silently.

"Would it help if I told you that until his recent problems, Melville – Malvolio as you so cruelly call him – was convinced that you were the most brilliant man he had ever met?" Breamore tried as a last throw of the dice.

"Indeed it might," The Vicar said, breaking his silence. "Flattery will get you everywhere, as you well know. And you are generous to have taken an interest in my career, if not in the music that I produce."

He seemed extremely amused by the whole thing.

"So you have come here to hire James Bond. Licensed to kill with a DAT machine and a roll of AMPEX tape. All very wonderful. You seem to overlook the fact that the affairs referred to in those Music Week articles concerned poor downtrodden musicians who were being maltreated by large greedy record companies. I suspect that if there were to be a civil war in the record business, I would be fighting against you rather than with you."

"Why do you insist on seeing this business as a conflict. Is it not a partnership between management and the musicians?"

I think the question was meant to be rhetori-thingy, you know, one that doesn't need an answer. But The Vicar would never let something like that go.

"A partnership in which the management gets rich, and ends up owning everything, including the music written by the musicians, while the musicians do all the work."

"Can we not save this argument for another day?" Breamore held up his hands as if surrendering. "We shall agree to differ. Billy G is a musician, who can benefit from your help."

"I am sure that the police would serve you better. Although this is close to the most exciting offer I have ever had. I have never been hired as a trouble shooter before."

I could see that The Vicar was tempted by the idea.

"Nor would you be now!" Breamore snorted. "You would come on board as part of her crew. Only, hopefully, while you are there, you can apply that bright little mind of yours to the problem of preventing anything like this happening again."

"Does Billy G need a record producer? Best beware. We might make strange music together."

"No. She does not need a record producer, and I would not let you within a mile of her recordings. She does, however, need a sound engineer to go with her on tour. It begins at the Sun Plaza in Japan in three weeks time. Although we would of course need you to start tomorrow."

"Good God, Richard, you are just as absurd as ever. You come here in the middle of the night, bringing me all your problems, expecting me to drop everything and come at the snap of your fingers. You forget that I have an album to finish. Which I fully expect to take me another week." The Vicar pulled Breamore's chair away.

"Not content with that, you then insult me, by offering me the post of *sound engineer.*"

He made the word sound disgusting, as if he had just trodden on a dog turd.

"Simple souls like Punk here do *sound engineering.* We producers concern ourselves with loftier matters."

Breamore was doing his best to resist The Vicar's attempts to force him out of the room.

"When my album is finished, and assuming that my little wife is willing to humour me, I may come and see what can be done for Miss G. But now..."

He had finally wrestled Breamore as far the door,

"...Goodnight. You have a chauffeur to catch, and I have a duty to ruffle my sheets before getting up again, as otherwise the chambermaid will be out of a job. If I accept your offer, my office will be in touch with you to discuss a suitably ruinous fee for my services. I am sure I can endeavour to be the most expensive *sound engineer* you have ever hired."

And with that, Breamore and I found ourselves standing side by side on the landing, as he calmly but forcefully closed the door behind us, making a loud show of turning the key in the lock.

And that is how it all began.

The Vicar was as good as his word. For the next week, he put the excitement about Billy G out of his mind. Even at meal times, he never discussed anything other than the current album. Which was some feat, as supper at Real World is a complete gossipfest. Where else would I get to sit down and gossip with the likes of Peter Gabriel, Sting, or the gorgeous Diva? (the first victim for my newly planned, less than a few seconds old, 'indiscretions videos' – dodgy footage of big-time stars, available from my website www. bigfuckingpipedreams.com. I have this great picture of a blob of mayonnaise escaping from her sandwich and landing unceremoniously on the side of her face. If you like that sort of thing.)

And everyone at the table had only one subject of conversation – Billy G's performance, or lack of it. When asked, The Vicar would simply say "Tabloid tittle tattle". And Tabloid tittle tattle it certainly was. They were universal in their condemnation of her. You can imagine the sort of thing: *'Billy gets Lippy and Don't she look Silly'* – front page of the Daily Whatever.

From the amount of brandy I drank, I might have thought that the whole meeting with Breamore was a dream, were it not for some notes that I found on the back of a studio track list. They were written in The Vicar's immaculate hand writing, and no doubt deliberately left where I would find them. They read:

Who gains
– other acts?
Revenge
– ex record company?
– ex publisher?
– other band members?
– loony fans?

And then in large underlined writing across the bottom, he had added

"WHY NOT THE POLICE?"

CHAPTER TWO

Well, now I know why books have chapters – so that the writer can get up and have a toilet break (and yes, I did wash my hands afterwards). I thought that completing the first chapter would be a triumph. Far from it, The Vicar was upset! I have apparently made the whole thing sound rather like some sort of spy thriller. "Richard Breamore did not really come down and hire the Vicar as a private eye".

Well, of course he frigging didn't, but I am trying to turn this into a whodunnit. Isn't that what I'm meant to do? Read my lips: Rule One: Absolutely no rewriting. There's less than ten days before we get on a plane to Cannes to meet with some literary agent from America, and I've got to have at least five chapters of this story finished.

While I'm here, I have just realised that I've forgotten to mention the final morning at Real World. Now hey. It may have nothing to do with the plot, but nothing is going to make me miss that out. That was the day when I ceased to be simple Punk Sanderson, and became PUNK SANDERSON, THE NAKED ASSISTANT. With capital letters. It was like this. I invite Siobhan through to the studio to look at my videos. We have a drink and then…well then, I can't remember a damn thing. But, believe me, anyone at Real World will tell you about the day when Punk Sanderson woke up stark naked on the studio floor with his manhood under threat from an industrial strength vacuum cleaner and his memory completely obliterated.

Now I'd love to claim that the cleaner was waking me up after a night of great sex with Siobhan, but who knows. I certainly don't. And Siobhan claims she doesn't, although I have my suspicions. I know something went on. I smelt my whatsit and…well never you mind. Let's just say that was the night I got to live the rock n roll life.

It was also unfortunately the night that someone nicked the Vicar's video camera. So whatever happened, it cost me over five hundred quid. And if I can't remember it, it can't altogether have been worth it.

On the good side, the video of Diva wasn't in the camera, so I've still got that. www.bigfuckingpipedreams.com lives to fight another day.

Onwards and upwards I say. Or downwards, in fact, towards the next paragraph.

TTFN

☺

The
Naked
ASSISTaNT

WE LEFT REAL WORLD ABOUT A WEEK AFTER THAT
first meeting with Breamore. The Vicar had spoken
with his wife and apparently got approval for an "extended
holiday" working with Billy G. I could rant away about the
Vicar's mysterious wife, but now is not the time. We went
up to London, in The Vicar's horribly boring, very sensible,
elderly Volvo estate, to stay on his boat, The Betsy – a large,
very unsensible, 38 foot concrete monstrosity that he built
himself, long before I knew him.

"See if you can take the CD that Billy G mimed to on the
National lottery and load it into the digital editor, without
losing your underpants," he joked, once we were on board
(I was getting tired of the jokes about naked engineers). "It's
bad enough having your face exposed every day, without
adding the dubious pleasures of your groin".

I took the CD and recorded it into his computer. The
waveform of the music came up on the screen.

"It is most unlikely that this will tell us anything," he
warned. "It would be a simple matter for anyone to buy
the single, load it into a computer and simply switch the
song around on a digital editor. I imagine virtually anyone

with a home studio could have done it."

After the fake CD, I loaded in a copy of Billy G's real CD. My guilt had got the better of me, and I'd 'fessed up to the fact that I already owned a copy. In fact, who am I trying to kid, I had four, with different covers, plus the exclusive remix from iTunes. Not the sort of thing to admit to down the pub, where I'm more of Muse and the Kaiser Chiefs, with some of the godfathers like the Jam thrown in for good measure. But she hails from Manchester (always a good thing), makes great music, and, well, that poster of her with the python. If I wasn't such a calm, sensible, restrained individual, I would have that nailed to the ceiling above my bed.

But perhaps this isn't the time for my private obsessions.

"Let us see how we are doing, my dear Punk." The Vicar took the mouse from me and looked at the two versions of the song that were now laid out one above the other on his 20 inch flat screen monitor. "All of these bits are absolutely identical."

He slowly scrolled through the song, starting with the introduction, and then the first two verses.

"Exactly the same. The beautiful voice of your beloved Billy G warbling away as nature intended." He pointed to the waveform of the real CD, which filled the top of the screen, and the fake CD, which I had aligned perfectly underneath. "Identical. Someone has simply taken the real CD and copied it. Careful. I think your socks are trying to escape. Your clothes are trying to get away again."

He carried on scrolling through the song, until he came to a point where the two waveforms were different.

"And this is where they started to alter the song."

He double clicked on the version of the song at the top of the screen, and the music started to play. Billy G was singing the third verse of her song.

'Little girl cried herself to sleep'

He stopped the music, and double clicked at the same point on the fake version on the bottom of the screen. Rather than the third verse, she was singing the first verse.

'Little boy walking in the park'

"Hardly the work of a criminal mastermind," he chuckled. "That will be the point where her luscious lips became rather less than synchronous on the Lottery. They have simply taken the first verse, and put it where the third verse should be. As easy as moving a paragraph around in a word processor. So let us try."

The Vicar may love playing with his computer, but he is nowhere near as quick as I am.

"That's my jo…"

He slapped me away, and I twitched silently as he took an ice age to perform the ten second task of copying their edit.

"Good!" He sat back, proudly. "My edited version of that verse is now just the same as theirs. What other delights await us, I wonder? Is there to be nothing more challenging?"

He carried on listening to the fake version. Where I expected the third chorus, Billy G was singing the words of the first chorus.

"They've put…"

"And finally they have messed it around by switching the choruses at the end." He smiled smugly at his own brilliance. "So let us do the same."

He slowly made the edit, saying quietly to himself "Eternity is a dreadful thought. I mean, Mr Stoppard, when is it going to end?" (Quite appropriate given the speed of his editing).

As he finished his eyes lit up with that demonic look of his.

"Finally, my naked assistant, we have something to attract our interest." He hurled a triumphant fist into the air. "My edit, perfect though it is, does not match theirs. The mellifluous tones of Miss G are the same, but the backing music is different. Do those words happen anywhere else in the song?"

I read through the lyrics, which were printed in the CD booklet. *Don't Touch What You Can't Afford,* Words and Music by Edward Broom.

"No, definitely not. The words to the chorus change every time. Why?"

"Because if you are right, my fine friend, then the number of possible suspects has been cut from just about everyone in the known universe to a very much smaller, more identifiable group."

"And you can tell all that just from the editor?"

"Let me enlighten you. On the real CD, Billy G can be heard singing these words only once. In the first chorus, over the sparse empty backing. Correct?"

Yes, I nodded.

"On the fake CD, they have reused those words at the end of the song to confuse her, but the backing music is totally different. To do that you would need access to the multitrack tapes of the song. You would have to obtain a recording of her voice on its own, and then recombine it with the music. We have therefore in a matter of five minutes reduced the possible suspects from any Tom, Dick, or Harry who, like your good self, was misguided enough to purchase a copy of the CD, to a very much smaller band of people who, unlike yourself, would have had access to the original tapes. We have, in fact, successfully eliminated you from our enquiries. A good thing too, as I am not sure that I would have been willing to put up bail for you."

He smiled in a self satisfied way and lent back in his chair. I almost thought he was going to put his feet up on the table.

"No, I suspect that you and all her other fans are in the clear, and that this will prove to be what your TV detectives would call 'an inside job'."

He wiped the table with his hand.

"All this and we have not even had time to sample that excellent pot of Earl Grey tea that I have skillfully prepared in a warmed pot, with fine bone china cups. Shall I play mother?" he asked, picking up the teapot.

A FTER OUR DISCOVERY ABOUT THE CD, THE VICAR WAS impatient to visit the studio where Billy G recorded – although not sufficiently to hurry his beloved Earl Grey. I, too, was excited at the chance of meeting her. Before leaving, The Vicar muttered something about petty rock stars always having ridiculous security, and spent a few minutes downloading an image from her website, and playing around in one of the graphics programs on his computer. He took the results off his printer, and hustled me off The Betsy.

It was one of those times (those very frequent times) when I hated the Vicarmobile, and wished that he owned any one of a number of perfectly satisfactory sports cars, so that we could have arrived in something resembling style. What makes it worse is the fact that he always asks me to drive, so I look like a bloody chauffeur. He had some calls to make, and he would never dream of using his mobile phone while driving.

He sat in the back seat with his phone, Filofax and Palm pilot. Everything but his laptop, which was being mended, for reasons we don't need to go into. He loves mobile gadgets, particularly ones that store phone numbers. I think he even has a credit card with phone numbers in it. Out of his clutch bag, he brought the sheet of paper that I had seen at Real World. He looked it over, and then read aloud what he had written across the bottom

"Why not the Police?"

and then again more slowly

"Why...not...the...Police?"

He thought for awhile, during which time I manoeuvred us safely along Old Kent Road (street name supplied at random) before turning into (yes, you Monopoly players guessed it) Whitechapel Road. He looked up a number in his filofax. I learned later that it was 'Angela Barnett', a columnist with the Financial Times. *(In real life 'Angela' was actually a man, but there seem to be so few women in this book that I thought I had better give him a quick sex change. I hope his wife doesn't mind.)*

"Hello Angela, The Vicar here."

I am not sure if the voice at the other end knew who he was.

"We met over lunch at Sir Edward Heath's many moons ago."

Well, if you have to drop names, I suppose saying that you met over lunch with a former Prime Minister pretty much comes top of the list.

"Yes...Fabulous view. I remember Sir Edward saying that he had been told that it is one of the top ten views in the country. And his reply was that he could not imagine what the other nine could be."

The Vicar put his hand over the receiver and told me.

"Edward Heath's house overlooked Salisbury cathedral.

Breathtaking!"

He returned to the conversation.

"Angela. A favour, if I may. A simple financial query."

He asked her advice on some Lloyds insurance funds he was interested in, gave her his email address, and then rang off.

It was difficult to see what that conversation had to do with Billy G, if anything.

He looked up to see where we were, and then went back to his list. He went to the very top, where he had written '*Who gains?*'

"So who gains, Punk?" he asked me. "The other members of her band? If you could keep hold of your own slightly soiled underpants and were less interested in the inside of Billy G's knickers, who would you be buying?"

"I'm sorry, Bishop. I absotively posilutely fail to drift your catch?" I said obscurely.

"If Billy G stopped making records, who benefits?" he repeated.

"Emma B, of course. It's been in all the papers."

I shall spare you the ritual argument about the newspapers which followed. I, as always, stoutly defended the right of the working man to have ever larger breasted topless girls on page three, and articles explaining how to eat my way to multiple orgasms, while the Vicar espoused the quality of his beloved FT, which doesn't even have sports pages. I ask you.

"Well, which of us knows about the rivalry between Emma B and Billy G?!" I said finally, pleased to have won the day.

"Ah! but did this insightful journalism, written entirely in words of less than one syllable, wonder if it might not be a manufactured rivalry? Even Punk Sanderson must know that those apparently great rivals, the Beatles and the Rolling Stones, used to secretly co ordinate their releases to ensure that they did not coincide?"

I, as ever, remained resolutely ignorant of any fact more than twenty years old.

"Your modern day battle of the alphabet girls is no doubt equally phoney. But a little analysis of their sales figures might prove fruitful. Careful that truck is stopping!"

I dumped the Vicar's mobile office unceremoniously onto the floor.

We had been in the car forty minutes and had only just reached...The Angel Islington.

"Time for you to follow your roadies' instincts, my dear boy. Follow your nose towards the river. I'll see if Sean Fitzpatrick can give us some sales figures."

He kept Sean's number in his watch, and in my mirror, I could see him pushing a button on his watch scrolling through to the right number.

"Sean. How wonderful. A small favour, if I may."

Sean. Sean. Sean. What can I say? Well, firstly, of course, that his name is not Sean. I shall probably have to buy him several pints and a couple of hundred Rothmans to apologize to him for giving him such a lame new name, but 'Sean Fitzpatrick' was the best Irish name I could do on the spur of the moment. A total character, he has worked with The Vicar for years – 'A&R hero and frequent saviour of my vegetarian bacon'. Sean, as he shall forever more be known, had a brief career as an excellent, but penniless, musician, before he noticed that even the successful rock stars only had a couple of swanky sports cars, while record label executives owned entire racing teams. Or in Richard

Branson's case, a whole airline. He therefore promptly did the 'poacher-turned-gamekeeper' switch, and went to work for a record label, gaining the obligatory expense accounts and limited edition sports cars along the way.

There is no such thing as a quick conversation with Sean.

The Vicar held the receiver away from his ear, and I could hear Sean mouthing off in his thick Irish accent.

"It's *fucking* ridiculous! You waste your day playing *fucking* power games with the *fucking* accountants. What the *fuck* do they know? Have they had three *fucking* million selling records in the last year? All they have to do is sign the *fucking* piece of paper and they will make more *fucking* money than even they can *fucking* add up. And I get to make a *fucking* great record. But no. None of them are willing to make a *fucking* decision. They just shove it further and further up the *fucking* food chain. I might as well not bother and just go straight to the *fucking* top myself. No one else has got any *fucking* balls at all."

The Vicar smiled as Sean vented his fury.

"Acts of heroism, Sean. Supreme acts of heroism. Without you, there would be no hope for any of them."

Sean continued regardless.

"It's all so *fucking* stupid. We all know we're going to make the *fucking* record. This business could be such fun if we could just cut the *fucking* crap."

"The music business is unfortunately more concerned with business than it is with music. We all need challenges. And yours is to make the suits do the right thing despite their complete inability to know what is good for them, even when it is staring them in the face."

Sean was slowly cooling off. It must finally have occurred

to him to ask why the Vicar had called.

"An insignificant trifle, Sean. I am almost embarrassed to ask you to concern yourself with such a trivial matter. I need some soundscan figures. UK sales figures for the last couple of months, and then the sales for the next couple of weeks as they come in."

"You can? You are too kind. I would need them for both Emma B and Billy G."

Sean obviously had a lot to say about Billy G. Again The Vicar held the receiver away from his head.

"It's going to *fucking* kill her. I was laughing so *fucking* much, there were tears rolling down my cheeks. You could imagine some bastard changing her song lyrics on the autocue and putting up the story of the Flopsy *fucking* Bunnies or something..."

"You are probably right," The Vicar said, when Sean finally ran out of steam. "If you can please email the figures as soon as you have them. I shall be forever in your debt. As I already am."

That should have been the end of the conversation, but Sean obviously had more to say. I saw the smile on the Vicar's face start to fade.

"You have no idea what you are asking, Sean." He made a display of shaking himself as if he had a chill. "This is more than a simple favour. Even the thought of it brings me out in a cold sweat."

He listened as Sean said something further.

"This is something that I would rather you did not ask of me. I have not so much as set foot in 'The Place We Do Not Talk About' for seven years. You have no idea what would be involved. There would be all manner of aggravation and complications."

He sat silently and then drew a deep breath.

"If you can find no other solution, I will agree. I do business with people, not companies. I will do it as a personal favour for you. But I would ask you to please try your damnedest to find an alternative."

He rang off just as we approached the river.

"A live radio show for the Glamour Twins. Broadcast from Malvolio's office. We go as far as despair and then say 'Lord have mercy'".

He turned his thoughts back to the journey.

"Turn left along the embankment, and we are nearly there," he commanded, winding down the window, and blowing an imaginary cloud off the palm of his hand. "Let's blow that dark cloud away. It may never happen."

West End Studios

CHAOS CALMED

O UR FIRST VISIT TO WEST END STUDIOS WHERE BILLY G was recording. So much for glamour! Some studios, like Real World and Abbey Road, have got it, and some...well, some haven't. I need not have worried about the Grannymobile letting the side down. This was nothing more than an anonymous building on a rundown red brick industrial estate. Above the expensively designed logo mounted on the front of the building saying that this was indeed "West End Studios" was a large number 11, pointing out that this was really just the 11th unit on the estate. Number 10 was an international freight business and Number 9 was a stationery business. I could have been coming to buy car spares rather than going to meet Billy G.

"The tragedy of England is the tragedy of ugliness," The Vicar quoted from God knows where. "Ugliness, ugliness, ugliness. Ugly surroundings, ugly ideals, ugly religion, ugly hope, ugly love, ugly clothes, ugly furniture, ugly houses, and now ugly industrial estates."

The front door was completely blocked by two large security guards. The one furthest from us was being pummelled by a blond haired woman wearing a jacket with No Meat No Man emblazoned across the back.

"But you've gotta let me in," she was screaming. "Do you know who wrote her new hit? Me that's who. She fucking stole it. I just want to look her in the eyes and laugh. Life owes me that. Take your hands off my jacket, you tosser."

It must be scary to be stalked by people like that. Completely mad. Even my auntie knows that Billy G and Emma didn't write their own songs. They were all written by two guys, Gaydon and Broom.

"I am sorry, sir," the other security guard barked, as we approached him. "No one gets in the building without a pass. Absolutely no exceptions."

He'd obviously had a long day, and must have heard every excuse going – members of the family, former employees, royalty, US presidential staff, arse-tronauts, public health inspectors, rodent exterminators... The two guys were both frigging enormous, absolutely square – as wide as they were tall. Not so much a brick shithouse as an entire toilet block. Where do security firms find these freaks? I hadn't seen men this big since the last time I was thrown out of the girls' changing room at Wimbledon. There was going to be no way past without a pass. It seemed we would have to wait for our meeting with Billy G.

The Vicar had no such doubts.

"Absolutely right," he oozed graciously to the guard. "The last thing that Billy G needs now..." he looked over at the demented woman in the jacket, "...is unauthorized visitors, or, even worse, members of the press. Fortunately, gentlemen, I am a current employee, and I do indeed have a pass. I am Billy G's sound engineer, at your service."

And he produced a laminated "Access All Areas" pass

for Billy G, complete with her logo, and his photograph.

The guard examined it, and stepped aside.

"Where on earth?" I exclaimed, as the Vicar pushed open the glass door and walked into a small lobby area. "Isn't that illegal?" I carried on, as I realised that this pass must be the result of his work on his computer.

"Why?!" he taunted, as if shocked at the suggestion. "I am her sound engineer, and I do have access to all areas. Her manager would be happy to confirm it, as you well know. It simply saved an unnecessary waste of time standing outside making phone calls. Spit Spot. Best foot forward."

We entered a building in turmoil. The receptionist was being hassled by two pretentious young arseholes – little greenhorns, as they would say in the US, fresh out of college. They obviously fancied themselves as future record company executives, complete with designer clothes, haircuts, and even designer glasses, not to mention Billy G passes not dissimilar to the one the Vicar had created for himself. They were at number eleven on the stress-o-meter. There is that scene in a Bond movie – *'Never Say Never Again'*, I think it is, where Bond is playing a game that sends electric shocks to the controls he is holding – slowly raising the level of pain. These two were well into the red zone. You could almost see their hair starting to stand on end as the voltage increased.

And here, Punksters, we face a small problem. I have no idea how to do dialogue when there are three people yelling, all at the same time, not listening to a word anyone else says, coupled with the constant sound of the telephone ringing off the hook. But, hey, Rule Two applies. No complaints about bad grammar. We boldly go where no Punk has gone before. Into the literary unknown. In alphabetical order:

"Arsehole…"

"Bugger me. This is serious…"

"Can't you just leave the frigging phone alone…"

"Damn. One of the tabloids has logged on…"

"Everybody shut up…"

"Fuck me. There's got be someone to talk to…"

"God. This is a bitch…"

"Hell. Leave the damn thing off the hook…"

"Idiot. Don't talk to anyone…"

"Just think of something…"

"Kunt. (OK I had trouble with K). Keep quiet until Richard Breamore gets here…"

"Luvvy. The trouble is there's nothing to say…"

"Might I ask you to keep your hands off my arse…"

And so it continued. You get the general idea. A hive of absolutely useless activity.

The Vicar waited patiently for a chance to speak to the receptionist. He has this way of apparently being the most patient person in the world, while some unconscious part of his body language makes it very clear that he is not accustomed to being kept waiting. Perhaps it is the way that he refuses to do anything other than remain totally focussed on waiting. Everyone else becomes distracted, they get a coffee, sit and read, or in my case, they stare at the talent. Like the receptionist, for instance, with whom The Vicar was to have frequent battles over the coming weeks.

She was sitting in a raised area behind a large curved desk. Well, not exactly a desk. More like a bar, all painted in a cool blue colour to tone in with the walls. The BHBB, or Blue Haired Booby Bird, had a large blue streak in her blond hair to make her match the furnishings: hence her name. Well, it explains the blue haired bit. I'll leave the booby bit to your imagination. Although she didn't.

"Good afternoon. I *am* The Vicar." He had walked over and lifted the phone off the hook.

"I have come at the request of Richard Breamore. I shall be working with Billy G on the tour of Japan".

"Well Richard Breamore isn't here at the moment, and when he gets here there is a long queue of people wanting a bit of him" one of the two aresholes snapped rudely. "Can't you see we've got a crisis on our hands?"

The Vicar lent over and looked at the little prick's pass.

"I see you are in the PR department," he read his name "... Michael. A tough job at present. You will achieve nothing until you lower your levels of stress. Look at your shoulders. You are so uptight."

And with that the Vicar began to massage the young guy's shoulders.

"Hey, wait!" the guy squealed, but he gave up. He was in the grips of a superior force.

"Now, how may I be of service to you?" The Vicar urged.

"I – I'm sorry?" the guy stammered, completely fazed by this old man who had come in, started giving him a massage, and was now offering to help him.

"I have been employed by Richard Breamore to help with Billy G's problems. It would seem that you are currently having difficulties. So how may I be of service?"

Still no reply.

"It may be, for example, that you are concerned with that woman outside?" The Vicar persisted.

This suggestion received an instant response. Not from the young guy, but from his partner in crime. A girl of a similar age.

"What are you talking about, dopehead? We've got a major horror on the internet and you think we are worried about some deranged fan?"

The Vicar appeared not to notice her rudeness or her aggression. He continued very calmly to pour more oil onto troubled waters.

"Now we are getting a little closer. And what exactly has happened on the internet, pray tell?"

"You haven't seen it. I thought the whole world and his mother had been there," she wailed. "If you want to gloat. Be my guest." She wrote something on a piece of paper and handed to him. "Go sample the action. But you can't do it here. The whole system is down while they sort out what happened."

"You should learn to trust in the good fairy, young lady," The Vicar trilled. "If you become too cynical, when she comes knocking, you might just slam the door in her face. I shall return."

And with that, he bowed to the arsehole who had got the free massage, smiled at me, motioned me to walk through the door ahead of him, and made his exit from the building.

It was an amazing performance. Vintage Vicar. Within a few minutes, he had reduced a complete clusterfuck to the silence of a zen monastery. Well, almost.

HORRORS
ON the Internet

THE VICAR AND I LEFT WEST END STUDIOS, AND LOOKED around for the most likely source of an internet connection.

"If only you had not spilled tea on my laptop," The Vicar reminded me, before adding "International Cargo, I think," and walking into the freight unit next door.

Regular Vicar watchers will not be surprised to learn that, less than five minutes later, he had successfully commandeered one of their offices, complete with an ageing PC to access the internet, and had also gained something of an audience, admiring their exotic visitor from the studio next door. It was one of those moments when you feel this sudden surge of power just following in his wake. Like Hugh Hefner must feel when he snaps his fingers and fifty women instantly drop their bikinis.

Nor did he disappoint in his duty to put on a show for his audience. When he had first walked in the room, he had picked up a newspaper – the tabloid newspaper – and tut tutted at the headline news about a recent rampage by England football fans.

"They will break panes of glass and smash the windows of coaches and also knock you down without the slightest compunction," he quoted from the top of his head. "Would anyone be interested to know what that is? It is a description of a English football match…" he paused for effect, "…In the Eighteenth Century. Is it not reassuring to know that we are not going to the dogs? We have always been there."

He turned and smiled politely to his audience, who would immediately look away, pretending to be actively engaged in some form of gainful employment – like a playground game of grandmother's footsteps.

"The tavern is rather worshipped than the church. Gluttony and drunkenness is more abundant than tears and prayers." He paused again. "The Archbishop of Canterbury. Speaking in 1562. You see things are not as bad as they seem. They are worse than that. They are also better than that. Unfortunately thuggery is something we English do well. Unlike sex. As Jeremy Paxman points out in his excellent book *The English,* how we reproduce is one of the mysteries of the Western world."

This comment produced the desired level of tittering. We had typed in the URL that the girl had given us – *www.whatif. com/BillyG* – and were waiting for the computer to make an archaic dial up connection. What kind of International Cargo business doesn't have broadband?

One day the internet may truly become an 'information super highway', but right now, there are still places where it is more like, in The Vicar's words that day "a traffic jam in the bra of a New York drag queen – painfully slow and crammed full with rubbish that no-one wants".

A young guy had asked The Vicar if the music industry was very incestuous.

"What a strange question. Do you mean musically or

sexually? I am probably the wrong person to ask. Jac Holzman, the founder of Elekctra records, used to claim that, pre Aids and at the height of antibiotics, if you made a family tree linking who fucked who in the business, it would be pretty much solid black. That is why the whole industry could never get up in the morning."

More quiet chuckling.

"I am not the perfect person for such anecdotes, but I do recall a story about Warren Beatty, the famous womaniser, who was confronted by a woman he had been chasing at an industry party. She turned round to him and said 'Warren…I have fucked him, him, him, him and him…and I'm never going to fuck you.' Poor Warren was apparently downcast for weeks."

General laughter.

"If you ask me if that is true to my experience of three decades of jumping in and out of vans, travelling the world, playing and recording music in the most unlikely and inappropriate venues, I would have to say that it is."

The site eventually appeared.

'Click here. Billy G exposed', a window popped up, inviting us to download a song. The Vicar clicked on the icon.

"It would seem that I can finally stop spouting elephantosities, and we may actually have some music to play you, although the sound on these computers is normally appalling."

It downloaded painfully slowly – 10%, 20%, 50% and finally, wonder of wonders, 100% – by which time the audience for our little concert had grown to perhaps twenty people. We heard the introduction to Billy G's new single 'Don't Touch What You Can't Afford', the same track that she had sung at the lottery. The singing came in as expected, but on the first high note her singing was painfully out of tune. Everyone in the room winced. The Vicar looked at me and raised his eyebrows as if to say 'What is this girl of yours up to?'

As the song went on, the entire audience was ducking in advance of all the high notes to try to shield themselves from the worst of the pain. It was unbelievably embarrassing. Enough to make even the most ardent fan question her ability. The phrasing was the same as the single I had played hundreds of times at home, but the tuning was simply appalling.

"Quad erat demonstrandum," the Vicar said incomprehensibly (fuck, I hate latin).

"What a fine web we weave when first we practice to deceive," he continued poetically, scrolling down to the bottom of the page, where there was some form of discussion board, where fans were posting their comments.

"Perhaps we should see what the judges made of that fine performance," he suggested to his amassed audience. "Rebel says *'Listening to this, I am felling'* – I think he means feeling – *'sad and depressed. I lurvved that girl but she was just pissing'* – I apologize for the language – *'in the wind like the rest of them.'* Not exactly up to the standard of Simon Callow on Rockstars, but I sympathize with his point of view."

He cleared his throat.

"Waterbottle – a more intriguing web handle – says *'God she's the pits. Anyone want to buy my collection from me before I throw it in the trash'"*.

He looked at the gathered crowd.

"If anyone wants to buy some cheap CDs, probably from America, given the reference to 'trash', Waterbottle's your man, or woman. Royaltrude – these people do choose interesting names – says *'She was always a phoney. Anyone who could make that much fuss about lip syncing had to be hiding something'* – a case of methinks the lady doth protest too much from Royaltrude. There might be something in that. Finally Raging Bull says simply *'anyone for a lynch mob'* – a little severe, although I would agree that singing of that kind should probably carry a mandatory custodial sentence, or possibly an optional frontal lobotomy."

"Enough!" He closed the program. "We have taken up far too much of these good people's time. Now, if someone would like to give me a large invoice for the time I have spent on your computer, I will be happy to see that Richard Breamore pays it."

Someone gave him a piece of paper and a pen.

"Oh No. You do not want my autograph. I am not that famous. And I only ever sign my own work."

He pushed it away.

"No really. Have Punk's. He is the drummer with the Hellboys."

I, of course, would have been happy to sign, but the paper and pen had mysteriously disappeared.

The Vicar was impatient to get back to the studio.

"It would seem, Punk, that Billy G has been pulling the lamb's wool over everyone's eyes and someone is out to expose her. I think it is high time we went to meet the young lady in question, and I ask her some very direct and painful questions."

He turned and smiled to me.

"Although I still doubt this case will change my deep seated conviction that anything can be settled over a good cup of Earl Grey tea."

CHAPTER THREE

Billy G
Fact File

Perhaps now would be a good moment to cut away from the scene of The Vicar and me walking back to the studio, and, in the best tradition of television films, use this moment to capture the key moments in Billy G's past. Bonobos@aol.com emailed me, asking to know more about my "superfandom" for Billy G. Seems there's about as much privacy in telling this story as in standing stark naked in the middle of Piccadilly Circus. Something I have done more than once. So, here goes. Punk's Billy G Factfile.

Scene number one, and my story's just begun, roll me over lay me down and do it again (do it again)...Roll me o-over in the clo-over, roll me over lay me down and do it again (do it again)...

We start in the basement of the Grand Hotel in Manchester, where Billy G and the G strings as they were then called, had somehow got a twice weekly slot. Billy G has bright orange hair and in the audience a young seventeen year old, probably spotty, Punk Sanderson is wondering if it is true that she always dyed her pubic hair the same colour as the rest of her hair and if she is really wearing a G string. Well, these sort of things are important to seventeen year old boys. Next to me is a tall, beautiful, leggy, blond, Swedish language student, scantily clad in little more than a bikini, looking lovingly into my eyes and hanging on my every word. Or perhaps not. Billy G is on stage, pausing between numbers to tell one of her riotous stories about her polite convent education, saying such things as –

"I'm a nice girl, I am. I looked very smart in the uniform, it's just that I had a G string where my regulation green knickers should have been".

She then launches into her slogan "Go Go G strings" before starting the next song. This might be any one of a number of unreleased classics such as *'Green Spiky Hair'*, (memorable for its opening line: "Woke up this morning and threw up on the bed") or the provocative *'Look Don't Touch. Rich Man's Slut'* – particularly apt when you are seventeen with nothing but loose change and wishful thinking in your pockets.

The first three or four rows were always filled with her hardcore followers, the G stringers – a group of big, tough, leather clad lesbians – pretty intimidating (and exotic) to a young snotty nosed boy – which is why I was always to be found near the back, banging my head against the low ceiling...

Scene number two and my hand is on her shoe, roll me over lay me down and do it again (do it again)... Roll her over in the clo-over, roll her over, lay her down and do it again (do it again)...

Cut very professionally, with my dreams of a Swedish blond fading into the background, to a smart terraced house in Kings Road in London, plastered in slogans such as *'Sign Billy G'*, *'Billy G's the greatest'*, and other unsubtle graffiti. The story goes that the G Stringers had decided to daub the house of Chris Blackwell, owner of Island Records, in Billy G graffiti, to encourage him to sign her. Unfortunately, they got the right address (70 Kings Rd), but the wrong Kings Rd – the house they daubed actually belonged to Richard Breamore, a very wealthy lawyer, who at this stage had nothing to do with the music business. He was intrigued to find out the reason for the graffiti (after no doubt trying to sue the brown stuff out of anyone he thought was involved), and, to cut a short story even shorter, this was how he first met Billy G, entered the music business, became her manager, brought her and Emma B together as the founder members of TITS 'N' ARSE (what a great name that is!), and moved towards his now current legendary status...

And now our third and final flashback. Sing a long. You should know the tune by now:

At last scene number three and my hand is on her knee, roll her over, lay her down and do it again (do it again)... When it's o-over in the clo-over, she'll knee you in the groin and leave you doubled over in a pathetic heap moaning in excruciating pain (That doesn't scan quite right. Suggestions in an email, please).

We return to the Grand Hotel in Manchester, and the small local launch of their first single – which became prime time national TV due to the fantasmagorical way that the girls arrived at the press conference. The girls apparently jumped onto the huge ornate chandelier, which hangs eight floors up right in the centre of the stairwell (a terrifucking, five pairs of underpants, leap from the top of the bannisters, I've tried it) and then got a friend to lower the chandelier all the way to the ground floor, as their single was played on the PA system. The first the press saw of them were two mad girls, with grins like two cheshire cats, posing provocatively, and descending from the heavens on a seemingly diamond encrusted chandelier. Even Marilyn Monroe could not have conjured such an entrance. The other two band members greeted them at the bottom, showing that even then, there was a strict hierachy in the band.

Breamore had no doubt arranged that the event was perfectly timed to make all the papers, and TV stations. The rest, as they say, is history.

No time for number four and she firmly slammed the door, roll her over, lay her down and do it again (do it again)...

Enough. Enough. This flashback stuff may well work well in films, but it's high time that I got out my blowtorch to unfreeze our heroes, and send them back into the studio to do battle once again with the Blue Haired Booby Bird and the forces of the evil empire.

This time The Vicar was in no mood to be patient – although he asked his first question:
"In which of the studios will I find Billy G?"
in the same patient, gracious tone he always used.

When the answer was not immediately forthcoming, he added simply "Are you willing to be responsible for the repercussions of your failure to allow me to help Billy G? If so, I shall leave everything in your capable hands."

The BHBB quietly raised two fingers (stuck together, you perverts – meaning 'studio two', not 'fuck you') and gestured in the direction of the studios, which were on her right. She then looked away as if she had other far more important things to be doing.

"I thank you, Madam," The Vicar sang with a smile, as he waved me through the heavy metal door with the large TWO over it.

The studio was laid out very differently to the ones at Real World. The whole wall on the left was given over to electronic keyboards, on neat sloping pine shelves. We had entered through the door at the back, and between us and the mixing console was a large pine bar, with a ten-seater (or so it seemed) cream sofa and two equally vast easy chairs. The Vicar could not resist giving the evil eye to the television mounted in the wall, showing the 'obligatory MTV clips', as he marched round to the other side of the bar (which was, of course, an equipment rack, stuffed with sound processing gear, not a drinks cabinet – silly me). Two people slumped on the console at the front of the room drifted into view.

He walked up and introduced himself.

"Good evening. *I am* The Vicar," pronounced in the same time-honoured way. "A friend in need. I am sorry to intrude. And you, I assume, must be the famous Billy G. I am honoured to meet you."

The lighting was really very dim, but one of the two

faceless people at the mixing desk had bright dyed hair, and it was to her that he addressed himself.

As the other one was a man, it was not a difficult piece of detective work.

THE GIRL AT THE MIXING DESK GOT UP. BILLY G. AND she looked absolutely stunning.

She had lost a lot of weight recently – the papers had been filled with pictures of her on a beach holiday looking close to anorexic – but in the flesh she seemed to glow with good health – which was, I suppose, pretty surprising, given the events of the last few weeks. She was shorter in the flesh than I pictured her (isn't it funny how that's true of virtually everyone – with the exception of John Cleese, who is simply enormous?), but she had that magnetic quality that made it difficult to take your eyes off her . My mother would no doubt have commented that "if God had intended you to gawp like a goldfish, he would have made you small and brainless, going round and round in ever decreasing circles. OK so my son's a goldfish."

I can still tell you exactly what she was wearing (Billy G, not my mother). White NikeTrainers, white ankle socks, which were neatly folded down at the top, baggy grey jog pants, and a white T shirt with "Madonna" emblazoned across the front (one of the ones shaped like a vest, with no arms and open at the neck). I could see no signs of a bra strap showing under the straps of her T shirt, so I can even inform you that she had probably 'gone commando' as you might say. She had gained a few tattoos, and a strange metal protrusion from her chin, since the last photos I had seen of her.

"Good bloody evening," she snapped, in her thick husky Mancunian accent. "I am sure you plonkers think you have a very good reason for being in here. But this is my studio. I booked it, and I have told mission control that I wish to be left undisturbed." She was as used to getting her own way as The Vicar. "So if you gentlemen don't mind…" she goaded in a mocking middle class voice "…Life ain't exactly a bed of roses at the moment."

She turned back to the mixing desk, assuming that this broadside would be sufficient to drive us from the room. The Vicar, however, is not one to flee in the height of battle.

"Which is exactly why I am here," he trilled, his head bowed and his hands behind his back. "Richard Breamore felt that I could be of some assistance. I *am* the Vicar."

"So you said," she snorted, turning round again. If she knew who he was she wasn't letting on. "How thoughtful of Richard. To get a Vicar to perform the last rites over my bloody career."

"I think it was more the resurrection that he had in mind."

"Fat frigging chance I would have said."

"Oh ye of little faith. Jesus may be able to feed five thousand people with just five fishes, but I can set the whole world singing with just three chords."

"Oh my god. A clever cleric. God spare us."

"I am sure he will." The Vicar smiled patiently. "But first I may be able to perform a few miracles of my own. All I need is the answer to one question."

"Which is?"

"Is that your singing on the internet?"

"Well, you can piss off out of here right now. You come in here with your la-di-da friend of Richard bloody Breamore accent and accuse me of singing flatter than a..." she was lost for a suitable comparision "...squashed...chapati. No one could sing that badly."

"You must admit it does sound very like you. Even Punk here, who has followed your work closely for along time, seems to be fairly convinced that it is your voice".

"Well he can go fuck himself too. I tell you nobody could sing as out of tune as that recording".

"Exactly what I thought. But could it not be something like a rehearsal recording. Perhaps you were warming up with your headphones on, so that you couldn't hear yourself? Even the Angel Gabriel would sing out of tune in those circumstances."

She thought about this for a while.

"No. It's completely im-fucking-possible. Nothing I have ever done is as hideously atonal as the recording on the internet." She stared at The Vicar defiantly. "It must be an impersonator. So you have your answer. Now, will you please kindly leave."

"But the tone, the inflections, everything is yours," The Vicar persisted, standing his ground.

"Are you calling me a fucking liar. Are you saying that it's me on that recording and I sung that out of tune?"

She was close to losing her pretty legendary temper. Her first meeting with Emma B, in Scamps bar in Manchester, had apparently occurred because she thought that Emma had spilled a drink on her as she walked past, so she had thumped her. They were both thrown out, and had got to know each other standing outside in the rain. Not exactly the quiet retiring type.

"I am suggesting nothing of the sort," The Vicar maintained. "I simply said that I do not think it is the voice of an impersonator."

"So you do think it's me singing on that recording?"

"I think it is undoubtedly your voice."

"Perhaps you had better get the fuck out of this room before I hurl something at you. Something large. Like your frigging ego. How dare you stand there and accuse me of singing like some drunken karaoke trollop."

"I did no such thing".

"I rather think you did. I can play the la-di-da barrister just as well as you. Did you or did you not say that it was my voice on the internet."

"I said that it was most unlikely that it was an impersonator," The Vicar agreed.

He appeared to be enjoying himself, as if he knew something that the rest of us did not. Billy G, however, was reaching the end of her very short tether. She turned to the engineer, who had been sitting silently throughout this confrontation.

"Ben, would you please show this idiot out."

Ben was short and slight, probably in his early twenties. He had blond hair, and a goatee beard that I would have shaved off in embarrassment as it was mostly bum fluff. A bouncer he was not.

"I also think," The Vicar persevered, ignoring Ben completely "that it is most unlikely that anyone, let alone a professional singer of your standing, could be that out of tune."

"So, you do accept it wasn't me."

"I thought that I made it quite clear that I am one hundred percent sure that it was indeed you."

"I don't understand!" She threw her arms in the air in frustration.

"That is quite obvious. It does not seem to have occurred to you that it is perfectly possible that it is both your voice, as I have been saying all along, and that you have never sung the song in the least out of tune."

All three of us looked at him quite baffled. As ever, The Vicar enjoyed his moment of superiority. He drew up a chair and sat in the centre of the console, with Billy G on his right, and Ben on his left. "We need two things to resolve this issue. Firstly, a little toy." He spun around and pointed at one of the processors in the rack between the console and the studio door, "such as that one, and secondly…" He looked at me and I completed his sentence for him.

"… a pot of Earl Grey Tea."

HEADS or TAILS

By the time I returned with the tea, Ben, the studio engineer, had already plugged in the FX unit that The Vicar wanted, and he was awaiting his chance to perform. As he pressed 'play' on the remote control, the new song that Billy G was working on burst from the speakers. Something of a departure for her. It was a cover of 'Respect' by Aretha Franklin (well, Otis Redding, actually, but let's not split hairs). You know the thing '*R.E.S.P.E.C.T. Find out what it means to me.*'

The Vicar pulled down a slider, removing her voice from the mix.

"And if we want to hear what's coming out of my little wonder beast?" he asked.

Ben pointed to a channel further down the console. The Vicar proudly slid up the fader – to universal disappointment. It brought back the sound of her voice, but it sounded much as before.

Not that this appeared to worry The Vicar, who was altering the settings on his chosen toy.

As he turned the dial, I felt her voice shift off key and go flat. I looked at The Vicar, who was smiling. At the beginning of the next line, he span it further, and she hit the most atrociously out of tune note.

The Vicar was enjoying himself.

"You would agree that that is your voice, would you not?" he asked Billy G, "and that the tuning is simply diabolical?" As he said that, he gave the big black dial on the front of the processor a final spin and her voice went so deep that it seemed more like a man singing.

Billy G let out a huge sigh of relief. She too was now smiling, as at least part of the mystery was revealed to her. In my official capacity as Chief Ignoranus, it fell to me to ask The Vicar what he had been doing.

"Elementary, my dear Watson. Welcome to the wonderful world of weird!" He smiled in a self-satisfied way. "My favourite toy, The Eventide Ultra Harmonizer. Although any harmonizer would do – even the one that's been reliably wrecking decent records ever since Cher first suggested we 'Believe'. Did it not occur to that pea-sized brain of yours that any toy that will generate fake harmonies, or correct an out of tune voice, can be used to do exactly the opposite – make a perfectly good voice sound out of tune?"

"So the singing on the internet is Billy G...but she sung perfectly in tune...and someone has doctored the recording to make her sound out of tune?" I asked, making sure I understood.

It sounded so simple that I couldn't believe I hadn't thought of it.

"And anyone could have doctored the recording that we heard on the internet?"

"Not anyone. You would need access to the original recording, as you would need to be able to process the voice separately from the music..."

"...exactly as with the lottery performance!" I added, finishing his train of thought.

"Voila. So Exhibit A, the internet tapes, as we shall call them, are simply another way of using the same ammunition that was already used in rigging the lottery performance. Almost certainly done by the same people. One really does have to admire their ingenuity."

"Hello! Excuse me!" yelled Billy G. "I know I am just a woman, and I hate to disturb your private little men's club." She smiled at us sarcastically. "But I am not just any lady, I am *THE* lady." She shook her hands like Al Jolson. Jazz hands, I think they call it. "I think I deserve some explanations. Did you say that whoever did this must have come from this studio?"

"No." The Vicar turned to face her. "They could have done it in any studio – even at home on a cheap computer. They would, however, have needed access to the original tapes."

"Well, I doubt they have ever left this studio, or even this control room, have they Ben?" she asked.

We all looked at the humble little Ben.

"They'll all be in there," he muttered, pointing to some glass doors behind him. "Do you mind getting them out, Gabriel?"

I turned and noticed a young guy, wearing a garish KMFDM T-shirt, who was cleaning up at the side of the studio. I followed him as he disappeared into the small tape room.

"All the tapes from Billy G's new album are here. It's a 48-track recording," he explained.

Now, don't ask me why, Punksters, but no-one has invented a 48-track tape machine. If you want more than

24 tracks of that 'warm analogue sound' made by conventional tape machines, as Billy G clearly did, it can only be done by 'locking' two 24 track tape machines together.

It was the enormous tapes these machines play – 12 inches wide, 2 inches thick and weighing more than one of my more anorexic girlfriends – that were stored in large boxes on the metal shelving.

As Gabriel lifted down the first of the two reels that had been used to record Billy G's single, I instinctively knew that the box would be empty. He was very slight, and he was carrying it far too easily. He walked out of the machine room, and laid it down on the edge of the console to open it up.

"Well that's how it was done," I cried, keen to show that I had spotted it so quickly. "Someone's stolen the multitrack tape."

Ben opened the box that Gabriel had brought over…and there inside was a reel of tape, shielded in a white protective guard, just as it should have been. What an anti climax! So much for my instincts! The Vicar looked at me with raised eyebrows, amused at my embarrassment.

Gabriel wandered back to get the second tape, which would hold the other 24 tracks of the same song. He carried this to the console in the same way, and once again, the box was opened to reveal…the tape in its protective wrapping.

Billy G jumped up.

"So if the tapes are still here, and you say that someone had to use those tapes, does it mean that it's been done by someone inside this room?"

The Vicar didn't answer. His eyes were fixed on the reels of tape. He got up and tore off the protective wrapping from one of them.

"Did no one ever teach you to store your tapes tail out?" he almost bellowed at Ben. "You certainly would not get work in a studio with me!"

We all looked at the reel. We could see green leader tape. The start of a tape is always green, and the end is always red. It is a strict convention within studios that tapes are always stored "tail out", with the red end showing. *(BTW willing as I am to kick the crapoli out of meaningless rules – more willing than most as they might be a creepy 'sit at the front of the class' goody two shoes – there are very good reasons for storing tape like this – impressive insider knowledge at no extra cost – because of something called 'print through', which is when you can hear a faint echo of a song before the music actually starts.)* Suffice to say that The Vicar is a stickler for such things.

Ben looked confused.

"I always store my tapes tail out. Never like this," he insisted, and as if in his own defence, he pulled the protective wrapping off the second reel of tape. This one was indeed stored correctly.

"Interesting. One stored one way, and one the other. In that case, I would put a large wager on the fact that this..." The Vicar picked up the reel that had offended him by being wrongly stored, "...contains the vocals." He turned over the box to read the track list.

He was, of course, quite right (when is he ever wrong?).

"My deductions would seem a trifle more accurate than yours, my dear Punk." He sat triumphantly back in his chair, as if to wait for the applause. Ben further pampered his already inflated ego, by asking how he knew.

"Simples," he joked, slipping into Sherlock Holmes mode. "Someone has been in here and played that tape in order to make a copy of the vocals. That someone either did not know or did not have time to store the tape properly afterwards. All that they would then need would be a copy of a dub mix."

A dub mix, Punksters, is a version of the track, which does not contain the lead vocals. Ready made karaoke.

The Vicar looked at Ben.

"You did make one, I assume?"

"Yeah, of course," Ben answered. "We always do, in case Billy G wants to sing live over the recorded backing."

"And it would have been a fuck sight better if Breamore had let me use it on the bloody lottery, instead of being hung out to dry," screeched Billy G, caustically. "Then the luuvverly lady would still be a sex goddess, not an ex goddess." A phrase I suspect she had used before.

"The DAT will be in here," Ben muttered, ducking away from Billy G's carping as he opened a drawer, "with all the others from the current album."

He ran his finger down a neat row of tapes.

"I can't see it, but it must be here somewhere. I remember doing the mix."

He pulled out a large A4 pad, a detailed inventory of all the recordings made for the album.

"Here we are. It is DAT number 14."

He looked back at the box of tapes, but between Number 13 and Number 15 there was an ominous gap.

"It would appear that DAT number 14 has mysteriously disappeared." The Vicar raised his eyebrows in mock surprise. "I think that proves my version of events."

THE VICAR WAS NOT ALLOWED TO MILK HIS MOMENT OF glory for long. All this talk of missing tapes had distracted us from one important fact – namely that the recording with Billy G's hideously out of tune voice, fake or otherwise, was still available on the internet for anyone to hear. We were quickly brought back to earth, as the telephone in the studio flashed and Ben answered it, before handing it over to Billy G.

"Yeah, you had better come in and get it over with," she groaned, and almost immediately the studio door opened and in walked our friendly PR girl from reception.

She was not looking any happier.

"I am sorry to disturb you, Billy..." she started. "This internet thing is getting bigger and bigger. Apparently Radio One Newsbeat have just announced it on air, and given fans the URL to go to."

"Trust bloody Radio One. They'll kiss your ass to get an interview when all's going well. As soon as you need a little help, they open up that great big corporate sized waste pipe of theirs and dump all over you." She may have grown a lot richer since those early concerts, but it was good to see that her language remained just as fruity.

"We are going to have to make a press release. Do you have anything you want us to say?"

"Yes. That if I get my hands on whoever is doing this I will personally tear their throat out and feed it to my pet budgerigar!" A fair punishment under the circumstances, I thought.

"Come back in five minutes," The Vicar suggested, "We'll see if we can get you something worthwhile," and he motioned the girl back out the door. I noticed that she no longer questioned his authority.

"But it's simple," I said, putting in my oar where it was not wanted, "You have proved the recording is a fraud, so you simply have to tell that to the press – "

"But you must remember," The Vicar interrupted, struggling with my naivete, "that the press do not want to be told that Billy G sings perfectly in tune. Hardly much of a story. The fact that she sings hideously out of tune is a far better prospect as far as they are concerned."

"But couldn't you show them how it was done?"

"I doubt that we could fit all the music journalists in the country into this studio," he continued, patiently, "even if they wanted to come, which they do not."

"Then what?"

"What we need is a second recording involving someone of impeccable reputation. If I were to produce a recording of Pavarotti singing out of tune, for example, then they might believe us."

"Superb!" I cried, impressed as always by his ability to find the right idea at the right time. "You've got the CD of the three tenors in the car. Nessun Dorma out of tune. Quite brilliant."

"It would be if I could do it. But I cannot. You are forgetting, my dear Punk, that I need the voice and the music separately. Otherwise, it will not sound like the singer going out of tune, it will simply sound like the whole tape machine speeding up and slowing down, a quite different effect."

"Well, where are we going to find multitrack tapes of some well known singer in the next five minutes?"

"That is the problem that is currently occupying my mind. We need a recording where the music and the singing are separate."

"Like the Beatles," said Ben, who had almost been forgotten, as he sat quietly at the far end of the console.

"I beg your pardon?" said The Vicar.

"Like the Beatles," repeated Ben, "You know, their early recordings, which have the vocals on one side of the stereo and the music on the other."

This was such a brilliant suggestion, that I am sorely tempted to rewrite history and claim that it was me that made it. Only Rule One prevents me. If you have ever listened to any of the early Beatles albums on headphones (which I, of course, have never done, as they are an old phogey band), you will know that these albums often have the voice in one ear and the music in the other. The Vicar tells me that this strange arrangement was apparently caused totally by accident. The original recordings were all mono (made for people with only one ear, growing in the middle of their face). When, in the middle of the 1960s, people suddenly grew two ears and wanted stereo recordings, someone found recordings of the Beatles which had the voice on one track and the rest of the music on the other. These were never intended to be released. They were made so that the sound and volume of the voice could be changed at a later date. However, because there was apparently a 'ruling from on high' that all Beatles recordings should not be altered, they were released exactly as they were – with mad stereo. Well, that's the story anyway.

The Vicar, as you can imagine, was impressed by Ben's suggestion.

"Benjamin, you are a genius! If ever Punk is man enough to admit that he has not the slightest talent for his job, then please feel free to apply for the post as my assistant. In the meantime, Punk," he said, throwing me his car keys, "I think you will find the CD of the Beatles Double Red album in the car. Spit Spot. Time waits for no-one, least of all you."

I ran to fetch the CD, and it proved a simple task for The Vicar to prepare a hideous version of Eleanor Rigby, with vocals even more ridiculously out of tune than those on Billy G's track. He then recalled our beloved PR girl, and suggested that she announce to the press that the recording of Billy G was indeed a fraud, no doubt done as a joke, and that she had obtained this recording of Eleanor Rigby prepared in the same manner.

"You can then ask them if anyone doubts Paul McCartney's ability to sing in tune," he added. "Perhaps we could also put it on a website, so that everyone can hear it. Maybe even persuade Radio One to give out the URL. Totally illegal, of course, putting out an atonal version of the Beatles on the internet. We shall probably get sued by Paul McCartney."

He laughed.

"Well, not me. I am merely your humble servant." He looked at Billy G. "You will get sued by Paul McCartney.

Sir Paul McCartney. And your manager of course. If he had not mysteriously absented himself during this moment of crisis, we could ask him to try to get some form of approval. As it is we will have to trust to EMI's..." he turned and pretended to spit on the floor, "...spirit of goodwill. If that is not a contradiction in terms."

He turned to the mixing desk.

"Now Ben, I am sure you can make me an MP3 file of our Beatles classic."

(I am sure I don't have to explain to any of my readers – thieves one and all – how to "rip" a track, make an MP3 copy and put it on the internet. If the record industry had their way we would all be behind bars). It took Ben no more than ten minutes to have a great sounding version of the track uploaded to Billy G's website, together with the press release, saying that the original recording was a fake.

I was convinced that we had completely solved the problem.

"Congratulations," I enthused, impressed as ever. It was moments like this that made me proud to work for him. "That will certainly silence the press."

"I agree that if anything will shut them up, then that will. Although there is an obvious reason why it will not work." He looked at me questioningly. I shrugged back. "Because, my dear Punk, a singer that cannot sing remains a much better story than some fan playing a practical joke. I fear it will take more than the fact that it is not true to change a juicy story like that."

"You old cynic," I mumbled.

"Read tomorrow's papers! In the meantime, we have indeed done all we can." He got up. "It is time to leave Billy G and Ben in peace. It is most rude to disturb an artist when she is working."

He bowed ceremonially to Billy G and headed to the door.

"Now, I think we deserve one of those large beasts of delight from that fine café just around the corner. I do hope it will still be open. Something suitably gooey..."

And ideally we would close this chapter with The Vicar and I heading off in search of large sticky cakes and, of course, the obligatory cup of Earl Grey tea. Although, unfortunately we never made it. Before leaving the West End Studios, while *'hitting the tickler'*, (does anyone else use that phrase?) The Vicar had a 'bright idea' that sent him marching straight back to studio two. Where would the world be without all the bright ideas that have been conceived in the little boy's room? At the beginning of Chapter Four perhaps, and one stage closer to a much needed pint of Speckled Hen.

CHAPTER FOUR

The Vicar has just handed me a late Christmas present – a stack of Beatles albums, (works of fucking genius one and all, if he is to be believed) labelled "essential listening". He has even made helpful suggestions about what order I should play them in. This trend clearly has to be avoided, so it is time for a new rule.

RULE SEVEN: No music by dead people.

No doubt there will be a few exceptions, but that should be good for starters. After all, The Beatles didn't even play all their own stuff. The Vicar tells me that he has an old Mellotron keyboard thing that'll play the whole of a Beatles intro – with just one finger. So much for Music Gods!

Perhaps the CDs can help me stop this desk from wobbling so badly...

TTFN

☺

A *Priest Hole* Uncovered

BACK TO OUR OWN LITTLE MAGICAL MYSTERY TOUR. I keep hoping that I'll be able to jump forward a few days, but I must be careful not to get ahead of myself. There are a few more things that you should know about our first visit to West End studios.

Firstly, and most annoyingly, on his return to Studio Two, The Vicar somehow managed to invite Billy G to come and have dinner with him on his boat the following evening. I know, it's absurd! I almost died of embarrassment. Picture it. A fabulously wealthy, successful singer being asked to visit him on the Betsy, which can best be described as a floating council house. How can someone that intelligent not realise that when he says 'we could meet on my boat', it tends to conjure up an image of an expensive gin palace, rather than a floating flagstone? How could she fail to be disgusted when she turned up? I tried my best to cough in the corner, and shake my head at him, but The Vicar was, as usual, clearly in no mood to accept my advice.

Anyway, that problem was for the future. On a brighter

note, we also made an important discovery. Worthy of a drum roll, and a loud bish bish on my best Zildjian cymbals (endorsements gratefully accepted). The Vicar – wait for it, barbecue my bollocks if I tell a lie – to the funbelievabubble delight and wonderment of the assembled applaudience… the great Victator found a hidden room in the studio. A veritable 'priest hole', in fact.

It was next door to the machine room, a small booth, shut off from the main control room by sliding glass doors, probably intended for vocal overdubs. Not much of a priest hole or hidden room you are probably thinking, but bear with me. On this recording, the booth had been used by the bass guitarist to house his amplifiers. He had stood in the control room to play his parts, while his amplifiers were no doubt turned up to deafening levels inside this little booth. Nothing unusual. An average rock 'n' roll day. What was strange, however, was the positioning of the amplifiers inside this little booth. He had built a huge stack, about seven feet tall, with two speakers on top of each other, just to the right of the sliding doors, sticking out from the wall. I'd love to draw you a diagram, but that would be cheating. Grown up stories don't have pictures. So, Punksters, it's down to your imagination. Imagine that you open the sliding doors, and there on your right are the amplifiers, looking as if they were up against the end wall. Except – and this is the fabulastically exciting bit – that they weren't! They were actually about six feet from the end wall, leaving a six foot square room behind them that was completely hidden from view. A perfect hide away.

As far as I was concerned that pretty much closed the case. The bass guitarist was obviously guilty. Go straight to jail, do not pass "Go", do not collect £200. And for you, dear readers, and for this exhausted writer, that should have been the end of the story, pack up our bags and go home. No one could have put those amplifiers there without the deliberate intention of making a hiding hole.

That was on the Tuesday, and by the Wednesday morning, I fully expected The Vicar to have gone off to arrest the bass guitarist, or whatever one does.

But I was to be disappointed. The Vicar made absolutely no attempt to get in touch with the mystery bass guitarist. I met him (The Vicar, not the bassist) early on the Wednesday morning, on board the Betsy, where he was, in fact, far more interested in an email he had just received from Angela Barnett, the journalist he had spoken to at the Financial Times (she of the instant sex change), regarding some investment possibilities. I almost felt that it was my duty to point out to him that we were meant to be working on 'the case of Billy G', not checking out his investments. I didn't, of course, as I had no desire to seek employment elsewhere. I simply made the tea (remembering to put the lid back on the jar so that the "essential Bergamot oils" don't evaporate) and kept quiet. The first indication that he had not entirely lost interest in the case, was when he suddenly looked up from his computer and asked me to get Billy G on the telephone.

"And how am I meant to get her number?" I whimpered, pathetically.

The Vicar looked despairingly at me.

"You are allowed to work from your own initiative, you know. The job description did not say *Must leave brain at home and have no original thoughts while at work...*" he paused as it became apparent that I still had no idea how to find Billy G's number, "...such as telephoning the studio where she records," he added painfully slowly, as if despairing of a child that can't learn some simple task.

He continued poring over his email, while I spoke to the studio, and eventually persuaded Ben to part with Billy G's home number – no mean feat as such things are normally guarded more closely than the Crown Jewels, or the age at which you finally managed to dispose of your unwanted virginity (as opposed to the greatly enhanced fictitious versions). When I finally did manage to get Billy G on the telephone, The Vicar would not even speak with her.

"Ask her if all her royalties are paid up to date."

"Pardon?"

"Ask her if all her royalties are paid up to date," he repeated, in a despairing voice.

There then followed a clumsy conversation, with me asking her about her royalties, which I knew nothing about, and her saying that it was none of my business, which clearly it wasn't. The Vicar remained an amused spectator, merely repeating "Tell her I need to know if all her royalties are paid up to date" until finally Billy G took pity on me and admitted that she was two periods late (We're talking accounting periods here, not menstrual cycles. But then you knew that). She explained that Breamore had taken out business loans on her behalf to cover her until they were paid.

"Good," chanted The Vicar, still seeming very distracted and tapping away on his computer.

"You can put the telephone down now," he added, when he noticed that I hadn't rung off. "Blow the luuvverly lady a kiss. We cannot sit on the telephone all day. Fine invention though it is. Nosey nosey grindstone".

I apologized to Billy G for disturbing her and rang off. The Vicar was becoming increasingly animated.

"We have no time for pleasantries, time is fleeing." He stared at his computer. "I have a plane to catch. To Edinburgh. There are two flights still available. One from Heathrow and one from Gatwick. The Gatwick flight leaves a little sooner, but Gatwick..." He shook his whole body as if suffering from a fever. "Such a proletarian departure point. Full of screaming children and discarded cigarettes. Heathrow it will have to be."

I assume he was on some travel website, as he clicked on his mouse as he made his decision.

"As Richard is going to pay personally, it may as well be first class," he chuckled. "If they do such thing on short flights. No point in sitting next to the great unwashed if you do not have to. Club Europe. A wider seat and a free glass of Champagne. That should ease the pain. And even a free copy of the Financial Times, if my luck holds."

He clicked on the screen again and began to pack up his laptop computer. He may have been in a hurry, but he was nothing if not systematic. Even on a quiet day, I just shove everything into the nearest bag and charge out of the door. Not so the Vicar. He placed the laptop carefully into its carrying case, wrapped the cable neatly, complete with cable tie, and put it equally carefully into a small bag he kept for the purpose.

"Onward!" he then ordered, thrusting his left arm into the air and pushing me from the Betsy.

Punk
Wins the Lottery

THE VICAR HAD NO INTENTION OF TELLING ME WHY HE was flying to Scotland, when the perpetrator of the crimes was obviously a bass guitarist living in London. Unless he didn't live in London, of course. Perhaps The Vicar had tracked him down, and the bass guitarist lived in Scotland. It seemed unlikely, but it was worth a stab.

"So why does Billy G use a bass guitarist living in Scotland?" I asked casually as we negotiated the pontoon.

"I didn't know she did," he replied, showing no interest, "You would have thought it would be easier to use someone based further South."

No, it definitely seemed to me that he had lost interest in Billy G, and was moonlighting. It surprised me. He is famed for his forthright views on propriety and business ethics. It was difficult to imagine him charging Richard Breamore for a flight that had nothing to do with him – but then how could Edinburgh fit into this case?

"I think I shall drive today," he announced, heading to the driver's door of the car as we approached. "You are always inclined to dawdle."

Dawdle?! Even Michael Schumacher could not persuade

the Grannymobile to do anything other than 'dawdle'. But I had no time to nurse my wounded pride, as no sooner had The Vicar taken the wheel, than he was firing instructions at me. He had arranged for a stopover of around 3 hours in Edinburgh, and the soonest he could be back was seven thirty.

"That will be a little tight for my debut celebrity boating dinner party, but it is workable. You will simply have to do all the preparation for me."

He smiled broadly.

"Buy in all the food, of course. Some of that excellent Carrot and Coriander Soup from Covent Garden for starters, and then something Italian, perhaps. Do I remember reading somewhere that Billy G is a fellow vegetarian?"

I said I was sure she was.

"Good. I find it most difficult entertaining carnivores. Unhealthy throwbacks."

He looked over at me.

"But I shall leave the choice of menu entirely up to you. Buy plenty as it is possible there will be an extra guest. It depends on how today goes."

As ever, he was enjoying keeping me in the dark.

"I doubt our extra guest has ever eaten a meal that does not contain any meat, so that will make it doubly interesting."

He had a wicked twinkle in his eye. "If it does not work out for you as a recording engineer, you can regard it as a day's training for a possible career as a butler."

He looked across at me, while dodging through the traffic.

"Although I am not sure you have the looks for it. Or the necessary sexual orientation. If we did not live in an age of equal sexual opportunity, I would definitely demand that any butler of mine should be gay. And of your many

– 76 –

undoubted qualities, I fear being gay is not one of them."

As we approached the M25, the traffic got busier, and he finally had to stop trying to annoy me, and concentrate on manoeuvring the great ship granny through the traffic. He made it to the airport with the obligatory hour to spare (this was before they extended waiting times to several days due to the terrorist threats).

"They will be screening the mid week lottery tonight," was his final parting thought, "and I am sure Richard could get you a pass if you want to check out the studio. You had better keep my mobile phone in case I need to get in touch with you."

With that he disappeared into Terminal One and I was left to drive back to the Betsy.

I know I have referred to the Betsy before, but perhaps I should try a little harder to describe her. Firstly, as I have already said, she is made of concrete. Or at least the hull is. From sideways on, the dreaded Beasty resembles a concrete bath with a roof on.

And The Vicar may have done a lot of work on the inside, but it still doesn't stop you from feeling that you are inside a well appointed coal bunker, or perhaps a prefabricated garage. His guests were unlikely to see the slickest bit, which was definitely the double bedroom in the stern – that's the back, to land lubbers like you and me – complete with an invitingly large curved double bed and ensuite bathroom. A veritable babe magnet, in the hands of a sex-perienced professional, like yours truly.

Which reminds me. Why is the khazi on a boat called the '*head*'? Why '*head*'? I ask. Why not some other part of the body, such as the '*Arse*'? It would seem more appropriate. The only time my *'head'* goes anywhere near the pan is after a lengthy night on the town, and even then, as I am sure you can imagine, I miss more often than not. My *'arse'*, however, visits the throne far more often and is considerably more accurate. I suppose that's sailors for you.

I digress. Back to the matter in hand. How could I make such an ugly duckling into a swan in the space of a day? In less than a day, in fact, as I was determined to take my chance to visit the National Lottery Studios.

Outside caterers were the only answer.

Some flowers, a well laid table, some candles. Is that too much to ask for?

For most of the companies I called it clearly was, as my fingers had to do some extensive walking. In fact they probably completed a half marathon, before I finally tracked down a company in the Yellow Pages, who were willing to take on such a bizarre situation.

"Darling, if we can decorate a marquee, then why not a concrete coal bunker?"

They promised to meet me at the boat at five o'clock.

Which left me exactly five hours in which to visit the National Lottery studios, assuming that Breamore could get me a pass. I was as nervous about talking to him as I was excited about nosing around the studio. In the end my excitement won – although I tried very hard to persuade his secretary to arrange things herself, without 'putting me through' to her lord and master. Isn't it strange how secretaries will never put you through to someone when you desperately need to talk to them, but will insist on doing it when you would rather not?

"I am very sorry to disturb you, sir," I began. "The Vicar suggested that you might be able to get me a pass to TV centre to have a look at the National Lottery Studios."

"Where is David?" he demanded.

I tried to sound important. "He has been called away to Scotland on business. He has asked me to go to the studios on his behalf."

Breamore made it very clear that he would rather wait until the Vicar could go himself. I was not going to let him steal my moment of glory.

"Unfortunately, sir, it has to be today, as they will be preparing the midweek lottery. It really would help our investigation very much if I could get a pass."

I thought I had slipped in the phrase "our investigation" most professionally, but he was having none of it.

"Just remind your Vicar," he bellowed, "that I am paying him, not you, to look after Billy G. If he telephones, tell him I wish to speak to him. Immediately. In the meantime, I will see what I can do. Phone my secretary in quarter of an hour."

He got me the pass, of course, and I duly went off to Television Centre. I would love to relate my visit in detail, but what's the point – unless you are interested in a mediocre description of a BBC TV studio, or the fact that the warm up comedian is far more interesting than the show itself, or the absurd-icrous way that the audience 'clap' or 'laugh' like sheep when they are told to by an officious floor producer, who waves her arms around like a frustrated conductor. And that was just the rehearsal.

To begin with, I ascertained very little, except that the winning lottery numbers were 5,9,19,21,23 & 39 (none of which were mine) and that absolutely anyone on Breamore's guest list could have switched the CD. Billy G had a rehearsal before the show, at which time the music must have been correct. Between then and the main show, Richard Breamore's entire party traipsed through the control room, at his request, so it could presumably have been any one of them.

Although I did get something of a result, as we might say in the trade, with the bass guitarist. An assistant particularly remembered him as he was wearing a black leather kilt, and had seemed really quite interested in the way the control room worked. She suggested I talk to the guy in the KMFDM T-shirt who brought the CD from the studio, as he was also there the whole time. Unless there had been an unexpected and frankly unlikely outbreak of KMFDM fans (even I had to look them up on the internet to see who they were), this must have been the assistant who I'd met working with Billy G, so hopefully he may have noticed the bass guitarist make the switch.

Altogether not such a poor piece of detective work, even though I say so myself.

The ORDER of
the Boot

WHERE WERE WE? OH YES, MY GREAT PIECE OF DETEC-
tive work at the lottery. I was on a real high, when
I was, as ever, brought down to earth with a resounding
crash by a call from The Vicar, who was in a phone box
at the airport in Scotland. He told me to ring Breamore
and invite him to dinner on the boat.

"Tell him 8 o'clock sharp. He will, no doubt, claim to
have a prior arrangement, so tell him that *Gooda Walker*
should give him ample reason to be on time. Have you got
that? Oh, and pray do not mention that there are any other
guests. We will leave that as a pleasant surprise."

He was not impressed by my suggestions that he might
perhaps make the call himself, saying he was running out
of change and had a plane to catch. How bloody conve-
nient, I thought.

So for the second time in the day I found myself talking to Breamore. He did indeed say that he was otherwise
engaged. He tried to humour me.

"Tell David that it is very kind of him to invite me aboard
his luxurious cruiser" (something about the way he said
'luxurious' made me suspect that he had visited the boat

before) "but it is quite impossible. I have a most important prior engagement that is simply impossible to move. However much I would like to."

I could almost imagine the greasy insincere smile that would have come with the last phrase. He was saying polite things, but making it quite clear that he really meant 'Bugger off you impertinent little S H one T. I have better things to do than mess around in The Vicar's bathtub.'

So I repeated what The Vicar had said about *Gooda Walker*. This caused an instant change of attitude.

"What exactly do you know about *Gooda Walker*?"

"Absolutely nothing," I replied quite truthfully.

"And so what did David mean by it?"

"I have absolutely no idea," I repeated, feeling that my genuine ignorance was probably my best protection against some unknown fate.

"And so why does he think that these magic words will bring me to dinner?"

"I'm sorry. I'm merely the messenger. I know nothing more than I've already told you".

"How bizarre, because I know no more than you do."

But you do, I thought, or you wouldn't still be talking to me.

"David obviously feels he has found something of immense importance. I would hate to let him down. I will see what I can do about this evening. Can you hold on a minute?"

The line went dead, and I was no doubt meant to imagine that he was trying to cancel his 'most important prior engagement'. The power play was clearly with The Vicar and there was no doubt what Breamore was going to say.

"I'll be there. Eight o'clock sharp. Tell him to prepare something decent."

This time the line really went dead.

The taxi carrying The Vicar arrived at the boat at ten to eight. This gave him just enough time to shower, and put on some clean clothes, before preparing to welcome his guests.

"My, my, we have been a busy beaver," he said, surveying the dinner preparations. The caterers had brought in a table, chairs, tablecloth, silver cutlery, the lot. "I was imagining something a little less lavish, perhaps a TV dinner spilled over our laps, but your career as a butler has not started at all badly. Perhaps you had better consider changing your sexual proclivities."

He rearranged the flowers that had been put near the wheelhouse entrance.

"Unfortunately," he looked at the four places laid at the table, "the butler will not be able to eat with us. I personally would be most happy to have your company. As indeed, I always am," he bowed slightly to me as he said this. "But I rather suspect that I would never be forgiven for allowing 'lesser mortals' to hear what is going to be said. In fact, I am not sure that I will be forgiven, full stop".

He went down into the saloon and began to clear away the fourth place.

"However, if you were to stay a while, so as to be here to help our guests make the treacherous journey from the quayside, along that deathtrap of a pontoon and see them safely onto the boat, that would be most useful. We will be doing sufficient injury to our guests' pride, without injuring their persons as well."

He folded up my chair and gave it to me.

"After that, I fear, I will have to give you the night off.

Whether you wish to go into the city or sample the nightlife of Hampstead is entirely up to you."

He looked at me in a conspiratorial way, like a school boy planning a midnight feast (Punksters in the great US of A may not be fully familiar with our strange tradition of toffee-nosed, 'jolly hockey sticks', pillow fights in the dormitory, late nights with matron, boarding schools, so beloved of old British TV shows. In which case you get to go hungry. Scrap the reference to midnight feasts).

"If, of course," The Vicar hinted, "you were to choose to stay closer to home and happened to overhear some of what was said, that would be entirely beyond my control." He looked me in the eye to see if I was following his meaning.

"Now, perhaps, you had better show me what delightful food I have been preparing with my long hours sweating over a hot stove."

I showed him what was in the various pans, under the grill, and in the oven, and did my best to hide my immense disappointment. After doing all that work, I had certainly expected to join them rather than being turfed out into the cold. Bugger this life as a butler, I thought. Who the hell would do this for a living? I was just planning my future career as a revolutionary, when a car drew up on the gravel outside, and I went out armed with a powerful torch to try to shepherd the prospective lamb to the slaughter.

It was Billy G. She had arrived in a two-seater Vauxhall, coloured metallic orange to match her hair. Flash, but not one of those really expensive sports car that I used to pin up on my wall and salivate over ('salivate', not 'masturbate', you perverts. Whoever heard of someone masturbating over a car? Except Jeremy Clarkson, perhaps). Billy G certainly had not dressed up for the occasion. Underneath her long Nazi style leather coat, she was wearing jeans, with the obligatory split on the knees, and an untucked white shirt. No doubt expensive stuff, but hardly your designer dresses. All horribly sensible for an evening on a boat. God, how I hated all this sensibleness. The Vicar's disease must be catching, I thought.

I lit the way along the pontoon as best I could, and showed her the way up onto the boat.

"My God, so it really does exist," she gushed, in that fantastic husky accent of hers. "But hey, it's not nearly as Heath Robinson as I expected."

Clearly, someone had had the good sense to warn her what to expect.

"And I bet I am not the first luuvverly lady to be lured out here. Should I have brought my bodyguards with me?"

We went up onto the back deck where The Vicar had come out into the dark to meet her. He took her hand and ceremonially kissed it.

"Dark was the night as pitch or as the coal,
 and at the window out she put her hole,
 and Absolon, him it befell no better or worse,
 But with his mouth he kissed her naked arse,
 Full savourly, before he knew what it was".

He always pronounced Chaucer in such a way that it wasn't possible to work out exactly what he was saying – which is usually quite a good thing.

"Welcome aboard The Betsy," he trilled. "If you have survived the shark infested swamps of Hampstead, and our peculiarly man-eating pontoon, then I doubt anything inside will hold any perils for you."

THE VICAR OPENED THE CABIN DOOR TO WELCOME BILLY G onto the boat.

"I've never been greeted with poetry before," she giggled. "Am I wrong, or was that a little bit 'risque'? Perhaps I should get you to help with my lyrics."

She went down below into the cabin.

"Hey, is someone getting married?" she laughed as she saw all the decorations inside. "I hope you haven't laid all this on just for me? I'll be needing to spread a few cigarette stubs and crisp packets around the place to create a bit of working class club chic. This could ruin a carefully crafted reputation."

I could feel myself going red in the face.

"Punk was worried that you would not be willing to eat at a table that was not laid for a princess, complete with silver cutlery and candles," The Vicar explained. "Please don't disillusion him and tell him that you expected chicken McNuggets in a bag."

"Ciabatta and jam is more my style. Ciabatta 'cos it a little bit poncey and jam to keep it real." She smiled and looked round at me. "How chuffed is he, or what! No, the boy's done good, as we're meant to say up North. Very many thanks. I am sure you will get your reward in heaven. If not sooner, in the arms of several beautiful ladies, if you know what I mean."

She had a wonderful way of pronouncing words. 'Beautiful' with a long 'u', like 'beauuuutiful', and 'ladies', with a long 'a', more like 'l-ay-dies'.

"It looks like we have everything we need for a riotous party," she agreed, "so long as there is some beer available."

The Vicar cast me an anxious glance. He only drinks 'Champagne, sparking water or beerless beer' (alcohol free) at parties, and certainly would not have had the foresight to buy in some cans of John Smiths. Fortunately, I had – although I had been hoping to drink them myself – and I produced a cluster of cans with the necessary flourish.

"And is there somewhere on this boat I can have a leak?" Billy G crossed her legs. "I was stuck in that car for so long I was afraid I was going to pee in my knickers."

"Or in your G String!" is obviously the slick smooth answer I should have given. It's so easy to think of these things months later. But at the time, I was goosebumping uncontrollably (I blame it on the hormones) and could do little more than grunt unintelligibly as I showed her down the steps into the back cabin.

I told you about the magnetic qualities of that bedroom. The first thing she did as she entered the cabin, even before having a leak, was to fling herself onto the bed.

"How fantastic is this?!" she laughed. "All these naughty naughty rumours about the state of this boat, but hey, it's really quite together."

Life can be a bitch, can't it? If you had told a spotty seventeen year old Punk Sanderson that he would one day be in a bedroom with Billy G bouncing up and down on the bed, he would have died and gone to heaven. But here I was, in exactly that situation, and it was more like hell than heaven. It was The Vicar's bed, on The Vicar's boat, and that same goddamn Vicar was about to turf me out onto the street. Where was I when the luck was handed out?

I had yet to say a word to her. I was rehearsing some simple phrases such as 'who told you about the boat?', or 'what did they say?' or the obligatory 'I suppose oral sex is out of the question?' when the Vicar called down to say that he had heard a second car drawing up on the gravel. Time to jump up and do my angel of mercy bit, before Breamore ended up in the Thames.

So that was the end of my one and only bedroom scene with Billy G. Snuffed out, before it had a chance to get going. Story of my life. If you're expecting romance, Punksters, you're in the wrong place.

So. Breamore's arrival.

He had parked his suitably expensive Rolls Royce next to Billy G's car. He certainly travelled in style, although I was relieved to see no sign of a chauffeur. Seeing the difference in the cars made me wonder if there wasn't something in Sean Fitzpatrick's theory about managers and record labels getting rich while musicians never make any money. I remember reading about Gilbert O'Sullivan, I think it was, who used to live in a caravan at the bottom of his manager's garden, while he was writing all those number one hit songs. Duh! Am I mad, or is there something wrong with this picture?!

Either way, Breamore was certainly not afraid of splashing it around. He obviously had plenty of the folding stuff left after buying the car, as he was dressed in full dinner suit complete with dicky bow and white scarf. He also had one of those flashy belts trying to hold his stomach in check. A moribund, or whatever it is. And I bet the rocks on his fingers were worth a bob or two. It made Billy G look very underdressed.

He had already got out of his car, and was looking at Billy G's as I walked towards him.

"I see we have some other guests. Who is there?" he demanded.

"Just you and Billy G," I mumbled, guiding him along the pontoon.

I could tell by the look on his face that she was the last person he was expecting.

I don't know if you know the scene at the end of the musical "Oliver!", when all the wooden walkways start sinking into the mud of the Thames, as the Victorian coppers chase Scrooge and his army of pickpockets along the backs of the buildings, but walking along that pontoon always reminds me of it. Squelch, glorious squelch! I think the rebel in me quite fancied seeing a bit of Thames mud on Breamore's dinner jacket and patent leather shoes. He placed every foot very carefully as if picking his way through a field of cowpats.

The rebel in me was disappointed, of course, as he arrived quite safely on deck, to be greeted by The Vicar.

"Come below and get warm, Richard. I have just opened a bottle of Champagne. Unless you prefer to join Billy G with a glass of beer."

"I'm not sure that I am in much of a party mood." He pulled the Vicar to one side, but not far enough that I couldn't hear. "I hope you know what you are doing, David. I got some fool's message about *Gooda Walker*, which clearly does not concern you. Whatever you want to discuss, let's do it quickly and privately, with just the two of us. Certainly not in front of Billy G. And then I must be off, I was going to the opera, and I don't want to miss the whole thing."

"And I thought you had dressed up on my behalf!" The Vicar exclaimed, addressing a larger audience and pushing Breamore down into the boat. "I cannot guarantee that I will let you escape so lightly. As you can see we have gone to a lot of trouble. Punk will be most disappointed if you don't sample all the food he has prepared. And I am sure there is nothing that you can say to me that you cannot say in front of the beautiful Billy G."

He acted as if he was introducing them to one another.

"You have met I suppose. You do manage her after all. It's her royalties that help to pay for that magnificent Rolls Royce".

"I can see you are in one of your light hearted moods. I am afraid I am not. Perhaps we should meet later tonight." He pulled The Vicar aside again. "This is not something to discuss in front of women."

"Ah yes, I remember your views on women. Not exactly very new man. Employ them if they have large bosoms, make money from them if they can sing, sleep with them if they will have you, lie to them whenever necessary and never treat them as an equal. Have I left something out?" The Vicar smiled as he looked Breamore straight in the eye.

Woah! If this was to be the style of conversation, I began to see why The Vicar felt that my presence might be slightly undesiri-whatsit.

"Not now," Breamore whispered loudly through his teeth.

"No, it must be now," The Vicar said equally firmly, leaving Breamore in no doubt that he still held the big, thick gnarly whip hand. He then put the big grin back on his face "Perhaps Punk can get you a drink before he leaves us. Billy G, I trust we have not been deserting you."

The Vicar and Breamore went over to join her in the saloon.

"Hi Richard. Have you had your hair cut or your ears lowered?" I heard her say. "You look depressed. I heard on the radio driving here that the Japanese have discovered that clenching your buttocks one hundred times a day is an excellent cure for depression. And you have such fine buttocks. Come on, let's try."

She held her arms up and began closing her buttocks, in a comic dance somewhere between suggestive pelvic thrusts and someone struggling with constipation. The Vicar was in for an exciting evening. The combination of his two guests seemed fairly explosive.

They had all moved down into the saloon, leaving me standing alone in the galley. The Vicar looked up at me.

"Am I right that you have other plans for this evening? I am sure we can cope if you need to leave us."

My signal to leave. I am flattered to say that Billy G was good enough to say "Aren't you staying. I had assumed you would be eating with us", but I was in no doubt that Breamore, for one, was pleased to see the back of me.

Before going, I asked The Vicar if I could borrow his big boating jacket. It is waterproof and lined with the wool of about twelve sheep. Just the thing for a cold April evening. He handed it to me with a simple "don't get too cold", and I clambered off the boat.

CHAPTER FIVE

IT WAS BY NOW VERY DARK OUTSIDE, AND I HAD LEFT THE torch on the boat, knowing the party goers would need it later. I also knew that I would have no use for it. I was on covert ops – if I had any black shoe polish, I would have been smearing it over my face, and doing my Al Jolson impersonation.

Fortunately – very fortunately given the standard of my singing – there was no shoe polish, and so no Al Jolson. But the scene is set. A dark, cloudy night. Can I use the words 'pitch black'? Some jack ass will no doubt point out that London is never 'pitch black', what with the constant orange glow of the street lights and all.

"Ah ha! But how can you be so sure?" I ask. "Is it not possible that the little old man who goes around switching on the street lights in London could have been late for work that night, after a long day visiting his younger sister, who paints the dew drops on the flowers at the bottom of the garden, who lives across the road from her uncle who turns off the light in the fridges, near the dirty little boy who puts the dust onto the top of the picture frames, and just upstairs from the elderly lady who puts the mould on all the strawberries less than an hour after you've bought them?"

Touché. This is my story, so if I fancy 'pitch black', 'pitch black' it shall be. I should know, 'cos I was there.

BTW – Seeing that word '*Touché*', reminds me of the joke about George W Bush, who asked a waitress for a 'quickie'. She was very upset, thinking that he was following the "errant sexual path" of Bill Clinton. Turns out he was reading the menu, and trying to order a 'quiche'...Thought you might be amused.

Back to me leaving the boat. I went up onto the rear deck, and then made a show of announcing my departure by jumping loudly down onto the pontoon, a brave thing to do at the best of times, and absotively posilutely stupid in the dark without a torch. Imagine the headlines:

'Idiot drowns in mud on the Thames. Too dumb to deserve to live.'

Fortunately, the ageing timbers of the pontoon did not choose this moment to give up the ghost. I waited for the boat to stop rocking and then walked very quietly, and rather more gingerly, along the pontoon towards the bows of the boat. The saloon had two small portholes and I positioned myself carefully in the blank spot between the two, before gently clambering my way back onto the boat. As I reached the side decks, I could hear the muffled sound of voices inside. For some reason they were discussing *Hello* magazine, which, unless I am getting my Harpers confused with my Vogues, is the magazine that specialises in luvvy duvvy couples pictured inside the glossy interiors of their expensive houses.

"That was straight after Cambridge," The Vicar was saying. "They had no interest in me. It was all down to my then female companion, Miss Camilla Fry-Hillier. Her father was the British ambassador in Paris at the time – a mover and shaker of the highest order..."

I couldn't hear the next few words correctly. It sounded like "A formal kennel with the arses and now on empty", but that can't be right. Anyone who thinks they can decipher it, please send your suggestions. Answers on a postcard to the usual address.

I moved slightly closer to the porthole and could hear The Vicar continuing

"...I was in fact so far beneath her that her mother felt I needed a stepladder just to kiss her beloved daughter's buttocks."

I had heard that joke before, but it was always well received.

"I think that the editors of *Hello* magazine were keen to make the poor Betsy look as seedy as possible, to show just how far Camilla had been forced to demean herself in the search for love. We always suspected their main reason for featuring us was that they thought we were good candidates for the *Hello* curse. Are you familiar with this phenomenon?"

I couldn't see anyone, but I could imagine a general shaking of heads.

"No?" the Vicar went on. "The fact that most couples

split up soon after an article about them is published? I am pleased to say that we did not prove an exception to the rule. We lasted barely a month after publication."

"Any well bred woman would have far too much sense to consider actually marrying you!" Breamore snorted, still sounding impatient to be elsewhere.

"Our futures did indeed lie in different directions," The Vicar replied. "She is now happily married to George Berenstein, the chairman of Coutts bank. I met them for dinner recently."

"But I thought everyone at Cambridge was gay!" Billy G yelped. "You know, all those spies, Philby and Burgess, and Stephen Fry."

"Stephen Fry is not a spy, as far as I know. And unfortunately I must confess that I was not part of the trendy bendies. Although I have nothing against it, you understand. It was an all male college at the time and young men are inclined to follow the direction of their erection, so who knows what was going on inside the seat of learning, as you might say."

I missed Billy G's answer, as I had decided to move positions. One of the three hatches in the cabin roof was slightly open. I lay full length on the roof, and slid my way across until I could peer in through the hatch lid.

The pleasantries were continuing.

"But did I hear on the grapevine that you did finally tie the knot some time ago?" Breamore was jabbering. "I would be pleased to invite you and your wife out to dinner if you are ever in town."

"We lead a very private life," The Vicar answered. "But we thank you for the invitation. Perhaps at some time in the future."

"That'll be the day," I thought. "Not a hope. Not some much as a rat's patooty. I would bet a year's salary on it. I would bet all the money I will ever earn..."

The Vicar's wife. Trust bloody Breamore to bring up the subject of the Vicar's goddamn wife. Just when I had the story moving along so smoothly and professionally.

I am sorry, Punksters, to let my private obsessions derail your enjoyment of this story, but I have promised to be honest, and honest I shall be, right down to the stains on my underpants. Perhaps now is, therefore, the time to come clean about my obsession with this mysterious lady.

Or maybe not.

It could prove a lengthy detour, I hear you thinking.

And you are right, of course.

I resisted the temptation a few chapters ago, and I suppose I can do again. Although, believe me, it's the worse kind of itch – and itches are something I am well qualified to talk about – *'Bitches keep bitchin' and Clap just keep itchin'* as the song goes. The more I think about it, the more the itch just keeps growing. If you imagine it started in my groin, where, let's be honest, itches normally start, it would now have spread all the way down both legs and up my entire upper body. I would now be nothing but bright red, itchy flesh. There would even be itches on the ends of my fingers that are trying to scratch the itches everywhere else.

Oops. There I go. I almost got carried away. I told you, it's really is an unhealthy obsession. Time to get a grip of myself. A pause, a deep breath, a smart slap in the face, a couple of pints of beer, and we continue – ignoring all references to the Vicar's wife...

The Vicar had got up from the table and was fetching the carrot and coriander soup from the galley.

"Time to move from the aperitifs to the starter, and from the pleasantries to the business of the day." He served both Billy G and Breamore, before serving himself, and taking his seat at the table. He put his napkin in his lap. "First a grace, perhaps. Or just a pause before we launch into this excellent dinner and the business at hand."

He bowed his head in the same ritual I have described before, taking a series of deep breathes, before thrusting his left fist into the air and shouting the word "Yes!", rocking the boat a bit as he did so.

"And what exactly, may I ask, is the business at hand?" Breamore demanded as soon as the Vicar had broken the silence.

"I would suggest that the subject is…redemption." The Vicar paused. "Which is very real, and is available to all of us on a daily basis. But how to earn it? That is a tricky one."

He paused again.

"The offending party must put themselves inside the circle of healing. We have some rough terrain, to cover so the sooner we set off the better." He tried the soup. "Excellent, as always."

"What terrain?" Breamore bellowed. "I assume you are going to give us some signposts, or even better a map."

"Actually I am certain of only one thing. And that is the uncertainty of the outcome. Where we are going is how we get there."

Those familiar with Vicarspeak will have heard such phrases before.

"All I can give you is a starting point. We will all three find out together where it leads. The starting point is this."

The Vicar took another spoonful of soup before continuing. "I have a colleague, of many years standing, who I fear may have been involved in some financial misdealings. Should I allow him the chance to address these issues in front of a select group of friends and colleagues, to take advantage of the redemption of which I spoke earlier...

...or should I allow him to slowly but surely impale himself on these problems of his own making?"

A BED TIME STORY

S O THERE I WAS, PERCHED ON THE ROOF OF THE VICAR'S boat, listening to him lecture Billy G and Breamore about 'redemption' of all things.

"The repercussions of our actions are remorseless and completely unavoidable," he was saying. "The best we can do is to hold our hands up, admit defeat and to try to cut a deal."

I felt some raindrops starting to fall on my head. I looked up at the sky (why do we do that? where else is the bloody rain going to come from? What did I expect to see? A woman's squatting over me and peeing on my head?).

I pulled the collar of my coat up around my neck.

"If neither of you has anything to say then perhaps I shall describe the landscape of our mythical journey in greater detail. We have a nice friendly management company that is apparently two periods late in paying royalties to its artists."

As he said this Billy G, who might have been bored by all the preamble, gave him her full attention. I carefully wiped some of the raindrops off the hatch to improve my grand-stand view, nervous all the time in case anyone looked up.

"The accounts of this management company make interesting reading. The delay in paying their artists is not due to late payment by big bad record companies, as may have been suggested. The company is in debt because it has paid huge fees to two other companies, both, surprise, surprise, controlled by the same single director, who controls the management company."

Billy G had heard enough. "Are you saying that my royalties…"

The Vicar raised his hand. "Let me finish. Now I have started I had better lay out all the facts, unless anyone else would like to finish our cosy little bed time story?"

He looked at Breamore, who remained silent. From above I couldn't see the look on his face. All I had was an excellent view of a small balding spot on the top of his head and some suspiciously grey looking roots. I carefully wiped the hatch again.

"Very well, children," The Vicar continued. "Let us use our imagination. Let us imagine that these two other companies paid this money straight into the ever needy bank account of this director. It is impossible to tell if this is in fact so, as, both these other companies are nearly nine months overdue in filing their accounts, and are no doubt incurring serious penalties." He again looked at Breamore.

A motor boat went by, kicking up a large wash, which caused the boat to rock. They all looked up, and I backed away from the hatch, trying to find something to hold on to. The cabin top was now quite wet, and it was not blessed with such simple things as hand rails. I gripped the edge of the hatch, and waited for the wash to subside, wobbling precariously on the roof of the boat.

The Vicar resumed.

"What we must now consider is why the behaviour of this mythical director, which had until then, we suppose, been a model of ethical business practice, might suddenly become less straightforward. My trip to Scotland has furnished me with one possible reason."

Still Breamore kept silent. I pushed my nose right up against the hatch cover to get a better view. It would have been a terrifying sight if someone had looked up. A large snotty nose staring back at you.

"Some years ago, I had the dubious pleasure of attending a college reunion with my then manager," he lent over and pretended to spit on the floor, "and a new colleague of his."

There was now no doubt he was talking about Malvolio and Breamore.

"A wonderful event, for those who like old fashioned ceremonies. You dress up in all your academic finery, including a large black gown," he turned to Billy G, "making you look like an overgrown bat," he explained to her. "And there I sat with the great and the good, receiving advice as to how I might improve my financial situation. This new colleague suggested that I become a name on a certain Lloyds syndicate of which he was a member. The Gooda Walker syndicate. I don't know if you know how Lloyds works?"

Billy G shook her head "no".

The Vicar wiped his hands on his serviette, reached behind him, and placed a copy of a paperbook book on the table in front of him.

"*Ultimate Risk* by Adam Raphael. It makes interesting reading. As recommended to me by Angela Barnett of the Financial Times. By becoming a member of a syndicate, and doing absolutely nothing, not even putting in an investment, you can earn a percentage of the vast sums of money that are paid in insurance premiums every year. Money for free. And the British are the most overinsured nation in the world." He quoted from the book. "Once upon a time smug, fat men sidled up to one on shoots and smirked horribly: *'Just got the Lloyds' cheque. Very nice number – pays for the wife to go to Portugal with her boyfriend, settles the school fees and takes care of the cartridges. You really ought to think about it.'"*

The Vicar closed the book.

"I declined, fortunately as it turned out. I have often remembered that conversation as I have read about the horrifying demands placed on the Lloyds names, and about how it has driven many of them to bankruptcy, even suicide. The problem with being an insurance underwriter is that when there are very large claims, such as the billions that are currently being paid out over the health risks from asbestos, you are financially liable. And there is no limit to your liability. You can lose your bank account, your home, your car, even your gold Cartier."

As The Vicar said this, Breamore took his hand off the table and hid it in his lap.

"Such is the fate that has befallen many of those illustrious Lloyds names."

I again wiped the hatch with the sleeve of the jacket, and peered up at the sky to see if mother nature was going to stop peeing down the back of my neck.

"A well-informed insider was kind enough to share his research on Lloyds with me. I flew to Edinburgh to look through his papers. He estimates that that the losses to each individual on the syndicates in question could have been in the region of..." he paused for effect.

"…two million pounds."

Fortunately there was a loud intake of breath from Billy G, which was loud enough to disguise my own.

"Now if our imaginary director were a member of these syndicates, one could imagine that the need to find two million pounds might have caused a slight cashflow problem at the imaginary management company in question".

He got up and cleared away the soup bowls.

Billy G and Breamore sat in stunned silence.

"There is now an excellent tomato, basil and mozzarella salad," he announced. "I personally recommend these beans, but perhaps now is not the time for a discussion on the importance of diet. Oh I am sorry, Richard, no meat". He laid a large, beautifully prepared dish in the middle of the table, before again regaining his seat.

"It is possible that this entire story is inaccurate, in which case I have made a supreme fool of myself. Or it is possible that at least some part of it is correct. Either way, that is our starting point. I suggest we now all travel the road together to see where it may lead us. Alternatively, we can each carry on seeking the truth individually and present the facts to an uncaring, unfriendly world. The choice is yours."

BREAMORE
COMES CLEAN

I TOOK ADVANTAGE OF A PAUSE IN THE CONVERSATION TO reposition myself. I had been lying stretched out on the roof – but unfortunately the rain seemed to be trickling straight from The Vicar's waterproof coat onto my jeans, which were uncomfortably damp. But I could hardly wander back in and ask him to lend me his waterproof trousers, so instead I tried sitting cross-legged on the cabin top, with my legs pulled in under the coat, and my head huddled deep into the collar. It was considerably drier, but my grandstand view was less good. To the couple over by the parked cars, I must have looked rather like an enormous bright red garden gnome planted on top of the boat. No more ridiculous than usual, I suppose. I lent forward and again peered through the hatch. It was Breamore's turn to do the talking.

"May I ask what led you in this direction?" he bleated.

"I could never understand why you did not bring in the Police, or some professional investigators. It made me wonder if there was something you did not want them to find."

"It never occurred to you that it is possible that I brought you in because I knew what you would find? Melville warned me that you were always too intelligent for your own good. You idealists should learn not to attack the hand that is paying your bills."

From where I was sitting, I couldn't tell if he was crying or smiling.

"It would seem that I have some explaining to do," he wheezed.

Too bloody right, I remember thinking. There he was sitting in comfort in his dicky bow and patent leather shoes, while I was outside in the cold, and all the time he was ripping her off.

"Or rather some apologising as the explanation has been done for me. David's facts are all basically correct. I am sorry, Billy G, I have misled you. As David has rightly suggested your royalties could have been paid on time, but the money was paid to my other companies, from where I used it to pay the Lloyds debts. I had already borrowed as much as I could. I have sold everything worth selling. My house is mortgaged so heavily that I would gain little by selling it. True, I have kept the Rolls Royce, but it is not worth as much as you might think, and a manager without status cannot properly serve his artists…"

At that point I almost slipped off the boat, I was so angry. He shouldn't have said that. I thought he was doing well at covering his arse until then. He even had a hard hearted revolutionary like me feeling quite sorry for him. But a man who regards a Rolls Royce as a necessary accessory does not deserve sympathy. Hang him, I say. And in the meantime fix some bloody grab handles on this boat before I fall off.

"It seemed," he was gibbering, "that the obvious thing was to use your royalties and to take out a loan for you.

Except for the interest payments, you would have been no worse off. I had always intended to somehow refund you the cost of the interest."

I am sorry to keep butting in, but what he said still makes me angry – even now, months later. Even in this naughty new millennium of ours, it seems a bit rich to claim that theft is alright provided no one finds out. Or am I out of touch? Call me old-fashioned , but I would chop his hands off, gold cufflinks and all, and I wouldn't blame Billy G if she wanted to cut off a lower piece of his anatomy as well.

"Legally, I must tell you I have done nothing wrong. Those two companies to which David refers simply sent invoices for my services, which were paid in the normal way. Morally, I know I should have paid the royalties to you first…"

Well that's something I suppose.

"I had considered doing this, and asking you for a loan, but there was no reason why you should grant it. Perhaps, I was too proud to ask. I shall, of course, resign. As for the royalty payments, the company is effectively bankrupt, so I cannot guarantee how easily you will get them. However, you can always try and lay claim to any personal money that I have, including the tiny part of my house that is not owned by the bank, assuming you get there before Lloyds do."

At this point he looked up at The Vicar, probably to see how well he had done at extracting himself from the large pile of manure he had dumped on himself.

"I think that completes your hypothetical journey for you," Breamore scowled, and then, more defiantly, or even sinisterly "We shall see if it is the end of the road for me."

The Vicar remained totally unmoved, if that is the right expression. At least, what I mean is that he showed no emotion whatsoever. No sign of forgiveness, or of blame. He merely continued with his dinner party, as if all this was innocent small talk. He got up to clear the plates.

"I make no judgement. As I said at the outset, redemption is freely available to all. All we need do is allow it to take place within us. And we must be willing to pick up our own tab, or for someone else to pick it up on our behalf."

He carried the dishes up to the galley – or at least, I assume he did as he went out of my view.

"And I fear we are not yet at the end of our journey. We have only just begun. And there are still several more courses of dinner."

He was carrying something back to the table.

"Do you also owe royalties to all the other members of the group?"

"No, I no longer manage them. They left my company when Billy G split up the band. Surely you knew about that?"

"No, I recall seeing some headlines in *Music Week*, but sadly I passed them by as being of no interest. Vegetable lasagne?" he asked Billy G, silver serving most professionally with the hot dish balanced on one hand, and a spoon and fork in the other. He was enjoying his role as party host. "Do I gather that the parting of the ways was not entirely amicable?"

"That depends what you mean," Billy G chirped. "We still talk to each other when we meet, you know. We even, like, use the same studio. Emma B's currently in studio One at West End studios, where you came yesterday. Hey, after working with people for several years it is difficult not to be friendly when you meet in a corridor. Doesn't stop us suing the Armani bra straps off each other's backs, though."

She smiled as she said this. It was good that Billy G was

entering the fray, as I had a clear view of her face. The rain was now dribbling off the end of my nose, and if the meeting had not been so riveting I would long since have given up. In fairness to The Vicar, I could see why he thought that they might resent my presence. But the rain wasn't that bad. I have been in some clubs where you can get that wet listening to the band. And that's far worse as the liquid falling on your head sure ain't water.

"And what is the dispute about?" The Vicar asked.

"Well, it's a bit of a long story..." Billy G started, before Breamore cut in.

"If Billy G is going to spill the dirt, do you mind if I go and have a cigarette. I need to settle my nerves. I am not sure I can do justice to your dinner at the moment."

"Revolting habit!" The Vicar pulled a disgusted face. "But be my guest. Not in the boat, though, as the smell lingers forever. You will have to go up on the back deck."

Breamore got up, clearly intent on heading outside to have his cigarette. Time for me to panic. As soon as he reached the back deck, he would have a perfect view of me, sitting perched on the cabin roof. Bond may be cool in these situations, but most of us, I discovered are darnright awkward. I rolled off the cabin as quietly as I could, although from inside I probably sounded like a herd of pregnant elephants charging over the cabin roof. I was sure they must have heard me as The Vicar got up and closed the hatch I had been sitting near. It couldn't be helped. By then, I was already dashing along the side deck, causing the boat to rock, before flinging myself down on the foredeck, where I would hopefully be hidden by the front of the cabin. I had just ducked down, when the night sky lit up, as Breamore opened the galley door and stepped out onto the back deck.

The rain had eased off a bit, and he was evidently happy to stay outside for a while – no doubt reflecting on the fine mess he had gotten himself into, as Laurel would say to Hardy, or the other way round. I could only pray he would not be too long as the foredeck was very damp and very uncomfortable. I lay there panting and listening to my heart trying to tell me that I don't take enough exercise.

After several minutes, when it became clear that he was not exactly hurrying to rejoin the party, and that no one was coming out to investigate the noises I had made, I began looking around the foredeck to see if there was somewhere better to hide. There was a hatch, similar to the ones on the cabin roof, which had also been left open, no doubt to allow fresh air through the boat. I slid across, eased it further open and lowered myself into the forepeak of the boat.

IT WAS WONDERFUL TO BE OUT OF THE RAIN. I SAT ON THE bed and took off my trousers and The Vicar's hefty coat. I could still hear him and Billy G talking in the saloon next door. If they were to find me, I would have literally been caught with my pants down.

The forepeak had two berths, which were laid out in a V shape, so that one person sleeps on each side of the boat, and your toes play tickle-your-partner in the middle. Those of a boating persuasion will probably know what I mean – and if you don't, it is hardly critical to your enjoyment of the story. Take a day off and go to the boat show in London. What is important is that I was now dry, relatively safe, and as an added bonus, I could still overhear the scandal that was going on next door. Unlike The Vicar, who had passed over the Music Week articles about the dispute between Billy G and Emma, I had followed the story blow by gorgeous blow, so I already knew most of what Billy G was telling him. The essence was as follows. Billy G had decided to fold the band to pursue a solo career, but the other three members had decided to continue using the band name without her. She had tried to stop them, supported by Breamore, which is why the rest of the group left his management company. The recent talk in Music Week was of high court writs and ever growing legal costs.

"Why are you so determined to prevent them from continuing?" The Vicar was asking.

"Come on. How chuffed would you be if a group you invented, with a name you thought of, went on without you? You're something else you are. Anyway, I need to hold on to the name. Richard said that if my solo career doesn't take off, I should consider reforming the group."

This was news to me. If I was not an honourable underpaid assistant, I could probably have sold the story to a gossip magazine.

"At present, though, I want a solo career."

"More money?"

"And more pressure! You'd never believe what it was like to be all alone live on national television, miming to a tape that is singing the wrong fucking words. I died. Had that been the four of us, it would have been a lot easier to handle. In fact, we would probably have stuck our arses up the cameras and acted as if it was all deliberate. It's easier in a group. It's the same with this internet thing. When it's focused only on you, it's so frigging personal. If much more of this happens, I probably will reform the group, because it takes the pressure off. Who needs it?"

"Have you any suspicions about who might be doing it?"

"No, some nutter maybe?"

This eavesdropping business was tiring work, so I lay down on the bed with my hand behind my head, and settled in for a long hard listen.

"Do you have many?" The Vicar was asking.

"My fair share, I suppose. There's a guy in Germany who

writes to me every day to tell me what he's been dreaming about, and how he's gotta spend five minutes in a room alone with me. *'I have had no sexual life since my pacemaker and my artificial heart flap. I am infinite frustrated.'* You know the sort of thing. Richard's been trying to get the cops to stop him writing. You also get stalkers whenever you go on tour. For two or three months, they'll go everywhere you go. They'll be at your hotel before you get there, at the airport before you check in, at the venue before you soundcheck. Just everywhere. You gotta blot 'em out of your head, darling, or it would drive you craaazy."

"But crazies don't normally have access to studio master tapes, and editing equipment."

"So who then?" she asked.

"You tell me. That's why you are here this evening. Ah, Richard…"

I heard the sound of steps. Breamore must have been rejoining them.

"…I was asking Billy G who she thinks might be behind all this trouble. I assume you did not do it."

There was a silence.

"Come, come, my fellow it is a perfectly simple question. And I shall undoubtedly find out the answer sooner or later, so if it is you, it would be best to get it off your chest now."

There was another silence. I moved over to the door that separated my front cabin from the main saloon, and eased it slightly ajar so as to be able to see the action.

"Am I being unreasonable in some way?" The Vicar taunted. "Billy G, have I not been entirely fair with him? Was it not a simple question?"

Billy G did not answer. We all waited for Breamore. It was a long while before he spoke.

"I cannot describe quite how much it hurts to know that you were serious in asking me that. I suppose, after the crimes I have already committed, it should not surprise me, but it does. Whoever is persecuting Billy G is cruel, and I do not think of myself as cruel. Misguided, maybe, but not cruel. No. I had nothing to do with it."

"I know!" The Vicar cackled. "But it is good to hear you say so. I asked myself 'Is this kind of behaviour true to the Richard Breamore I know' and it was not. Whoever is persecuting Billy G is also creative and inventive, not at all like you."

"I am not sure whether I should be pleased or insulted!"

"I do not think you would wish to be described as artistic. Artists are very low down on the food chain, well below managers, and in a completely different dining car to record company executives. I suppose Billy G hasn't offended any of them recently?"

"No, not to my knowledge." Billy G masturbated an imaginary penis in the air. "You know, I'm pretty good at giving them all the right kind of hand job when they deign to visit me backstage."

"Well I would strongly recommend you do start offending a few of the blood sucking little leaches. It is no more than they deserve. But that is a different story. And your manager would strongly disagree with me...Now. Who else might you have offended, pray tell? There was some crackpot outside the studio the other day claiming that you had stolen her song."

"There's always someone or other. Which reminds me, Mr Brainless Breamore." Billy G stood up to stare him straight in the eyes. "What about my publishing money. I suppose you syphoned that off too?"

Breamore nodded.

Billy G fell back into her seat "Ten minutes late and your dinner's in the dog."

"But I thought someone else wrote your songs for you?"

Both The Vicar and I asked her the same question at the same time – except that my question was in my head, as I wasn't exactly part of the conversation, if you know what I mean – which I assume you do.

"Oops!" Billy G put her hand across her mouth. "No one's meant to know about that." She acted like a tipsy schoolgirl. "It's a secret, you know".

She laughed at The Vicar.

"Hey! You've got steam coming out of your ears." She patted him on the head. "Would your macho pride be absolutely gutted to learn that Emma and I, two incapable little girlies, wrote all those great songs. We just called ourselves Benedict Gaydon and Ernest Broom, because they got paid more money."

The Vicar and I mirrored each others slightly bemused expressions.

"You know. The clausely controlled composition thing?"

"The controlled composition clause." The Vicar nodded.

At this point our expressions parted company as he knew what she was talking about, and I didn't.

"A particularly hideous invention of this caring industry of ours – at least in the US. If you write your own songs, you get paid far less money."

"So we invented two different people, Benedict Gaydon and Ernest Broom, who get paid all the *luvvly jubbly*," Billy G sang.

"Smart," The Vicar admitted. "And, no doubt, totally illegal. What about Emma? Do you still write with her?"

"No."

"And what about your bass player?"

My ears pricked up at the mention of the bass player. I had been wondering when The Vicar would remember that he was surely the prime suspect.

"Who, Kevin?" she asked. "Funny you should mention him because he's been spending a lot of time with Emma recently. I think he may be planning to start work on her projects."

Bingo! What did I say! The buggery fucking, arse licker's guilty as sin! Just as I said several chapters ago.

"A traitor in the camp?!" The Vicar exclaimed, getting up. "Almost as bad as a spy in the closet. Which reminds me... You can come out now, Punk!" He had raised his voice and was now talking directly to the door to my cabin. I felt like he could see straight into my eyes. "Perhaps you can make me a pot of tea. I think that's quite enough snooping for one night, don't you?" he laughed.

I almost pissed myself. There I was crammed in the cabin, soaking wet, with no trousers on, and he knew I had been there all along. I was terrified he was going to push open the door, which was already ajar.

"I think my guests are ready to be off now," he announced, still obviously talking to me through the door, rather than to them. He was going to throw them out. The man is incorrigible. One minute he is the perfect host, the next, he is shoving your arse out the door.

"It has been ever so exciting," I could hear him saying to them. "But I fear we have an intruder, so it might be best to leave now. For security reasons...We must do this more often...Perhaps cucumber sandwiches next time, while we make Richard confess to all those awful infidelities. So distressing for his wife."

I couldn't see what he was doing as I was struggling to put my trousers back on, but I could imagine him finding their coats and pushing them towards the door. Billy G and Breamore had not said a word. They were probably too shocked to know how to respond.

"The Vicar's scandal parties!" I could hear him continuing. "They could become a high point of the social calendar... perhaps you could oblige us, Billy G, by having a lesbian lover who has inseminated herself with the sperm of your dead grandfather. Something suitably tabloid..."

I lost track of the next bit.

"And we never got round to those fantastic desserts. Do take one with you... I cannot think what is keeping him. Perhaps he has got some under age girl with him...I think under the circumstances it would be best if you saw your-selves out. Take the torch, I can always get another one. No please, I insist."

I was now ready to come out, but far too embarrassed to show my face.

"I am sorry to throw you out so suddenly, but I am very tired...Come along, come along...It really has been most exciting. A very good evening to you...Some more Chaucer perhaps. A valediction, courtesy of the Wife of Bath.

I pray Jesu short their lives
That will not be governed by their wives
And old and angry misers of dispence
God send them soon real pestilence."

I waited to hear him shut the door before creeping out

very sheepishly to make yet another pot of Earl Grey tea.

CHAPTER SIX

*Check it out. We're in Cannes. Well, not exactly Cannes –
Cavaliaire, which is about an hour away by farm track, but
let's not split hairs. We've flown in to meet Luke Hutchence,
literary agent extraordinaire. I've just printed out the whole
story down to the bottom of the last page (108 pages of A4),
so if you actually get to read this (in a published book as
opposed to a stolen print out) then presumably that means
he likes it.*

*For those who wanted to enter the competition to decipher
the Vicar's weird comment that I misheard on the Betsy:*
"A formal kennel with the arses and now on empty",
*I now have the official version straight from the horse's
mouth, as it were. The Vicar assures me that Camilla Fry-
Hillier's father was apparently:*
"A former colonel with the SAS and now an MP"
*I am tempted to say that I think my version is more
interesting.*

*Anyway. Nosey nosey grindstone . Back to the boring old
story before we lose the plot. It gets pretty surreal. Before we
left to come here, I went to use the photocopier in "the place
we don't talk about", and guess what, in the next chapter, the
Vicar and I are going to do exactly the same thing…cool huh!*
*In fact, the other day, while I was there photocopying the
Vicar's business plan for these psychedelicious Chronicles, I*

also did a quick photocopy of my whatsit…but we certainly don't need to talk about that. Or perhaps we do. What makes a grown man do something like that? Did I just want to make up for the Christmas party when all the girls were photocopying their pert little bottoms? Or is there something more complex going on. Maybe it's

Sorry about that. The Vicar just walked in, perhaps we really had better get on with the story.

XOXOX

☺

The PLACE
we do not TALK
aBouT

REMEMBER THAT DARK CLOUD HANGING OVER THE VICAR? I think it's fair to say that it burst the day after the boat party. I met him standing outside 'the place we do not talk about', 30 P*****e Lane, Notting Hill (one tube stop from my flat – £1.20), with his eyes closed, breathing deeply.

"We English are inclined to grasp at the clouds and ignore the silver linings," he said at last, "but I must confess even I am struggling to find a way to turn this seeming disadvantage into an advantage."

He started to walk into the building, but as his foot was about to touch the step, he stopped.

"I know you don't believe in Feng Shui, as I do, but I should warn you that this is not a happy space. It is filled by not one but two very powerful, malevolent personalities."

He closed his eyes again. He opened them and smiled.

"But I have promised to do this as a favour to Sean, and, no doubt, his Irish luck and the stench of Guinness will protect us. Onward." He thrust his arm into the air, and pulled open the door.

Unfortunately, things did not improve as we entered the lobby. The first thing that The Vicar saw was the original artwork from his first album hanging on the wall in bright sunlight.

"That picture!" he shouted at the nearest available body, so angry that he could barely speak. "What complete idiot hung it in full sunshine? Look how the colours have already faded. That is both a classic work of art and a piece of rock and roll history. Move it, or I'll come and take it down myself. Can this company not be trusted to do anything properly?"

His lips were pushed so tightly together, that they were little more than a thin line.

"I'm sorry. Who should I say is here?"

"I *am* the Vicar. Here, much against my better judgement, to produce a live radio show with the Glamour Twins. I assume the beautiful boys are in the studio?"

The body twitched to get up.

"No thank you. Stay where you are. I know my way. Unless the studio got up and moved in the last seven years. And it looks to me as though nothing much has moved in here for a long time."

All of this 'impending doom' may seem a little extreme. All we were doing was entering an office building. Admittedly it was the one still shared, in separate parts, by Malvolio and Breamore. But how bad could that be? It was one of those times when you wish you knew then what you know now. Little did I realize that it was not so much Malvolio's presence (all spit together) as Breamore's that was troubling The Vicar.

"We are embattled, Punk. Embattled persecution. That is what the English do well. And, as ever, we shall triumph against the odds. I shall put that in my letter to Breamore."

I still had no idea what he was talking about.

He pushed open the door to an empty studio, a simple, dirty affair, nothing more than a few tables and chairs in a drab brown room. It obviously saw more use as a games room, as there was a Scalextric track running round the walls.

"An uncreative space." The Vicar ran his finger along one of the tops and looked at the dust "I tell you the soul has gone out of this whole building."

He had taken a paper towel out of his pocket and begun to clean the tops.

"Seven years ago they brought in a table tennis table, and I knew that it would be the end of the company. It invited a confusion between work and play. And now this." He pointed to the track.

This was not the time to tell him about modern views on labour relations. Or the 30 yard, 6 lane Scalextric track at Universal Studios in LA.

"Still, it will do. Set up your box of delights in that corner, and work your magic from there."

He looked around. "Fortunately, it would appear that the pretty boys are not here yet. I am afraid I shall have to leave you to get all plugged up by yourself." He picked up his laptop. "I have an urgent letter to write to Breamore. In reply to a happy little tome that I received from him by courier earlier this morning."

And with that, he headed out the door again, leaving me the perfect opportunity to secrete my video camera behind the console – any chance to add to my collection of 'indiscrete footage' gratefully accepted.

I did not get to read that famous letter until much later, as, by the time The Vicar returned, brandishing it in his hand, Alex and Chris, the pretty boys, had arrived, bringing with them several crate loads of LPs, and a turntable. Two woolly hats, but no musical instruments – welcome to the new generation of DJ musicians.

"Good morning, boys," The Vicar chanted, as he walked through the door, greeting them both with his customary left handed greeting. "A moment to gather our thoughts perhaps."

He used his hand to dust off a chair for each of them, and went through his normal routine, except that this time, he sat still and silent for what seemed like an eternity.

"So," he said finally, as he thrust his arm into the air, "it would be best to put all our cards openly on the table. I only agreed to produce this radio show as a personal favour for Sean FitzPatrick, A&R hero of the first order and frequent saviour of my vegetarian bacon."

He looked at them to gauge their reaction.

"I very much doubt that I am first on your shopping list, either. But since we are together, let us make it worthwhile. If ever I was in need of the divine healing presence of music," he cupped his hand and looked up at the heavens, "it is today. When Malvolio planned this live radio concert, what exactly did he think you would play?"

Alex scratched his beard "Oh he told us what to play. Play the last album off the CD player, and just spin a few samples over the top."

"Malvolio's thoughts are grimly inevitable and inevitably grim. Such safe options are death by a sweeter name."

The two young rock stars looked at him.

"Let us embrace this live radio show as an opportunity for a spectacular creative leap."

"Spectacular?" Alex muttered. "In your twenties, nothing's spectacular. Babies can be perfect, teenagers can be happy. After that it's all down hill."

I could see we were in for a happy day.

"And why, Mr God's fucking cock, would we want to do any of this, anyway?" Alex added, taking off his sun glasses and preening like a rock star, before tipping over backwards in his chair and starting to laugh at himself.

"Why not? Besides it's the only way you can afford me. At my normal rates, you certainly could not, and I will not demean myself by going cheap." The Vicar struck a simi-larly haughty pose. "So pay me in music. A truly creative leap. One for which the outcome is wonderfully insecure and totally hazardous."

They looked at each other and shrugged.

"Good. So if for one night only you could play anything, what would it be?"

"Russian." Alex said, taking some LPs from such exotic names as Pushkin Boom Beat, Huun Huur Tu and Malerija.

Which is how the famous Russian session by the Glamour Twins was born. Any lingering thoughts I had of the Vicar's mysterious letter to Breamore were soon lost in the magic of the moment. It was fascinating to watch The Vicar take samples of these records, distil their essence, twist them around and help Alex and Chris create the building blocks they needed. The Vicar was having a blast.

And yet he never imposed himself upon them. The music was born from Alex and Chris. He simply encouraged them to look in places that were unfamiliar to them, and the further and further away they went from any territory they knew, the more exciting it became.

After three or four hours of intensive work, the three of them did a trial run through for the radio show, recording it onto DAT. It was astounding. One of those moments, as The Vicar would say, when "the heavens open and music leans over and takes you into its confidence."

'Inspired and inspiring, it joined East and West, visiting places dark and light, poignant and terrifying. Moscow trans-planted into the heart of the English countryside, accompanied by the urban rhythms of New York.' was just one of the many reviews.

Thinking back, The Vicar's performance that day was even more astounding, once you realise that he was doing this, while conducting his own private war with Breamore. It was not until after three o'clock, when we stopped for a late lunch, that I got my first chance to glance at The Vicar's long letter to Breamore, complete with a yellow post-it note saying, *'Please photocopy and circulate to all concerned, Yo V'*

It took little more than the first sentence for me to forget all about the session we had just completed.

The Vicar's letter to Breamore, which I read at lunch during our session with the Glammer Twins.

Vicar World Central
The Vicarage
Winterbourne under Lyme
Wilts

Dear Mr Beermore, (I assume the spelling mistake was deliberate)

I am in receipt of your unsettled and unsettling letter, dated April **, in which you inform me of your decision to sell my publishing catalogue to BGM. It is ironic that I should receive this letter the day after I extended you the hand of friendship and healing, and on a day, when, for the first time in over seven years, I shall be working in your office.It may seem surprising to some that you did not choose to tell me this news personally. Or not. I suspect that my riposte – which is that this catalogue is not yours to sell – will not surprise you. Perhaps my intention to serve you with a high court writ to halt this sale may help to focus your mind.

The circumstances under which my publishing catalogue came under the administration of R&B management are quite clear.

When, while still at University, I first began receiving money for my production work, Melville Olver Spence, a promising student of Politics and Economics, and general good egg, undertook to be my manager. We never had, and still do not have a contract. We were two idealists dreaming of a relationship founded on partnership rather than opposition. We believed that an Englishman's word might still be his bond, and that business might be conducted on a basis of trust and goodwill. Distant times indeed.

When I began to get publishing credits, Melville administered these, on a basis of shared ownership – until the rock and roll lifestyle finally eroded Melville's health and he merged his management interests with your own. In effect, your firm, R&B management, took over his business.

Immediately on your arrival as my manager, you requested that I formally assign my publishing interests to you on the basis that this would enable you to "collect my royalties, and protect my copyright interests around the world". I asked you what would happen in the event of a sale, and was told that I would receive my share.

From the substance of your recent letter, I assume that you are now "unable to recall" this conversation.

It would appear that you, as my manager and lawyer, recommended to me a course of action which was clearly detrimental to me – I lost control of my copyright – and hugely beneficial to you – you gained a valuable asset. In *not acknowledging your conflict of interest and not recommending third party counsel, you fell below acceptable practice, and on these grounds I dispute your right to sell my catalogue for, as I understand, a seven figure sum.*

I terminated my relationship with R&B management less than two months after the merger, when I realised that the new firm no longer represented those ideals which the old one had professed. I also discovered that the partners had been party to an insurance scam, where they were claiming large insurance payouts for cancelled concerts which had never existed. Somewhat strangely, given his almost total absence from the business at the time, Melville's signature was on all the incriminating paperwork. He left the firm and served his sentence. He is now to be found managing The Glamour Twins, with whom I shall be working today.

Indeed, if you yourself were not mysteriously absent from your own office, you would be able to hear the healing sound of music as you work.

Yours disappointedly,

The Vicar

Postscript. Might I also take this opportunity to point out that my publishing royalties for the last two accounting periods remain overdue, apparently due to a shortage of funds, despite the fact that you have continued to pay yourself numerous large fees, far in excess of my pitiful royalties

cc. Stan the Barrista
The office staff at R&B management
Punk Sanderson
Music Week
Rolling Stone
Billy G
The Queens Equerry.

The Vicar pulled me aside as soon as I had finished reading the letter.

"The company no longer manages and protects the interests of the artists. It now works to protect the interests of the managers." The Vicar sighed. "Things are not as bad as they seem. They are worse than that. They are also better than that."

I didn't know what to say. I pointed to the list of CCs.

"Why all these people?"

"Richard will hate nothing more than washing his dirty linen in public. It is his achilles heel." He looked at the list. "Stan the Barrista runs the small coffee stand across the road, so you can hand him his copy while ordering yourself an excellent Cappucino." He ran his finger down the rest of the list.

"I have no idea if the Queen's Equerry is the right person, but hopefully, nor has Richard the B. He has been working for several years with a number of charities in the hope of landing himself a knighthood, or an OBE, and hopefully, this might set them right."

"And what of Billy G?"

"Yes, she must have a copy. Oh, you mean shall we proceed with the case. Why, of course we shall. I shall, however, raise my already extortionate fee by exactly the amount that I am paying to my lawyer, so that Richard the B can bear the full costs of his foolishness. This is all a powerplay, because of his loss of face last night."

I took the letter and set off in search of the photocopier, which I discovered hidden under the stairs. It's difficult to imagine that an inanimate object could cause such chaos in my life. A faulty condom, a black leather belt, a pretzel, but a photocopier? It is not exactly easy to give it the necessary sense of importance. Perhaps a name would help. After all, this particular machine was almost alive. It had this unfortunate habit of flashing in your face (yes, yes, calm down in the cheap seats), whenever you lifted the lid too high. Let it therefore, by Punk proclamation ("Punklamation"), be known as the *Dragon Under The Stairs*.

But all this drama was for the future. I made twenty copies and returned to the studio. It's difficult to believe, but this rollercoaster of a day was not yet over. It had a whole nother – should that be *'other'*? – act left to come. For as I walked into the studio, I was greeted not by the pretty boys, but – dramatic pause, while the camera pans around the room, the sinister music kicks in, CUE general sounds of booing, hissing and spitting from the children in the audience – by Malvolio.

Melville Olver Spence himself.

MEET
MALVOLIO

"WHERE SHALL WE THREE MEET AGAIN, IN THUNDER, lightening or in rain." Malvolio chanted theatrically, as he entered the room (well, if he didn't, he should have done).

He was accompanied by the obligatory young assistant – not so much a girl as an uneven struggle between a large pair of bosoms and a low cut – extremely low cut – tie-dye T shirt. Malvolio's employment policy was similar to Breamore's. He once famously asked his bookkeeper "how the hell did I employ anyone with boobs that small?". To which she replied "You didn't. I'm self employed."

"Punk Sandleforth." Malvolio came over and shook me as if I was a rag doll. "You looked so much better with your make up on. It was almost worth being fired by The Vicar in order to see you in all that gorgeous girlie make up."

The Uneven Struggle raised her eyebrows at me.

"And you looked so butch with my crash helmet on."

If you are waiting for some explanation of this comment, then dream on. He was referring to an event, which I shall henceforth call the Airbrush Event, as I shall be removing it from history.

The Vicar was irate.

"I thought I made it very clear that I would only do this session on the condition that you absented yourself."

"Which you must have known was the only guaranteed way of ensuring that my perverse, beautifully rounded little arse would show up."

Malvolio looked little different from when I had last seen him – the Airbrush Event seven years before – same black suit, same black T shirt, same jet black hair. A modern version of Alan Rickman's Sheriff of Nottingham. He also had the same distant stare in his eyes, an unfortunate combination of natural arrogance and illegal narcotics.

"The boys tell me that their run through before lunch was perfect. So I sent them home. Which means we won't be needing your services any more."

He moved over to a row of master switches, and took great delight in very slowly and deliberately switching each one off. Each click was accompanied by a theatrical intake of breath, as if it was some great sexual pleasure.

"So this is what you have become." The Vicar's lips were pursed so tight that they had all but disappeared. "One of the last surviving members of The Breed – safe in taxis, fearless in shipwrecks, dominating the natives firmly but fairly with nothing more than the occasional months old copy of the Times and a tin of your favourite pipe tobacco. Reduced to this. A truly pathetic sight. And what of the radio show? Our beloved BBC, funded by us taxpayers, has paid astronomic sums of money to equip this pathetic little space with a row of ISDN boxes," he pointed to a neat row of white boxes on the wall, "so that a live show can be sent directly from here to Broadcast House."

"Oh, they shall have their show," Malvolio laughed. "And

it will be spectacular, I assure you. We shall play them this." he snapped his fingers and his assistant handed him a DAT tape, "The tape that you so kindly recorded earlier."

"If all you wanted to do was play a tape, you could have biked it over to them. It would have been thousands of pounds cheaper."

"But it wouldn't be the same. You really don't get it, do you? It's not the truth, but the myth that is important. The audience must believe that it is live." He turned to leave the room. "And don't give me all that tosh about 'play up, play up, and play the game'. I don't go round wearing some hairshirt, pretending that being uncomfortable is the same as being moral. I am playing the game. It's just that you don't know the rules."

He slammed the door behind him, leaving The Vicar to sink into a chair.

The Uneven Struggle had stayed behind, meekly suggesting that "I need to arrange payment".

The Vicar shook himself with horror at the very thought that he might be expected to touch Malvolio's money. "But you can make a cheque for £500 payable to Punk Sanderson. There is no reason why he should suffer for my pride."

"Coutts. It had to be," he added on seeing the cheque. "The aristocrat who banks with Coutts, the aristocrat who hunts and shoots."

I had never seen him so deflated.

"There was a time when Malvolio and I thought almost with one mind," he said after the girl had left. "Which is perhaps why it troubles me so much to see what he has become. Such an internally powerful man, who could be such a force for good, had he not gone so far off the rails."

"A man that needs to get out of the rut and back into

the groove." I offered helpfully, as he carefully packed his computer back into his bag, before sitting quietly for a while.

"But these are not our problems. We go as far as despair, and then say '*Lord have mercy*'. If all else fails, put your trust in Art." He got up with a smile on his face and walked back through the office, to the spot where his album artwork was hanging exactly as it was that morning.

"Snaffle, I think." He lent over the astounded person still sitting at their desk and took it down from the wall, looking lovingly at it.

"Good. My soul feels better already."

I helped him carry it to the car, and install it safely on the back seat.

He apologized for leaving me to tidy up. "I am sorry. I would rather not go back in that accursed building. Malvolio can pay to have my rack shipped back to me."

He carefully folded his coat and put it on the passenger seat.

"Besides," he said, feeling ever more cheerful, "I have a radio show to listen to!"

Which is how The Vicar came to be driving home to his Vicarage in Wiltshire, achieving the seemingly impossible task of driving down the motorway, listening to himself simultaneously performing live in a studio in the middle of London. I myself performed a more interesting time bending feat by climbing through the window of the flat next door, and enjoying the forbidden fruits that have been so frequently offered by my attractive Russian neighbour, while her husband is away. Well, it seemed like an ideal time. Like one of those Jonathan Creek mysteries – without the murder. After all, no-one can be in two places at once, can they?

CHAPTER SIX AND A HALF

(I'm not sure if the last one, 4,126 words, made up of 18,505 characters, was long enough to qualify as a chapter).

SO MUCH HAPPENED IN THE WEEK AFTER THE RUSSIAN sessions – named after the recording session, not my extramarital activities – that I'm having trouble remembering in what order it all happened. This amnesiwhatsit can absotively posilutely not be blamed on the weird stuff that happened in Cannes a couple of nights ago – in the immortal words of Homer Simpson "weird, strange, sick, twisted, eerie, godless, evil stuff, and I want in", nor on the bottle of Wine Society Sparkling Saumur that The Vicar gave me as a present for finishing the first six chapters (the greatest breakthrough in labour relations since the cat of nine tails). It is simply down to the fact that we spent the week in question running around faster than a ferret in Richard Gere's underpants, and my forgettory is easily confuddled. It all began with a flurry of emails. As the Vicar is the sort of man who files his boarding passes for posterity, it is not surprising that he has kept every email:

-----Original Message-----
From: The Vicar [mailto:theVicar@theVicar.com]
To: Donnie Greenhair [mailto:Donnie@Greenhair.com]
Subject: Billy G

Dear Donnie,

A favour if I may. I need to trace the origin of an MP3 file – a version of Don't Touch What you Can't afford doctored to make Billy G sound hideously out of tune – that was featured recently on the Whatif.com website. Does your astounding network of connections stretch to a person suitable for some discreet "internet detective work"?

I still have fond memories of the time we spent together in Seattle. A time of spiritual renewal, accompanied by numerous cups of the healing brew, and excellent company.

Best,

V

From: Donnie Greenhair [mailto:Donnie@Greenhair.com]
To: The Vicar [mailTo:theVicar@theVicar.com]
cc. Steve LaBalle
Subject: Billy G

Sir,

I can indeed recommend someone for the task you require.

Steve Laballe, please meet the Vicar. Steve is a program manager at Microsoft, but there is no reason to hold that against him.

He is a genius at computing, and a music lover to boot. He also sports one of the best haircuts in Seattle.

Happy hunting,

Donbledore

Donnie Greenhair, The barber of Seattle, Party guest extraordinaire, Friend to the stars

---

To: The Vicar [mailTo:theVicar@theVicar.com]
From: Steve LaBalle
Subject: Copyright infringement.

Reverend Sir,

Suggest you send the following attachment to webmaster@whatif.com.

Before we resort to hi tech solutions, it is worth trying traditional methods. An honour to work with you. I hope to attend one of your retreats someday.

Steve.

From: The Vicar [mailTo:theVicar@theVicar.com]
To: Steve LaBalle
Subject: Copyright infringement

Dear Steve,

Attachment would not open on my Mac. Please resend as a text file.

Best,

V

From: Steve Laballe
To: The Vicar [mailTo:theVicar@theVicar.com]
Subject: Attachment

Reverend Sir,

Apologies for Microsoft centric view of the world. Worldwide domination obviously not quite complete. Have resent Mac friendly version.

Best,

Steve.

From: legal@whatif.com
To: The Vicar@theVicar.com
Subject: Copyright infringement
-----Original Message-----
From: The Vicar [mailto:The Vicar@TheVicar.com]
To: Webmaster@whatif.com
Subject: Copyright infringement

>You said:

>Dear Sir,

>It has come to my notice that you are currently featuring copyright material on your web
>site. It is possible that the audio you are featuring also makes you liable for a defamation of
>character claim.

>My client has agreed not to proceed with any claims against you, in return

>for complete
>disclosure from you of the source of the recording.

>Your immediate co-operation is expected

>For and on behalf of Billy G

Dear Sir,

With regard to your claim regarding defamation of character, Whatif?.com rejects any assertions that any of the stories it carries are in any way libellous, or might lead to defamation of character. All articles on our website are preceded by the words "what if", and it is made very clear that they are merely suppositions:

"*WHAT IF* man never went to the moon?"
"*WHAT IF* Diana was murdered by Prince Charles?"
"*WHAT IF* Bill Clinton's cigar had an affair with Monica Lewinsky?"
"*WHAT IF* George Bush is a weapon of mass destruction?"
"*WHAT IF* Elvis Presley is still alive and living in the house next door?"

Furthermore, we strongly reject your assertion that our website "features" any copyright material. We merely linked the article in question to an audio clip hosted by MySpace.com. If there has been a breach of copyright, it has been by MySpace.com, and I suggest you pursue it with them.

Yours faithfully,

Legal Dept

From: Steve LaBalle
To: TheVicar[theVicar@theVicar.com]
Subject: Worry Not

Dear Vicar,

As they suggested, I am tracing the origin of the file via a contact at MySpace.com. Unlike Whatif?.com, they may be wary of copyright infringement (after all they are part owned by News Corporation) and are being very helpful. They claim the file was mislabelled, so that they did not realise it was Billy G(!!). It was placed by a user called whisteblower@randb.co.uk.

Steve.

From: The Vicar[mailto:TheVicar@theVicar.com]
To: Steve laBalle
Subject: Excitement Excitement

Dear Steve,

Excitement. Excitement. Randb.co.uk is the email address of Richard the B's (spit spit) management company. Does this mean that the culprit is someone at his company? Much as my Christian upbringing advises against schaden-freude, that Germanic joy that comes from watching other people's misfortunes, if there has to be a culprit, I can think of few places I would rather find him, or her (not wishing to blame all the ills of the world on the male sex, you understand)

Best,

V

From: Steve.Laballe@Microsoft.com
To: The Vicar [mailTo: theVicar@TheVicar.com]
Subject: Schadenfreude

Regret that the email address is a decoy. Our criminal created a fake email address and bounced his messages off
the computers in Breamore's office to hide his trail. There
is absolutely no security on their computers. It would be
easy to do. I have just got in myself and left a message on
every screen reading "Suggest you get some security" in
large letters. Should give'em quite a shock.

The culprit has nothing to do with Breamore.

Steve

From: Steve.Laballe@Microsoft.com
To: The Vicar [mailTo:theVicar@TheVicar.com]
Subject: Schadenfreude

Have now received details from MySpace.com of the exact
name of the file, the time it was sent, and the internet
address of the computer that sent the file. Unfortunately,
this doesn't equate to anything you can use – just a series
of numbers, something like the postcode of the computer.
Have contacted the IT guys at West End studios on the
offchance.

Still trying.

Steve

From: Steve.Laballe@Microsoft.com
To: The Vicar [mailTo:theVicar@TheVicar.com]
Subject: Bingo, Home run, Grand slam

Dear Vicar,

We now know the exact computer that sent the file. The one in Studio Two at West End. It actually came from the following folder: Westend/studiotwo/my documents/mymusic

The file was transferred at 5.30 am GMT April 5th

Steve.

PS. If it is not too presumptuous, I have attached a copy of a business plan, I am considering for an internet startup. Your thoughts would be invaluable

---

From: The Vicar[mailto:TheVicar@theVicar.com]
To: Steve laBalle
Subject: Congratulations

Dear Steve,

My thoughts on your start up would, on the contrary, be quite valueless. I have forwarded your email to Punk, who is more up to speed with such things,

Good luck and many thanks,

The Vicar

So there you go.

Today's news. We now know exactly where and when our culprit uploaded the doctored version of Billy G's track. West End Studio Two. 5.30 am. April 5th. Now all we needed to know was *WHO WAS THERE??*

ROUND 3
with the
Blue Haired
Booby Bird

"FINALLY, SOME CONCRETE EVIDENCE. OUR CULPRIT WAS in Studio Two at 5.30 in the morning last Friday April 5th," The Vicar said, as he finished reading the last of Steve Laballe's emails. "West End studios, James, and don't spare the horses. Time to start shaking a few trees. Come on, come on, how often must I tell you. Time waits for no one".

It was round three of The Vicar's world title bout with the Blue Haired Booby Bird. Time to push home his advantage.

"A very good morning to you. I *am* The Vicar," he intoned, bowing to the BHBB. "Would I be correct in assuming that this reception area is manned twenty four hours a day?"

When his prey said 'yes', The Vicar demanded an immediate interview with whoever had been manning the desk at 5.30 on the morning of 5th April.

"It matters nothing to me if he is hunting zebra in Timbucktoo. Could you kindly ask him to come to work immediately. It is of the utmost importance."

The BHBB, feigned defeat, a little like Ali's rope trick against Foreman, obediently looking into the reception diary.

"It was old Wilf that night. He's on again tonight, so you

can see him then," she squeaked.

"I am sorry, we clearly have a failure in communication," The Vicar said, trying to restrain his impatience. "I thought that I had made it abundantly clear that it was an immediate interview I had in mind. Let me spell it out for you. Could you find 'old Wilf''s telephone number? Could you perhaps then pick up the receiver and dial it for me. Could you then perhaps tell him that if he wishes to keep his job, he should come to work immediately to answer some questions regarding the morning of 5th April?"

"Who do you think you are?! You're not his employer." The BHBB was not done yet. "You've got no say in whether he keeps his job".

I grimaced. Saying such things would only provoke him.

"You make three points," The Vicar replied calmly, rising to the challenge. "Who do I think I am? – A metaphysical question. Most of our sense of self is delusional. In its simplest form, I have already addressed this point. I *am* the Vicar" He again bowed to her. "Secondly, you claim that 'I am not his employer'. On this point, I am happy to admit that you are most correct, excellent employee though he may be. Thirdly, you claim that I have no say on whether he keeps his job. On this point you are sadly mistaken. Do you not think that if I were to prove that things had been stolen while old Wilf was on night duty, that this might affect his job prospects?"

"Are you saying there's been a robbery?" she asked.

"My dear lady, much as I am enjoying our conversation, there are places that I would rather spend my limited time on this beautiful earth. Yes, I fear there has been a theft. Intellectual property rather than physical. But theft none the less. And may I now politely suggest that you make that phone call? How far away does he live? Can he be here in half an hour? Good. Tell him, I will expect him at 11 o'clock sharp."

The Vicar walked past reception towards Studio One.

"But what if he isn't there?" the BHBB was asking, but The Vicar didn't answer.

Of course he would be there. If The Vicar willed him to be at home, then that is how it would be.

He marched into Studio One.

"Good morning. I am looking for Emma, is the famous lady in yet?"

The engineer did not need to turn around for me to know that it was the assistant we had met in Billy G's studio. He was wearing yet another KMFDM T shirt. This time with *'Juke Joint Jezebel'* on the front, and *'Kraut'* on the back. Scarydelic stuff.

"No, I haven't seen her," he answered. "She don't normally start much before eleven. What do you want her for?"

"Sex" I thought "if the photos I have seen do her justice."

"Sex," The Vicar said, "is what Punk is thinking…" smiling at me from the corner of his eye.

"Shit, shitty, shit, shit! Am I that transparent?" I thought, staring at the floor, and hoping my ears would not go bright red.

"But it was oral rather than sexual intercourse that I had in mind," The Vicar went on.

"I'm s-orry?" the engineer spluttered, clearly confused at The Vicar's comments.

"I am hoping to speak with Miss Emma B," The Vicar explained.

"Y –you're The Vicar, aren't you?" The engineer was visibly shaking, as he shook The Vicar's outstretched hand. "I'm er I'm Gabriel. I have admired your work for a long time. I've even used it on some club mixes. I was wondering. What made you work with Billy G, if you don't mind me asking?"

"A damsel in distress. I find myself cast in the role of Billy G's knight in shining armour. And I thought Emma might be an appropriate person to..." The Vicar looked at me and raised his eyebrows "...poke with my lance."

I was beginning to get worried by all the sexual innuendo. I had a terrible feeling that I knew why he was teasing me in this way. I quietly prayed that I was wrong.

"I er I d-on't...?" Gabriel stammered.

At least I was not the only one who was embarrassed at The Vicar's behaviour. Gabriel was also turning a delightful shade of red.

"I need to speak with Emma concerning the recent problems Billy G has been having," The Vicar explained again.

"I doubt she will show much sympathy. A lot of people think Billy G deserves everything she gets after the way she treated the other band members. There are a lot of ugly rumours."

"What a faithful little hound you are, sticking up for your mistress like that. And you really should learn to be more tidy in the studio." The Vicar removed a cup from the mixing desk. "Please let Emma know that I will be coming to have a word with her. About half past eleven."

He turned around and left the studio. I stayed behind to have a quick word with Gabriel – I thought he might want to come to one of my gigs – and then followed after his Viciousness, more than a little worried at the way he was behaving.

"You can't go round treating people like that," I nerved myself to say.

"Why on earth not. Did I hear him complaining?"

"No, but you must have hurt his feelings. And he was a fan!" I said.

"So fans have feelings, do they? I think not. I am sure it is far more flattering that I do him the honour of saying what I think, rather than hiding behind platitudes and discussions of the weather. What a soft character you are! You cannot have made a very convincing punk".

And with that, he wandered back through reception, with a nod of his head to the now submissive BHBB, and then through into Studio Two. He was increasingly behaving as if he owned the entire building.

The faithful Ben was hard at work in Studio Two preparing a mix for Billy G.

"Ah, Ben!" The Vicar enthused, "An earnest bearded young man like you will, I am sure, be gifted with a good memory. What, pray tell, do you remember of last Thursday night?"

"What about it?"

"Nothing personal. How late did you work, who was in the studio, the genital disorders of the person, of whichever sex, with whom you shared your bed. That sort of thing."

"I'm afraid I spent the night on my own," he said, smiling, "but I spent the evening in the studio with Billy G. We worked through until about 10 o'clock, I think. If I remember rightly, Kevin, the bass player, came in a little before we finished, saying he wanted to work on some new ideas. Billy G said she would like to hear them, but he wanted to work on his own, so he waited until we had finished."

"So you left him on his *own* in the studio?"

"Yes. I didn't need to stay. Kevin knows how to use all the gear. He likes to work through the nights. He comes in when we go to bed and works through until morning."

"I have had the pleasure of working with more than a few musicians like that." The Vicar smiled. "And a right pain they are one and all. This business of music would be so much easier if it did not involve musicians. Fortunately for all of us, music is so desperate to come into the world that it does so despite the gross inadequacies of most of those involved." He turned to leave the room. "I thank you, young Benjamin, you have as always been most helpful. Not a day goes by without me planning some wicked way of poisoning Punk so that I can lure you into my employment. Unfortunately, Punk not only has the looks of a donkey, he also has the stomach of a donkey. All known poisons pass through him without so much as a bad case of flatulence. But worry not, I shall succeed. I bid you adieu."

He made a theatrical exit from the studio, pausing in the doorway to glance at his watch.

"And there is still just time to visit the café on the first floor. Perhaps, Punk, you could wait in reception, and bring our Mr Wilf up to see me at eleven o'clock. Shall I bring you a cup of Earl Grey tea. No arsenic, I assure you."

I WOULD LOVE TO SAY THAT THE VICAR'S COCKY CONFIdence was misplaced and that Wilf, the night watchman, was for some reason 'indisposed', or, even better, chose not to come and talk to him. In truth, of course, old Wilf hobbled through the door at a little before eleven o'clock, exactly as The Vicar had requested, and I ushered him 'into the presence'. It was a fairly brief interview, but highly informative. The Vicar was keen to know who might have been in Studio Two at 5.30 am on the morning of Friday, the fifth of April.

Wilf was in no doubt.

"Mr Kevin and Miss Emma were both in there," he wheezed. "I remember as how Mr Kevin came out at about eleven o'clock – that's the Thursday night – and went to find Miss Emma in Studio One. They then both went into Studio…Two, isn't it, and worked through 'til morning. I was thinking at first that they were going out somewhere as she was carrying her great big sheepskin coat. But they went into the studio and never came out all the while I was on my shift. And I never leave my post until the stroke of 8 o'clock in the morning. I prides myself on that. Not so much as a bathroom break."

The Vicar assured Wilf that he was not questioning his efficiency.

"Mr Kevin and Miss Emma are real night birds, as you might say," Wilf went on. "I particularly remember because the cleaner always does the studios in the early hours at five or six o'clock and I was worried that he would disturb them. It's not unusual for them to work like that. They did it the night before as well, you see."

The Vicar thanked Wilf for coming so promptly, apologized for taking up his valuable time, and assured him that he need worry himself no further over the events of that night.

"And now for the famous Emma and Kevin!" he said, sending me down on a fruitless visit to Studio One: her manager had phoned in, saying she was going straight to 'Metropolis', where she was due to master a single that afternoon.

In true story book style, The Vicar and I therefore jumped in our Aston Martin and raced across London, leaving a trail of burning rubber and dead bodies in our wake. Metropolis studios, on Chiswick High Street, is one of my favourite mastering facilities in London ("and I should know, I've seen a few" to paraphrase the one and only Monty Pythons). It is a spectacular building – a huge old power station. It always strikes me as one of the few buildings in London large enough to contain The Vicar's personality (unless you include St Pauls and Buck House, I suppose).

He was still in no mood for pussyfooting, but the surroundings made him seem less abrasive.

"Good afternoon. *I am* the Vicar," he said to the receptionist (no blue hair or boobies on view). "I understand that Emma B is here to attend a cut. Would you kindly tell me which studio she is in?"

"Who shall I say wants her. The Vicar? You are one of our clients, aren't you?"

"The Vicar," he intoned, nodding his head to show that she was correct. He looked at me as he continued.

"...If you lick her after liquor
 and prick her and then dick her,
 you had better call The Vicar

is the catchy little rhyme currently doing the rounds on the websites. I cannot think where it originated."

My heart sank. It was as I had feared. Visions of a P45, my pink slip, floated before my eyes. I had put that catchy little rhyme at the bottom of an email to a friend, who had then 'helpfully' posted it on the guestbook of a fansite. The Vicar was grinning from ear to ear, revelling in my discomfort.

"I understand that Emma B's cut is not until one o'clock." He turned back to the receptionist. "And so I had hoped to speak with her beforehand. Do you know if she is here yet."

"If you go up to mastering reception on the second floor, up the staircase and past the café, they may be able to help you there."

"I thank you most kindly. Have a nice day, and I mean that most sincerely," he gushed, ushering me towards the stairs.

We never got as far as the mastering department, as Emma was sitting in the café on the second floor, talking to the girl in the No Meat No Man jacket that we had seen outside West End Studios.

Do I need to describe this café? It's not like anyone hurls themselves off the balcony or anything. It's really just like a street café, with a counter inside and table and chairs outside on the pavement. The only difference is that instead of being on a pavement, the table and chairs are actually on a balcony half way up the inside of an old power station. Will that do? Check out their website.

The two girls were sitting at one of the tables right next to the railings. As soon as they saw us, the girl in the jacket got up and left.

Which left us with Emma B. Not at all my type, Punksters. Enough toffee in that nose to coat a whole barrel of apples. Where Billy G is bubbly, daring and perhaps a little punk-ish, Emma is classy, suave and sophisticated. Billy G has a mop of dyed orange or blonde hair, while Emma is a neatly trimmed brunette. The Audrey Hepburn of pop music. I certainly can't imagine her bouncing around on the bed on The Betsy. A girl to admire from afar, rather than rush up and say hello to.

Not that that stopped The Vicar, of course, because that is precisely what he did.

"Miss Emma, I presume. I am Dr Livingstone, or perhaps I have got that the wrong way round"

He bowed and offered her his hand, which she accepted.

"You are 'The Vicar', are you not?" She wiggled her fingers to make fake quotation marks. "You're working with Billy G." She pointed at her salad. "This is not a good time, I am afraid. You know the game. Go through my manager." And with this she dismissed him, and went back to her meal.

"Oh dear, my fame precedes me," The Vicar trilled, ignoring her comments completely. "How simply terrifying. Please assume that I am the devious mischievous character of legend and then you will not be disappointed or dismayed." He smiled at her "Whatever they are saying, it is all completely untrue, of course. I couldn't possibly have done it. I spent the entire day stuck in my bedroom trying to remove a penile wart."

Despite her desire to be rid of him, Emma could not help laughing and looking back at him.

" Or perhaps you had heard only good things," The Vicar went on, "in which case there is even less chance of any of it being factual, but I shall be most happy to take the credit."

Emma pushed her salad to one side.

"Now that you have disturbed me, did you actually have something you wanted to say? I am due to start mastering at one o'clock, and was hoping to finish my lunch beforehand...If that is alright by you?"

"I must confess that my young, extremely handsome sidekick and I have ventured all this way with the express purpose of grabbing a few minutes of your precious time. May I?" He motioned towards a chair. "Or would you really rather that I called your manager. I do hate to impose on an artist in this way."

He had succeeded in 'buttering her biscuits'. She nodded her approval, and he sat down at the table with her. There were no other chairs at the table and so his handsome sidekick was left standing around like a spare part.

"I would like to discuss last Thursday night. Would I be right in thinking that you worked through the night in Studio Two?"

"I said you can sit down, not conduct a fucking inquisition. What's this about last Thursday?"

"That was the night before all the excitement with the internet posting about Billy G. I assume you didn't miss all that?" The Vicar asked.

"Oh no. I logged on together with the rest of the world. Great fun. Completely bogus, of course, but then you know that. She unfortunately has a wonderful voice. Although as she goes down, I go up so long may it continue. I wouldn't even mind giving her a push to help her on her way...

...*B I T C H !* "

A Rapier-like Strike

THE VICAR WAS QUESTIONING EMMA ABOUT HER NIGHT in Studio Two. The very night, – as our friendly Microsofty, Steve Laballe, had proved in his emails – that the doctored MP3 file was uploaded from the computer in that studio.

"Yes," Emma admitted. "That was one of the nights I worked with Kevin. We are working on some ideas together."

"And were you really in the studio all night? The night watchman remembers seeing you go into the studio shortly after eleven o'clock, and says that you were both there until at least 8 o'clock in the morning."

Emma slammed the table.

"Have you any right to go round asking questions like this? I hope for your sake all this is leading somewhere? The local charities are constantly benefiting from the work of my libel lawyer. And I am sure he would love the chance to empty your coffers". Her playful manner didn't hide the fact that she meant every word.

"Please bear with me. I just want to get one thing straight. Are you sure that you never left the studio in those nine hours? You never went to get a drink or something?"

"OK. Let's get this over and done with. We were in the studio all night. It's very comfy. I may have dozed off for a while on the chairs at the back, I don't remember. There's no need to leave the studio. There's tea and coffee and all the booze you could want in the cupboard beside the TV set."

"It really is important. Did you never set foot outside the studio? Not even to go to the toilet?"

"We were there all night. Not that it's any of your business, but Billy the 'I can have a solo career without you' can testify to my famously strong bladder. Unlike her, I have never had to resort to peeing in a tea pot!"

It was The Vicar's turn to be shocked. This was sacrilege. Peeing in a beer bottle, maybe. But a teapot. That is a sacred object.

"And now will you tell me where all this is leading?" She was tiring fast – like Billy G, she was used to being in control.

"Simply this. I received an email this morning that seems to offer incontrovertible proof that the source of the bogus recording of Billy G was the computer…"

He looked at her to watch her reaction.

"…in Studio Two. The sound file was uploaded to a myspace.com website…"

He paused again, his eyes firmly fixed on her.

"…at 5.30 am on Friday morning. A time at which, by your own admission, the only people in the studio were you and Kevin".

She seemed truly shocked.

"But s-surely emails and the like can be sent from anywhere. I can pick up mine from any computer in the world. Can you really prove which computer they have come from?" she demanded.

"I am not an expert. Our culprit did indeed use a fake

email address to help disguise his tracks. But it is apparently possible to track the exact source of the sound file, and it was sent from Studio Two at 5.30 am GMT. A time at which you and Kevin were apparently the only people in the studio."

"Well, I can assure you that we did not do it, however it might appear."

"Of course, you did, you sassy little bitch!" I thought. "The Vicar has caught you with your knickers down. He makes all this play of being an eccentric, and then, when you are not concentrating, he delivers a rapier like strike to the heart". I was totally impressed.

"There's just one other thing that is troubling me," The Vicar added slowly. "Why did you work in studio two when you were booked into studio one?"

The question was obviously totally unexpected. She did not have a ready answer.

"I...I'm not quite sure." She tried to think of a reason. "I guess it was for the keyboards. We don't have the same selection in studio one, so we went to studio two."

"I didn't know you played." The Vicar toyed with her.

"I don't," she snapped. "Kevin does."

She became more aggressive.

"You know, it is no doubt very kind of you to try to help Billy, but I should point out that she is far from being a saint. I don't mind telling you, as far as I am concerned, she deserves anything she gets."

"You are the second person today to tell me that."

"That few? You have been leading an isolated life. You should talk to Mair on the subject. The girl who was here a few minutes ago? Now there's someone who really hates Billy G – ever since she kicked her out of our backing band to bring Kevin in."

"Oh yes. The young lady in the "No Meat No Man" jacket. Interesting tastes for such a lady. She also thinks that Billy G stole her song, does she not?"

"Yeah, well that's rubbish." She stood up, showing that we had outstayed our welcome, and the interview was now at an end. "That song was written by Ernest Broom." She was a totally convincing liar. "And now, sir, it's time for you to leave, so that I can finish my lunch."

"I thank you. You have been most gracious and most kind." The Vicar offered her his hand, and she took it. He kissed hers with a flourish, and then turned and left.

"You are not going to let her get away with it are you?" I asked, as we clanked our way down the metal steps." Shouldn't you call the police or something?"

"Things are not quite as they appear, my dear Punk. You are forever jumping to conclusions."

"Jumping to conclusions?!" I shouted "You mean you don't think she did it. When she and Kevin were the only people in the room? I suppose it's possible *he* did it while she was asleep at the back of the room".

"No. She never went to sleep at the back of the room. That was just part of a tissue of lies so transparent that it might have been invented by Kleenex, if you will excuse a very poor joke. Look. There's young Mair. A word if I may?"

The Vicar might call her 'young Mair', but she wasn't that young. Late thirties, I would think. And bitter and twisted as hell. Her nose and chin were slightly hooked together like a witch in a story book. And she had been doing her research. The conversation was barely twenty seconds old, before she told The Vicar:

"Do you know who's the managing director of Gaydon and Broom's publishing company? Richard bloody Breamore, that's who. Billy G and Emma B's manager. . Coincidence? Coincidence, my arse. They were the only two people I sent a copy of my song, and the next thing I know Billy G has kicked me out of the band and released it as a single."

She prodded the Vicar with her finger each time she made a point.

"So please excuse me if I don't go crying about everything that's happened to her. Emma's cool. She's supportive. She told me at the time that she didn't want me thrown out of the band. Unfortunately, she don't remember getting a tape from me, otherwise I could prove it."

It was a sad story, and probably true, but nothing to do with the case.

"And you are playing with Sascha Konietsko's mob now?" The Vicar asked.

She looked blankly at him.

"The jacket? 'No Meat No Man'? A Germanic industrial rock song?"

"Oh No!" she said. "The jacket's not mine. It belongs to my boyfriend".

"That explains it." The Vicar looked relieved. "It has been troubling me ever since I first saw that jacket. It seemed so unlikely."

He tossed his phone to me. "And yes Punk, I know you are about to tell me that we have a case to solve. Time to meet the famous Kevin. Could you please call Richard the B's office and get his address."

CHAPTER EIGHT

I have just had a text message from The Vicar. He must be the only person in the world, except my sister, who spells out every word correctly. He probably even has a spell checker on his phone, although he wouldn't need it, of course. He wants to know if my latest chapter about our meeting with the elusive bass player is ready. Give us a chance. I've only just woken up!

While he's waiting, he can read my Fool's guide to text, courtesy of the concise Oxford Punktionary

ATB	*All the best*
BBLR	*Be back later*
BFN	*Bye for now*
CUL8R	*See you later*
HAND	*Have a nice day*
TGIF	*Thank God its Friday*
TTFN	*Ta ta for now*
XOXOX	*Hugs and kisses*
MYOB	*Mind your own business*
GAL	*Get a life*
FU	*Fuck you*
FU2NITE	*Fuck you tonite*
FU2NITEPLS	*Fuck you tonight please*
NE1?	*Anyone?*
SOM1?	*Someone?*

THE MYSTERIOUS CASE OF BILLY'S G-STRING

PLS?	*Please?*
GR8	*Great*
XLNT	*Excellent*
TX	*Thanks*
WU	*What's up?*
RUOK	*Was that good for you*
LOL	*Laugh Out Loud*
JK	*Just kidding*

☺

A WEE DRAM
with KEVIN the
BASS PLAYER

ENOUGH. ON WITH THE STORY. OK. WELL, FIRSTLY, ONE of the most surprising bits of news to come out in the aftermath of Breamore's financial misdealings was the fact that he was to remain Billy G's manager. I had personally expected her to castrate him, before quietly supping on his intestines.

"Perhaps a good decision on her part," The Vicar said at the time, "leaving aside my own personal bias, of course. If she stands by him, he will certainly work hard for her. Sometimes better the pickpocket you know than the jewel thief you do not."

Whatever the rights and wrongs of her decision, her manager he had remained, and it was the snooty tones of his secretary that gave me the address of our famous bass player. Kevin McCallister, 15 Kings Rd, Kings Stanley London W1.

A brief glance at the A-Z, and half an hour cursing the traffic, and we were standing outside his door. Or more correctly we were driving past his door. It was a typical London journey. Half an hour to drive to the house, twenty minutes finding somewhere to park, and then ten minutes walking back to the house you found half an hour before. There must be a better way.

I suppose it's called a taxi.

"Mind you, Richard the B had better watch his back," The Vicar warned, as we walked back along the street. "There is nothing so dangerous as a musician with a grudge. Have I told you the story about Nearly Noseless Nick, the head of *Be Randy*'s US record label?"

I shook my head "no".

"*Be Randy* were on the point of breaking in the US. The band needed their label's support to finally break into the mass market. The head of the label initially promised a massive advertising campaign, but then changed his mind, and the band's career took a terminal nose dive."

We were moving into a slightly run down area.

"Some years later, Nearly Noseless Nick, who still had his nose in those days, bumped into the band in a studio in London, expecting a hostile reception. He was surprised when they welcomed him like a long lost friend, and invited him to attend their sessions. They even asked him to join them in a line or two of coke. In fact, during the week he was in England, he joined them in more than a few lines."

We had arrived at Kevin's address, but paused outside while The Vicar finished his tale.

"When he got back to New York, he began suffering from nose bleeds, which got progressively worse. By the time, he visited a doctor, his septum..." The Vicar fingered the skin between his nostrils to show me what he meant, "...had completely rotted through. The friendly boys in the band had apparently been mixing white bleach with his coke."

He raised his eyebrows.

"And so now he is known as Nearly Noseless Nick. A warning to all against the wrath of an aggrieved musician. I trust Kevin McCallister will be altogether more civilized."

We walked up the steps to Kevin's house. The Vicar rang the bell, and Kevin's wife, as we later found her to be, answered the door. I word it in that way, as my first impression was that she was perhaps a cleaner. Some of The Vicar's snobbery must be rubbing off on me.

"A very good afternoon to you madam. I *am* The Vicar. I trust that we are not disturbing you. My manservant tells me that Kevin McCallister lives here. I expect to have the good fortune of working with him on the forthcoming tour of Japan with Billy G. Is the man of the house available? I would very much like to have a word with him, please."

She didn't say anything to us, but moved out of the way to let us through and shouted into the house

"Kevin. There's people here to see you."

We walked along the narrow hall and waited at the foot of the stairs, to be greeted by Kevin, who came bounding up from the basement.

He was nothing like I had expected him. Why is it that the name Kevin always conjures up someone with dyed blond hair, a girlfriend called Sharon or Tracey, white ankle socks, and driving an XR3 convertible? I could not have been more wrong. I should have paid more attention to his surname, *McCallister*, for Kevin was nothing if not Scottish. He was a big bear-hug of a man, with long, messy red hair. He was wearing a Black Sabbath T shirt, with the arms cut off, to expose tattoos on both his shoulders.

"You're The Vicar, are you not?" he said in a thick Scottish accent, "You'd better be coming downstairs."

Fortunately The Vicar refrained from any jokes about penile warts and we followed Kevin down into a large messy family kitchen at the back of the house. It was piled high with so much debris that it had either been rampaged by a herd of rhinoceros, or he had a large, extremely healthy tribe of children, or perhaps both.

He walked over to the sofa, and with one sweep of his arm, pushed all the junk onto the floor, while moaning at his wife, who was standing in the doorway.

"Woman, can you not (or was it *'nay'*) tidy the children's toys occasionally?"

Having found us somewhere to sit, he picked up some clothes off one of the armchairs, and dumped them in a pile in the corner, shouting

"and why do the wee one's clothes have to live in here and not in her bedroom?" before closing the door, almost in his wife's face, and coming to join us.

"Do I detect that you have a large brood of dirty urchins locked in a cupboard somewhere?" asked The Vicar, brushing his trouser leg as if something might be contagious.

"Oh, aye. We've got four of them, though fortunately the eldest three are with their grandmother today, so we should have some peace."

"It is safe to say that the NHS will not exactly be needing to fund fertility treatment for you. More the opposite, perhaps!"

"We got off to a quick start, as you might say. Ewan was born when we were only seventeen. They're all right. Their mother needs to learn to keep them under control, that's all."

"Oh, I don't know. All mothers are inclined to be a trifle lenient. My own dear mother should no doubt have stifled me at birth and saved the world a good deal of heartache.

Fortunately for Punk here, who would otherwise be jobless, it was not until I was in my late teens that she realised to her horror that I was entirely worthless, and that all her efforts had been in vain."

The Vicar smiled and moved his attention from his trouser leg to the dirt on the sofa around him

"It is in the genes. After all, if every mother looked at her newborn baby and saw a disgustingly ugly, noisy, smelly little thing, that is going to cause nothing but problems and enormous expense for the next twenty years, few children would survive."

He pulled out a toy from underneath his trousers and placed it carefully on the floor. Even in a room as messy as this, The Vicar could not resist the temptation to try to put everything in its place.

"No, all mothers are fooled by nature into thinking that their children are beautiful, valuable, and deserving of their attention. I am sure your wife is no exception."

"That's as maybe. I still think the little wifey should be more strict with them. There's never a moment's peace in this house!" Kevin shouted.

"Fortunately, we have one now, so perhaps, I could ask you a few questions."

The Vicar then ran through the same details that he had discussed with Emma, and Kevin confirmed that they had both been there working all night, and that no-one else had been in the studio. The Vicar asked the same question about why they had used studio two, not studio one. It caused Kevin to hesitate in the same way that it had with Emma.

"I do nay remember," he paused. "I ken it was because my bass rig was in Studio Two. I would have been needing it to get my full range of sounds."

"Yes, of course." The Vicar nodded. "Do you only play bass? Do you also play keyboards?"

"No, I could nae get on with them. I'm a half way decent guitarist, though, which is what I use for my writing".

"Yes, I can see that the guitar would be more your style than the piano. I would be interested to hear some of the work you have been doing with Emma. She is clearly very committed to it."

"Well, I would nay want Billy G to go thinking that I'm not fully behind her album, because I am. It's a pity that Emma and her can nay just forgive and forget."

"I think that would be easiest for everyone," agreed The Vicar. "In the meantime, we must manage as best we can". He got up.

"Will you not have a wee dram while you are here?" Kevin offered.

"Thank you, but no. I only drink sparkling water, beer-less beer and champagne, and I do not think it is quite the moment for any of them. Another time, perhaps." The Vicar shook Kevin's hand, which was simply enormous. "Thank you for your help. We can see ourselves out. I look forward very much to working with you in Japan. It promises to be an exciting time."

Short and sweet, you might say. In less than ten minutes, he had effectively established Kevin's guilt.

The GROPE and WANKER

ARE YOU AS CONFUSED AS ME? THE VICAR CATCHES Kevin and Emma in his little web – effectively proving they're guilty – and yet he still plans to let Kevin come on tour.

"You are surely not serious about letting Rob Roy go to Japan?" I asked as soon as we'd left his house. "You have proved that he and Emma did it. They cannot even agree about what instruments they were using that night. He's probably desperate for money, and she's paying him to do it. You can't risk him coming to Japan and sabotaging her concert."

"Have no fear. No one will sabotage her concert. I shall see to that. I intend to catch our nasty little villains red handed. It is a game of chess. Me against them. And I never lose at chess."

"That's only because you never play anyone who's better than you." I thought. But I kept the thought to myself.

"In the meantime, we have not finished our little round of interviews. I am sure Sherlock Holmes would not have felt he had done his job properly until he had spoken to the other person who was in the studio that night."

"But Kevin and Emma have both said they were by *themselves* all night."

"Indeed they have, but the night watchman said that the cleaner went in to do the studio some time early in the morning."

"So what if he did? You think he might have caught them at it? It seems most unlikely."

Now, you might be thinking that we should gloss over this interview with the cleaner. You probably stole this book from the back shelf in the bargain basement of your local used book store in the misguided hope that it would contain some dirt on the music business, not to hear tales of me driving in The Vicar's Grannymobile talking to *'hygiene sanitation operatives'*. But bear with me. That little chat with the cleaner proved to be pretty important. If not for me, then for Harvey, the 'toilet-clogging, last-cookie-eating, collect-call-making-sponge' who lives with me, and plays in my band.

It was like this. The cleaner turned out to be none other than the angel Gabriel, the tea-maker/tape op/DJ who we had met in the studio that morning – and the first place we could track him down (assuming he showed up with the guest pass I'd given him) was at my gig at the Grope and Wanker in Islington – which was fantasmagorically significant as the Vicar had never once attended any of my gigs, and for some time I had clung to the slightly pathetic belief that if he could just see my potential, he would immediately release me from my life as his mediocre sidekick, and give me a spangly new one as a fully fledged demi-god rock drummer.

Not that I was putting any pressure on myself or anything.

I don't know if you know the Grope and Wanker. It's a suitably disgusting London pub, with a small, sweaty, and, back then, very smoky cellar.

I should never have let The Vicar come. A Punksaster from the moment he walked in. He spent our entire set jumping around the room like a knight on a chessboard. He would stand still, with his hands neatly behind his back, listening intently, until some smoke (tobacco or otherwise) reached his nostrils, at which point his nose would twitch in disapproval, and still facing the stage, he would manoeuvre himself into an empty slot. Only to repeat the whole farce less than a minute later – all the while shaking his head and hiding his face behind his hand whenever a fan approached him.

How is a man meant to concentrate faced with such an absurd performance? I died that night. I completely missed the ending of two of the songs and forgot the words in most of the others – pretty craptacular, bearing in mind that I wrote half of them. I shall go to my grave knowing that it was only the Vicar's obsessive hatred of tobacco that ruined my chance for stardom.

That and a slight lack of talent.

Dominic, our bass player, coped pretty well. And Harvey. Well, Harvey was spectacular. Better than that, even. He was in his Ritchie Edwards phase (Don't worry about it, I didn't know who he was either until Harvey told me). Whatever it was, it worked well. He was intense. The engine, the heart, the whole lot. He was so far gone, that when some guy in the front row criticized him as he walked off the stage, he took a knife out of his pocket, lifted his arm above the guy's head, and slashed the back of his arm, letting the blood run into the guy's hair. I saw a photo of him that night. He seemed to be looking right through the camera and into your soul. What can I say? He just looked like a star.

The Vicar had just one thing to say to him after the show. "If you can sort your life out and find some discipline, you are ready to work with me."
I don't think he knew how much I wanted him to say those same words to me, as he dragged me off to meet with Gabriel in the pub upstairs.

"I'm sorry I fooled you," Gabriel mumbled, as we sat down beside him. "I was so flattered that you thought that I was the engineer, not just a tuppenny ha'penny cleaner. It's just so difficult to get on in this business".
He looked at me. "Great gig."
But then ruined it all by adding
"Your singer's great."
Bitter as I was over his indifference to my extraordinary drumming talents, I liked Gabriel. He was about my age and had taken the job in the studio as a first step on the ladder. You know the score, this week you brush the floor, next week you make the tea, next year you operate the tape machines, and one day you may get to make a recording.

The Vicar took me down a further peg or two by referring to me as his personal version of "the maggots that Thomas Beckett kept writhing in his undergarments". It may be a good story (apparently when Thomas Beckett was buried, after being decapitated by some rogue knights, they discovered that he'd filled his underpants with maggots, to keep himself in a constant state of discomfort) but, hey, it's hardly flattering to hear The Vicar announcing that your role in life is little more than a glorified form of jock rot, or dobi's itch.

Anyway, Gabriel seemed a good enough guy. He confirmed that he had cleaned the studio in the early hours of the morning, but was adamant that neither Kevin or Emma were there.

We were therefore left with the seeming impossibility that both Kevin and Emma *and* the cleaner were claiming to have been in Studio Two at the same time…but that neither had seen the other one. Anyone for parallel universes?!

In my own little universe, the main upshot of the meeting with Gabriel was that I badgered The Vicar to take him to Japan as a technical assistant. After all he needed a break. To begin with The Vicar sounded less than convinced.

"If Gabriel's work is necessary, he will find the right people to support it. With commitment all the rules change."

I suspect that he probably felt that giving house room to one sexually incontinent imbecile, namely myself, was quite sufficient.

"Let us not be distracted from our mission," he insisted, as he asked me to chauffeur him back to West End studios. "The next step is to ensure that there is no exit from Studio Two except past old Wilf in reception."

And so an hour later, one sweaty Punk Sanderson, reduced from rock hero to rock zero, found himself back at West End studios doing a quick security check. There was a fire door, but that wasn't the answer. It could only be opened by breaking a glass panel, which would have set off the entire fire alarm.

"And I think someone might have told us if there had been a fire alarm and a fleet of fire trucks," I muttered sarcastically, trying to sound as misunderestimated as I felt.

The answer had to lie in the famous priesthole. Kevin and Emma must have hidden in there when they heard Gabriel coming.

"But why would they hide?" asked The Vicar, "They were booked in. They were quite allowed to be here."

He squeezed past the loudspeakers and disappeared into the priesthole. Suddenly, he shouted with glee.

"Ah ha! I have it. I have it! I knew it, but now I have the proof. Get Emma on the telephone. Let us confront her with the truth."

I got a number from the switchboard, but she was not answering.

"No matter, I can ask her another time."

He was suddenly in a generous mood. "I think we will perhaps invite your friend Gabriel to join us in Japan, after all. You will have to room with him, though, as there is no way that I can persuade Richard the B to pay for another hotel room. One night in Tokyo would buy you a month's sex anywhere else in the world."

"And you are going to let Kevin come?"

"Of course, Kevin must come. He is the main stay of Billy G's rhythm section."

"And you are not worried that someone will try to sabotage the concert?"

"I think it is now one hundred percent likely that someone will try to sabotage the concert."

"You think that Kevin might try something without Emma?"

"Oh I do not think we will be entirely without Emma. She'll turn up in Japan alright. I would bet my last Yen on that."

And on that mysterious note, I'm off to powder my nose.

CHAPTER NINE

Too hungover to tell you anything today, so this is going to be the shortest Chapter in history.

CHAPTER TEN

See! Here we are already in the giddy heights of Chapter Ten. Maybe I'm onto something. After all, I could decide to do this...

CHAPTER ELEVEN

(Just kidding. It's still Chapter Ten really). I suppose I could write a whole book that had nothing but chapter headings, and no writing at all – the literary equivalent of a blank canvas or those absurdicrous piles of bricks in the Tate Gallery. But isn't that cheating somehow? After all, isn't the idea to fill up all the pages and get to the end of the book without losing too many readers on the way?

Anyway, enough time wasted. At least I can tell The Vicar, in my very best French, that I've finished the last chapter (or two).

☺

The MILE HIGH CLUB

BACK TO OUR BARGAIN BASEMENT PLOT AND OUR CHECK-in at Heathrow airport on the way to Japan – unfortunately without my trusty video camera. Another strange tale of the rock 'n' roll lifestyle, which I should probably share with you. Siobhan – remember her from Real World – had turned up at our band party, and bewitched me with her underhand use of a loaded girating arse. How is a man meant to cope? One minute she won't talk to me. The next minute she is sidling up to me backwards, and massaging my ever attentive groin with her delightful little patooty. You can probably guess where this is going, and, yes, you'd be right. Like the fool I am (come on, who wouldn't have been?) I took her back to my flat – ostensibly because she asked to see my Diva video – and then, yes, the next thing I remember is waking up in the morning stark naked. My camera wasn't stolen, it was smashed, probably when it fell off the mantlepiece. I can think of three possible explanations:

1. She is irresistibly attracted to me, and is making pornographic films of our fucktacular lovemaking. I reject this

theory because it is the stuff of every schoolboy fantasy, and thus highly unlikely.

2. She is being paid by Diva to steal the video from me. This is the most likely theory, and if so, I can look forward to more of the same, as, she will be Divastated to learn, tee hee, that I've still got it.

3. I can't remember what the third reason is.

Anyway, more about this weird camera stuff later, as it happened to me again the other day in Cannes.

Back to the check-in, without my camera, at Heathrow.

As you might expect, The Vicar had insisted that we arrive several hours early. He was flying Breamore class, of course, and asked to be seated as far away from everyone else as possible.

"So that I can behave like the pig I am..." he said, as if sharing a confidence with the girl, who was checking his bags "...I pick my toe nails, you know."

Gabriel and I on the other hand decided to sit together.

"Have fun in the cheap seats. Noisy children, smelly trouser coughing and appalling food. Other than that it's fine. Except, of course, that you are squeezed in so tight that you cannot breathe, and have to perform amazing acts of athleticism every time you need to siphon the python. I cannot say that I envy you. 16 hours in coach. I would wish it on no-one – with the exception of both of my former managers and their solicitors," he said with a smile as he sauntered through the fast track passport controls, leaving us to queue with the rest of the world. "Meet me at the Red Carpet club, I shall introduce you to a style to which you would like to become accustomed. Delight and wonderment. You will be happy boys".

Actually, it was something of a miracle that Gabriel and I were going at all, as there had been no time for Breamore to get us working visas. The Vicar already had one, but Gabriel and I had to go in as tourists.

"If there is one thing I know Punk can do," he had assured Breamore, "it is lie convincingly. Almost as well as you. After all, he fooled me into giving him a job. And to think that I employ him instead of the boy Ben."

That joke, like the previous ones about the Naked Assistant, was wearing about as thin as an extended foreskin. But it was worth suffering all The Vicar's insinuations just to sit on the plane, however full. Free booze and free films. It's hard work but someone's got to do it. I bored our waitress by becoming the gazillionth passenger to ask her what it would take to become a member of the mile high club, using my carefully prepared Simpsons line.

"I have this empty spot. I tried to fill it with family, religion, community service. But those were all dead ends. I think the mile high club is the answer."

But all to no avail. Whatever happened to compassion? She assured me that such services were not even available in First class, although it has to be said that the Vicar did arrive in Japan looking very refreshed and with a big smile on his face, so you never know.

"Hello Vicarsan. It is good to see you again."

The promoter had laid on the red carpet treatment at Tokyo Narita airport.

"Hello, Tetsu. It is good to see you again." The Vicar bowed to the three people who had come to meet us. "Are we travelling to Tokyo in your wonderfully lavish limousine?"

This from the man who, the last time we had travelled in one, had complained that it was 'more of a political statement than a mode of transport.'

"No. You have arrived in rush hour. We think the train will be best."

"Ah! you have reserved the limousine for The Rolling Stones," The Vicar teased, noticing that one of them was wearing a Rolling Stones jacket.

"The Rolling Stone finished. Now is Billy G." (I am sure you have seen enough B movies to imagine the Japanese accent. The "R's" and "L's" are totally interchangeable, so that it becomes "Lorring Stones" and "Birry G".)

The train, which arrived punctual to the second at a station directly under the airport, put our privatized mess to shame. As if it was not sufficiently spotless on arrival, we were not allowed to take our seats until every carriage had been scrubbed, polished and vacuumed, and the swivelling seats had been turned around for the return journey.

"But British trains are better because you can smoke on them," said Tetsu, who smoked, or rather spoke, the best English of the three.

"Fortunately no longer," The Vicar assured him. "They only allowed smoking because it covered up the smell of the decaying carcasses of travellers who died waiting for the trains to arrive. Your trains are punctual, so there is no need to allow smoking."

"I see," said Tetsu, who clearly didn't.

"I recently met a London taxi driver, who had just taken a passenger to catch a 9.30 train. It was nearly 10 o'clock, so the taxi driver had asked if his passenger would like to catch a different train. 'Oh, there's no hurry,' his passenger replied, 'The train will still be there. I am the engine driver'. Such is the state of public services in our beloved motherland."

"It is good to have you back, Vicarsan." Tetsu smiled. "It is sad it will be so brief. And we have much work to do. We will please be needing the production meeting as soon as you arrive at the hotel."

"I am here to work. My brain is more than a little scrambled. 'Dribblans in extremis' is the medical term, I think. Regrettably even first class passengers get jet lag. But my body is yours. And my wife tells me it is my best asset, anyway. Do with me as you will. Just lead the way, and pick up any pieces that drop off."

More VIP treatment greeted us at the station. Maybe our minders were used to ageing rockers who were too infirm, or too sozzled, to walk even a few yards unaided – we were met on the platform by the most lavish 'people van' I have ever seen, with tinted windows and sumptuous interior, and it drove us to within literally inches of the hotel door. Tetsu sat in the front, constantly chattering into his mobile phone.

"When the Japanese answer the phone they say Mushi, mushi," The Vicar advised us, in his role as tour guide. "You will find that saying *'washing machine'* in a Japanese accent works perfectly well. Remember to bow politely whenever you are introduced, and they will bow in return. Do not keep bowing, as the senior person will always want to bow last. If you keep going, you will end up like a pair of nodding donkeys."

The absurd level of service continued inside the hotel. We were greeted by numerous porters, who felt we should not carry our own bags, door attendants, who felt we should not open our own doors, even lift attendants who felt we should not select our own floors. In fact, there was a lift attendant waiting for us on each floor, whose only job seemed to be to bow to us and tell us which floor we were on, before placing his hand against the door, in case, as The Vicar put it "the door should have the temerity to try to close automatically, while you were half way in or out." I later discovered that there was even someone to turn down your bed and lay out your slippers for you. Gabriel suggested that at a price there was no doubt someone who would come and massage you, and do other things that you might normally do for yourself – but there will be more time for that later.

Personally, I'd have been more comfortable if instead of bowing politely to me, some of the attendants had either been downright rude, like in Britain, or unbearably friendly and chatty, like the States.

"Hello, I'm Samantha. I'll be your waitress for the evening. My hobbies are windsurfing, and dressing up in skimpy clothing. If there is anything I can do for you, just pull on my skirt. Have a nice meal ". You know the spiel.

Here in Japan, they would simply put their hands together, smile and bow politely, which is exactly what the lift attendants did as we headed to the conference rooms on the first floor. Time for The Vicar to tell Breamore and the rest of the crew how he intended to stop anyone sabotaging the concert.

If he had a plan, he certainly hadn't shared it with me.

T HE WHOLE JAPANESE PRODUCTION TEAM HAD ASSEMBLED to hear The Vicar's plans for Billy G's concert and it was time for him to perform. Before starting, he, as usual, suggested "a pause for thought", and made the whole team sit in silence, taking "great gulps of fresh air", before he finally thrust his left fist into the air with his enthusiastic cry of "Onward!"

I was, as ever, impressed by the ease with which he took total control of the situation.

The first item on the agenda was to finalize the specs for the PA system for the concert, which The Vicar was happy to approve with some minor amendments. Then he examined the layout.

"Well, if you think I am going to mix the concert stuck away in the back corner, I fear you are sadly mistaken. You might as well put me in the broom cupboard or the ladies' toilets. In fact, I will be able to hear so little that you could have saved yourself the cost of an airfare. I would have been able to hear just as much sitting in my drawing room at home, so I could have mixed the concert from there."

"But Vicarsan, every engineer is happy with the mixing

desk there."

"Then get every engineer to mix it. If you want me to the mix the show, then the mixing desk must be here." He pointed to a schematic diagram. "Right in the centre of the hall, in the middle of the stereo. Where I can hear."

"But that is impossible. There are seats there."

"Then cancel the concert, because I shall not be mixing it." He smiled across at Breamore, who was sitting in the corner tapping his fingers impatiently. "I think if you talk to the promoter you may suddenly discover that those seats can be moved and the mixing desk can magically appear in the middle of the hall. What next?"

They ran through numerous other points about which The Vicar was equally forthright. Some of the things that he demanded appeared bizarre to me at the time. He insisted that each member of the group should use tiny little in-ear monitors, like miniature headphones, to hear themselves on stage.

A technician queried this decision, but The Vicar was adamant.

"Nothing that I do is arbitrary," he scowled, surprised that someone should be so insolent as to question him. "I offer you an informed opinion based on years of experience. And pain. And suffering. Interspersed with just A sufficient quantity of sheer joy as to make me keep the faith. Might I be so bold as to suggest that you trust me? Richard the B is paying me the equivalent of the third world debt for my views, and I would like him to feel that he is getting something for his money."

As he spoke, he picked up a half empty cup of coffee that I had left on the table, and tidied it away on the sideboard behind him.

"There is an appalling sound reflection off the back wall of the theatre. I attended a concert here," he looked at his watch, "nine months and two days ago, when half the band was playing in correct time, and the other half was playing a second behind because they were listening to the echo. I am sure you would not want Billy to get her G string out of time."

Also, The Vicar would allow no conventional stage monitors for the band. Instead he announced that he wanted a large speaker on each side of the stage which he would feed with the same sound as the main hall.

"..so that Richard's expensive guests, who will no doubt be supping on Gin and Tonic back stage can hear what the great unwashed are getting."

The only problem that he had not foreseen came when Tetsu asked him how he would like to cope with the TV feed.

He looked angrily across at Breamore.

"I think that More-Beer has been keeping teeny weeny secrets from me. Again. Do you not know the parable of the detective and the manager? The manager hires the detective to stop his singer being poisoned to death. He unfortunately forgets to tell the detective that he has just handed a loaded rifle to the singer's ex boyfriend. Net result one very messy singer. Unless we are lucky and the boyfriend misses and hits the manager in the balls. Did you not think that I might need to know about something like a TV broadcast of the concert?"

Breamore did not like being spoken to in this way in public.

"The TV broadcast is my business. You are being paid to tell Tetsu how you will supply him with the sound."

"Is this the usual Japanese satellite TV deal? A recording for PowWow to broadcast later?"

"No. It is Live Broadcast. Because of 'Lip Sync Scandal', it will be good to show Billy G really can sing live (or more accurately "Birry G learry can sing rive)," Tetsu replied.

"My my. A live TV Broadcast," The Vicar looked over at Breamore. "We do keep big secrets. But then again I knew that already. If that assassin were to hit you in the balls, you would not only be in danger of impotence, but brain damage as well."

"I will not be spoken to like that. Who do you think I am?" Breamore bellowed. "Not in front of the hired hands," he hissed more quietly to The Vicar – it was obviously not so much the comment that Breamore objected to, but more the fact that The Vicar was saying such things 'in front of the servants'. I am tempted to suggest, Punksters, that come the revolution, our Richard the B would be one of the first to receive a haircut courtesy of our friend Madame Guillotine.

"If you keep up your insinuations, I will to have to consider suing you for defamation of character and loss of my good name."

"That would never fly." The Vicar never missed a beat. "You have no good name to lose!"

The veins on Breamore's neck began to stand out.

"I am sorry. Have I been pissing in the communion wine?" The Vicar returned to the subject at hand. "I suppose it has occurred to you that by broadcasting this concert, if there were to be a case of sabotage, you risk Billy G being held up to ridicule all over Japan".

"That is why you have received a big fat cheque," snorted Breamore, who was getting very heated. "I hope my trust is not misplaced, because I have just allowed Pow Wow to license the broadcast in America too. Billy G will show that she has nothing to hide."

"So not only Japan, but the rest of the known world as well. Might I suggest that you also throw in 'the known universe and universes yet to be discovered', as you do in your record contracts? That should at least make it mildly exciting."

He collected his things together.

"I think, under the circumstances, gentlemen, that I had better forgo the luxury of a brief rest, and head straight to the venue. Unless someone has something appropriate to the moment that they might wish to say." He looked around.

"Good. When you are ready, Tetsu.."

Before leaving, he remembered something and turned to Breamore.

"Did you at least manage to get Hawk as head of security?"

Breamore asked the door attendant to open the door, and in walked a vast man – simply ginormous. His head was shaven, except for a large mohican down the centre, and his entire body seemed to be one large tattoo.

Breamore pulled The Vicar to one side.

"Are you sure he's the man for the job?"

"I am sure you know his reputation as well as I do. And he has no previous involvement with anybody here. Including you." The Vicar walked over and shook his hand.

"Ah Hawk, I am pleased to see you again. It has been a long time. Perhaps you would like to join us? Given Richard the B's latest news, I may be relying on you even more than I had suspected."

WE HAD JUST FINISHED THE PRODUCTION MEETING, AND were travelling to the Sun Plaza in Tokyo in the same luxury 'people van' that had brought us from the station. The Vicar still appeared somewhat disturbed by what Breamore had said about televising the concert.

"Do you know how easy it would be to sabotage a concert?" he warned. "Let us take one small component. The guitarist's rig, for example. During the set, he uses some thirty or forty sounds, which he recalls by pushing on a footpedal. It would be a simple matter for someone, even with your lack of intelligence, to go to his rig before the concert and alter any one of those sounds. That would be quite sufficient to ruin a song."

"So what can you do to prevent it?" I asked.

"In the case of all the digital information, I have that in hand." He leant back in his seat, regaining his composure. "Hawk has arranged for everyone to store their sounds on to a computer disc. Before the show, we will go round the equipment racks and load the sounds back in again. That way, if anyone has tampered with them in advance, we will have corrected them. Our problem lies with things that people might do during the show."

"People such as Kevin?" I suggested. "After all, he is on the stage."

"The very fact that he is on the stage means that he will do nothing. He is hardly going to thrust his bass guitar through a speaker cabinet in full view of everybody. Jimi Hendrix may put his guitar on the floor and set light to it, but I think our musicians will be rather more restrained." He pointed out the window. "Look, that's the Imperial Palace on the other side of that lake. And those are all cherry trees. Give it a month, and the whole of Tokyo will be out sitting underneath the cherry blossom, getting drunk. "

"So our problems lie off the stage," I probed, bringing him back on track.. "With Emma, perhaps?"

"Well, I still maintain that the delectable, ever scrumptious Emma B will certainly arrive in Japan before the concert. But no, our weakest link is here…"

He leafed through the equipment specs that he had with him.

"…Radio microphones." He pointed to the reference. "They are a nightmare. Too many possibilities for interference. I went to a London show a few years ago that was deliberately ruined by the Tetradyne effect."

Neither Gabriel or I knew anything about this.

"What do they teach you at these colleges?" he mocked, grabbing a piece of paper and writing the heading 'An idiot's guide to radio microphones'.

"Unlike the beasts I grew up with," he explained, "modern radio microphones all operate in UHF. You have the transmitter, which is the microphone, on the stage". He drew a microphone. "You then have the receiver, which has aerials like a radio, at the side of the stage". He drew a radio. "The microphone is set to transmit on a particular channel, and if you set the receiver to the same channel, you will hear the singer's voice as the good Lord intended. Any questions at the back of the class?"

"No, sir!" we shouted together like American GIs.

"Good. Now imagine a set up where you have a microphone transmitting, for example, on channel 12, and a receiver picking up channel 12. What do you think would happen if some mischievous person was to bring another microphone into the hall also tuned to channel 12?"

"The receiver would pick up the sound of both microphones?" I suggested tentatively.

"Not bad, Bloggs minor, that is possible. A bit like hearing two radio stations at the same time. Sometimes, if one of the microphones is much closer than the other, you might still get something intelligible. The most likely result, however, is what is called the 'Tetradyne effect', something that will put the fear of God into even the most experienced sound engineer. It is as near to the sound of complete chaos as you would ever wish to hear. Something like BBC World Service in Outer Mongolia." He paused for effect. "On the opening night of the London show to which I referred they were using sixteen radio microphones. Someone from an opposing theatre, a jilted luvvy, no doubt, booked a seat in the theatre and sat there with sixteen microphones in his bag transmitting on all channels. It brought the sound system to its knees and the show was cancelled."

He handed us the piece of paper on which he had drawn his diagrams.

"Something for the Brown Album. I would not like to have smelt the underpants of the sound engineer that night. Our Achilles heel, gentlemen, is Billy G's radio microphone…"

We had now arrived at the venue and Tetsu came round and opened the door for us.

"…which is why I am going to send Gabriel on a little expedition."

He asked Tetsu to give Gabriel one of the spare radio microphones, and arranged for one of the Japanese crew to take Gabriel around the various PA hire companies. His task was to track down one of the old VHF transmitters and receivers.

"They may well be illegal now. But if you can persuade someone to hire one to you, it will be our safest option. A radio microphone with which no-one can interfere."

Meanwhile The Vicar and I went inside the hall. It made me nervous just to stand on the stage in the empty building, it was so big. At least 5,000 seats (or should I type "five thousand" – I never know if you're allowed to write numbers in books). The Sun Plaza was immaculate, like everything in Japan. The dressing rooms – proper posh rooms, not backstage corridors – were on the floor above the stage, and you went in a large lift down to stage side. I sneaked into Billy G's dressing room, where a series of flight cases were being unpacked. She had a huge wardrobe, built into five or six flight cases, which fitted together to make her own mobile dressing room, complete with mirror, table and lights. I could see some of the dresses that she was going to use for her costume changes.

And then I realised, with a large gulp and severe chest palpitations, that I could also see none other than Billy G herself sitting in the corner with her back to me.

"I'm s-sorry," I stammered. "I didn't know you would be here."

Billy G stood up and turned round – except that as she walked towards me, I realised that it wasn't her. Identical height, hair, clothing, but the face was slightly different. Not that I would have known, if I had not seen Billy G in the flesh recently.

"Hi, I'm Chelsey." The girl introduced herself. "I'm just Billy G's dresser...though I think you knew that."

"You could tell that I'd realised..."

"You're smarter than most. You must know her very well"

"I had dinner with her recently," I lied a little.

"Most people don't notice. I started just doing her set up for sound checks and photo shoots, as I'm the same size and same colouring. But now I get to do half of her appearances for her. I go out the front door, while she goes out the back door. Quite a giggle."

It was uncanny how much she looked like Billy G. I suppose in her job, she deliberately used the same hairdresser and the same clothing, but even so, it was quite disturbing.

"Perhaps we could meet up later tonight and do a home movie," I suggested. "Could be very lucrative. Something like that one of Pamela Anderson and Tommy Lee. Except that it would be me and Billy G. Or rather me and...?"

"Chelsey," she reminded me.

"Chelsey," I said.

"Thank you, but no," she smiled. "If you want a fuck with Billy G, you'll have to ask the real thing. This girl ain't for hire."

"Damn!" I said jokingly, clicking my fingers. "Worth a try". She smiled and went back to her work.

And so Punksters, unloved and unwanted, must I.

O N STAGE, AT THE SUN PLAZA IN TOKYO, THEY WERE assembling the equipment for Billy G's show, and, as The Vicar did his tour of inspection, all the workers would stop and bow politely. It was rather more like Prince Charles on a royal walkabout than a sound engineer rigging a concert. Particularly an engineer who could be about to face the biggest disaster of his career. Anyway, this Japanese stuff is all very fine, I thought, but it's not a proper venue if it's not covered in graffiti and if you can't smell the toilets as soon as you walk in.

The Vicar moved over to the drum riser and regaled the bemused workers with some of his vast repertoire of drummer jokes.

"How can you tell when the snare drum is level?" he asked "When the spittle rolls off both sides at the same time".

"What do you call a drummer without a girlfriend?... Homeless!".

(It was 'Penniless' last time he told it, but it comes to the same thing, I suppose.)

"What do you call the person left in the room after all the musicians leave?...a drummer!".

He turned to introduce me.

"Let me introduce, Punk, my able assistant, hero of the first order...and a very fine drummer! His band have been thrown out of all the best pubs in London."

The crew now all bowed to me.

It is difficult to imagine anything more ridiculous. It was almost embarrassing. Here I am, a confirmed revolutionary, with a series of Japanese roadies bowing to me, saying "Hello (which, of course, sounds like 'Herro') Punksan".

The Vicar was highly amused at my discomfort, and wandered away, laughing to himself, to talk to Tetsu about a photographer for the following night.

"He must be very discreet and must wait up there." He pointed to a gantry on the stage right high up above the lighting rig. "He must observe and photograph but not interfere. You must make that most clear."

"Trust me, Vicarsan, I will see to it."

"I do trust you Tetsu. You are one of very few people that I think I can trust. You and Hawk."

One of the Japanese crew came over carrying a mobile phone.

"It is Mr Richard for you, Vicarsan."

Breamore had phoned to say that he had heard on the grapevine that Emma had checked into the Capitol Tokyu Hotel. He was also trying to track down Kevin, who had apparently failed to turn up for a band meeting.

"That surprises me very little," advised The Vicar. "I should not let it worry you. I am sure he will turn up for the sound check tomorrow if not before".

Breamore's response to this was so loud that The Vicar pulled the phone away from his ear and waited for him to finish.

"You look after the musicians, Richard, and I will ensure that there are no problems at my end."

He handed the phone to me.

"See if you can get Emma B for me. Capitol Tokyu Hotel," he asked, before wandering away to inspect the mixing desk.

Tetsu found the number for me, but the very polite receptionist was "very sorry to inform me" that there was no Emma B staying in the hotel.

"Ask for Mrs McAllister," the Vicar shouted over.

I looked at him wondering how on Earth he could know such a thing.

He smiled, as if to say 'I have my contacts, you know' – and I was duly put through to Mrs MacAllister.

Hello, Emma," I said rather embarrassed. "I have the Vicar for you".

"Not him again!" she yelled. "Who the hell does he think he is? And how the effing hell did he get this number? Does he never give up?...No, I'll speak to him. Put him on."

I was carrying the phone over to him, but he just shouted at me.

"Ask her what contraception she uses."

I stared at him in disbelief and put my thumb over the mouthpiece, before mouthing to him.

"I can't do that."

"Go on, ask her," he said.

"I can't," I continued.

He grabbed the phone from me.

"Hello Emma. Welcome to Japan. I have an important question for you. I trust you will not let any ridiculous feminine sensitivities get in the way of a perfectly sensible question. What contraceptive do you use?"

There was silence.

"She has put the phone down!" he said. "Women really are a strange breed. Do you understand them? Ask a man if he has had the snip and he will tell you all about it. Perfectly acceptable dinner time conversation. Ask a woman if she puts a small white tablet in her mouth every night, and she rings off on you. I suppose there are other alternatives, though. She could be using the coil. Though that sounds so painful, you wonder if anyone would be mad enough to try it. Surely it must be preferable to have fifteen children rather than a large piece of metal implanted up you know where. What do you think, my young friend?"

I stared blankly back at him, trying to decide if he was playing some complicated psychological game, or if he was quietly taking leave of his senses.

He called Tetsu over. Fortunately, he did not ask him about his wife's contraceptive habits.

"I think we have finished here now, Tetsu. Make sure that I am given the valve compressors I have asked for, and all will be well. The positioning of the mixing desk is perfect. Now Punk is beginning to fear for my sanity. Time to leave it all in your capable hands and go back to the hotel for a rest. Has Hawk finished checking the place out?" He carefully surveyed the scene again before heading away.

"I will see you later, at dinner with honourable Mr Udo," Tetsu said.

Mr Udo was the Japanese promoter for the show. I had seen his name on all the posters.

The Vicar shook himself as if he had a chill.

"If I ever thought that attending Mr Udo's dinner was a necessary part of this job, I would have declined. You must understand, Tetsu, the deep seated loathing I have for such events. I have not yet had time to visit my hotel room and yet I am expected to mingle and press the flesh. I am sure Punk would be pleased to attend on my behalf."

Tetsu looked shocked at the suggestion.

"You would enjoy it, Punk. It is undoubtedly one of the most expensive meals you will never eat. Large slabs of animal being cooked on hot stones in front of you. Unfortunately," he bowed to Tetsu to show that he was accepting the invitation, "I shall have to attend. The Japanese take these things very seriously. Mr Udo would regard it as a personal slight. In any case, you are far too short and smelly. Only tall clean people are allowed. It is a very strict rule."

We took the lift back towards the dressing rooms and the stage door. He had recovered his good humour.

"Sadly, Mr Udo does always feel obliged to invite the artists – although Billy G is surprisingly housetrained. There was a rock guitarist several years ago who got up on the table and pissed all over the food. God only knows what the Japanese made of that. There are times when you are embarrassed to be British."

I followed him back to the van.

"If Gabriel makes it back alive, I would suggest that the two of you go in search of a sushi bar. I was taken to one last time I was here. Bizarre. They know I am a vegetarian, and yet choose a sushi restaurant. Something failed to connect. A carnivore like you would probably enjoy the live eels, chopped and skinned in front of you."

I pulled a revolting face.

"Not to your taste? No, Try a different three Japanese inventions: Geisha Girls, Saki, and Karaoke. Perhaps you will strike it lucky and be able to do all three at the same time...

There was a young man called Punk
Who drank Saki and got very drunk
He sang karaoke
And wanted some pokey
something something something spunk."
He lay back in the large seats of the van.

"And you thought my poetry stopped at Chaucer. You have got all the time until tomorrow morning to think of the last line. Home, James. Don't spare the horses. I wonder if the Imperial hotel can run to a decent pot of Earl Grey tea?"

CHAPTER ELEVEN

The Morning of the Concert

NOW THAT WE ARE APPROACHING THE CLIMAX OF THE story, I have been instructed to cut the silly chit chat. No more talk of toilet breaks and Sparkling Saumur. No more editorial ad libs, as it were – no more telling you about the scandals that happened in Cannes, or the fact that we should far better have trusted Luke Hutchence, our crooked literary agent, with the photocopies of my penis, than the ones of the Vicar's business plan. My lips are sealed. I hereby promise to avoid any further unnecessary deviations, hesitations, repetitions. Except a quick one, perhaps, about the night before Billy G's concert as its indelibly etched in my forgettory. I couldn't sleep because of this sense of impending doom. After all, it could hardly be a coincidence that Emma had followed Billy G to Japan.

Emma was here for a purpose, and we hadn't even succeeded in changing our vulnerable radio mic system.

Over breakfast, I tried to persuade The Vicar that he must
do something, rather than sleepwalking his way to disaster.

"You're like that emperor fiddling while Rome burned."

"Yehudi Menuhin. Now that is serious!"

The jet lag had not dampened his sense of humour, nor
his appetite, as he was working his way through the largest English cooked breakfast I had ever seen. Carefully
pushing the bacon and sausage to one side, as if touching
repugnant life forms.

"Even the working classes are allowed to eat, you know,"
he said, when he saw me looking, "They serve you over
there. It is all or nothing. No vegetarian options."

"I am far too nervous to have an appetite. You must do
something about these radio microphones. Persuade Billy
G not to use one."

"Would that not be rather like giving in to terrorists?
We English do not do things like that. We march slowly
towards the guns dressed in all our finery." He paused
to eat a mouthful of scrambled egg, carefully wiping his
mouth with his napkin before continuing. "It would not
help anyway. Trust me. There is nothing to worry about.
Buy yourself a coffee and calm down."

"Personally, I am terrified," I confessed, and I certainly
wasn't going to buy a drink. I had made that mistake the
night before, and my cup of coffee had cost me more than
I bet Hugh Grant paid for the full shabang with Divine
Brown – including a tip.

I went and parked my bottom on top of the dwarf wall
that separated the café from the rest of the lobby.

It wasn't all doom and gloom. There was this great moment when The Vicar was spotted by a young Japanese man with a camera, who went over to speak with him. I had seen the same man at the production meeting – a journalist, I think, writing a diary of the tour. Regular Vicar watchers will know how such encounters usually go. First, The Vicar hides his face with his hand and turns away when accosted by the unwanted intrusion. When that fails, as it did here, you don't need to hear a word of the conversation to know that it will go roughly as follows:

The man asks if he can ask a question, and The Vicar replies *"If it is the right question"*.

The poor man then proceeds with his questions, at which point, The Vicar says *"That is two questions, pick one."*

The man tries to re-ask a question, at which point The Vicar cuts in *"The quick answer is yes"* (or sometimes *"no"*) before returning to his Financial Times and completely ignoring further questions.

Vintage Vicar. Completely unhelpful and totally infuriating.

I was still chuckling at this display, when The Vicar was joined by Kevin. This brought back all my fears. It was a conversation I desperately wanted to hear, but I fear even the eavesdropping skills of GCHQ might have struggled. They were too far away to hear what was being said, and I don't speak body language (body odour, maybe – but I promised to cut the crap jokes). The Vicar was his usual assured self, and was quizzing Kevin about something. I couldn't see Kevin's face clearly, but he looked fairly shocked by whatever The Vicar had to say. It would almost have been worth the price of another cup of coffee to know what they were talking about, but I could hardly go and plonk myself right beside them – and I still think Hugh Grant got better value for money.

I was so engrossed with watching the pair of them that I did not notice Gabriel sitting down beside me.

"So Kevin has shown up then?" he observed, following the direction of my gaze.

"Yes, and I'd love to know what The Vicar's saying to him. I trust he's blackmailing his sorry arse so he behaves himself this evening. Although he's convinced Kevin's not a threat as he'll be on stage the whole time."

"You worry too much," Gabriel said. "Look at The Vicar. He's relaxed. It's hardly your problem anyway. You're just a hired hand."

I felt quite insulted.

"I have this horrible feeling that *we* should have done more," I said, stressing the *'we'*.

"Well, it's too late now. Here comes Tetsu."

I looked round to the hotel entrance, to see Tetsu, prompt to the second, ready to whisk us off to the venue.

I had been given a schedule for the day. Soundcheck at two o'clock. Doors at half past five. Showtime at half past six. It seemed absurdly early, but apparently it was normal for Japan.

"In order to save on travelling, concerts happen straight after work before people leave the city to go home," The Vicar had explained. "There is a strict curfew at nine o'clock by which time the building must be empty. You watch at the end of the concert. It is an impressive sight. The audience will barely have left before a large squad of roadies will appear as if by magic and the whole PA will be dismantled in the time it would take a western roadie to pull his trousers up and put his gloves on." He smiled knowingly at me. "The truth is, of course, that the Japanese have to finish the concert early so that they can all go out plastic food shopping afterwards."

A joke that went straight over my very small and mostly empty head.

"Oh, I must insist that you take a walk around the back-street restaurants that lurk underneath the raised railways and tram lines. The plastic food displays that they have in their windows are fascinating. There is an entire industry in Japan devoted to nothing other than the production of plastic food. No doubt, there is a ministry of plastic food, ensuring that no restaurants put posh looking food in their window while serving mouldy offerings inside, or vice versa. It is one of the sights of Tokyo. To miss it would be rather like having a weekend in Paris without a French kiss. Although I would, of course, advise against actually eating at any of the restaurants."

Such flippant talk had seemed wholly inappropriate to me. I kept wondering if I should perhaps go over The Vicar's head and warn Breamore how lightly he was taking the dangers of the concert.

"You are still not a happy bunny, are you?" he asked, as we drove towards the venue.

"Too right," I thought.

"Then perhaps we should get you and Gabriel to mount a guard over the stage. It will serve no useful purpose, but I can see it will make you happier. I suggest you position yourself on the gantry on stage right, above the monitor mixing desk, and Gabriel does the same on stage left, where he can keep an eye on the microphone receivers. Is there anything else?"

I mentioned the fact that a 'friend of The Vicar's' had asked if they could meet him after the show. The moment the words left my mouth, I regretted them.

"You know my feelings on this subject exactly and precisely."

He looked at me.

"So why would Punk do exactly and precisely what I have exactly and precisely asked him not to do? You know that I see no visitors before or after a show. Unless I find my feet walking towards them."

He sat back in his chair, half joking and half serious.

"So I must ask myself why Punk has deliberately chosen to disregard my wishes. That is an interesting one."

The cloud of my gaffe hung over us all the way to the venue, where I was able to hide myself away on the gantry, as The Vicar had suggested. I moved into position as soon as we arrived at the venue, and, with the exception of the odd toilet break (my bladder has the capacity of an eggcup) I stayed there until the end of the concert.

I, at least, was taking my responsibilities very seriously.

T HE SOUNDCHECK FOR THE CONCERT PASSED WITHOUT incident. The Vicar took up his position at the mixing desk – which had, of course, been placed in the centre of the hall as he had requested – and was his usual authoritative self. He ran through the sounds of each instrument by itself, before everyone played together to check the sound of the whole band.

"Kevin, your bass guitar sounds like a limp dick. Have you had a hard night, or something?"

The Vicar had a microphone at the mixing desk and was able to hurl his abuse directly into the musicians' earpieces.

Everything worked perfectly. Chelsey did the first part of the soundcheck, although I am sure most of the liggers and general arse-lickers thought she was Billy G. The lighting crew used her to check the focus of all the spotlights, and she checked Billy G's microphone.

"Oh dear. I've gobbed on the microphone," she giggled to an empty hall. "Perhaps we could auction it off – one microphone, almost gobbed on by Billy G."

She was wonderfully confident and pushy. She even

complained about one of the TV cameras that was being set up for the broadcast.

"There's no way you can put a f*****g camera straight between me and the audience," she yelled at a Japanese cameraman, who stared blankly back at her. "Who's in charge? Can someone make him move it. That's ridiculous."

The majority of the broadcast was going to be done by remote robot cameras on stage. But the director was adamant that he needed a view from the audience, and there were lengthy negotiations, in pidgin Japanenglish, about the correct placement of this camera. Breamore was hardly going to let Chelsey dictate camera positions.

"Back to the dressing room, young lady. If your head grows any larger, you won't be able to do your job. I have seen the cameras in the mobile truck and they look wonderful. Let them do their work."

Chelsey stormed offstage, and was replaced by Billy G, who looked stunning, fresh from make up. She had obviously been listening. She carefully removed the microphone from its stand, as if handling a dog turd, and tossed it into the empty theatre.

"I'll have a clean one please. And Chelsey's quite right. Move that f*****g camera."

Breamore stared back at her.

"Hey! I pay the bills. And I have to stand on this stage," she taunted. "Unless you want to sing tonight?"

In the end, they laid a camera track in front of the first row of seats, but Billy G insisted that it must always stay low enough that the audience could see her.

Breamore tried to point out that from that angle the pictures would not be so good.

"Couldn't give a toss. The pictures always look good. My concern is for this concert and those people out there." Billy G pointed into the auditorium. "That's the main event. The broadcast comes second."

"But millions of people will see the broadcast and there are only 5000 people in the audience."

"Then get rid of the fucking audience, and take me to a TV studio. If you want a live concert, with live people, then the concert comes first. All the other people are just peeping toms, jerking off in their living rooms."

"I am sure it will be fine," oozed Breamore, with one of his best smarmy smiles, deciding not to push it any further.

"Are you happy, David?"

He looked over in the direction of the mixing desk, but The Vicar was nowhere to be seen.

"Are you there, David?"

The Vicar had been lying stretched out in the aisle, and slowly surfaced.

"I do hope I am not disturbing you. I am paying you a great deal of money to be here."

"And you are getting my full attention, I do assure you. Sometimes when you are looking for something, it is best to close your eyes and find it in your head. Hours and hours spent rushing around in ever decreasing circles, when all you had to do was look inside."

"Yes. Well I suppose we are in the right place for all that Zen stuff. If you could be brief. Billy G has some interviews to complete before the show. And more make up."

"All we need is one track. Whatever the "luuvly lady" fancies."

Billy G asked for a note from the guitarist, and then

burst into a stunning solo rendition of "R.E.S.P.E.C.T.". It sent shivers down my spine. There was nothing but me, her voice and an empty hall. One of those moments that live with you a lifetime.

Half way through the track, the rest of the band kicked in. A great sound, but not the same intimate magic as before. They didn't even bother to get to the end of the track. Billy G waved her arms like someone flagging down a car, and the song petered out.

"OK. Save it for tonight. It don't pay to come too soon. Not that any of you guys would understand that. See you later, gorgeous."

She blew a kiss in the direction of The Vicar. She, at least, seemed confident in his hands.

"You are most welcome, my darling," he answered through the talkback. "All I need is a set list."

He muted the sound in the PA and the stage monitors, and with a brief "I shall be here if you need me" lay back down in the aisle.

That was at about half past three and the couple of hours before the doors opened passed quickly. I stayed up in my little roost, while Gabriel was occupied with a ghetto blaster he had bought that morning. My only moment of alarm was at about half past four when Emma suddenly appeared on the side of the stage. She had no backstage pass, but I suppose if you are famous enough these things don't matter. I once turned up for a show at the Albert hall, walking in through the stage door and realising that I had forgotten my pass. I assured the door man that I would get a new one from the stage manager, and he let me in. When I got to the stage, I realised that I had turned up on completely the wrong night and had just blagged my way into someone else's concert. You've just got to be confident enough, I suppose.

"Emma! So you have come to see our little presentation. Perhaps we can persuade you to sing a song or two tonight. Some of the tunes will no doubt be familiar." The Vicar had spotted her.

"You again. I think it will take a lot more than that to get me back on stage with Billy G."

"Oh come, come, my good lady. I trust you do not envy her. Such an English disease."

She looked at him with daggers in her eyes – not literally, you understand.

"Perhaps you could be a celebrity guest," he teased, "and we could slowly lower you on a wire at the end of the show."

She turned away to ignore him.

"I imagine the Japanese have one that is strong enough, although it does look as if you are putting on a few pounds," he taunted.

That had the desired effect of making her turn round.

"My God," she yelled. "Just where do you get off. Thank you so much for the insult. If you were a burglar in my house, I would happily grab a kitchen knife and hack you into little pieces. And then feed you to the cat. I am looking…"

"…For Kevin. I know," he said finishing her sentence for her.

She looked at him as if to ask how. He smiled back, victoriously.

"I am sure he is expecting you. Go up in the lift on stage left and follow the signs to the dressing rooms. Be gentle with him. At soundcheck, he seemed in need of a little…"

He paused, as if choosing his word.

"... Viagra".

He then lay back down again and took no further interest in her, as she wandered backstage. He certainly was cool. In fact, I don't think he moved again until doors opened, when he had to, as he was blocking the aisle. I just hoped that Hawk was doing his job, and would keep an eye on her antics.

I T WAS HALF PAST FIVE AND THERE WAS THE USUAL BUZZ of expectation as show-time came nearer. I had a birds-eye view from my spot on the gantry above the stage, with Gabriel opposite me on the other side. The side of the stage underneath me seemed to be one huge mass of people. Billy G's 'onstage bar', for friends and family, might make for a party atmosphere, but it was a security nightmare. I prayed that the huge figure of Hawk would spot any trouble. The Vicar was having a quiet word with him, after making final checks on all the gear on the stage.

"The witching hour approaches, when devils will do their worst, and all good men will be put to the test," he whispered to me, with a gleam in his eye.

"You are actually looking forward to it, aren't you?" I gasped.

He was very calm and focussed.

"This case was far too simple. Let me ask you. What do you do when you are at a point of maximum peril, and have no option for escape?"

I looked blankly at him.

"Come, come," he urged. "There is a technique. You should know this."

I made a guess.

"You run like hell?"

Wrong answer. He shook his head disappointedly.

"No, my fine fellow. You do exactly the reverse. You raise the odds. It is an entirely practical technique, like the person who is caught red-handed with a suspicious suitcase, who walks towards his enemies, and says 'Excuse me, officer, do you want to have a look in here?'…I needed to raise the odds to a level at which they were challenging. To give me a chance to perform. Let the devil do his worst. I am ready for him."

"Have you told all this to Breamore?" I demanded.

"Richard is a prosaic soul. He does not believe in devils. They are only visible to true believers."

"And what do I do if I see one?"

"You must observe and not interfere. Those are the instructions I have come to give you. You must follow them precisely and exactly. It is very possible that you will see or hear things that will make you panic, but on no account must you desert your post. You can look, but must on no account touch."

And with that, he turned and left me. I next saw him standing at the mixing desk at the centre of the hall. The house lights were beginning to dim, and along with five thousand fans, we were all waiting for the players to take to the stage. The dry ice machine was building up a mist. 'It was the early dawn and expectation was in the air,' as a more lyrical writer might say.

Some of the party goers underneath me started to clap.

The lift doors on the other side of the stage had opened to reveal the band standing inside. As I counted them through the mist, I realised to my alarm that there were only four of them, plus the three backing singers.

Where on God's poopy-stained planet was Billy G?!

I had no time to wonder before the other four rushed on the stage and the lights went up. The audience roared their appreciation, and the band struck the opening chord of the first number.

The lighting effects, transformed the band from ordinary mortals with whom you share a coffee, into glamorous rock stars. Kevin was wearing a kilt, and his huge posturing as he hammered his bass, made him seem like an ancient warrior. A bit like the hero that Mel Gibson played in 'BraveHeart'. William Walter. No Wallace. Wallace Walter. That's right. The guitarist, who was a total babe, just in case you sexists have forgotten that girls can play guitar, prowled round the stage, flicking her tongue at the audience, and the drummer stomped on his two bass drums, knocking his sticks together above his head to make the crowd clap. The keyboard player would play a few lines, then step out from behind his rack, spread his legs to fondle his groin, and gestured with both arms to make the audience clap louder.

And still Billy G was missing.

I had visions of Emma gagging her in her dressing room, or perhaps even a shooting. Even now, Breamore might be frantically trying to break down the door to rescue her.

"Answer me, Billy G, Answer me!"

I wondered if I should go and find Chelsey and persuade her to stand in.

Finally, I saw the light inside the lift, and prayed that it would be Billy G. I didn't have long to wait. She burst onto the stage, wearing a pair of ice blue hot pants and a skimpy white boob tube, and danced around, her heels flashing as they touched the ground. Her delayed entrance had clearly been planned to heighten the audience's anticipation.

This was not the same girl that we had met in the studio and seen at the soundcheck, this was a star performing to her audience. I noticed the radio microphone in her hand and did yet more praying that when she finally started to sing all would be well.

She moved to the front of the stage, lifted the microphone to her lips and her voice rang out clear and true. I was so relieved, it is possible that I cried.

After those opening moments, I just sat back and enjoyed the show.

"Oh my God! My tush was in a rush," she gushed after the first song. And then, pointing at the guitarist, who was literally bursting out of her leather jacket, "I mean. You know what I mean. Good luck to her and all that. But cripes. She's got her pops out. Her dirty pillows. Put 'em back in darling. I'm the star of this show."

She hadn't toned it down for the TV audience. Every song, new and old, was perfect. At one point, Emma B walked out onto the stage, gave Kevin a drink, a huge kiss, and waved to the crowd. It seemed designed to steal some of Billy G's thunder, but it made no difference. When Billy G left the stage at the end of the set, she was triumphant.

This Japanese audience was cheering and screaming like a crowd in London or New York.

I could already see the headlines in the papers.

'Billy G sets world alight...'

'The angelic voice of Billy G never missed a beat as she lit up the night in Tokyo...'

After five minutes of stamping and cries of "more, more, more, more" (in English), the band ran back onto the stage, with their arms raised aloft to take the cheers of the crowd. Billy G seemed genuinely moved by the warmth of the reception. She beckoned to the cameraman down in front of the stage.

"I have something I wanna say to all of you out *there!*" She waved to the crowd, who screamed back. "And to all of you out *there!*" She stuck her face right into the camera.

"I wanna dedicate this song to all of you who believed in me. And to think the fuckers said that I couldn't sing it! So thank you."

She planted a kiss onto the camera lens.

"Hey, Chelsey, wherever you are. You only get to gob on microphone, I just gobbed all over the fucking camera. Now that will be worth some money. OK, 1,2,3,4."

The band launched into *'Don't Touch What You Can't Afford'* and, with a leap that would have cleared a microphone stand, she began the first verse. There was a hint of feedback on the microphone, but her voice rang out clear and strong.

And then, at the beginning of the second verse, her triumph turned into disaster.

As she began to sing the second verse, her voice disappeared completely. It then returned, but out of time. It was like history repeating itself – in slow motion. The lip sync scandal all over again. I could see her mouthing the words, but the voice I could hear was almost a bar behind. It then leapt forward, as if someone was spinning through a tape, and when her voice returned it was now ahead of the beat. It was bizarre. The voice that was coming out of the speaker immediately below me was now singing the words a good second before I could see Billy G mouthing them on stage. She carried on like the true professional she was, but it was obvious that we were listening to a recorded voice being played on a tape somewhere. For all the world, it would look as if Billy G had been planning to mime to the track, but that the equipment had gone wrong.

"The Vicar should have persuaded her not to use that fucking radio microphone," I thought, staring at the gantry on the other side of the stage to see if Gabriel was doing anything to solve the situation.

What I saw made me sick to the bottom of my stomach. There were several flashes, like those from a camera, and frozen in them, I could clearly see Gabriel, playing with a microphone and his new Ghetto blaster. The guy who had taken the CD to the BBC studios. The same guy who was in Studio Two at 5.30 that morning. It seemed so obvious, that I couldn't understand how we had failed to see it.

Far from protecting Billy G, The Vicar and I had personally invited the arsehole who was ruining her.

CHAPTER TWELVE

As the final chords of Billy G's disastrous last song died away, there was complete silence. Gabriel was being led away by Hawk, and Breamore was yelling at The Vicar down a headset. His words were all too audible to the shocked crowd standing by the stage.

"To think I trusted you, you complete imbecile. Billy G's career has just been ruined by the cretin you insisted I take on tour. And from what I hear, you even personally told him how to do it. I shall murder you. Don't come backstage, because if you do, you will be lucky to walk out alive."

And still the hall was silent, as if the whole audience was shocked. It was one of those moments when the cliché of 'time standing still' seems almost real. We were all hanging in suspended animation waiting for something to happen.

And then it did. The audience erupted into the loudest cheer of the evening. Billy G and the band who had been standing like statues at the end of the song, moved to the front of the stage and bowed and waved to the audience as if nothing had happened. They couldn't have looked happier, and the audience were ecstatic. The applause went on and on, and Billy G bowed and waved to all parts of the theatre, flicking her tongue stud, and throwing them sweaty towels, water bottles and anything else she could find, before the lights finally went down and she moved off to the safety of the lift and the backstage dressing rooms. The house lights went up in the hall, and at the same time, I noticed that the light was flashing on the monitor engineer's headset. He relayed a message to Breamore.

"That was The Vicar. He says that he personally wishes to address all the media and other worthies that you have assembled backstage. He will be in the backstage bar in five minutes."

"No doubt, he wishes to tell them that it was his fault and that Billy G is innocent," bellowed Breamore, who was still raging, "It won't cut any water. After that display, nothing will persuade them that she wasn't trying to lip sync. But I am happy to let him take the heat. He and his assistant deserve to roast in hell."

And with that he headed round the back of the stage towards the lift, leaving me on my gantry, frozen to the spot.

I think I would have stayed there forever, had not The Vicar appeared at the foot of the ladder a minute or two later and called me down. Most of the party goers had dispersed from the side of the stage, in search of the bar.

"Come along, my dear Punk, the best part of the evening is upon us, and we must not miss our cue."

He seemed impossibly jovial.

"I do hope that Breamore has not said anything unfortunate to you. He really can get very hot under the collar."

"Well, fairly justifiably," I cut in.

"From his point of view, I suppose, yes. But there is always more than one of point of view. Come along, I do hate to be late." He led me round the back of the stage. "Have I not told you of the Spanish writer, Unamuno?"

This hardly seemed the time for philosophy.

"He described your four faces: the one you see in the mirror, the one other people see, the one you think other people see, and finally the one that God sees. There is no *one* version of the truth."

"Try telling that to Breamore," I thought, as we entered the lift, and headed up to the backstage bar, on the floor above the dressing rooms. "What other ways of seeing it are there?"

"Perhaps we had better find out," he mused, as the lift door opened and we walked into a passage, filled with people all pressing in the same direction.

The backstage bar was filling fast with all the worthies who had been given the chance to meet and greet the band – but thankfully, the band themselves had not yet arrived. They would be at least ten minutes, showering and changing, before putting in an appearance. I spotted Breamore lurking near a side door, pushing away anyone who came near to him. The Vicar found an empty spot near the corner of the room, put his hands behind his back, and stared patiently into the noisy crowd, waiting for silence.

"Fat chance!" I thought. "If you want to talk to these people you are going to have to jump up onto one of the tables, clap your hands above your head, and shout for silence."

I was, as ever, completely wrong.

The Vicar's presence seemed to weigh on the room, and one by one people turned around to look at him, until the general murmur of "sssh" became louder than the talking, and the place fell silent.

A few people tried to take a photograph. The Vicar stared at them as if they were trying to steal his soul, and shook his head, no.

Still he had not said a word.

The only noise left in the room was that of the cash register at the bar.

"If you please!" The Vicar commanded, looking at the barman, and even that fell silent.

The Vicar then hung his head and made us all wait for what must have been at least a minute.

"Good," he said finally, raising his head and smiling at the crowd. "Ladles and Gentlespoons, as my father might have said, I do not have the pleasure of knowing very many of you, and I would not be so presumptuous as to assume that you should know me. Let me introduce myself. I *am* The Vicar." He bowed his head. "And for my sins, I was the sound engineer tonight."

There was a very polite, Japanese style, round of applause.

"You are too kind. Unfortunately, Richard the B, Billy G's manager does not share your opinion of my abilities. I think it would be fair to say that he would describe tonight's concert as an unmitigated disaster."

"Too right," shouted out an American voice at the back. "The sooner Billy G stops pretending to be a singer the better. That broad's a goddamn embarrassment."

There was a large intake of breath around the room, at the directness of the comment – which, no doubt, mirrored what most people were thinking, but would never dare to say.

"I can see that you, sir, are not Japanese. Might I ask what brought you here, and where you were during the concert?"

"Yessir. I flew all the way here at Richard's specific request, and watched the show from the side of the stage – not ten yards away from that girl. I know what I saw. And that last number was one of the worst performances I have ever had the misfortune to witness. Just 'cos her fans give her a standing ovation, don't make the facts any prettier."

There were some general murmurs of agreement.

"I may be a friend of Richard's," he scowled, "but I write it just how I see it. I've bought a few of your records in my time, but there ain't no sweet talking from no goddamn Vicar going to make me change my mind," he said forcefully.

"Thank you." The Vicar smiled at him, completely unfazed by his comments. "And I very much hope that you will give maximum publicity to what happened here tonight. I have no desire to compromise your journalistic integrity."

"Unfortunately," I thought. If ever there was a time for a large bribe, this was it.

"But first," The Vicar demanded, "how many other people here were backstage? Don't be shy. In England we are trained to raise our hand at the drop of a hat. To catch a bus, to buy an antique, to go to the tickler..."

A few hands started to go up, and by the end there must have been a total of about twenty.

"Well I am sure it will surprise those of you who were backstage to learn that Billy G's performance of the last number was, in fact, immaculate."

The American journalist let out a loud disbelieving "humpf" sound.

"Is there anyone here who saw the concert in the hall or on TV who would like to tell these gentlemen how well Billy G sung the last number?"

"Birry G sing absorutely excellent!" chirped a Japanese voice.

"Here, here, brilliant!" chorused some other people, before the whole room burst into applause.

"Well, I know what I heard," shouted Breamore from the side of the room. "I know you have a way with words, and can harangue a crowd. But none of it covers up for your gross incompetence. Or the size of the lawsuit."

Again there was a sharp intake of breath.

"We know what we heard," he repeated, as if spelling out the words.

"Yes, perhaps I had better explain to you what you heard." The Vicar smiled. "But first we had better allow all these other fine people to return to their drinking."

The cash register had already begun to ring again.

"Perhaps everyone who was backstage would like to join me in that side room over there, including you, sir," he bowed to the American journalist, "and you, Richard the B, manager and erstwhile publishing thief." He waved to Breamore, who looked as if he was ready to burst a blood vessel.

I could not understand how The Vicar could remain as arrogant and confident as ever.

The Absurd Nonsense
of
The Orange Eyebrow

CHAPTER ONE

The
ABSURD Nonsense
of The
ORANGE EYEBROW

9am Saturday 23rd January
Heathrow Airport

66YOU CAN'T END THERE. WHAT HAPPENED NEXT?" VENUS
Crappenleigh cooed.

We were waiting for our 11.30 flight to Nice. Five days
in the sunshine at the annual music industry gathering in
Cannes, and a long awaited meeting with Luke Hutchence, literary agent extraordinaire, to show him the first
five chapters of *'The Mysterious Case of Billy's G String'*.

"I should have thought that is obvious."

The Vicar carefully rearranged the table in front of him.

"I led them through to a rather messy room, and gave a
very impressive, if I say so myself, impromptu press conference. To give Richard the B his due, he had, as requested,

succeeded in getting a number of hacks from suitably large international publications to watch the show backstage. There was even someone from *Rolling Stone*, but then we all have to start somewhere, I suppose."

"And you did what? Bribed them to keep their mouths shut."

"Tut tut tut, young lady. I would never do such a thing. No! I told them how we caught the man responsible for persecuting Billy G."

It was an ingenious sting, you know," I cut in.

"One which went horribly wrong?" Venus grimaced.

"No, young lady. One which went wonderfully right." The Vicar looked at the menu. "Now what does one drink?"

He had recently given up drinking tea after reading an article about the harmful effects of caffeine.

"Hot chocolate? I am sure that contains caffeine as well."

He finally stunned the waitress by asking for a mug of hot water, and pouring a little milk on top as if it was tea.

"Earl Grey, without the Earl or the Grey. More like Commoners White. Certainly not a drink for the likes of Lord Crappenleigh." He looked at his watch. "Who is already 33 minutes late."

He raised his eyebrows at Venus, as if to say "Where is that husband of yours?"

"I hope that I do not live to regret the decision to share a villa with him, as much as I regret the size of my recent telephone bill."

I tried my best to distance myself from any blame. After all, Lord Crappenleigh was my flat-mate Harvey's father, and this grand reunion of old sparring partners had been his idea, not mine.

"So what did you tell them about this *'ingenious sting'*?"

Venus probed.

"That I knew full well that Gabriel was our saboteur, but had no substantial proof. I had therefore contrived to catch him in flagrante delecto, as it were."

"But you hadn't told Punk?"

"No. There is that. He was quite upset at the time."

I avoided his amused stare by glancing through my copy of Music Week.

"Oh Punk, please do not embarrass me by reading that rubbish here of all places. Do you not have a copy of Playboy that you can hide it inside. Look at all the posers. I would rather that the world did not know we have anything to do with them."

I looked around at a café now filled to bursting with pilgrims joining us on their annual outing to Cannes.

"And might I recommend a serviette for wiping your hands, not your trouser legs," The Vicar added, producing a carefully folded paper napkin from his pocket. "You really are a very proud member of the music industry club, are you not, my dear Punk?"

"And what is so wrong with being one of the lucky few going off to have a good time in the South of France?" I thought.

"You were telling me about the sting," Venus was saying.

"It was most simple," The Vicar smiled proudly. "I brought Gabriel to Japan and explained to him how it would be possible to interfere with Billy G's radio microphone. What I did not tell him was that *that* particular one was only rigged up in the loudspeakers on the side of the stage. In effect, his virtuoso performance in ruining Billy G's vocals was solely for the benefit of those who were standing backstage. No one else heard it."

"Are you telling me that the broadcast was perfect?"

"It is funny that you should say that," The Vicar nodded. "That is exactly what Breamore asked."

"And wasn't there a danger that the musicians would be put off?"

"No," I said, still impressed by his meticulous planning. "If you remember he had insisted on them all using stereo in-ear monitors."

There was a commotion as two people pushed past us to sit at the next table.

"And what about the motive?" Venus coaxed. "Do you know why he did it?"

As if the Vicar wouldn't have all the answers.

"Cherchez la femme. Isn't that what all the detectives say? Gabriel was the plaything of a bitter and twisted woman – the band's former bass guitarist, Mair. She had never forgiven Billy G for throwing her out of the backing band."

"Or for stealing her song," I added. "It all came down to that jacket that Mair was wearing *'No Meat No Man'*, which she said belonged to her boyfriend".

"It is a song title by KMFDM, just like the T-shirts that Gabriel always wore," The Vicar explained. "All it needed was an internet search. A quick visit to Google. As I said at the beginning, it was all most simple."

The Metro café was continuing to fill up, and there was still no sign of Lord Crappenleigh. The Vicar looked at his watch.

"Perhaps we had better make our way through customs. I do so hate to be late."

I gathered up my printouts of the first half of *'The Mysterious Case of Billy's G String'*, and the photocopies of the Vicar's business plan. In my haste, I managed to drop one of the additional photocopies, of a certain part of my lower anatomy, on the floor.

"Interesting!" Venus beamed, picking it up. "Yours?"

"Yes," I mumbled. "But it's not that big. I – er, I used the enlarger."

"Pity! Don't be fooled by what they say. Size...matters..." She put her arm around me.

"And what happened to Gabriel?" she purred.

"I'm not entirely sure." I blushed. "I think it was up to Breamore. Ritual disembowelment, I suppose. Although The Vicar had already planned a sort of punishment. He had bought Gabriel one of those bucket shop special tickets that can't be changed. He was effectively imprisoned in Japan for a whole month. A prison without walls, and a large compulsory fine, as it will have cost him a bloody fortune to find somewhere to sleep. You don't want to get on the wrong side of the Vicar."

As I was to find out, Punksters, over the next six days.

We had now arrived at baggage control, where they, of course, pulled me to one side to give me a quick frisking. What is it with these customs officers? Do I look like a terrorist, or do they all fancy me?

"So what about Kevin and Emma?" Venus pressed, as we reached the departure lounge. "I bet they were just banging each other in that priesthole of theirs."

"Yeah! How come *everyone* saw that but *me*?!" I moaned. "The Vicar apparently twigged that very early on, as he found the corner of a condom wrapper jammed in between the two loudspeaker cabinets. Not an essential musical accessory, you might say, and not a good advert for condoms, as it turned out, because Emma was actually pregnant."

"That must have been the baby she had a couple of weeks ago. I read about it in the paper. Small world. To think you were almost there at the conception."

"The sad thing," The Vicar announced, as we walked towards the plane "is that Mair had picked the wrong pony so to speak. It was her *'friend'* Emma B, not Billy G, who wanted her out of the backing band. It may have been Billy, as band leader, who broke the news, but the deed had Emma's fingerprints all over it. After all, she is the one who – how shall I put this? – was hot for Kevin. And I rather suspect that the writer, Ernest Broom, who ripped off Mair's song, will also turn out to be the less than Ethical Emma."

Venus looked at him dubiously.

"Emma B and Ernest Broom. Do you not spot anything? It was Emma, not Billy, who listened to Mair's tape and stole the song – although, of course, when the band folded, it was Billy who, unwittingly, released it."

"What a mess."

The Vicar shrugged his shoulders.

"Absolon hath kissed her bottom's eye
 And Nicholas is scalded in the butt
 This tale is done.
 God save all of us."

W E TOOK OUR SEATS AT THE BACK OF THE PLANE, RIGHT behind Venus and Harvey's dad, the famous Lord Crappenleigh – the very last person to board, just as they shut the doors. Nothing like Harvey – mousy brown hair, fading to white, a light blue cotton suit, so crumpled that he could have spent the night on a park bench, a bright yellow cloth waistcoat, checked shirt and maroon tweed tie.

He had the most strange way of speaking. At first, I thought that maybe he had a lisp. But it was more that he spoke without moving his lips. Add this to the fact that – how shall I put it – he was not exactly abstemious in the alcohol department, an expert in drinkmanship, you might say, then you will forgive me if I say that at times I was not quite sure if we were speaking the same language.

I stood up and introduced myself.

"Ah yes. Punk. My sin, ahem son, Harvey's flatmate. And the Vicar's lapdog and poodle. Pleased to meet you. I'm Giles Crappenleigh. Not Crapwell, or Crapalot, or any of the other names that a vicious and vindictive press have tried over the years."

He threw some things onto his chair.

"But you, dear Heart, must call me Crap. Crap as in the game, that is, not the shitty slimy stuff that occasionally stains the Crappenleigh undergarments. Mayhap, you are unaware of the fact that I was famous for it. Shooting crap, that is. Not having a crap. Although, erm, my previous wife, I tell you this with a smile that is both weary and wry, was very bad at it. Constantly constipated, poor thing. Used to pull faces of the shaven arsed dog walking backwards variety." Can you believe this guy? I can't, and I'm the one who's making it up.

Venus kicked him in the shins.

"He's teasing you I'm afraid. It's a ritual performance. He enjoys shocking people."

Lord Crappenleigh was now making a big show of bowing to The Vicar, calling him "Your Vicarious Highness" and offering him his left hand, mimicking The Vicar's left-handed hand shake.

"So kind of you to join us, GC," The Vicar said, not rising to the bait. "We have enjoyed meeting Venus. How do you manage it? Was not your last wife called Aurora? Who would have thought that there were so many beautiful women with latinate names?"

"Surely you have heard of deed poll?" he slobbered. "In this world of enlightenment, where you can choose hair that is blond and bleached, breasts that are firm and curvaceous…" he caressed her thighs, which from where he was sitting were roughly level with his head "… why use the old hatted name that two parents dreamt up some thirty years ago in their, erm, shall we say youthful exuberance?"

At that point we were interrupted by the stewardess, who "humbly suggested" that we should take our seats, belt up and actually allow the plane to take off.

"And that is the man they wanted me to share a live television broadcast with," The Vicar whispered, as Lord Crappenleigh pulled Venus into the seat beside him.

It was the first time that the Vicar and I had sat together on a flight since, well ever actually – he usually turns left to preen himself in the pointy end, leaving me to fend for myself in the cattle truck at the back. And that, you understand, is the way we both like it.

On this flight – the music biz special I suppose – there was just business class throughout, so we found ourselves side by side, with one precious foot of no man's land between us, where they had converted a row of three narrow seats into two wider business class seats by placing an over-wide armrest in the middle.

The Vicar pointed to it as he sat down.

"They had to put that there as otherwise our chairs would have been too wide and too comfortable. We have only paid for two foot three inches of space and so that is all we shall be given. Better to have wasted space than let us be more comfortable than we deserve. Such is corporate Britain."

I prepared myself for a lecture, but he broke off to busy himself with his blow up neck cushion and eye mask, and settled back to sleep.

"There is no need for you to waste your time daydreaming," he said, without moving. "I am paying you to work not to enjoy yourself. You can always take some notes to use for the next Vicar Chronicle."

"Well, nothing interesting could ever happen at a conference about bootlegs," I bleated, little realising how wrong I could be.

"Then might I suggest that instead of scanning the adverts

for pictures of scantily dressed young women, you actually read some of the news items in that copy of Music Week you insist on waving around. On the third column on page four, you will find an article about a music publisher who recently had his legs broken by the Russian mafia because he attempted to clampdown on bootlegs in Moscow. And the front page of the October 1st issue last year was entirely given over to the murder of a record company executive who attempted something similar. But then you were probably more interested in the poster size advert for Janet Jackson, which filled the back page, if I remember rightly. Which I am sure I do."

"Although it's conveniently impossible to check," I thought to myself, sneaking a glance at page four of the current issue, which sure enough carried a story about bootlegs in Russia.

I folded the paper and went to stuff it back in the seat pocket in front of me.

"You really should read that article," The Vicar persisted, still lying back apparently asleep with his eye mask and neck cushion in place. "You have persuaded me to come and talk at this conference, much against my better judgement. You may as well learn what you have got me into..."

He was disturbed by the arrival of the drinks trolley.

"Ah! A glass of your best Champagne, please Carol," he boomed, surprising the stewardess by knowing her name. "Together with a separate glass filled with ice. You never serve it sufficiently chilled."

The stewardess gave him two bottles of champagne, and then, looking round to check no-one was looking, gave him a third bottle. How does he do it?!

"Many thanks!" he chanted, bowing his head to her as

she left.

"Snaffle!" he bragged. "They will come in most useful if we have anything to celebrate. Such as successfully avoiding most of the other people on this aeroplane for the next three or four days."

He chuckled in that wheezy way of his.

All the talk around us continued to be of music – or more correctly about the business connected with music.

From the man diagonally in front of us…

"…I collected him £500 that no-one had ever bothered to ask for, and he thought '*you* know the music business' and asked me to manage him. It's mad. No-one's stealing these artists' money. It's just leaking through the floorboards, being pissed away by incompetence not theft. U2 are the only people who have ever audited Performing Rights Society…"

Or from behind us…

"…I persuaded Van Morrison not to play Bush's inauguration because of all the sleaze surrounding his election. It was pretty ironic. They got Ricky Martin to play instead, and he was a declared Gore supporter during the campaign…"

Or on the other side of the aisle…

"…You've got the backstage pass, so it doesn't matter if I am late. Is Tom Jones coming? No no, we talked about this before…"

My kind of people. My world. I had heard sufficient stories about parties on expensive yachts to make the next few days sound pretty appletizing. The Vicar had, of course, heard exactly the same stories, and decided the exact opposite.

"I can think of little that would fill me with more dread than being stuck on a boat surrounded by boorish drunks spilling expensive wines on my shirt, cigarette ash on my shoes, spraying garlic flavoured spittle in my ear, and, no doubt, trouser coughing in the canapes."

All of which sounded perfectly fine to me.

The plane had started its slow descent down towards Nice airport, a tricky runway, particularly when the Mistral is blowing hard – as we were soon to learn. We were just about to touch down, when the pilot put the engines full on and pulled back up into the sky. It was the first time I had ever experienced an aborted landing, your real intestines sucked up through a straw moment.

This was nothing compared to the shock of hearing the announcement over the aircraft's tannoy.

"Attention everyone. Remain calm. WHAT IF this aircraft has been HIJACKED?!"

"WHAT IF *this aircraft is now the property of the Free Music Forum?!"* the announcement continued. *"WHAT IF you were being held hostage until all copyright ownership on the music you exploit has been returned to the people?! The FREE MUSIC FORUM believes that music should be free on the internet. Big business killed Janis Joplin, Jimi Hendrix and Kurt Cobain. WHAT IF the new order were coming and you knew nothing about it?!"*

You can imagine the stunned silence that followed.

The Vicar once told me about a legendary performance by Yehudi Menuhin, I think it was, at the Albert Hall during the second world war (I don't know if he was actually there) of the – whatever the solo section is called – in a Beethoven violin concerto. Menuhin, so the story goes, played all alone slower and slower, with the whole audience holding their breath, until when he finally reached the end, everyone in the building let out their breath at the same moment.

Well, this moment on the plane was nothing like that.

This was the eye-of-the-storm calm of sheer terror and disbelief. I doubt you could have heard a pin drop as the floor was well carpeted, but you would certainly have heard the sound of Lord Crappenleigh living up to his name and losing control of his bowels.

The silence was eventually broken, however, not by crapping, but clapping.

One person, all on their own, clapping very slowly, gradually becoming more and more enthusiastic. It was only when the needle on my personal terrormeter returned to normal and everyone started turning and looking towards me, that I realised that this solitary applause was coming from the Vicar, who was lying back, with his neck cushion and eye mask still in place, chuckling to himself.

A stewardess came running down the aisle.

"Excuse me, sir. Do you know what's going on? Can you tell us something about that message."

She may have been polite, but she was as white as a sheet (well, not my sheets, you understand).

"What exactly would you like to know, my dear Carol?" he smiled, pulling off his eye mask. "And here was I thinking that British Airways had finally excelled themselves by putting on some worthwhile in-flight entertainment."

He gently took her hand.

"I am sure that you will find that your plane still functions just as badly as it ever did. The Free Music Forum cannot even build a decent web site, so I think the taking of hostages is rather ambitious, would you not agree? Although that message is one of the best advertising stunts they will ever pull. They certainly had the undivided attention of all the worthies on this plane. Even I found myself listening to them…"

He chuckled.

"...Although if you recall the exact wording of the announcement with its use of the phrase 'What if' four times in about as many sentences, I suspect the message was really intended to draw attention to the infamous *What if?* Newsletter," he pretended to spit over his shoulder, "if any more is needed."

He reached for my copy of Music Week and pointed to the large advert for *What if?*, corporate sponsors of MIDEM, which filled the back page.

"...And now if you will please excuse me, I was trying to get some sleep, and Punk has still not finished his newspaper article. Third column page four."

And with a triumphant smile, he slipped his eye mask back in place, and lay back in his seat, leaving the stunned stewardess to slip quietly back down the aisle.

"Are you sure?" I gulped, struggling to regain my composure. It is not every day that you think your plane has been hijacked.

"Undoubtedly!" he assured me, calmly looking out of his window as we circled the airport, preparing for another landing. "Although I am equally sure no connection will ever be proved. And the head honcho, Vincente Smagala, himself will not be on this plane. He will be coming to MIDEM by private jet. If he did deign to use public transport, he would only fly first class and would need two seats, one for his arse and the other for his inflated ego."

I laughed nervously.

"You think I am joking. Believe me, it is remarkably common for music executives to demand two first class seats side by side. I have heard that Biff Melcovsky, the radio plugger, often does the same thing. No, that little stunt was a reminder to all those record companies that have not yet paid their multi-million dollar subscriptions into Vincente's blackmail fund."

I looked shocked.

"Come, come, my dear Punk. You cannot really be *that* naïve! The *What if?* Newsletter does not plan to make its millions from small subscribers like you, paying their $20 a month for a weekly newsletter on '*Breaking News within the Industry*'. It wants the large corporations to pay mega bucks for – how shall I put this? – a certain immunity from having their own news disseminated at inopportune moments."

The plane finally touched down and we jolted forwards.

"You will have the opportunity of judging for yourself. Vincente is one of the other speakers on the panel you forced upon me. Such delightful company we shall be keeping. And to think that I have you to thank for it. How would I cope without you?"

The plane came to a halt and the seatbelt sign went off.

"Now. Can we get up yet? Good."

He carefully folded his copy of the Financial Times.

"What about the delightful Venus? Can I perhaps help you with your bags? Are you familiar with Chaucer's *Wife of Bath*, Venus? A mine of useful information for the newly wed.

'If I be standoffish, God give me sorrow
My husband shall have it both eve and morrow.'

I am sure Crappenleigh would approve of those senti-ments, wouldn't you, GC?"

He looked teasingly at him.

"Although, Venus, there are other parts of the Wife of

Bath's prologue that might I think be more appropriate in your case:

   'I would no longer in the bed abide
    if that I felt his arm over my side
    'til he had paid his ransom unto me;
    Then would I let him do his nicety.'

"Yes, much more appropriate, I think," he said mysteriously, as we arrived at Nice Airport, Cote d'Azur.

CHAPTER TWO

I've just received my customary ear-bashing from The Vicar over my writing of the first chapter

"How dare you choose a name like Crappenleigh?" he asked.

"How dare you make me write a book about The Orange Eyebrow?" I replied. "It hardly constitutes a proper adventure. Why should I write a book about what a complete arse I made of myself?"

Fortunately, Harvey thought Crappenleigh's name was very amusing, and it's his dad, after all. Encouragement I can use.

I read something in the paper yesterday about huge payouts for over-stressed employees. 'The scourge of the compensation culture', I think it was. I am sure all this typing is damaging my fingers. Perhaps I could put in a large claim for repetitive strain disorder? If there are any lawyers out there, I'm sure we can do a deal.

UP THE REVOLUTION!

JK

☺

2pm Saturday January 23rd

WHY WOULD ANYONE CHOOSE TO LIVE IN LONDON, when paradise awaits in the not so distant South of France?! We were finally released from flight 109, and walked along the glass corridors through to Customs Control – sorry, '*Douanes*' – and then '*Livraison Bagages*' to collect my suitcase (easily spotted by the large photo of a topless woman taped to the front for the purpose) and finally the airport foyer to be greeted by palm tree skies, left hand drive packets of Gauloise and elegant women talking French. What more could life possibly have to offer?

Venus and I went in search of the AVIS car rental stand, while the ageing duo received the worst thumb screws, soft cushion and lukewarm treatment that BA had to offer over the 'criminal offence of tampering with on board equipment'.

As if the Vicar would have been involved!

And while they are there, I have a bone to pick with the aforementioned AVIS rental company.

The case for the prosecution is this. The Vicar had

arranged for a hire car to await us, but on discovering the model that he had chosen, Venus seemed less than happy.

"A Vauxhall estate car? Surely we can have something more exciting. How about one of those?"

She pointed provocatively to a series of photographs of sports cars headed "Special offers for Midem".

The fact that the sign was in English should have been enough to set alarm bells ringing in my head – Not so much *'Offers'* as *'Rip offers'*.

"Go on," Venus purred. "Ask how much. I am sure Giles will pay the difference". She put her arm round me and pushed me to the counter, where I found myself asking about a Mercedes coupe.

"That will cost 80 Euros a day more than the car you have ordered," came the reply in perfect English in a sexsational French accent. Is it only me that finds the sound of French women talking English impossibly sexy? It's getting so serious that watching 'Ello Ello' is almost as good as a one of those in-hotel pay-per-view movies.

(Any French girls wishing to indulge a young man's pathetic fantasies can email me at Punk@thevicar.com)

"Let's do it!" said Venus, dragging my thoughts away from my groin and back to the subject of sports cars.

"And how exactly are we going to pay for the difference?" I remember asking, trying to retain a degree of sanity.

"Don't you have a credit card?" she replied, staring at me wide-eyed.

And I found myself pulling the plastic out of my pocket and asking for our car to be changed to a Mercedes coupe.

"Brilliant!" Venus cooed, giving me a kiss on the cheek, "and don't forget to have me put down as one of the drivers.

I can't bear to be a passenger."

I have no complaints with AVIS over any of this. I am not complaining that they knowingly displayed provocative pictures of sports cars, nor that it is unreasonable to employ French girls to work at their stand at a French airport. I am not even complaining about the way that I found myself paying for a sports car for Venus to drive – when I'd understood that I would be doing the driving and she, or at least her husband, would be doing the needful. Did I really look that stupid, I can remember wondering?

On balance, I decided that I probably did.

No. My complaint over my treatment by AVIS relates to what happened after the Vicar and Lord Crappenleigh emerged from their session with the Spanish Inquisition.

Venus had rushed to meet them, carrying the keys like a trophy of war. Even at a distance of thirty yards, I could tell that all was not well. The Vicar's lips were pursed so tight that they had almost disappeared. Never a good sign. I caught the end of their conversation as he strode towards me.

"...I am sure, Lady Crappenleigh, that the car I had booked will be quite sufficient for your needs."

I was struck by the almost mocking way in which he spat out the words '*Lady Crappenleigh*'. Had I been more on the ball, I would have realised there and then that all was not as it seemed.

He grabbed the keys from her hand.

"And now, my dear Punk, you will please hand these back to the receptionist, and take delivery of the Vauxhall Astra I ordered. If I wished to be seen in a Mercedes coupe, then I would own one, which as you well know, I do not."

He moved towards the door.

"Giles is in need of a cigarette to calm his nerves after his intensive grilling by MI6. A foul habit, but a sane, if slightly bitter man emitting cancerous fumes, is probably better company than a pair of dimwitted pigeons."

He escorted Lord Crappenleigh out through the door. I tried my best to apologise to Venus, but she seemed totally unconcerned.

"Well, it was worth a try," she shrugged, smiling at me, and for the second time she put her arm round me and pushed me to the counter.

Which finally brings me to my complaint against AVIS. My five minutes rental of that bloody Mercedes coupe cost me one hundred frigging pounds, pardon my French. That's twenty, five-pound notes. Or fifty pints of beer. Or 1.3 cheap tricks on the back streets of Soho. And I never so much as set foot in the car. Beware of fine ladies flashing their eyes, and sexy-voiced receptionists. They can seriously damage your bank account.

But then, I suppose, Punksters, we already knew that, didn't we?

To cap it all, Venus never even apologised to me. She simply made sure that she was put down as a driver on the Vauxhall Astra.

"I really do get terribly car sick when I don't drive," she begged." Why don't you sit in the front and we will put the two wrinklies in the back? Shall we go and get them? You will carry my luggage for me, won't you? You are such a darling. Bless!"

I could see that nothing in my history had prepared me

for the next few days with Venus Crappenleigh.

Or for her driving.

"The engine is so quiet that I can't hear whether it's on or off," she wailed, as we stalled our way out of Nice towards the Sunny Riviera and the fleshpots of Cannes.

"Yes, music. That's what I need," she added illogically, as Lord Crappenleigh, ("Thing is, man, I do the DJ thing best around here") produced a travelling pouch full of CDs.

He had reckoned without the lack of a CD player in our budget rental car.

"Nothing but a radio offering a woeful diet of French music, and an ageing cassette player," The Vicar intoned. "Surprising. I am sure even Punk here could have told Vauxhall the relative market share of the CD versus the music cassette. Could you not, Punk?"

I'll spare you the conversation that followed. The Vicar, of course, knew the exact figures.

"Vauxhall give us a cassette machine that, according to recent IFPI figures, only 3.6 percent of us want. While the CD, which is totally absent from this otherwise fine automobile boasts 85.3 percent of the market. The mind boggles. I am sorry, GC. We will have to travel in *silence*."

Although he wasn't, of course – sorry, that is – as was very clear from the blissful way that he whispered the word '*silence*'. Of course, he was pleased to be spared the Crappenleigh CD collection.

Which explains why I felt so wonderfully smug and a smirkfully cool dude, as I pulled my portable CD player out of my bag, plugged it into the car stereo with the special cassette adapter, and asked Lord Crappenleigh which CD he would like to play. Unfortunately, the Vicar was sitting straight behind me, so I couldn't see the expression on his face. Although I hope he saw the big smirk on mine.

The scene is therefore set, and it was to the strains of The Waterboys singing '*The Whole of the Moon*' (an excellent choice by Lord Crappenleigh, who went up in my estimation) that we arrived in Cannes at about 3 o'clock on a sunny Saturday afternoon – ready for the delights of MIDEM.

"THERE ARE FEW COUNTRIES THAT I LIKE SO WELL AS France..." The Vicar commented, as we walked from our car park towards the Palais des Festivals "...if it were not for the *French*. Elizabeth Inchbull summed them up rather well. The most disputacious, arrogant, unreasonable, self- satisfied set of beings on the face of the Earth."

"A tad unfair, don't you think?" Lord Crappenleigh gurgled.

"I think not. A country with such fine architecture, and yet they still have their Christmas decorations up 17 days, 14 hours and..." he checked the time "...ten minutes after the twelfth day of Christmas".

"They have presumably left them up for MIDEM," I suggested.

"Presumably? Why would I presume?" The Vicar smiled at me.

"Well, I have fantastic memories of Cannes." I went on, ignoring his provocations. "I spent six months here when I was seventeen."

"Sowing oats, which were wild and passionate eh?" dribbled Lord Crappenleigh, who was walking beside The Vicar, with Venus and me following behind.

"Not so much *'oats'*, more *'boats'*. I earned 100 francs a day, which is more than I get paid now, for scrubbing and painting those bloody great things." I waved my hand towards the million pound yachts that lined the wharf.

"It is amazing," The Vicar was saying. "Every country and every city has its smell. Tokyo has the smell of soy sauce mingled with the smell of the drains. France is the smell of foul black tobacco, sea air and,..." he sniffed the air "...sun baked dog shit. Look at the stuff. It is everywhere. How can a civilised race, living in a twenty first century city put up with all this dog crap." He started to walk on tiptoe, as if avoiding imaginary droppings. "What amazes me is how the stuff gets on the pavement in the first place. Look around you. All you see are fluffy little poodles in the arms of overpainted old ladies. Does it come out of their arses while they are being carried along, or are they put down specially so that they can defile the place? In fact, are they being carried because their owners find the pavements too dirty for them..."

At this point the Vicar was thankfully forced to break off from his thesis on the toilet habits of French poodles, as we had reached our destination, the Palais des Festivals, with its enormous awning, proudly announcing MIDEM.

"Hardly a great advert for modern architecture." The Vicar was still not happy. "All these fine nineteenth century buildings on one side of the street, and this modern, brutalist monstrosity on the other. It owes rather more to a concrete car park, than a palace."

A sign on the main doors sent us to a marquee round the side – a marquee unlike any I had seen before. A bit like the immigration section of a large US airport. You know the sort of thing. A row of maybe thirty booths, and those long wiggly queues that you always follow round even when there's no-one there. What's that about?

Pay attention to what happened when we got to the front. It's important.

All four of us went to the same booth, behind which sat two Sexy French Bimbettes. The Vicar asked me to use my best schoolboy French, which (in the new improved version) went roughly:

"Nous sommes quatre. Est-ce-qu'on peut tous registrer ensemble, silver plates?"

The Vicar then produced a letter – not a French one – showing that he was an invited guest, as he would presenting an award at the opening gala, and Lord Crappenleigh produced an invoice showing that he had been forced to pay for him and Venus.

"I, too, would be presenting at the awards ceremony, if my colleague's ageing postures were more flexed and less ego-centric," he ranted.

"'Zat's good," said the SFB (Sexy French Bimbette), although it wasn't. "If you will please stand over 'zere and look at the camera."

On her lips the word *camera* seemed impossibly suggestive. She motioned the Vicar over to the far side of the booth, in front of the other receptionist and pointed to a small stalk coming out of her computer.

"'Zis is the camera. Ready?"

She tapped on her keyboard, and the pass came out of a little printer on her desk, with a big yellow heading saying MIDEM and his photograph underneath. The SFB showed it to him before taking it away and laminating it, so that he could hang it round his neck on a ribbon (no chance), or clip it to his shirt (a poor thousand to one shot).

The next victim was Lord Crappenleigh. His photo was taken by the girl at the other computer, so he had to stand on the opposite side of the booth from the Vicar. Do I need to draw a diagram? Don't worry. It's not important. All you need to know is that SFB number one (she of the premature ejaculatory accent) produced passes for the Vicar and myself, while SFB number two photographed Lord Crappenleigh and Venus. As well as our passes, we were each handed an enormous black bag embossed with, yes, you guessed it, the word MIDEM.

The Vicar handed his disdainfully to me, with the tips of two fingers as if its contents might dirty him.

"Take mine too, Punk. A present for your nieces and nephews."

And with that, he put his pass in his pocket and strode out of the marquee.

Talk about a million dollar view. The Croisette, the main street of Cannes, lined with palm trees, lay before us. Eyes left for the old port, with the old town on the hill beyond. Eyes right for the Carlton hotel, with its overtones of Meg I'd-give-her-a-French-Kiss Ryan. Straight ahead for the bars: all six or seven of them, most of which had put up large awnings to keep out the cold. It was, after all, still only January.

"Time to try some of the local poison, dear Hearts. Essential to maintain me in my current dilapitated state of health," Lord Crappenleigh burbled, diving through the traffic.

A man after my own heart.

"You will join us, won't you?" Venus purred. "I am sure

they do other drinks if you think it's too early for some-thing alcoholic."

"I doubt you need to teach Punk about French bars, *Lady* Crappenleigh," The Vicar spat the word '*Lady*' out, before smiling, and adding more politely, "I had intended to ask Punk to guide me to a good bookshop, but we would, of course, be delighted to join you while Giles does the needful…"

"…And do mind the traffic," he added as he started to cross the road. "This may look like a pedestrian crossing, and may be called a 'passage protégé', but no self-respecting French driver will ever stop for you. Even if your legs are rather more shapely than mine."

I will not bore you with all the details of our first visit to Café Mediterranee. There'll be enough time later to acquaint you with the peculiar delights of that watering hole. The Vicar spent most of the time discussing breast cancer.

"A great friend of mine has asked me to research the validity of all the various alternative cures, about which one hears," he explained to Venus.

"Mayhap you have heard that cancer can be cured by dining upon Apricot kernels," Lord Crappenleigh slurped, through his beer.

And so we continued. I hardly think you need all the details.

Fortunately, for those reaching for the delete button, the weighty 'meat and two veg' of this story was awaiting us very shortly at that evening's opening party aboard the wonderfully named yacht 'ToyBoy'.

Allow me to set the scene. When I say 'yacht', I certainly

do not wish you to picture sails. The yachts that line the wharf of the old port in Cannes are all motorized gin palaces. Large white creatures, luring you inside with their curvacious lines and their promise of adventure. And the boats are fairly attractive too.

"Get on in," shouted the bouncer on the gangplank. "Nibbles, wines and beers are on this deck, the bar is on the top deck".

The Vicar went first, followed by Lord and Lady Crappenleigh and my good self, all obligingly showing the bouncer our Midem passes. If that's all it takes to get a free drink, then it's a small price to pay. If he had asked me to take down my trousers and wave around the contents of my underpants, I would probably have obliged, looking at the considerable array of goodies on display in the boat.

It was while showing my pass that I first noticed a large lime-coloured Post-it on the back, with some writing on it. I was about to read it, when the Vicar passed me on his way back down the gangplank. I was still on my way up and we met in the middle.

"I think not. No host to greet you. And I have already been accosted by Malvolio, who seemed rather surprised to see me. He has invited us to the launch of the Glamour Twins album on Tuesday. No doubt deducted from their advertising budget. I do not wish to ruin your evening, but this is not for me. You and the Crappenleighs stay as long as you wish. When you are ready to leave you will find me waiting in the car."

And with that he turned and left – completely distracting me from the mysterious message stuck to the back of my pass.

Toy Boys & Big Girls

"LOOK AT THE CEILING ON THIS BOAT!" VENUS SHRIEKED, as I squeezed my way beside her. "It's wonderful. Wouldn't it be great to have something like that at home."

The ceiling was one gigantic mirror. I got the feeling it was intended to be fairly walks-like-a-woman-talks-like-a-man-Ray-Daviesly-kinky.

"I think I can imagine what sort of Toys these Boys like playing with," I said, not exactly excelling myself in the wit department.

"And if this is the lounge, what the hell must the bedrooms be like?" Venus cooed, getting up and wandering towards a set of curved stairs.

"I er doubt we're meant to go down there," I hesitated. "No-one else is."

"But we're not everyone else. No-one tells a Lady what to do. Fancy coming, Toyboy?"

"Uh…N-No," I stammered. "I must go and find Lord Crappenleigh. I have a message from the Vicar."

I sounded self important, but, who am I kidding, I was just bottling out.

"Please yourself. I hope you don't always miss out on

the fun."

I headed up to the top deck to find Lord Crappenleigh.

Being a simple soul, I had imagined that the top deck would house something practical like the steering console. How ignorant can I get? Not a bit of it. The designer of this boat had bigger, better ideas. The top deck was an enormous bar, liberally stacked with every poisonous solution known to mankind.

Lord Crappenleigh had his arm wrapped around the man next to him for support.

"Evening friend (bend knees, nod helmet) Sgt Crappenleigh here. Reporting on the quality of my aim. Didn't touch the sides this morning, just a little stain on the left! Sprayed it everywhere, must have been that bloody curry!"

Astonishing though it may seem, even I can have too much toilet humour. I left him and wandered to the other side of the boat, where I saw the SFB (she of the instant orgasm), who had processed our passes for us. She was now working as one of the waitresses handing out nibbles.

"You were in the marquee earlier on, weren't you?" I asked (please note the skilful way I engaged her in conversation).

"It's a busy week. Pizza?"

Pizza? She had only said four words to me (well, five actually) and I would have got down on my knees and begged her to marry me. Imagine waking up next to that voice every morning. A man certainly wouldn't get much work done.

I thought better of the marriage proposal idea, and contented myself with a slice of pizza.

"Thank you. That'll seat my nudes exactly."

As she wandered away, I remembered the note stuck to

the back of my MIDEM pass.

"Thank you, God!" I thought.

She was the only person to handle it except me, so perhaps my luck had changed, and it was a note to meet her, with her name and address.

But then I think we all know that it wasn't.

RULE EIGHT: Punk never gets unsolicited notes from SFBs with instant orgasm accents, offering their phone numbers.

The message was in some small spidery writing, that was impossible to read in the dark. I was just moving to the lights by the bar, when I again caught sight of Lord Crappenleigh on the other side of the boat. He had now put his drink down, undone his belt and was preparing to take down his trousers. The man standing beside him was doing the same.

"Well, dear Heart, we are all part of the Urine Peeing Union now, aren't we? I bet I can fill up that dinghy even from this distance." I heard him say, before starting to piss over the side of the boat.

It is difficult to know how you will react to something like this until it actually happens to you.

You can:
1. Join in.
2. Deny all knowledge.
3. Run, run, run away.

I chose option three and ran to find mummy, or rather his wifey.

As chance would have it, she was holding court in the cabin – judging by the wet window – immediately below her husband. Beside her, on a completely circular bed, sat two other people, one of whom I recognized as Hugh Spiller. I am not very clear on the exact history, but I know that he and the Vicar had fallen out several years before, over a recording project. Whenever we meet, he always tries to quiz me about what he had done to upset the Vicar. How do you explain to a man that the main reason someone won't talk to him is probably that he has a terrible habit of spitting all over you whenever he speaks? And we are not talking about a gentle shower here, more a tropical monsoon.

"Hello Huge," I said, greeting him from the very far side of the bed. "Still, er, fit and filthy?"

"Punk Th-anderson, no less. Th-till with the Vicar?" he spouted, amid the usual shower of spittle.

"Yes, unless you're salivating over my unique talents," I said a little cruelly. "His Hairyness is not here though. Not his sort of a party. He is waiting for us in the car."

"What on earth is he doing in the car?" cut in Venus, and then eyeing up Herr Spiller, "You know Hugh, do you, Punk? He is interested in an album by Giles. Is his a good record company?" she teased.

What are you meant to say with him standing just across the room from you?

"I didn't know that Lord Crappenleigh still played?" I said tactfully.

"He has been trying to record a percussion orchestra for years," Hugh spluttered. "I thought we might be able to th-ettle th-omething. Where is Crappenleigh? Perhaps

I could speak to him myself."

"He's up on the top deck. But I don't think now would be a good moment."

He'd probably finished by now, but I thought I had better let Venus know, so I lent over and whispered in her ear. She laughed.

"You mean he's outside peeing into the water!" she squealed out loud. "Believe me, that's nothing. I am sure this would be an excellent moment for you to speak with him, Hugh. Perhaps you could shake his pecker off for him while you are there. Isn't that what record executives do? Massage their artists' ego?"

Hugh looked shocked.

"No. I'm serious," she said. "It probably would be a good idea if someone did go up and make sure he doesn't fall off the boat. This is your perfect chance to be a knight in shining armour."

He still looked doubtful.

"Although if the Vicar is really sitting waiting in the car, I suppose we had all better think about leaving. What do you think, Punk?"

I took her hand and helped her from the bed. Was it my imagination, or did she hold on to it a little longer than she needed to?

"Peeing and then rescuing of husbands," I decided. "In that order, otherwise, there's going to be some more damp patches. Shall we meet on the top deck?"

I went to shake hands with the unemployed – long queue, maybe Lord Crappenleigh wasn't so stupid after all – and joined Venus outside.

"It's stunning. Isn't it?" she breathed. "Imagine actually

living here."

"Well, I did for a while," I said. "I had forgotten how beautiful it was."

If I had ever noticed at the time. Teenagers have other things on their minds.

Over the stern of the boat was the park; the plane trees, draped with fairy lights, all recently pollarded, so that the bare branches looked rather like thick gnarled fingers.

"The trees look pretty stupid," Venus giggled. "Almost like they are upside down, with their roots sticking into the air. And it's bloody chilly. Here, keep me warm." And she put her arm around me, and pulled herself tight against me. Who was I to complain?

"Fancy losing some money on me?" Venus pointed teasingly at the casino.

"You have already cost me £100 on that bloody sports car," I moaned, as we walked to the very front of the boat.

Now Punksters, I know you are a hard-nosed bunch of people, but be prepared for a really romantic moment. Picture me in the arms of this gorgeous woman, with the lights from all the yachts beautifully mirrored in the totally calm Mediterranean sea, looking out on a row of little restaurants, with the castle floodlit on the hill behind. Be honest, Punksters, how much better can it get?

Not much, but it can get worse.

"Hey woman, are you going to carry me home? Punk, isn't it time we went to find that plagiaristic, back stabbing, insecure, bullying, control freaking, stage-too-small-for-the-both-of-us, Vicar of yours?"

Lord Crappenleigh come to disturb my dreams and

reclaim his wife.

"Good God, Giles. Pissed again." Venus removed herself from my arms, and put hers round him.

"Hold on to me, you idiot!" he spouted, as he tripped and fell down the steps, grabbing hold of my MIDEM badge, and ripping it from its clip.

I picked it up from the ground, checking the message was still there, stuffed it in my pocket, and helped Venus to carry him to the car.

CHAPTER THREE

11pm still Saturday January 23rd

I HOPE, PUNKSTERS, THAT YOU DON'T SUSPECT ME OF DELIB-erately trying to tease you about the message on the back of my MIDEM pass. I am not that clever. Nor would I presume that you would find it particularly interesting, when you have the whole of the rest of your exciting lives to lead. This book is not the place for sad, lonely gitfarts with nothing better to do. That's how the story goes. I just never had a chance to look at it.

Venus and I carried Lord Crappenleigh down from the top deck of the boat, avoiding the temptation to give him an unscheduled bath in the Mediterranean. As we neared the car, I could see the Vicar sitting in the front seat, staring straight ahead of him. What can you say? Any ordinary man would have put the seat back and gone to sleep, or maybe put the light on and read a book. But not The Vicar. He was sitting bolt upright, as if he was on guard duty.

"Good. I was hoping you would not be too much longer. Did you children have fun, or was it too atrocious even for your admirably downmarket tastes?"

"Well, Giles certainly enjoyed it," Venus said, shoving her husband into the back seat, "and someone is going to make him an offer about his percussion orchestra, so that can't be bad. Hugh Spiller. Do you know him?"

"Huge Spittler? I would not wish to speak meanly of him, but I think GC may find better options. Now then. Perhaps I should drive, given the general state of intoxication."

He moved into the driver's seat, and Venus sat beside him.

"Huge signs up records by fading rock stars on the principle that you can always sell at least a thousand, which is about enough to cover his costs. He then sits on the record, doing absolutely no work whatsoever, on the off chance that the old band might, through their own hard work, have a sudden resurgence in popularity. At which point he will claim all the credit and most of the money. If that is what GC wants for his record, then Huge is his man."

"Well, he was perfectly polite to me. Do you know where you are going?" She looked at the map. "We need to head West as if we were going to St Tropez."

Actually quite a long way past San Tropez. A small hut on the moon would have been about as 'conveniently placed' for commuting to Cannes. If you put a pair of protractors (compasses?) on the map of France, with one end on Cannes, and the other on Cavalaire and swing it around, we were going the same distance as half way out into the Mediterranean towards Corsica, or San Remo in Italy. Major suck-a-roony.

So, a lifetime later, we arrived in Cavalaire, and took the first turning off the coast road, onto a narrow, gravelled track that went up deep into the hills. Our villa was at the very top, with double gates which any normal person would, no doubt, describe as *'heavily padlocked'* – but being a pedantic crappipuss, I think I should point out that the padlock itself was quite light. It was the chains that were heavy.

Being perfect gentlemen, Lord Crappenleigh and I let Venus fight with the heavy-chains-light-padlock, before the Vicar drove down and parked just beyond the house.

Don't let the word *'villa'* fool you into imagining a large white building with marble floors, Burt Bacharach playing the piano downstairs and a blond movie star or two waiting for you in the bedroom. It did have a swimming pool, but it was one of those small, overgrown paddling affairs. Not that we had swimming on our minds. It was now late, on an increasingly cold and windy January night. Our main focus was a warm bed – and smashing the three locks on the front door – those peculiarly French affairs, which only work if the door handle is raised, the key is turned 2 degrees to the left, and Jupiter is in the fourth house.

"At last," The Vicar sighed, as the door finally gave up its fight. "A cosy home away from the shark infested pools of MIDEM."

"Giles and I will have the bedroom at the far end of the passage," Venus shouted down from upstairs. "It only has twin beds, but it has an ensuite bathroom, and a girl must have her bath. The Vicar should have the one at the top of the stairs, which has a private balcony, and Punk can bunk down in the middle room".

"Thank you, Lady Crappenleigh. If you think Punk will be able to help you extract GC from the car, then I will bid you a good night."

I could hardly have expected Venus to give me the best accommodation. And she hadn't. Although, after several days of my smelly socks and damp towels I can change even the poshest hotel room into a complete fug hole, so I suppose a small musky boxroom about seats my nudes.

This particular prison, complete with iron bars fitted to the window, had amazing textured wallpaper that went up the walls, over the ceiling and even covered both the main door and the door to a small built-in cupboard. A true French décor. Love them or hate them they are certainly original.

Not that I was interested in the decorations. Now that I was alone, I wanted to read the mysterious post-it message on the back of my MIDEM pass. I assume you are familiar with Post-its. There's one stuck to my computer now – a telephone number I copied down from a telephone kiosk in London – interesting but entirely private. If the session is successful, I will post a recommendation on my website. That one's bright yellow, but as I recall, the one on the back of my MIDEM pass was a garish shade of lime green – not unlike the colour of my bedroom (the one at home, not the one in Cannes).

I pulled the pass out from inside my shirt. My first surprise was that the Post-it wouldn't come off. Unbelievabubbly, it was actually on the inside of the clear plastic lamination. How was that possible?

I couldn't make out all the words, it looked something like:

"The Vicar must not p the conf
P ew tsing
O. the Org. Eye
Yo or I"

There is no point in taking you through the various ridiculous stages of my deciphering. Or perhaps there is. I think, at some stage, I had:

"The Vicar must not peel off the conifers
Pursue love whilst singing early
On the Orgy Eyesore all done out for years
You or I"

Which, as cryptic messages go, is pretty good. I am sure Nostradamus would have been proud of it.

In the end, I decided it probably said:

"The Vicar must not preach at the conference.
Persuade him without saying why
Or the Orange Eyebrow will do it for you.
You or I"

Hardly the love message I had been hoping for. Why does my whole life have to be ruled by the Vicar? Even when I get a mysterious message, delivered in a seemingly impossible way, it has something to do with his holiness.

Which brings me back to the way the message was sent to me – on the *inside* of my MIDEM pass. My Ferrari-like brain quickly worked out that there were only six people who could conceivably have handled my pass before it was sealed into its plastic wrapper: Either of the two SFBs, The Crappenleighs, the Vicar and me. It was most unlikely that we had chosen at random the one Sexy French Bimbette who wanted to give me a message concerning the Vicar. We'll leave coincidences like that to dodgy Hollywood movies. That left the members of our party.

I knew it wasn't me, and it was hardly likely to be the Vicar, which, by a nifty process of elimination, left the two Crappenleighs. And I knew that Lord Crappenleigh had been sending vicious emails to the Vicar recently – a storm in an Earl Grey teacup over the Vicar's refusal to co-present some award at the opening ceremony. Which meant all that was needed *now* was a brief interrogation to find out what was going on.

And staring out of my window, I spotted my opportunity. Venus was sitting outside.

"You'll never get a better chance, Punk," I told myself, as I put on my flimsy pink canvas jacket (yes, it is a bit camp), and braved the spiral staircase in search of the one and only Lady Crappenleigh.

A ROMANTIC
Tit à Tête

IN THE SEMI-GLOOM, THE SPIRAL STAIRS WERE YOUR French-special death-trap variety, steep and narrow with shiny tiled treads, specially designed to make unwanted British sound engineers slip and break their necks. In fact – and this is really saying something in the 'dangerous stairs stakes' – they were almost as treacherous as the Venus fly traps at the crematorium in Salisbury, where my grand-mother was cremated. As we fell down those particular steps at the end of her funeral, my grandfather made the now famous observation that they had been deliberately made as dangerous as possible to get new customers. Which was fairly ironic, as he did himself return several years later as a customer, although not because of a fall down those stairs.

Anyway, I arrived safely in the hall, and spotted Venus outside, leaning up against the patio doors. She had gone out through the kitchen. I did the same, picking up a glass of water on the way.

"Hi. I thought you had gone to bed". Not a classic pick up line, I admit. Having come down to pump her for inflam-mation, I had not the slightest idea what to say.

"No. I am not tired. And it's a fantastic view, isn't it? It is so wonderfully still."

Although it was now well past midnight, the view was, well, fantastic. High on a hill looking down over a patchwork of tiled roofs and olive trees. In the distance, we could see the sea and the old fishing port. All very picturesque (mispronounced picture skew, of course). If I remember, I'll upload a photo.

"And have you seen the stars? There are so many of them. The longer you look, the more you see," she said.

I stared upwards, and grew quite giddy. Venus was sitting on the concrete step with a blanket over her legs.

"Do you mind if I join you?" I asked.

"No, be my guest. But your arse'll go numb fairly quickly. This step's freezing. Here, you can share this".

Which is how I came to find myself sitting outside under the stars sharing a blanket with the beautiful lady Crappenleigh.

I don't normally bother describing people. After all, isn't it character that matters?

Oh come on. I think we all know my bulging eyes were not focussed entirely on her character. So for those who are interested, the fuck file – fact file – reads as follows:

Hair: The colour of a pint of Guinness.
Skin: Slightly olive coloured. Colour of a fine Irish malt whisky.
Height: Same height as the barmaid who served me the pint of Guinness with whisky chaser.
Eyes: Not the faintest idea. Big and dark. Dark brown? After all, I was distracted by her...
Bosoms: Finest parateets in captivity .

Perfume: I don't know, but I keep smelling it everywhere. Someone in my local wears it, and it
   always reminds me of her.
Clothes: Entirely unnecessary.

Enough. Unless we include the childishly obvious:

Sex: Preferably.

Imagine what you like, but the real thing would take some beating. Particularly when you have got her all to yourself underneath a blanket in the South of France.

"And er have you ever been here before?" I babbled, still working out how to get the inflammation I needed.

"MIDEM, you mean?" She shook her head "Uh huh. I think Giles has. But there are lots of places we have never been together. We have only been married a month."

"Really. I'd no idea. You should still be on honeymoon."

"Not that sort of wedding. Nothing too romantic. Brief and to the point. It's not exactly Giles' first marriage, and I am not quite the blushing bride. You can't keep taking honeymoons."

"Oh I don't know, Honey. Mooning can be quite addictive."

Best joke I've ever made.

"Naughty!"

She smacked me on the bottom.

"But nice. Well, Honey, mooning's not for us. We're not exactly conventional, you know."

There was a clumsy pause.

"How did you meet?" I tried again.

"Inquisitive little thing, aren't you? Well, it's no secret, I suppose. We met through a dating agency."

"Now you're winking my whizzler." I laughed "Someone as snoggly as you doesn't join dating agencies to meet people."

"I didn't say that I joined an agency." She elbowed me under the blanket. "I saw an interesting advert, and answered it."

"What did it say?"

"I think that's a little personal, don't you?" She raised her eyebrows.

"Yes, I am sorry".

Another long silence. Based on this performance, MI5 were hardly going to be queuing up to give me a job.

"What about you, Mr Handsome?" Now she was asking the questions. "No ring, so you'd not be married then?" She ran a finger across my hand. "And too young to have any punklets suckling away in a cupboard somewhere."

"Well y-y-yes and no. Or rather n-n-no and yes. Weddings are strictly for crashing, not "I doing", if you know what I mean – but I have got a son. He'd be ten now".

I'm not sure what made me tell her that. It's a secret I usually keep to myself. And now I've gone and put it in a goddamn book.

"You got off to a quick start." She gave me the full on Colgate-ring-of-confidence smile. "And you didn't marry the mother. More of a…" she paused "…a poke and run?"

Was I imagining it, or did she just prod me *down there* – if you know what I mean?!

"Are girls allowed to use phrases like that?" I pretended to slap her wrist. "No, I did try to do the proper thing. It happened in Cannes, actually, when I was here on the boats. She'd gone back home to America before she found out. I called and asked her to marry me – but I had all my fingers crossed praying that she would turn me down.

I didn't even pay for the phone call, there was this way of using a piece of wire to short out the coinbox and…"

My interrogation had gone way off course. I was suffering from a surfeit of testosterone, or whatever it is that flies around your body at such moments, and seemed to be doing all the talking myself. I tried a change of tack.

"So, er, what brings you to MIDEM?" I asked as casually as I could.

"You'd have to ask Giles. It's his business, not mine."

Yes, of course." I stared at my knees to avoid her big wide eyes. I was getting blurred breath and short vision. Or is it the other way round.

"I have been meaning to ask you." I finally blurted out. "There's a sticker on the back of my MIDEM pass. It wasn't a message from you was it?"

Subtlety personified. That's me. And completely incompetent.

"Is this a romantic tit a tete or an interrogation by Scotland Yard? You are asking some funny questions. No, you strange little thing, I don't know anything about your message. Come on. It must be bed time now. I think we had better go up before you start asking me what sort of underwear I wear. If I wear any at all, of course. Not that you'll ever find out."

And she got up, folding up the blanket.

Shit, shitty, shit, shit. So much for my future as a detective.

I followed Venus into the villa. And as I shut the kitchen door, I could swear that I heard the Vicar laughing on the balcony upstairs.

CHAPTER FOUR

I think that last Chapter might be a little too short. Only 3530 words, made up of 15,155 characters not including spaces, or 18,632 characters including spaces – assuming that Microsoft Word can count correctly. And if Microsoft can't count, then we are all in the poopy. It seemed like a good moment to change, as tomorrow was a new day, and therefore seemed to deserve a new chapter.

Perhaps we should do the girly thing and compromise. Instead of a having new Chapter, we could call the next bit…

"THE NEXT BIT"

???

☺

THE
TV SHOW
thAt PUNK
MisseD

The Next Bit
Sunday 24th January

A FINE BREAKFAST OF COFFEE AND FRESH CROISSANTS, purchased by Venus and me at the bakery (*Boulangerie*, I should say) at the foot of the hill – a short romantic stroll, if we overlook the slight public inconvenience of her being the newly married wife of our host. Mr Blue Sky was in his heaven, the Mediterranean crashed satisfyingly on the beach, and your senses positively swizzle-popped with the Cote D'Azureness of it all.

Even without our trip, the kitchen cupboard was not exactly bare. Essential items left by the caretaker:

1. A baguette,
2 A bag of coffee,
3. A bottle of red wine.

Don't you just love the French – they have certainly got their priorities right.

Not that The Vicar was happy. He was still continuing his *'caffeine cleansing'*, and ate his *'feeble little french pastry'* with a cup of hot water with a splash of milk.

"If a friend of mine can cope with the horrors of cancer," he said, "I would certainly hope that I have the personal discipline to cope without caffeine."

"But why would you want to, dear heart?" burbled Lord Crappenleigh, who had emerged apparently none the worse for his drinking spree. "Life is sufficiently riddled with lesser-potted holes, without making it any harder. Caffeine, nicotine, alcohol. The funky little darlings we need to help us get from one end of the day to the other. Crappy's little helpers. It's part of modern living. Like the calming scent of lavender that wafted from the Crappenleigh bathtub this very morning."

I still found his voice so slurred and gutteral, that he was hard to understand.

"These are personal choices, which work for you. I, for one, have no desire to be the servant of any substance," The Vicar answered. "Although lavender baths do sound good. It is also a form of pointed stick. Instead of sleep-walking my way through the day, with rhythms and habits that become so familiar as to be invisible, I am now more aware. But you know all this."

Indeed we do, do we not, Punksters.

"Although," he added, carefully placing his laptop on the table. "I hardly need a hairshirt, when my inbox is regularly disturbed by GC's Black Dog style Hogwarts sherbet lemonade fizzing e-howlers."

"Ah yes!" Lord Crappenleigh ran his hands over his eyes. "My droll offerings. Perhaps I have over elfined. I had an odd complaint or three to nudge forward. I just bounce ideas over the net."

"And this cruel heartless machiavellian creep has already made his position abundantly clear," The Vicar said, opening a bag. "I make no objection to you presenting the award this evening. It is a task that I will happily forgo. But if the organisers wish me to do it, then I shall to do it alone."

He toyed with an English/French plug converter.

"There is something to be said for Bill Gates' view on the benefit of worldwide standards, is there not?" He said, changing the subject. "The Victorians were the great creators of standards. You, of course, know why that was important?.."

Another of his unanswerable questions.

"...Because without common standards you could not have the industrial revolution – The Greenwich meridian, Greenwich mean time, the Whitworth standard for a flat surface, the Victorians even introduced standardized football rules. Until then, every club had their own. The French, of course, still have different rules. Or rather, they have the same ones, but they choose to disregard them."

I think he half approved of their approach.

"And now, what do we have on the guestbook today? Oh Joy. Bliss. The normal sniping and in fighting has been replaced by some educated postings in answer to the comments in my diary about breast cancer. I shall read these with interest..."

You may have gathered from the leisurely pace at which we had started the day that Sunday was a day of rest. Our only official engagement was for the much discussed live TV show, the traditional MIDEM opening , to be broadcast that evening from the Palais des Festivals in Cannes.

I say 'our' only official engagement, but, in truth, I, of course, was not invited – only the great, the good, and those with very big hair. The sort of event that the Vicar would normally have avoided like a pint of beer with the alcohol still in it.

"It would be hard to exaggerate my loathing for such events. Nothing could fill me with greater dread," as he might have said. And probably did.

On this occasion, he was forced to take his alcohol like a man, as he was presenting a lifetime achievement award to Dave Carling.

Dave, besides being a former band member with Lord Crappenleigh, was, in very large letters,

M I D E M' S P E R S O N OF THE Y E A R.

And, boy, did we know it. Inside our MIDEM bags was a 50 page magazine filled with such rubbish as
"Billboard congratulates you on this special honour",
or the sickly:
"Your musical friends in Sweden greet a friend and partner, who inspires, motivates and moves them".
Yukkety Yuk Yuk!

"A wonderful man. I loved working with him," The Vicar had said, "But note how the industry only honours him now he wants to be a record label executive. There's nothing they love more than a musician who actually wants to be a suit like them. It makes them feel that maybe they have got the best jobs after all."

Next time the BBC needs some good publicity because penny pinching misers with no art in their souls are moaning about the license fee, they should arrange to broadcast this MIDEM spectacular, as produced by French TV's very own EDF1. It was so bad, that I feel a poem coming on, working title "The TV show that Punk missed."

Who started the tape, so the band had no time
To find their place and start to mime.
Who filmed the compere combing his hair
And failed to say that he was live on air.
And who gave the drugs to the headline act
Who lost her place and asked to go back.
Which on a live show
Looks like shit
At the TV show that Punk missed.

Oh yes. the audience laughed til they pissed
At the TV show that Punk missed.

It was lucky the Vicar had the presence of mind
To forget the autocue and learn his lines
'cos most of the compere lost their place
and ended up with egg on their face
Which made the audience
Boo and hiss
At the TV show that Punk missed.

Oh yes. the audience laughed til they pissed
At the TV show that Punk missed.

All very amusing. But I am straying away from my plot (Plot? What's that? Does anyone have one they can sell me?). The TV spectacular, for all its glorious disasters, is nothing more than a sideshow. Several more important things happened during the day. The first was that the *Free Music Forum*, who had been involved in that scarifying little stunt on the plane reared their ugly heads again.

I had just finished the task that The Vicar set me for the day – completing a new chapter of *The Mysterious Case of Billy's G String* (my minimalist jewel – Chapter Nine – which I hope you've already read) when we received a telephone call for the Vicar from a certain Stig Blomquist, owner of OSV, the large Swedish record label. I called the Vicar down from his room.

He no doubt hurled his ritual question at me:

"Will this call enrich me? Will I look back in years to come and thank God for this call?"

before turning his annoyance on the caller.

And I think we've been here before.

Stig's
Polycarbonate
Crystals

66Why, Mr Blomqvist," the Vicar raged, "does everyone ask if I mind if they disturb me, as if I were free to
answer "yes", and magically find myself upstairs undisturbed,
still enjoying my essential Sunday reading, 'The role of
country houses in C19 England'? Would it not be better to
simply apologize and get on with the matter in hand? At
present you are simply extending the disturbance." A pause.

"Perhaps, you should have considered that before making
this phone call. Now I am here, perhaps you will kindly
let me know how I can help..."

"...The Free Music Forum. I like them more and more.
And I was so afraid that MIDEM was going to be dull.
Punk, kindly get me a copy of the OSV sampler from your
MIDEM bag."

I found one and handed it to him. He jammed the receiver
against his shoulder, and ripped open the CD. He folded
out the booklet, before shaking his head and throwing it
across to me.

"Not that one. Have a look in the bag that I was given,
or the Crappenleighs' bag. I need a few more copies."

I found several more. As the last came open, a card fell

to the floor. He picked it up, smiling.

"Oh yes, I have one," he said into the phone. "Rather amusing, don't you think…"

"…Well you Swedes never did have a sense of humour… Of course I can tell you how it was done. But do we have to play this game?"

Another pause.

"I suppose we do. Check out the stock you have left. I think you will find that exactly one in six has this little extra bonus. Ring me back if I am right. Which I imagine I will be."

And he put the telephone down.

"Take a look at this, Punk. If this is the new world order, then at least life will not be boring. Their politics may be dubious, but their methods are wonderful".

He threw the card over to me. On the front was a graffiti mural of the words 'Free Music' and, on the back, a message in several languages reading:

"The Free Music Forum opposes restrictive copyright laws. Free music from big business. Support the Free Music Forum."

"Where did it come from?" I asked.

"Inside this sampler promoting OSV's acts. And their new star, Elsa, in particular. Even you have surely noticed that MIDEM is featuring Swedish music this year."

"Bit of a pissbucket – having that stuffed in their sampler!"

"One might think so, although it will be excellent publicity."

The phone rang again.

"Ah Mr Blomqwist. Precisely one in six…exactly as I predicted." The Vicar was spinning the jewel case round and round in his fingers. He lifted the CD out of the case and turned it over.

"It does not mention on your artwork that this is an enhanced CD. What is on the CD-ROM portion?"

This question apparently caused some confusion.

"I assume you are familiar with enhanced CDs, Mr Blomqwist? They can be loaded into your computer to give you extra information…Well, I can assure you that it is. Punk, my laptop if you please."

There was a short pause as he loaded the CD.

"Oh my dear Mr Blomqwist." He chuckled to himself. "I do believe we have a problem, Houston. The disc contains another large advert for the Free Music Forum, with a link to their web site. It would appear that they have rather commandeered your product." A wide grin spread across The Vicar's face. "Anyone playing this in their computer drive is going to learn rather more about the Free Music Forum than they do about *Cool Sweden*."

The Vicar tidied the table in front of him.

"Well, yes I can tell you how it was done, but that would seem pretty obvious. Have you not visited a CD manufacturing plant? It never fails to amaze me how many people work in the music industry, but have no idea how a CD is actually made. I would recommend it, Mr Blomqwist. Quite fascinating how those small polycarbonate crystals are melted and stamped with the digital information from your master, before being coated with aluminium so that the laser can read them – making a perfect copy of the master disc you sent them. If, however that master disc was substituted on arrival for one that carried some additional information, such as, I don't know, some free advertising for the Free Music Forum, then all their work would simply ensure a perfect replica of the substituted disc. Ingenious, you have to admire them…"

"...No. I suppose it is not quite so amusing seen from your perspective..."

The Vicar was still finding it hard to keep a straight face.

"...Ah, the printing. You would have learnt about that as well. 24 page booklets are too large to be packed automatically. At your factory, DocData, they are hand-stuffed by six very bored and grossly underpaid ladies, usually of ethnic origin I am afraid to say, who sit at a table hour after hour packing CDs. I would suggest that one of those ladies has just retired, and earned herself a little bonus from the Free Music Forum before doing so..."

"...Yes, it really is as simple as that...I have no doubt that you will be wanting to talk to the factory...Thank you for calling. I am pleased I was able to help."

It seemed the conversation was at an end, when the Vicar unexpectedly continued.

"But before you go, a question if I may, Mr Blomqvist. Pray tell, Why exactly did you call me? I have told you nothing that could not have learned from the factory on Monday morning..."

A pause.

"...Ah. The daily MIDEM News. Much as I suspected. You want to issue a press release explaining the unfortunate incident. I must give you a suitable quote. I shall wait while you get a pen and paper."

He put the receiver on the table.

"The vandals have reached the gates of Rome, Punk. Pretty soon they will be tearing down the citadel. The old order changeth, as it does everywhere. Even with architecture, unfortunately." He patted his book. "In fact, perhaps, Punk, you could take down a version of my press release, as I somehow suspect that Mr Blomqvist will not be using it."

He picked up the receiver. I had no idea what was coming.

"The press release reads as follows: It is indeed possible that the Free Music Forum could have illegally usurped the OSV sampler, as OSV claim…"

He paused, for effect, with a huge grin on his face.

"It is, however, far more likely that Mr Blomqvist has deliberately wasted…" He looked at his watch "…six and a half minutes of the Vicar's Sunday morning in an ill conceived attempt to add credence to this unlikely tale. In the Vicar's professional opinion, as mistakenly requested by Mr Blomqvist, the most likely explanation is that Stig Blomqvist, one of the great self-publicists in the industry, fully authorized the use of the advertising space by the Free Music Forum, thereby ensuring excellent publicity for his sampler, and, if rumours are to be believed, the forthcoming sale of his label to Wendy Airhole's Regina Record Label…Yes, Stig, and I love you to. Thank you for your call."

He rang off and looked at me with a deadpan expression.

"Oh dear. I do believe that Stig Blomqvist has just removed me from his Christmas card list."

PUNK Warns
The VICAR

U NTIL THE PHONE CALL FROM STIG BLOMQVIST, I HAD
been undecided what to do about the message stuck
to the back of my MIDEM pass. I was half convinced
that it had to be a joke. All that stuff about *The Orange
Eyebrow'* sounded a bit like the *'The Black Fingernail'*, or
'The Scarlet Pimpernel'. But after hearing of the latest antics
of the Free Music Forum, I decided I had better mention
it to The Vicar.

We were lunching at Joseph's restaurant on one of the
back streets of St Tropez – where the head waiter surprised
us all by recognizing his Holiness, and welcoming him as
a regular client.

"Do not get excited, Punk. It is not me that he is remembering. The last time I was here I was with my wife, and
one of her friends, a rather beautiful actress, who insisted
on telling very risque stories about Hollywood stars and
small furry animals. That may have etched me into his
memory. Or it may simply be that I am the only Englishman who has made a booking today and that he wishes
to earn a large tip."

I wondered if this story was true. If so, I was tempted

to give the waiter a large tip of my own, in return for the dirt about The Vicar's wife, who, as all good Punksters will know, is something of an obsession with me. All that stuff about The Vicar only taking calls from "*My mother, My wife or Direct communications from God*". Calls from God are the most likely, because he certainly never gets any from the other two. His mother is actually dead, which rather takes her out of the running.

But I am wandering away from my sheep again. I didn't interrogate the waiter, nor unfortunately was this the time for a discrete word with The Vicar about the Orange Eyebrow, as the Crappenleighs were with us.

Lunch took an age. Venus seemed determined to sit around forever, playing infinite variations of desert island discs. What one film would you take to a desert island, what one person, which book, which sex toy.

I was hoping that the Vicar would lose patience with such frivolity, but he appeared happy to indulge her.

His favourite film was 'My Fair Lady', a surprising choice as he is a well known lover of high action Hollywood movies. His person was, of course, his wife (her again), his book was the bible ("I am a great lover of biographies"), and he was even willing to expound on sex toys.

"I cannot claim to be very authoritative on this subject. I recall a television programme about the young Conan Doyle, which featured the 'Berkeley horse'. I think you were strapped to it and beaten with stinging nettles, while someone had access to your 'pleasure organs'. Perhaps I should try that. Although I am sure the Japanese have invented something far more devious. I have memories of a telephone box when I was a young man seeking a liberal education – Would British Telecom be upset if I listed a telephone box as a sex toy? Perhaps chocolate. Does that count?" He flung his hands up in the air. "I think I shall have to defer to Punk on this topic. I am sure he has road tested most of the available options."

No Punksters, I am not going to reveal my poopathetic answers to these questions. Not my finest hour. Call me soft-cushioned, but I think bedroom toys belong in the bedroom, not at the dinner table, or even in this book. And all the while, Venus's big brown eyes (there, I do remember the colour) were staring straight at me, and she had this huge smile fixed on her face, as if revelling in my discomfort.

Venus Crappenleigh 1, Punk Sanderson 0.

I was rescued by the restaurant manager, who needed to throw us out to close up shop.

"Most unlike you, Punk," The Vicar taunted, as we left. "I would have thought you would be most happy to discuss the merits of," he paused, "telephone sex, for example."

I felt my face reddening. Why had I known that he would choose that example?

"Costly, but obviously enjoyable for some. I am told that WPC Paul Raymond, World Pornographer in Chief, was slow to enter the market, as he could not believe that people would pay to listen to such things. How wrong he was. Did you know that the turnover of the adult film industry is larger than that of Hollywood?"

I was worried about the direction this conversation was heading.

"Or that twenty percent of the users of the internet visit an adult site at some point every day?"

"T-That many?" I stammered, feeling that I needed to say something.

Fortunately, the flow of our conversation was disturbed by Lord Crappenleigh, who came to tell us that he and Venus were off window shopping.

"We will await you on the seafront," The Vicar said.

"There is something I have been meaning to show you," I began, as I finally got my moment in a café overlooking the port.

"As the Diva said to The Vicar?" he laughed. "Is this an official meeting? Perhaps we should first have a pause for thought."

He closed his eyes and drew in a deep breath. He then thrust his left fist into the air.

"Yes!" he cried enthusiastically. "Now what can I do for you? You wanted to tell me about the sticker on the back of your MIDEM pass."

I looked blankly at him. How could he have known?

"No-one else but you is wearing their pass today," he explained. "And you kept fingering it, and staring at that garish sticker on the back all the way through lunch."

I took the pass from around my neck, and handed it to him, pointing to the message.

"Not very inventive. Although quite clever in the way that it is sealed inside the plastic pouch. Whoever wrote it was evidently short of time. They should have been able to come up with a more exciting message."

He laid it on the table in front of him.

"It is just a game, Punk. Something to stop you getting bored while you are at MIDEM. Forget it. There may have been a time for such games, but it would seem that between the Free Music Forum and Venus Crappenleigh we are going to have quite enough excitement, without the need for these little extras." He lay back in his chair.

"Let us savour the moment. Life does not get much better than this. A sunny day in St Tropez. Beautiful yachts bobbing at the quayside. All that is needed is a good cup of tea, and a decent sticky cake. Perhaps I was a little rash in deciding to give up caffeine."

He was drinking an infusion called '*Verveine*' that the waiter had recommended.

"This drink tastes a little like boiled lawn mower clippings. Perhaps that is what it is. If they can eat snails and frogs legs, then I am sure the French are quite prepared to drink grass."

"It seems to me that this message must have been put there by Lord Crappenleigh," I pushed, not willing to let the subject drop quite so quickly.

"I think if you analyse the situation more carefully you will find that there is a far more likely suspect," he said teasingly. "But it says quite clearly that you are not meant to show me the message. You are not playing the game properly. You have to persuade me not to speak at the conference without telling me why. I think you have just cheated."

"I had not realised that it was a game".

"Well, then it would seem you had better beware the Orange Eyebrow," he exclaimed, getting up. "Shall we walk along the quay? Perhaps one of those paintings would make a suitable present for the Crappenleighs. How about this one of two lovers looking out over the sea? I can almost imagine what she is saying to him."

He looked at me, still with that amused smile.

"…Something like 'Is this an interrogation or a romantic tit a tete'?"

CHAPTER FIVE

Another short Chapter. I seem to be suffering from Premature Chapter Abbreviation. A cruel affliction that attacks young writers. There is no known cure.

I blame it on the poor working conditions. How can I realistically conjure up the mood of another late night of sitting out in the cold with Venus (after checking the balcony for Vicars) of the "How are you this evening? Is that a shooting star? If we wait up all night, snuggling together, we might see another" variety, – when I am stuffed here in the backroom of a studio with a computer struggling to operate Windows XP, and a mouse mat covered in some thick treacly substance that I hope was once ice cream.

If you are enjoying this, then rest assured that it was born amid discomfort and squalor, and vote for a left facing party at the next election, so that the workers can throw the Vicars of this world out of their palaces and can dine amid the splendour and the majesty.

Not that it worked with the last lot.

In the meantime we'll skip the late night romance, and head straight to Monday morning.

FU2NITE

☺

Monday 25th January

AN EARLY START. BREAKFAST AT SEVEN. WELL, LORD Crappenleigh, The Vicar and I had breakfast. Venus sipped pathetically on a cup of tea, and whimpered something about having "butterflies in her tummy". If it was meant to be cryptic, it was certainly too clever for me. Crosswords and the workings of the female mind were never my strong points.

As we got to the top of the drive the Vicar began what was to become a daily ritual by asking in his annoyingly 'holier than thou' voice.

"Shall we all check that we have our MIDEM passes?"

And I began my own daily ritual of running back to the house and retrieving my pass, from the begusting pile of clothes in the corner of my room, before we careered on down the road towards Cannes.

I again did the disc jockey thing – a difficult job as the bumpy French roads, made The Vicar's 'privileged pre release copy' of the new album by the Glamour Twins keep jumping.

"I do believe the music was intended to be enjoyed from beginning to end in one simple seamless experience," he sighed, as we failed to get to the end of the first track for the fifth time. "Can nothing be done about your contraption, Punk? Can you not find something to cushion it with?"

"Might I suggest, with the tongue well placed in the Crappenleigh cheek, that mayhap Venus has a suitable fine cushion or two?" Lord Crappenleigh drooled, like the worst kind of piggle-winking, dirty old man.

Venus didn't let it rattle her. She took the scarf from around her neck and handed it to me.

"Feel my hands. They are freezing," she said, touching the back of her hand onto my cheek.

I avoided her stare, and concentrated on wedging the CD player into the glove compartment wrapped up in her scarf.

The album finally stopped jumping – thanks largely to the discovery of tarmac. It (the album, not the tarmac) was an edited version of the infamous radio show produced by The Vicar – the strange blend of Russian samples and dance beats that I described in the Billy G story (note to self: insert page number). But then you probably know this already. What you don't know about is the dispute between The Vicar and Malvolio, who was 'assuming' that, as The Vicar had produced the radio show for free, he would receive no payment for the album. Cue large legal fees. Or, as Lord Crappenleigh put it:

"Employing the music biz tooth that is long, I surmise, dear Heart, that many scrupulous lawyers will happily earn a fee or three, at your expense."

Couldn't have put it better myself.

I had this cool description of the journey planned for you:

"The pine trees wept gently down to the minty cool sea, the foam rubbing on the masculine french underbelly, the white sails of the yachts filled like Jordan's triple D wanderlust bra."

But RULE FOUR (No Girly Poncey Language) prevents me.

So let's cut very professionally to a small joint on the far side of town, being smoked by Elton John...

Joke. More like:

9 am. Arrive Old Port, Cannes. Just late for The Vicar's first appointment.

Or, in Vicarspeak:
"We arrived at four minutes past nine, exactly punctual had we been on time."

Which, in Punkspeak, spells
"P.U.N.K.S.A.S.T.E.R."

And not just a small one. In Vicarworld, being late for an appointment is posilutely punkastrophic (totally my fault, but then what did you expect?), made even worse as the car park next to the Palais des Festivals was closed, with a row of bollards across the entrance, and an electronic sign saying 'complet'.

"This is ridiculous!" The Vicar shouted from behind me. "Do they not understand that I have a pressing engagement?"

He paused.

"Drive in anyway," he ordered. "They have simply reserved the entire car park for me. Sometimes I am amazed by my own importance."

Venus pulled into the slip road, but went no further.

"Come, come, my fine woman. In we go."

"Do you think we ought to..." she began.

Before she could finish her sentence, The Vicar had jumped out of his back seat, moved the bollards aside, and was striding down the entrance ramp, waving for her to follow him.

Venus looked at me, and I shrugged back at her.

"Do I have to remind you I have an appointment." He looked at his watch. "Five minutes and thirty seconds ago?"

Sensing that this was not the time for a discussion, Venus drove obediently into the car park. I half expected to be met by an armed guard, but it was deserted.

"Plenty of parking spaces," he crowed, triumphantly. "Take one of your choice and follow me to the conference centre. Punk, we are meeting Luke Hutchence at the Gramophone stand. Dawdle you must not."

He made a great show of directing us to one of the spaces.

"My talk is at eleven o'clock, but attendance is not compulsory. Shall we all meet for lunch at the Café Roma?"

He strode off into the distance.

And there we were. Deserted in a closed car park, accompanied only by the loud squealing of the tyres on the shiny green floor – almost drowned out by the loud 'ssssh'ing from your scarified author, worried about the impending arrival of armed policemen. I even found myself practicing excuses.

" I..am..sorry..officer...we..do..not..speak...french...We thought the bollards had been put there by mistake. It is a very common student prank in England".

Hell! Here I was making up lies to myself, when I was entirely innocent, and the real criminal had wandered off into the distance.

"What a shambolic cart of apples!" spluttered Lord Crappenleigh, getting out of the car. "I regret, dear Heart, that Venus and I must leave you to cast your lonely hook into stagnant water. We have our own shark-like meetings at which to debate the current worth of the minnow."

And then there was one. I walked out the in-ramp, and jogged in the direction of the Palais des Festivals. I never did find out why the car park was closed.

So. MIDEM. Six floors crammed with people, and each floor is as big…well, as big as …a car park. In fact, the Vicar's mocking reference to a multi-storey car park, the other day, is quite good. If you imagine a booth in each parking space, each representing some company, then you get the rough idea. Season with a large dose of decibels, as everyone pumps up the volume to try and drown out everyone else. Add a healthy helping of large drinks and small dresses: the universal language of trade shows, and there you have it. A seething mass of people, all wearing yellow passes around their necks and frantically doing the biziness of "doing biziness".

And it was into this resplendituneful environment that I stepped at about a quarter past nine, in search of his holiness. I'd had trouble getting passed the crowds gathered round the elderly, distinctly British, red double decker bus parked out the front with its huge poster advertising, you guessed it, the 'Free Music Forum'.

"Here, give this a read," said an ageing rocker with 'Rock out with your Cock out' emblazoned across the large white shirt that almost covered his beer belly. He thrust a pamphlet into my hand about the 'Free Music license', which I put in the nearest bin when I finally got through the doors, proudly brandishing my pass.

I studied the map, searching for the Gramophone stand. Level One 15J – home of the meeting with Luke Hutchence, that would hopefully lead me into a life of riches.

Although, let's be honest, Punksters, I think we all know that it didn't.

Another Message from the Orange Eyebrow

N O PRIZES FOR GUESSING WHY THE VICAR HAD CHOSEN
the Gramophone stand for our meeting with Luke
Hutchence. It is a respectable, grey-haired, Tory-voting, classical music magazine. Using my handy sex-based Universal
Music Filing System of *'Getting round to it'*, *'During'* and
'Afterwards' music, (all of life fits into one of those three cat-
egories), their brand of muzak was so long *'Afterwards'* that
most girls I know would have already gotten up and gone
home. It was surrounded by other *'Afterwards'* magazines.
An oasis of *'Afterwards'* in a building that was otherwise
entirely dedicated to *'Getting round to it'*.

And at one of the small round tables, sat the old wrinkly
himself, deep in discussion with a man, who looked more
like a rock star than a stuffy literary agent. Tall with black
curly hair and a large presence.

"Ah Punk," The Vicar rose from his chair and offered
one to me. "Please allow me to introduce Luke Hutchence,
from the Hutchence literary agency in New York. Founded
by your father, I believe."

Luke nodded.

"Luke, this is Punk Sanderson, the author."

The Vicar carefully rearranged the papers that had been placed messily on the table.

"I must confess, Mr Hutchence, that I had not heard of your agency until a few days ago," I muttered.

"Which is just how we like it," he boomed in a deep New York accent. "We are one of the biggest agencies in the business. Yet still something of a trade secret -"

"But you do come highly recommended, my boy," The Vicar cut in. "As you know, I sent a copy of Punk's pathetic offering to Karen Aires, successful author and long time friend. It was while sleeping on Karen's sofa in New York, being awakened by her cat, that I had the vision of what I would do with my life. The vision flew past from left to right, with the music of the first album I would produce going from right to left."

Luke raised his eyebrows slightly.

"Karen was sufficiently honest to confess that she had no desire to read the manuscript," The Vicar admitted. "Much as I have no desire to hear all the demos that I get sent."

"Although," Luke laughed, "I hear rumours that you'll listen to the first thirty seconds, if there is a ten dollar bill inside."

"I should have charged more for much of the rubbish I have endured," The Vicar scowled. "Fortunately, Karen needed no such inducements. She did it out of friendship. She reluctantly set aside her normal Sunday routine. One hour later, she was still reading, and sufficiently impressed to recommend us to her own agent. Hence this meeting."

The Vicar motioned towards Luke.

"Well, I certainly like what I've seen," Luke admitted. "And I think we can claim to be the best literary agency in the states."

"I did run a check on your company." The Vicar looked Luke straight in the eye. "I asked my lawyer, the black suited, pony tailed, beast of terror, Roger Borer, if you were indeed the four hundred pound gorilla of the literary world, as Karen described you. He told me that you were not."

Luke looked shocked.

"Roger tells me," The Vicar smiled, "that you are in fact a five hundred pound gorilla."

Luke relaxed.

"They sure don't come much bigger and better than us."

"Which is why we are here," The Vicar said. "Although it is actually Punk who has written the book, Luke, and any publishing deal would be with him, not me."

"But there's more than simply a series of books written by Mr…Sanderson, did you say your name was?"

"Oh yes, a complete multimedia launch. The Vicar may be the next James Bond, or, in the hands of cheap American television, perhaps Barney Rubble. Who knows? We must trust the process. In Punk's immortal words…"

He bowed his head and waved his hand to me like a conductor.

"Art plus truth equals shitloads of money," I chanted, taking my cue.

"Fine sentiments," The Vicar chuckled. "We have another important meeting this evening to discuss television rights."

"Champagne?"

The girl, who had first greeted me, hovered over us with a large Champagne bottle and wine glasses.

The Vicar shook his head. "It is most kind of Richard to let us use his stand, without us drinking his best champagne. I must introduce you, Punk. If anyone can rescue your appalling listening habits, it is surely Richard Whitelock, the editor of Gramophone. Music that appeals to the head and the heart, rather than the thighs and the penis."

"Ch-champagne, sir?" the girl giggled, as she turned to Luke

He too shook his head, at which point I realised that I would unfortunately have to decline as well.

"Well, I am confident that we can get a publishing deal. The trick will be to find an editor who likes Punk's style – those bizarre rules he keeps giving," said Luke.

RULE FOUR HUNDRED AND TWO: No-one gets to call my rules bizarre.

"Let me know how you get on with the television people. That will be critical. It's much easier to sell the book to a successful TV series. Mind you, you will have to be careful that no-one steals the idea."

This did not seem to worry the Vicar.

"I think that will be difficult, as it is based on the real events of my own life. You are the only person to see that synopsis and business plan. I only completed them on Friday, and there are just three copies. The master copy, and two photocopies, which Punk ran off in London before we flew out here. One for you and one for Michael Bernstein."

"Just be careful who else you show it to," Luke repeated. "And now I must go. I am really just another wannabe musician with a tape to tout." He took a CD out of his bag, and placed a ten dollar bill on top of it. "Perhaps you would give it a listen."

"For you, the first thirty seconds are free." The Vicar took it from him with both hands as if it was a valuable treasure. "Although I am not sure that I will be able to help."

They shook hands.

"There, Punk," The Vicar bragged, as Luke disappeared into the crowd, "I have just launched you on the path to stardom. I do hope you deserve it. It is amazing the amount of goodwill that is available to us."

He got up.

"And now I think there is just time to check our lockers, before I need to prepare for the conference."

The lockers were in a room on the fourth floor. Outside two girls were handing out yet more flyers.

"Fishnet stockings and roller blades," The Vicar observed. "An irresistible combination. They are certainly proving successful at handing over their worthless slips of paper. Looking at that waste paper basket, they are rather less good at making people actually read them. Such a point-less operation."

"I don't know," I began. "It offers employment to two cute snoggly young girls..."

"...and our locker will no doubt also be stuffed full of worthless flyers. Throw out anything not addressed to me personally, please Punk."

The MIDEM guide gave the box number of every atten-dant, and I soon located ours, which was, as The Vicar suspected, stuffed to overflowing with junk mail and free CDs.

"Unless it has my name on it, or a ten dollar bill slipped inside, file it in the bin," The Vicar instructed, bringing me a cup of tea, together with a croissant and a carefully folded napkin.

"Do you mind if I keep them?" I asked. "You're always saying I should wide-on my whore-izons. Accordion music from Finland, acoustic guitar arrangements of Duke Ellington. There is even another copy of that OSV sampler. That's a bit oggle the tits. They have already put one in everyone's MIDEM bag."

I picked the CD up and turned it over. I was *shocked* – no *flobblegobbled* – no *scarified* – to notice that it had a post-it on the back like the one on my MIDEM pass, with another hand written message.

"Are you alright?" asked The Vicar. "You look like you have seen a ghost."

"I'm er fine," I gulped, slipping the CD into my bag with the other ones. "I was er just thinking about all that trouble with the Free Music Forum".

I took a sip of my tea, and was so nervous that I managed to spill it all over my crotch.

"Come, come, pull yourself together. Look what you have done to yourself. You look a sight." He laughed at me. "Perhaps we should take a photograph. There are probably strange adult websites dedicated to people with wet crotches."

All his references to pornography were making me nervous.

"And now I must go and prepare myself."

While The Vicar slipped away, I looked at the CD. The post-it was on the inside of the shrink wrapping, and carried a note in the same terrible hand-writing:

"You should know I have eyes in the back of my head
'Don't tell the Vicar' is what I said
I am waiting in the conference room now
See you there…The Orange Eyebrow".

CHAPTER SIX

IT MAY BE VERY EASY WITH HINDSIGHT TO REALISE THAT a sticker on a CD is not an overly dramatic event. Not compared with planes crashing into the World Trade Centre, the third world debt, and the state of the seats in the back row of the Salisbury Odeon. But, at the time, I was more than a little agitated. Anyone brought up on a solid diet of James Bond and Die Hard, where a cryptic note on a CD inevitably leads to frantic chases, large amounts of gratuitous destruction, hopefully a little nudity and possibly the odd assassination, will know how I felt.

"Well, I'll be buggery snozzled. I hope this isn't going to get violent," I remember thinking, or words to that effect. I could picture The Vicar talking at the conference while a man with an Orange Eyebrow assassinated him with a rifle disguised as a video camera. Perhaps, this was the moment I had been born for. The defining moment in my life. Punk's fifteen minutes of fame.

Alright, alright. Let's not get too carried away here. I know I am just an underpaid production assistant with a strange attraction to internet pornography, but fate can come knocking on the most unusual doors, (and my door is pretty unusual. It has this strange drawing of a woman, with the handle just where you might want to fondle....)

I sat in the reception room, my pulse racing as if I had just run a marathon. What is it with adrenalin? Isn't it meant to help you be alert in a crisis? It seems to me that it has exactly the opposite effect. Here I was, needing to be clear-headed, and my body was fast being reduced to a jibbering wreck by my f******g adrenal gland, excuse my french. We may think we are so sophisticated, but in the end we are all controlled by our glands. Adrenalin and semen, the two defining substances in a man's life. With the possible addition of alcohol and caffeine, I suppose.

So there I was, suffering all the symptoms of a mild cardiac arrest, huffing and puffing my way towards the best course of action. It was too late to discuss this with The Vicar. I would simply have to survey the room and try to locate the infamous Orange Eyebrow. What I would do if I actually saw him, I didn't stop to consider.

I positioned myself halfway down the right hand side of the conference hall, surveying a crowd of a couple of hundred people. There was only enough seating for half of them, and the rest were squeezed into the aisles, or sitting on the floor in the front, crowded right up against the table where the speakers were going to sit. In the middle of the room, there was a large video camera. Have no fear, faithful readers, I had already checked out the camera, in best detective fashion. The cameraman had shown me a computer in the corner of the room where you could indeed see the pictures coming from his camera, ready for a webcast.

Imagine what it must be like to be a professional bodyguard. The Vicar likes to tell this story about George Martin and Brian Epstein watching a concert in the States (yes, another of his Beatles' stories) after the band had received some death threats, possibly over the 'We are more popular than Jesus' tiddliasco. Anyway, in watching this concert they realised how totally vulnerable the group were to snipers or assassins, and how little they could do about it. I looked around the conference hall. Most of the people in the room had either a camera or a mobile phone, and virtually all of them were carrying large MIDEM bags which could hide any weapon of choice.

Not that I was really getting too hung up on the weapon thing. And most of you will know that he doesn't get shot, because I have already told you that he is still happily (or unhappily) alive long after the events of this book, moaning about this book – rather ruins my dramatic tension doesn't it? But I was genuinely afraid that some crazed fan was going to make a disturbance, throw a rotten vegetable or some choice animal excrement.

I was concentrating so hard that I barely noticed the hand being slipped around my waist from behind.

"Hello Gorgeous. Haven't you been keeping a seat for me?"

I turned to see Venus standing behind me.

"Hi," I muttered sheepishly. "I thought you were in town stretching Lord Crappenleigh's credit cards."

"Plenty of time for that. I'm a professional. You'd be amazed at how much I can spend in less than an hour. Not that money buys everything." She gave me a friendly squeeze. "A good man goes a long way."

"I'm not sure you got that quite right."

"Whatever. Are you planning to stand here through the whole thing? Is it going to be really boring?"

"Not really. The Vicar will be…"

I realised she had skillfully distracted me from my Kevin Costner bodyguard role.

Shit, shit and double shit. Major Brown Pants Moment. What if she was involved with the Orange Eyebrow, and had been deliberately sent to disturb me? She and Lord Crappenleigh were top of my list of suspects for the note on the inside of my Midem pass.

"Wait a second," I said, hurriedly staring around the room to see if anything had changed.

You hardly need me to describe what moments of pure panic are like. Remember the first time a girl said yes to your constant demands to get inside her knickers, or when your mother walked into the chemist while you were being handed a packet of condoms. You step outside yourself and then, wham, you're back in the world again, complete with armpit stains and serious body odour.

"Are you OK. Have you got flu or something? I thought you would be pleased to see me," she joked in a spoilt child, my-friend-won't-play-with-me, kind of way.

"I'm fine. I was looking for someone," I mumbled, still slightly moggle-brained. "He must have left".

She stood looking at me, half smiling and half laughing to herself.

I cringe as I remember the short scene that followed. I am half tempted to omit it. But, hey, I have never claimed to be super cool. Laugh all you like. Some of us are, I discovered, more Austin Powers, than Hercule Poirot, or in my case, maybe even Inspector Gadget.

In fact, "Go Go Gadget Midem pass," would be a pretty good way of describing my plan as I casually started to play with the pass that was dangling round my neck. I kept glancing at Venus to see if she showed any reaction to this incriminating piece of evidence. You know the routine.

I smile at her,
She SmileAwkwardlyBacks
I toy with the pass
She SmileAwkwardlyBacks
I run the pass seductively through my fingers
She SmileAwkwardlyBacks
I take a closer look at the sticker.
She SmileAwkwardlyBacks

A bit like something out of a Woody Allen film. No. More like Laurel and Hardy, and the way he flicks his tie with his little finger, while smiling to himself. Generally a total fuckarooni.

"What's wrong with you?" she laughed. "Why do you keep looking at me like that? And why are you fiddling with your pass?"

She tried to take it out of my hand. Having worked so

hard to get a reaction out of her, I was now desperate to stop her from seeing it.

"No. That's mine," I shouted, trying to lock it firmly in my closed fingers. "You've got your own."

"What's so wrong with it? The photo can't look worse than the real thing. I'll show you mine if you'll show me yours…"

She fluttered her eyebrows at me.

Eyebrows!

Shitty, shit, shit. The Orange Eyebrow!

I turned and surveyed the room again. Quite what I was expecting to find I'm not sure. It was now so crowded that it was impossible to see anything.

There was a movement at the far end, and I squeezed forwards as a man walked up to the podium in front of the 'high table'.

It was about to start. Too late to warn The Vicar.

66 MESDAMES ET MESSIEURS." THE MASTER OF CEREMONIES had already started. "This conference deals with one of the central issues facing the music business today. I am sorry there is not enough room to seat everyone comfortably..."

You couldn't hear most of what he said, as hardly anyone stopped to listen. Although on the webcam, we'd all be fooled into thinking he was addressing a room of people, hanging on his every word –

– Not!

"...MIDEM is pleased to welcome Bruce Fanny, of Swapster.com, Vincente Smagala, of the What if corporation, and the producer, known to us all as The Vicar."

There was a ripple of applause, which grew slightly more enthusiastic as the three speakers took their places. The Vicar came out last and stood for a while carefully surveying the room, before quietly taking his seat. I toyed with the idea of rushing up and telling him to leave the stage.

Too late. Bruce Fanny, looked over and The Vicar waved his upturned palm, inviting him to begin. He then sat back, with his hands neatly placed on his legs, palms upwards, and his face totally impassive. A bit like those paintings of Buddhist monks you find in New Age shops (£2.50. The Spotted Duck. Wilton High Street).

"It seems I have to introduce myself." Bruce Fanny was on his feet, addressing the crowd. He looked like a college football player, complete with baseball cap. "I am Bruce, and I am the CEO of Swapster.com."

Even now, as he started to speak, the noise level didn't drop much. Half the room was listening, but the other half was far more concerned with generally being cool.

It was always going to be a rough ride for him, as no-one in the industry liked his software, even if it was a "devolved network with no central database, and encryption"...bla bla bla.

I doubt it will interest to you. And it certainly didn't impress Venus.

"Do we really have to stay and listen to this?" she whispered in my ear. "Nobody seems very interested".

"I want to hear what The Vicar has to say," I told her. "He's usually pretty contentious. It should be fun."

She gave me a doubtful look, as if unconvinced that anything about '*Bootlegs and The Challenge of the Internet*' could be even mildly interesting.

"It could change the whole way the industry works." I tried to convince her. "It may seem irrelevant right now, but it won't be in a couple of years time..."

Let's be honest. Own up time. Here was a beautiful woman, and I was keen to impress her with my knowledge. I told you, adrenalin and semen, the most powerful drugs in a man's life.

"...Right now you could say free downloads are not too much of a problem. Just another form of promotion, a bit like a song being played on the radio. Most people still want to buy the CD."

Even as I said this, I heard Bruce saying exactly the same thing from the stage. It gave me a real buzz. This is the way to impress a girl, I thought. Show her that you know as much as the guy on the stage. It was almost as if I had written his speech for him.

"But what happens next? I read that between Swapster and the other sites, there could be fifteen million illegal users, far more than the number of legal ones," Venus beamed. "And what if we all decide to stop paying, and download for free into our iPods. Bye bye major record labels. No more money for Paul McCartney and Elton John. No more income for Punk and the Vicar." She put an innocent expression on her face, and then grinned at me.

"F***k me!" I thought, "so much for impressing her. She knows as much about this as I do."

"Exactly," I blurted, trying to regain lost ground, "which, um, which is..."

"...why the major record labels have got their knobs in a twist and are trying to close the free download sites." She finished my sentence for me and gave me another squeeze round the middle. "Which still doesn't make this very interesting. Does it?"

Bruce was now being heckled by some members of the audience. He was fighting a losing battle. He sat down in the background, and wiped his slightly sweaty forehead with a handkerchief. I started to push to the front to warn the Vicar, but Smagala had already stood to take his turn.

He was not at all as I would have imagined him – a large, sweaty man, double chins and double stomachs, dressed totally in black, with the largest comb-over I have ever seen, complete with the grease necessary to hold in place.

Venus could not help giggling.

"How can anyone take a guy like that seriously," she whispered in my ear. I turned away and tried to ignore her.

"His hair is ridiculous!" she yelped. "It must be about a foot long. Why can't he admit that he is totally bald. Yuk!"

As I turned away again, she bit my ear, which made me jump more than a little. Well, come on, Punksters, it's difficult not to get a little distracted, when you have a vampire nibbling on your ear.

Oily Vince played to the crowd by denouncing the business practices of Swapster.com. Something like…

"…Everybody feels that the RIAA is being a bully, trying to protect the profits of the large record companies, by suing companies like Swapster. In truth, the RIAA is trying to protect the income of the musicians themselves…"

Or

"…People always think of the super rich pop stars, like Michael Jackson or Madonna, and imagine that they don't need the money. But most musicians need their royalties to survive…"

Or

"…Musicians care about their music being stolen. We all know about Metallica, who considered suing all the fans who have illegally distributed copies of their music…"

If you want the rest, read the transcript. Between trying to be sociable with Venus, and scanning the audience for a madman with an orange eyebrow, I cannot claim to have paid a great deal of attention. Unlike The Vicar, who sat impassively, his nose slightly raised and his eyes expressionless, as if he were daydreaming – although from painful experience I can assure you that he was not. He was listening attentively to everything that was happening, and no doubt memorizing it all.

In fact, he was probably the only person paying much attention. Smagala was beginning to overstay his welcome, and the audience was getting restless again.

"Are you sure there is nowhere we can sit?" breathed Venus, who was at least trying to keep her voice down so as not to disturb the speaker.

"Be my guest, if you can find a seat," I shrugged. "I'm going to try and move around and see if I can find my friend."

"What does he look like?" she whispered.

Could it do any harm to tell her? If she was involved in this fiasco, then she already knew about the Orange Eyebrow, and if she wasn't involved, then she could help me find him.

"He is easy to spot," I said. "One of his eyebrows is dyed orange."

"I'm not sure that's much help. What colour is his hair?"

"Oh! Er – that depends," I mumbled, stalling for time. "It's one colour on Monday, and a different colour on Tuesday. But his eyebrow, that never changes. It's a sort of calling card."

We started to look around, just as Smagala made his final comments, which were nothing more than an advert for *Whatif?*

"Keep ahead by subscribing to the *Whatif?* Newsletter. Our suppositions are right ninety percent of the time. The other ten percent are only wrong, because our newsletter made someone change their mind. We will be glad to see you at our stand. Thank you."

He finally returned to his seat, and looked over to The

Vicar. The moment I was dreading. Time for him to take his turn.

The Vicar's speech has become something of a cause celebre – extensively reported in the press and quoted in many of the internet music court cases, including the one against Swapster.com.

Almost as well-known as *my* actions which interrupted it.

CHRONICLE THE SECOND

THE Vicar Speaks

SMAGALA HAD FINISHED HIS SPEECH, AND THE MOMENT I had been dreading had arrived. The Vicar's turn to speak at the conference, and I had done nothing to warn him about the threat from the Orange Eyebrow.

At first, he just sat there impassively, while the crowd waited for something to happen. After a lengthy pause, he looked up to the heavens, with his right hand upturned in front of his chest, moving it gently up and down, as if seeking inspiration. He then put his hands back on his thighs before slowly standing and staring at the room.

He had still not said a word, when, smiling, he slipped out from behind the table, and made his way to the podium, where the initial announcer had stood. Why couldn't he just stay behind the table like the other speakers?! He was right out in the open.

He again stared silently at the audience, and, as the weight of his presence weighed on the room (not that he's that heavy, you know) they began to silence themselves, until finally you could have heard the proverbial pin drop.

Once he was satisfied that he had complete control, he relaxed his expression and took his wrist watch off his left hand, placing it on the podium in front of him.

"Anyone who wishes to take photographs. Now is the time," he said and stepped back from the podium slightly. He stood and smiled somewhat reluctantly for the numerous photographers who began to take their photos – any one of whom could have been the Orange Eyebrow.

As the last flash subsided, he moved back to the podium. A member of the audience tried to take one last photograph.

"The time has now passed," he said.

The photographer still stood there.

"If you please," he added, although it sounded more like a command than a request. He stared straight at the photographer, who meekly returned to his seat.

The Vicar smiled at the audience and picked up his watch from the podium.

"It is now 18 years, two months, three days, twelve hours and," he looked at his watch, "twenty minutes since I began working in the music industry. Throughout that time there have been numerous changes. The introduction of the CD, for example. None, however, has such far reaching consequences as the development of the internet…"

I was probably the only person in the room who was not concentrating fully on what he had to say. Even Venus looked slightly annoyed with me as I tried to squeeze past her and move along the side of the room. Now that everyone was so still and quiet, I had a much better chance of scanning the crowd for my villain, assuming he was really there.

"I work for him. I'm security," I barked at all the people who told me to sit down.

"…You have had two differing points of view presented. Both discussing the merits of this new technology for the artist. Swapster.com say it helps artists because more people can hear their music, even if it is not paid for directly. Smagala says it is stealing the very bread from the mouths of musicians..."

Having worked my way around, I was now nearly at the back of the room. It was virtually impossible to squeeze behind the back row of chairs as the passageway was crammed full of people.

"...what I find so interesting," The Vicar continued, "is the immense concern for the well being of the artist that both companies are suddenly showing. Let us start with Bruce, the founder of Swapster.com. I suspect that the majority of people who form internet companies do so in the hope that their stock will one day be worth millions. I wonder what his venture capitalists would say if they found that Bruce is apparently more interested in helping starving artists than making exorbitant profits. And believe me, no company can grow from a valuation of zero dollars to 30 million dollars according to the share price a few days ago..." he looked over at Bruce "without the promise of excessive profits one day..."

I finally made it across the back of the room and started working my way up the other side row by row.

"... It is, of course, difficult to know how Bruce will actually treat the artists, because, at present, of course, like so many internet sites, they are simply abusing copyright, and struggling to find a satisfactory business model. I recall Hank Berry, the then CEO of Napster, that most infamous of music sites, saying that he had noticed that most successful businesses have business plans, so he thought he had better create one. Most astute." There was a ripple of laughter in the audience. "I believe Bruce's background is in banking. Some people might suggest that a background in the music business might be useful if you want to start a music company..."

Cue large scale applause. This comment went down very well with the audience.

"...I, of course," The Vicar mocked, "would suggest that Bruce's total ignorance of everything to do with the music business is the only possible reason why his company might succeed."

I had got about halfway down the right hand side of the room, when I spotted Venus waving to me discreetly. She started to quietly point at someone on the floor in front of the Vicar. I couldn't see him from where I was because the cameraman was in the way.

"...Equally I am astounded that Smegma, I am sorry, Smagala, is suddenly so concerned about artists," The Vicar was saying, "and the fact that the internet is stealing their music. He didn't seem to be so concerned when his own company several years ago was found guilty of making thousands of extra copies of CDs and selling them without paying any money to the musicians. At least Bruce is giving the music away, not pocketing all the money and keeping it for himself..."

He turned to stare at Smagala, who was clearly losing it.

"I notice, Vincente, that you do not protest or accuse me of libel. Which is, of course, because I am telling the truth. Just as it is true that your United distribution company filed for Chapter 11 protection, bankrupting many small labels and their artists, while you continued to pay yourself a seven figure salary..."

I was trying to get back around the room to join Venus.

"...if everyone is so interested in the welfare of artists, perhaps now would be a good moment to conduct a simple survey…"

I was now climbing over chairs in my haste to get back to the front of the room where Venus was still frantically pointing at someone.

"…Let us do a little survey to see how trustworthy you feel the record companies are. Anyone who feels that they can name a major label that has always accounted fairly to their artists, even according to their own, hideously biased contracts, please raise their hand. If you put up your hand, and I cannot prove in two days that this company has been guilty of devious practices, then I will…"

He paused, and smiled,

"…offer to ruin one of your records for free. If on the other hand, you are wrong, then you will have to …come and work for me for free." He looked at me. "Punk is not allowed to put his hand up as he is already working for free."

The room turned to look at me, just as I made my way past Venus and saw what she was pointing at – a man sitting on the floor, not three feet way from the Vicar with one of his eyebrows…

D Y E D… B R I G H T… O R A N G E !

CHAPTER SEVEN

THERE IS CONSIDERABLE DISPUTE ABOUT WHAT HAPPENED next. I have been the object of ridicule at several dinner parties where The Vicar has told highly amusing stories about my "bungling incompetence and crass stupidity" in dealing with the events of the next few minutes. I prefer my version of events, and I reserve the right to lie unashamedly when it suits my purpose (and will claim any video evidence to the contrary is the fabrication of a skilled editor).

RULE NINE: The Truth is whatever I say it is.

So. My meeting with the man with the Orange Eyebrow. On fixing him in my cross hairs, so to speak, I blanked out all distractions, and pushed my way through the people crowded onto the floor. I suspect most eyes in the house were still fixed on me, fresh from The Vicar's latest 'Punk works for free' joke (whatever), but I neither cared nor noticed.

On reaching my quarry, I still had no formal plan. As rough a thug as I've seen – and I've seen quite a few, including the scarifying one that swears at me every morning from the mirror. That one, I must add, is particularly ugly when plucking his nasal hairs…

ABSOTIVELY POSILUTELY BEGUSTING!

Enough. This is not the place for poor attempts at humour.

I approached my villain from behind, and was a bit "shaken and stirred" to notice that he had eyes in the back of his head – literally. His scalp was scraped clean, with an entire phizog tattooed on the back. To cap it all – excuse the pun – he was wearing a backwards baseball cap. The effect, as I walked towards him, was of a rather shadowy face peering from underneath a hat, complete with the obligatory sunglasses sitting on the rim. Not what you want to see when approaching a suspect for the first time.

From behind.

If that were not enough, his back had more muscles than most men's chests, so that walking towards him with his ghost-like tattoo eyes, and his T-shirt saying '*This way up*', you could have thought he was facing you – until you realised that his legs were bent completely the wrong way round, like an Action Man doll, with its arms and legs back to front.

And despite all this, I percy-veered. The Vicar may mock, but I think I can justifiably claim to have showed great bravery in my efforts to defend him.

I tapped the man on the shoulder and he turned to look at me…with his *real* face – which was little more appealing than the fake one. One eyebrow was completely shaven and the other was indeed bright orange, with two small "nicks" taken from it. I would have felt less nervous if I had walked up to talk to an alien.

He had the full metal jacket – a ring in his nose, lip, eyebrow and a dozen or so hoops in his ears.

How do guys like that ever get through a metal detector?

"Excuse me," I said, doing a perfect imitation of PC Plod. "I need to talk with you. Can we please go outside."

As I said 'a cool hero in a crisis'.

The reaction to my simple request was astounding. He stood up, growing until he was almost exactly my height, but twice as wide. You know the type – so muscle bound that their legs won't fit together. He belonged somewhere on an army camp or in a rugby scrum, possibly a building site – anywhere other than one foot from me, and a couple of yards from The Vicar.

He stood there for a while and then he vanished.

One moment he was there, and the next he wasn't.

It was hard to believe that he had moved at all, let alone done a Harry Houdini. The room was so full that even Moses would have struggled to part the crowds. All I know is that, to misquote the song, (The live Tubes version, not the crappy Liverpudlian one) *'He left me standing there'* – and that I was suddenly very aware of all the eyes looking at me.

The Vicar had fallen silent. He was gently tapping his finger on the podium, his lips tightly pursed in a look that alternated between amusement and intense annoyance. *'Annoysement'*, as you might say. I had no desire to see which would win the day. I looked from him to the cameraman, and feeling the urgent need to be elsewhere, set off in hot pursuit of my villain.

There was, however, no easy escape. I was either far less agile than the dreaded Orange Eyebrow, or less willing to crush people. When The Vicar tells this story at dinner parties, he has me resembling a small boy hopping up and down with his legs crossed, desperately trying to persuade the seated masses to let him through so that he can crap to the dasher. A little unkind, of course (but then, isn't he always?). Who cares what I looked like? And who knows? How about we settle on a version that has me dancing on hot coals – an adult, not a small boy, with no references to toilets.

This story certainly doesn't need more toilet humour.

By the time I got to the door, Venus was waiting for me.
"Some friend," she cooed. "What did you say to him? It seemed more like a drugs' bust than a meeting between pals."
"I'll have to explain all that later," I shouted. "Do you know which way he went?"
"Yes," she said and pointed down the escalator.

Down I went. At the bottom were the half naked girls on roller blades handing out flyers. I bowled them over like nine pins, as I jumped off, and tore round the back to get onto the next flight downwards.
This brought me to the entrance hall, with the glass doors leading out to the street. I had no way of knowing which way he had gone, so I slowed up and stood guard just outside the building, getting my breath back. The pavement was full of people with their silly yellow MIDEM passes, just like mine, but no-one, thankfully, with either Orange Eyebrows or faces tattooed on the back of their heads. I thought for a second that I caught a glimpse of him inside

the Free Music Forum's red Double Decker bus, but the large black metal door at the back, a rather crude addition, was firmly padlocked.

Thank bloody goodness! As my pulse slowly returned to normal, I was increasingly relieved that I had not been able to find him – all three hundred pounds or whatever he weighed.

"So what was that all about?" Venus purred.

And I wish I knew, Punksters.

66 So are you going to tell me what it's all about?"

Venus put one hand on each of my shoulders so that I could not walk away and turned me to face her. "Is it usually this exciting?" That same seductive grin. "I think we had better go somewhere and talk about it, don't you?"

I encouraged her to avoid the seductive charms of the first few bars, in favour of 'Café Roma', which held special memories for me.

"This bar," I told her, "was the place, where all of us working on the boats would hang out. Pretty pricey. The idea was to have enough money to be able to order a drink and an ice cream."

"An ice cream? Why?"

"I am not sure. Maybe they soaked up the alcohol. Look at all those alcopops they are inventing now. We used to make our own. A perroquet and an ice cream in alternate mouthfuls."

"What's a perroquet?"

"Perhaps we had better order one," I suggested, raising a provocative eyebrow.

The menu hadn't changed much. Except the prices had

gone up.

"Pretty depressifying," I gulped. "You'd have thought I'd finally be able to drink here without counting the pennies. When I worked here, these things were so damned expensive I used to rootle through the pockets of the overalls on the boat to scrape enough coins together for a night out."

Innocent enough remark, I thought. But no.

"You mean you stole from the other workers?" she asked.

Knowing what I know now, it seems a bit rich that she was questioning my morals.

"No, not really. Or Yeah. I suppose so. Depends on your point of view." I wasn't sure what to say. "We all shared overalls, and if you left something in the pocket you didn't expect to see it again. It wasn't stealing. If there had been a note in there. But coins. No. They were fair game."

A waitress came over. One of those stunning brown-haired, brown-skinned mediterranean women who just ooze sexuality. I lent over to Venus.

"You know you were asking about French women," I whispered, "try this one for size."

She looked at me disappointedly, and barely waited until the waitress had gone away, taking with her an order for two perroquets and two ice creams, before belittling my tastes in women.

"I had expected you to go for something more sophisticated. Rich and classy."

"Sorry to disappoint," I blushed, "but that does it for me."

I am not quite sure why I should have been apologizing for my taste in women. After all, it's better than Robbie Williams. When asked what he looks for in a woman, he was recently heard to reply "a pulse."

I'll pause for a second while his joke sinks in. After all,

he no doubt worked hard on it, and it would be a pity to let it go to waste.

Back to my unmanly apologies for my tastes in French women.

"I am a slain and pimple fellow. What you see is what you get."

"Hardly that plain." She tapped me on the cheeks. "Nor that simple. Now come on." She grabbed my elbow and leant towards me conspiratorially. "What was all that about in the hall? Who is that guy with the orange eyebrow? He is certainly weird enough. Is he really a friend of yours?"

It could do no harm to let her into my bon-fi-dence, I reasoned. If she was part of the plot, she would obviously already know, and if not, she might be able to help. Am I repeating myself? I think I may already have given you the benefit of my charmingly naïve logic. If so, please feel free to wave the repeat sign liberally in the air. In fact, I feel a new rule coming on.

RULE (whatever THE NEXT NUMBER is): Whenever you spot an unnecessary repetition, all readers must wave the repeat sign in the air. It is made by forming your first two fingers into a number two (unfortunately identical to an international sign of abuse). Any complaints from the person working next to you, should be sent to thevicar@thevicar.com.

Back to Venus.

I reached for my Midem pass, and started to turn it over so that she could see the sticker on the back. As I did so, I heard The Vicar shouting to me.

"I would not advise you to do that, my dear Punk."

He was making his way through the cafe, dragging in his wake a man with long blond hair, ponytail and beret, and the ageing Crappenleigh.

"One of the worst photographs ever taken," he said to Venus, putting my pass back inside my coat. "One look and you will turn into an evil ghoul. My own is almost as bad." He reached into his pocket and showed Venus his own pass.

"But I am being rude. Punk Sanderson and Venus Crappenleigh, may I introduce Steve Laballe, who helped us in tracing the source of Billy G's computer files. Steve has been kind enough to express an interest in my concept of recorded music that never plays the same way twice. He wants to raise some money to develop the idea."

The Vicar looked around for a chair. I jumped out of mine, but it was too late.

"No. No No. This is not a good place for a gathering," he was already saying. "Shall we find somewhere more comfortable?"

What is it with him? We're all happily sozzled in a bar, and all he wants to do is uproot us.

"My dear Punk," he urged. "This is your town. What do you suggest? Lay on Macduff."

Steve Laballe (owner of the fine flat where I'm writing this) loves to tell jokes about his first 'lunch with The Vicar.' Nothing to do with the plot, but he'd never forgive me if I missed it out. Although, I'm not sure I've got the courage. We walked miles in search of something suitable for his holiness – with Venus gradually progressing from politely slipping her arm through mine to the full arm in arm thing. Call me soft-cushioned, but are women meant to flirt like this in front of their husbands? Particularly when they are a lord of the realm, standing three feet behind you, rather bizarrely lecturing your boss on chimney-cleaning:

"You must let me come and do the ones at your house. It's been a hobby of mine for years. These modern boxes aren't much fun, as you never get to use much rod. An old house like yours, you could be into a twenty or thirty foot length."

????!!!!

Eventually, we stopped at an appalling little fast food bar in the top right hand corner of the park. The worst fag end in the corner that time forgot. It was, of course, the one The Vicar chose. I say 'of course', but perhaps some of you have not understood his criteria, which are:

1. Smoke free
2. Quiet
3. No muzak
ie. Completely empty with no atmosphere.

He circled the completely empty room two or three times before finally choosing one of the tables, and then, after sitting in one of the chairs for a few seconds, got up and moved to the one next door. He shuffled this new chair a few inches backwards and forwards, before deciding "Yes, this will do perfectly. Not very decorous. But clean and functional. What do you think?"

He got up and offered a chair to the Crappenleighs, as if it were the Ritz.

"Please. Be my guest. No need to stand on ceremony here. Now. What will it be?"

CHAPTER EIGHT

I'm sure Steve Laballe will forgive my speedy editing of the last scene. Too painful. How can you come to France and eat a poopathetic lunch of soggy mini pizza food that even a roadside transport cafe would be ashamed of?!

Pardon me, "of which a transport cafe would be ashamed" I should say.

Can't end a sentence in a preposition, as the Vicar never ceases to tell me.

To which there is, of course, only one answer:

"Bugger off"

And it ends in a preposition!

Which reminds me. Have you heard that question the Vicar loves to ask "What is the first thing you do when reading a book?"

and before you start guessing, the answer isn't something sensible like "find a comfy chair", or "lock yourself in the toilet".

No, the answer is "wash your hands". I ask you. "Wash your hands"! Who washes their hands before reading a book? Other than his Hairyness.

Let us return to our bargain basement plot.

☺

Bernstein's
Not so Pretty
BLONDE BOMBSHELL

S O WHERE ARE WE, PUNKSTERS? WE HAVE HAD THE mysterious notes from the Orange Eyebrow, and the Orange Nutter has made his first appearance, surprising all those who thought he was just some sort of joke. And I was making a pitiful attempt to build up the tension over the question of "will he or won't he tell Venus". Which really means that we are still in the 'getting round to it' phase of our relationship. And we're nearly eight chapters in. Pretty good as foreplay goes.

And I am going to keep you waiting just a little bit longer, as we detour on the way back to the Palais des Festivals to visit the 'Swapster stand' or, more accurately, the internet café they'd set up in the bar directly opposite. A brillig idea. Way cheaper than paying MIDEM's exorbitant fees, and the coolest slut on the block.

The Vicar wants me to include more "technical info" about internet sites like GooTube, Ebay, MySpace, and Swapster, but I think we should tell the great Victator to keep his f***ing editorial decisions to himself.

Swapster is a way of swapping music from one computer to another (hence the name – duh!). I think that's enough.

"It is called theft, old hat," was Lord Crappenleigh's judgement on their software. "I see no reason why anyone should get my legendary musications for free. Music has never been free. How is a musician to pay the roof maintaining rent?"

"One point of view," The Vicar admitted. "Although it shows scant regard for the facts. It is only recently, my dear boy, that people have begun to regard music as personal property. That notion did not start until the late 1800s. It was reinforced by the copyright act, which as Punk can tell us was in..."

He must have known that I didn't know the date.

"...Oh come on, Punk. These are things you should know. The original copyright act was in 1911, September 15th to be precise. But..." he went on "...when Handel was paid to write a piece of music for next Sunday, he did not expect performance fees every time it was performed. Why should a musician continue to get paid for something they did thirty years ago?"

"Perhaps because people are still buying it?" sang Venus, to the tune of Eminem's *'You can suck my dick if you don't like my shit',* which she was playing at one of the terminals. Interesting lyrics.

"And I am most certainly in favour of a musician getting their fair share of any money that is paid," The Vicar agreed. "Hence my strong stance on bootlegging and piracy. But, in its purest form, music is free and belongs to everyone. An interesting dichotomy."

"Well, I think your system is great." Venus handed the

headphones back to one of the Swapster staff. "I stopped buying CDs long ago, and the sooner I can get movies this way the better."

"Which is why I shall fight your company with the tooth that is long and the nail that is rusty," spluttered Lord Crappenleigh. "Where shall we three meet again, the Criminal courts, the Old Bailey, or Capitol Hill?"

"And I am equally sure that it will all end in some wonderful compromise that serves the best interests of the major record labels," The Vicar advised the shocked assistant. "Be in no doubt, you poor deluded fool, that one of the companies, that is currently trying to sue your wonderfully anarchic little set up, will soon change their minds and decide to buy you. Enjoy your period of independence. It will not last long. Au Revoir".

And you first heard it here. For The Vicar was accurate as always. About two months later BGM (Big Global Monstrosity) bought Swapster, while still suing them in court. Baffles my poor little mind.

And so back to the Palais des Festivals and the glories of MIDEM. The Vicar had a few, long since forgotten, meetings in the afternoon. Blame my forgetteriness on the champagne that is served at most of the stands. Cheap bubbles may get up the Vicar's nose, but they all taste good to me.

A quick guide to my top stands:

1. Sonopress.
   A CD manufacturer. Very boring products. All the better for those of us who *do* call in.
   Alcohol content. 7/10.

2. Abbey Road Interactive.
   I've got the hots for Sam, who works there.
   Poor Alcohol Content. 2/10.

3. The Emperor's Palace.
   One to impress. Pony Canyon, Japanese Record label,
   have a room hidden on the top floor, protected by
   the "Asian Dragon Woman". Inside, Confucius say,
   many mysteries unfold.
   Alcohol content (Saki). 7/10

4. German Music Delegation
   Five o'clock on the dot, the beer flows.
   Hoffenbrau taps magically appear out of the top of
   their reception area. 8/10.
   Almost enough to make you like German music.

Almost.

I'll complete the list later. Right now, we must return to
our bargain basement plot, and The Vicar's 5pm meeting
with Michael Bernstein of the Music Network, the one he
mentioned that morning to Luke Hutchence. It conflicted
with the daily German beerfest, hence my slightly late
tanglefooted arrival. Another meeting of the 'old friends
network' – not quite 'old school tie', although Michael
Bernstein must have been the only person at MIDEM
actually wearing one.

He was very New York, very short and very Jewish.
(Does that sound racist? It's not meant to be, but you have
to be careful.)
Let it go.

"Michael Bernstein," The Vicar said, rising from his chair. "May I introduce Punk Sanderson. I should apologize, I suppose. There is, of course, absolutely no excuse for him."

I shook Mr Bernstein's hand, while he looked at me askance (what does that actually mean), to see what I had done to deserve such criticism.

"I am sure Mr Sanderson is quite excellent at his work," he said finally.

"Work?" The Vicar mocked. "I have long given up hoping that Punk will become a useful member of society. If we manage to train him so that the net results of his labours are not overwhelmingly negative, that will, in itself, be a triumph."

The Vicar was back to that old routine. Bernstein smiled at me.

"Pleased to meet you, Punk. What is it that makes us put up with this pompous fool? I allowed him to share my flat in New York, while we were both young men, and suffered nothing but abuse for the entire year." He looked at the Vicar. "And I am sufficiently mad to remember that year with great affection."

"We should not confuse closet homosexuality with complete incompetence. You, Michael, fancied my bottom. Nothing wrong with that. It is a perfectly fine bottom. Punk, on the other hand, is a complete incompetent who fancies his pay cheque. Nothing wrong with that either, I suppose. It certainly makes him behave himself…"

"Shall we sit down," Bernstein invited. "A glass of champagne, or is still Earl Grey tea?"

"Neither, I am afraid," The Vicar sighed. "I have regrettably given up tea. Right now, I am driven by a lack of caffeine, and a desire to launch the Vicar Chronicles."

"So. Tell me," Bernstein said, abruptly ending the polite preamble.

"The most exciting offer you will get all week to be sure." The Vicar handed over the synopsis I had copied for him. "A TV series based on my life, complete with all manner of commercial spin offs and online opportunities. Those pages lay it all out very clearly."

The Vicar did not watch Bernstein while he read. He sat there in one of his half meditational moods. I, on the other hand, fixed him very firmly with the old pork pies, and it was clear that all was not well. He became increasingly flustered, and flicked several times from the front page to the second page, as if checking that he was not imagining things.

He looked up with a nervous smile on his face.

"This is not some form of practical joke, is it David?" he asked eventually.

"Oh Michael, my dear man. You are not going to tell me that you do not like the idea?"

"Far from it. An excellent proposition. Exactly what a company like AOL Time Warner would have needed to make their mad merger work. Music, books, the internet, Films – a single artistic vision."

"Good. There is nothing I abhor more than trying to persuade someone of limited intelligence to do the blindingly obvious and make money for themselves."

"The problem," Bernstein cut in, "is that I have had this exact proposition, with virtually identical wording, presented to me already today."

He looked again at the piece of paper.

"In fact, with the exception of the name of the main character, I would have said that the two propositions are *absolutely* identical, *word* for *word*."

MICHAEL BERNSTEIN HAD JUST DROPPED THE NOT-SO-pretty-blonde-bombshell that someone had copied The Vicar's plan for his Chronicles – and was selling a proposition that was "absolutely identical, word for word."

The Vicar was never one for the usual reactions of 'You must be joking', or 'There must be some mistake'. Love him or hate him, he is the man for a crisis. While other people would have jibbered a million questions, he quietly took stock of the situation.

"I am, no doubt, correct in assuming that you are unable to tell me the name of the person who presented this proposition to you? A confidentiality agreement, perhaps?"

"Yes," stuttered Mr Bernstein, who appeared far more shaken than the Vicar, "one that covered both the subject matter of the proposal and the parties concerned. I suspect I have already breached it by telling you of the meeting."

"I think that can be forgiven under the circumstances. Blame it on the shock. Is there anything you do wish to tell me? I certainly would not presume on our friendship to make you act improperly."

"Under the circumstances, I think it would be improper

to reveal even the appointments that I have listed in my online diary. Mother's the word, I'm afraid. There is little I can say. And I fear their proposition is further along than yours. They claim to already have a publisher, a production company and online agreements."

"All in the space of a day. My my. They have been working fast. Eager beavers if ever there were."

"In a day? No. That would be quite impossible. They must have been setting this up for some time."

"Oh, I think not, Michael. Smoke and mirrors, I am sure. And now I must not take up any more of your valuable time. Come, Punk, it would seem that all these theoretical questions of the theft of intellectual property have been replaced by rather more real ones. A pleasure as always, Michael. Keep the synopsis. You will be needing it when we do business together. We are about to write a few more chapters about the art of smoking out a rat."

And with that, the Vicar turned and headed off towards the exit of the Palais des Festivals.

"So someone has stolen my ideas, Punk, and my children have been sold into slavery. We must rescue them."

A little overdramatic, perhaps, I thought. And anyway, the books are my children, as I am the one sitting here, scribbling away.

"There is, of course no monopoly on ideas," he continued. "They are out there waiting for the time and place that will give birth to them. You can be sure that if you have had a bright idea – most unlikely in your case, of course…" he pushed his way through a drinks party that was blocking the stairs to the exit "…that someone else has had the same idea. We are all one big humanity tapping into the same thoughts."

He sailed out through the glass doors, closing his eyes and taking great gulps of fresh air.

"In this case, however, I think someone has tapped into our ideas in a rather more literal way. If their presentation shares my exact words, then I think we can deduce that our miscreant has not tapped into the common humanity, but has placed their dirty dexters on a copy of our proposition. How and by whom. Those are the questions."

We headed straight over the road to the Swapster stand we had visited earlier. The same young attendant was still there.

"Good to see you again, my friend. I see the corporate takeover has not happened yet. Worry not. Your time here has not been wasted. I shall need access to a computer terminal for a short while."

The Vicar looked around, but all of them were being used. Undeterred, he simply walked to the nearest computer, and took the current user by the arm.

"Excuse me. May I?"

Not a question to which the unfortunate victim could say "no".

"If you want to hear some music, there is a perfectly good record store on the Rue St Antoine where they will be pleased to relieve you of some of those atrocious looking Euros."

The poor man stared up at the Vicar, wondering what was happening.

"If you please?" The Vicar boomed. "This computer has a higher calling" – pushing the man away from the keyboard, before sitting himself down.

The attendant came over to see what he was doing.

"How do I close down this awful software of yours?" The Vicar demanded. "It is hideously out of date. I am afraid you have three or four competitors who are light years ahead of you. Still, the best system does not always win. I myself was a Betamax user, and then we were stuck with that hideous VHS format. Thank heavens for DVD."

He succeeded in closing the Swapster software.

"Good. Now I assume you have an internet browser on here?"

The Vicar had effectively commandeered their machine to surf the net. He was looking for Bernstein's online diary.

"It was indeed most kind of Michael to subtly suggest I look here," he said. "This is how I booked my interview with him. His online diary for MIDEM week, where people can see when he is available, and request prospective inter-view times. Admirable, but not for me." He smiled at me.

"But I can, of course, see who else he has seen today. Who do we have?"

The Vicar was looking at a 'picture' of Bernstein's day, divided into half hour sections, shaded out whenever he was busy.

"What a busy man he has become. Twelve meetings today."

The 'admirable' system would not, however, give details of those meetings without a password.

"Strange. Why then, did he mention it to me?" For the first time, the Vicar looked non-plussed.

"Perhaps he didn't want you to come here. He said he wouldn't tell you anything. 'Mum's the word', as he put it."

"Yes." The Vicar sat back in his chair.

I pulled the keyboard towards me and began typing in

possible passwords. All my favourites, based on tits, arses and bosoms, didn't seem likely choices for Mr Bernstein.

"How do you spell Yom Kippur?" I asked.

"You will never guess the password. There are billions of possibilities. He must have told it to us."

The Vicar sat back in thought, while I ran through as many Jewish words as I could remember:

Yom Kippur
Hanukkah,
Rosh Hashanah,
Barmitzvah,
Shalom,
Circumcision.

"Mother's the word," he mused. "Those were his exact words. Go on, Punk, type in Mother."

I tried, but it didn't work.

"Try '*Mutal*'. M.U.T.A.L. That is what he calls his Mother."

YeeeeeeeeeeeS!

'OPEN SESAME' as Ali Babar's and his forty thieves would have put it.

The Vicar clicked on one of the meetings, and the details came up. He could even read the various emails connected with it. It felt somehow improper to be reading someone else's letters.

"We now live in a world where we must assume that everything we do and everything we say is available to all." The Vicar didn't share my concerns. "There is no longer any privacy. Those who act honourably have nothing to fear. The right action will have the right repercussions."

He closed the first email and looked down the list.

"I think we can exclude MMM@attbi.com. The email was sent last Friday. I rather suspect our miscreant will not even have known he wanted a meeting until after nine o'clock this morning. Still, note down the email, just in case."

As he searched through the diary, my mind wandered to all the bizarre things that had happened at this conference: the message on the flight, the notes from the Orange Eyebrow, this blatant theft of the Vicar's plan for the Chronicles. I couldn't help thinking that they must all be linked in some way. And that Venus Crappenleigh was almost certainly involved. Let's be honest readers. I was flattered by her attentions – a few crude remarks about "swellings in my head and my trousers" come to mind – but did she really fancy me, or was I being used in some way? That, it seemed, was the squillion dollar question.

Of all the meetings, only two were set up after 9 o'clock that morning. The first, requested by the unnamed ms2000@aol, said simply

Date: 25th Jan

Time: 9.30 am

Dear Michael,

Something of great interest for you. More in person.

**

And the other, sent at 9.34 that morning, barely minutes

after he would have left us – read:

To: Michael Bernstein

Date: 25th Jan

Time: 9.34

My Dear Michael,

Seems we both have a gap at the same time. Excuse me if I try to plug it. Something you must see.

From...

...L U K E   H U T C H E N C E !

CHAPTER NINE

Monday 25th January 7pm

THIS HAS BECOME NOT SO MUCH A 'WHODUNNIT' – AS A 'what do you do about it'. A bit like those great Columbo movies, where you know who did it, but have to keep watching to see how Columbo will catch them. We had caught our suspect, Mr Luke Starsky & Hutchence, but, as The Vicar had said "You cannot copyright an idea". If Luke was trying to sell the Vicar's business plan, was there anything we could do to stop him, short of setting him up with a fine French prostitute and blackmailing him?

His Hairyness's mind was already elsewhere.

"We are due at the Carlton in nine minutes and thirty seconds," he announced, cutting into my gruesome plans for a revenge attack. "I have a meeting with a very beautiful young lady. Pray do not tell my wife, she would be very jealous."

Did the twinkle in his eye mean that he knew about my bitchy wife obsession?

"I think we should start walking. Should we not?"

And we set off along La Croisette to the Carlton. Even in January, it is a spectacular walk.

"So how do we nobble Luke?" I asked.

"There will be time enough for that tomorrow," he chided, not wanting to discuss it further. "Our villain has already caused enough disruption, without ruining our plans for a pleasant evening."

He walked on in silence.

"You know that this is a gay haunt at night, don't you?" I couldn't bear the quiet.

"And how would you know that, my fine fellow?" he asked.

"A bit of an embarrassing story." I wasn't sure what he'd make of it. And no laughing, Punksters, or I will be less honest next time.

"I was wandering around here late one night after being kicked out of one of the boats I'd been working on. Just turned eighteen, with no place to stay. I met this guy who was out walking his dog, and he asked me if I was looking for somewhere to spend the night."

"And my sweet naïve little Punk thought that he was just offering a bed for the night."

"Well yeah. I thought 'great'. I'd already spent one night curled up in a hole in the rocks over there by the port, and I can tell you it was frigging freezing. So I went up with him to his flat, where he gave me a couple of whiskeys. He said there was only one bed, so we would have to share it. I didn't think anything of it. I climbed in, and curled up to go to sleep."

"Do I want to know the rest?" The Vicar laughed.

"Not much to tell. This hand came over, but I told him in my best French that that wasn't my thing and he stopped."

"Unless something happened while you were asleep, of course."

"I have wondered about that. Am I still a gay virgin? But I think I might have woken up."

"You astound me. So worldly wise and so naïve, both at the same time. Perhaps you would like to share your story with the Crappenleighs…"

They were waiting for us at the entrance to the Carlton – a huge tented tunnel, complete with red carpet, running all the way from the road to the main door. God forbid that the rich and famous should expose their hairdos to the pissing drizzle.

"And this is where I leave you," The Vicar said. "What plans do we all have for the evening?"

"I shall be passing the comb of finer teeth over someone I met at that party aboard the, erm, great ship, Toyboy," Lord Crappenleigh dribbled. "Mayhap Punk might care to, ahem, offer a gentlemanly arm to Venus?"

"A gentlemanly arm! What are you on, Giles? Don't ask him, just tell him," Venus pouted, taking my arm. "He might turn me down. Punk shall be my Prince Charming and take me to the ball. There's bound to be a concert on at the Palais. And we have some un-finish-ed business."

"We shall reconvene here at nine o'clock," The Vicar commanded. "The bar is a fairly dreadful place, but I am sure Punk will want to see it. One of the great sights of MIDEM."

And so we scattered to the four skins for a couple of hours. Venus and I suffered the 'Spanish evening' at the Palais. All very good, I am sure, but all a bit too mind-faltering for me: people dancing behind screens, and inside boxes. What will they think of next? Books where people write chapters with no words?

Not that the time was wasted. Venus and I were indulging in some strange kind of courtship, with rules that I didn't really understand. Hey, I'm used to relationships that involve kissing, sucking, poodle poking and other bodily functions. This was more like being sixteen, full of sexual tension, but with nowhere to go.

"So you were telling me about the way you used to steal from your mates when you were working on the boats," she whispered in my ear. "And the guy with the Orange Eyebrow, what's all that about?"

It couldn't do any harm, could it? I held my pass in my hand and showed her the note on the back.

"Is this for real? It must be a joke."

"You met him." I said. "And look, the note is on the inside of my pass. There were only six people there when that was made. The two receptionists..."

She looked at me with raised eyebrows.

"...one of whom I admit was quite a fluffy little feather mitten. But we chose them at random, so it's unlikely it was them. Which leaves just the four of us. You, your husband, The Vicar and me."

"You bumped into that same girl on the boat last night, didn't you?" she wheedled. "Are you sure it wasn't her?

"Can't see how," I shrugged.

"So it's one of us. How exciting."

She fingered the pass as she thought about it. It was still in my hand and her fingers gently walked from the pass, onto my hand and then up my arm. I tell you, Punksters, I can't remember when I was last so sensitive. Actually I can. I was fifteen, and lying next to this girl on the beach who wanted to put her hand down my trunks (as girls do. I can't help it. Call me irresistibubble). And I couldn't let her do it. Every time her fingers touched my skin – somewhere near my belly button – it was so sensitive that I had to push her away, or hold her hand to stop it moving.

And here I was, a grown man, feeling exactly the same. I just couldn't work Venus out. Not that she wasn't pervOggleTit. God knows, I would have said 'yes' to the sticky little romance that this book needs faster than...well, I'll leave it to you to decide how fast I would have been. The problem was that I wasn't sure if it was on offer. After all, her husband was hardly missing in action, and yet... and yet she kept giving these signals, if you know what I mean. And I think you do. It was like learning a new language. Was she winking my whizzler or not? Perhaps they were into threesomes. God, that would be pretty disgusting. The thought of Lord Crappenleigh naked was enough to make you sick.

Take what she was doing now, for example. She was watching the dancing (a man dressed as a bullfighter standing on an upturned dustbin). Not a hint that she had anything else on her mind. Except that every so often, her fingers would wander off the arm rest, and walk like a spider up my arm.

What did it all mean?

WHAT
DID
IT
ALL
MEAN?

Fuck it (which doesn't count as a swear word, as I only thought it and didn't actually say it out loud). A small delicate nibble on her lick-a-licious ear was the only way – a sharp slap in the face or a long slow kiss coming my way very shortly.

She turned her head, catching me in mid about-to-lick moment.

"You think it's me and Giles, don't you?"

"Well, yes," I reeled my tongue back in. "It has to be. Either both of you, or one or the other."

"Well it ain't me, darling. It could be Giles. He has known the Vicar a long time. Maybe it's a joke between the two of them. Bless."

"You saw the guy. Some joke."

She looked back at the stage (the bullfighter had turned out to be a woman, who had now reversed her costume to become some kind of giant turkey, at least that is what it looked like to me).

"Do you and Giles...like...sleep together?"

The question had been bubbling up inside me. It just popped out before I even knew I was going to ask it.

My boldness (crassness? stupidness? and other words not ending in 'ness') was greeted with a "sssh" from the people around us. I had apparently raised the old decibel level a little too high. Oops!

"Yes," she breathed in my ear. "He is my husband, and

we do sleep in the same bed..."

But the way she said it made me think that she could just as easily have carried on to say "although..."

The Carlton Hotel
9pm 25th January

VENUS AND I GAVE UP ON THE DANCING EXHIBITION IN the hope of catching The Vicar and his mysterious partner on my "Indiscretions" video. Picture the scene as I stroll up the long tented tunnel into the Carlton Hotel with Venus in one hand (still not quite sure about the 'arm in arm' thing) and Victoria Film'em, my trusty videocam, in the other.

I was doing my David Attenborough commentary bit:

"The voluptuous Venus and I make our way up the red carpet, through the revolving doors into this fine marble foyer. We creep through the undergrowth to this row of marble pillars, from where, we can examine the drinking habits of the high and mighty. At the bar, we get a fleeting glimpse of the lesser spotted Azzioli, head of Atlantic records, the largest hair in the business, and over there, is that not some poor soul being devoured by that rarest of predators, the Lord Crappenleigh, with his lethal tales of Prep schools, sexy Matrons' uniforms, and little boys in short trousers.""

Venus dug her toes into my shins. I panned around the room.

"And now viewers, we have spotted our prey. Over there, in the undergrowth, lurks the Vicar, preening himself before his prospective mate. As we move closer, we can get a clearer view. He's with…interesting, this is not at all what we expected…He's with…

….DIVA!"

Is there such a thing as Filmmakers Anonymous? If there is, better sign me up. I knew I should have put the camera away. But like the addict I am, I just kept shooting. I zoomed in to get a perfect picture as he leant over and whispered something in her ear before taking her in what in polite literature is I think normally described as a 'passionate embrace'.

Yes, Punksters, I have real live documentary footage of the Vicar necking Diva.

Talk about shocked. More like discombobulated. I looked at Venus and wondered what to do. It is, after all, one thing for the boss to have an affair, and quite another for him to know that his assistant knows about it. And after my previous experience with Diva (see opening chapter of *The Mysterious Case of Billy's G String*), I certainly didn't want her to know that I had filmed it.

"We need to creep back to the entrance, and then make a big display of coming in through the door," I whispered to Venus.

She shrugged her shoulders at me, and I glanced back around the pillar. They were now sitting side by side, holding hands, and staring into each others eyes.

Definitely not good.

Unfortunately, we were about six pillars from the door.

"We'll go one pillar at a time," I mouthed to Venus. I checked they were not looking, and we then dashed to the next one. Another quick look, and another pillar. A grown up version of musical statues.

We were three away from the door, when our oranges went pear shaped.

The Vicar and Diva, who seemed to be sharing a joke, got up from their table, and moved to the bar – standing straight between us and the exit. We slid back around our pillar, so that they couldn't see us.

"Perhaps there's an exit down the other end of this corridor," she suggested. "We could go that way instead."

"T-t-t..." I was frozen to the spot, as the Vicar and Diva left the bar and walked down the passageway towards us. We circled the pillar, so that they wouldn't see us as they went past.

Venus found the whole thing highly amusing.

"God, you do give a girl a great night out," she sniggered. "A new sort of barn dancing. Dozy doe your partner, and back against the pillar..."

I put my hand across her mouth as I saw the Vicar, who now had his arm around Diva, coming back towards us. They stopped at the table *right beside our pillar.*

"Steve, a wonderful surprise. May we join you for a minute?"

What a nightmare. Out of all the tables, in all the world, The Vicar had to know the person sitting at the table next to us.

"May I introduce Diva. As fine a chanteuse, as a producer

could ever ask to work with. Diva is here promoting the album that we made together at Real World," The Vicar said. "And I am exercising the standard rights in my contract for at least one night of, um…" He leant forward and whispered. "… *couch casting.*"

Diva giggled. I am pleased she thought it was funny.

"But we must not take up more of your precious time. Before we leave you…"

I heard them getting up.

"Yes?" Steve asked.

"Perhaps I should explain. We are merely putting on a display." He went into a stage whisper. "For the two professional eavesdroppers on the other side of this pillar…"

My heart sank. How could I be so stupid?

No. Don't answer that, Punksters. I know I'm stupid.

Ok. OK. So they saw us as we came in, and had been stringing us along. Very funny. Ha ha.

I haven't felt quite such a prime prat, since that time the toilet door opened automatically when I was washing my whatsit in the basin on a train. At least, that's my story.

"And now," The Vicar was saying, "if you would be so kind as to entertain Diva for a few minutes, I must nip to the tickler."

And then, turning to me.

"You should go while you are here, Punk. One of the most expensive '*pissoires*', you will ever have the pleasure of defiling. Larger and more richly appointed than the whole of your rather sordid flat."

I took this as an invitation to join him, and, believe me,

I was only too happy to drag my sorry arse away. I should have filmed in there (well, perhaps not) – Gold fittings, marble everywhere, and the most hi tech khazi I have ever had the pleasure of staining.

Have I already described the functioning of the toilets in the conference centre? There's been an enforced break of several months since I started writing this book – courtesy of a spell in her Majesty's prisons – and it's difficult to remember exactly what I've said. If I'm repeating myself, please wave the repeat sign joyously in the air.

No description of MIDEM or The Carlton would be complete without reference to the Magnificent Automatic Toilet Toy. Or MATT for short (silly joke at the expense of a friend of mine, called, yes, you guessed it, Matt).

Be warned. Approach these space age monsters with care. The seat automatically lowers itself, puts down a paper 'arse gasket', and lingers seductively awaiting your pleasure. Once you have finished dumping, defecating, shitting, pooing or other bodily ablutions, and stand up, it then automatically flushes, taking the paper cover away with all the excrement. A fun toy. In theory. The first time I met such a device – in the conference centre – it had me pretty confuddled. It prepared itself, a bit like a scorpion waiting to pounce. I sat down, and then got up to adjust myself, whereupon it promptly flushed and took the seat away. As I sat back, I nearly fell in the toilet as there was no seat. After two or three attempts, I managed to actually grab hold of the seat, and keep it in place. When I was finally ready to wipe my arse, I lent a little too far forward in trying to reach the toilet paper, and yes, you guessed it, the seat disappeared again.

A fine comedy scene for a Mike Myers movie, but what has this got to do with the Vicar? I hear you wondering.

Well, I shall tell you. This is not gratuitous toilet humour. For the Magnificent Automatic Toilet Toy in the Carlton plays a central role in this story.

I locked myself in the toilet in the Carlton, approached the throne with the necessary degree of caution, did my impersonation of Captain Kirk putting his hand through a light beam, and waited for the seat to lower. It came down slowly, and the paper arse gasket was neatly rolled out over the seat.

As it came out, and I know this is difficult to believe, but hang me by my crown jewels if I tell a lie, there was thick black writing on the flap of paper that falls into the middle of the bowl. Cue general blinking, rubbing of eyes and staring in disbelief. Another message from the f*****g Orange Eyebrow. Delivered directly to my toilet seat. How the hell does he do it?!

"Are you trying to spy on me
I have four eyes with which to see
Someone's lying to the Vicar
A message delivered to the tickler."

I had only just read the last couple of words, when I moved and the paper was whipped away, disappearing into the sewers below the hotel. Had I been a bit quicker, I could probably have grabbed it. But then would you want to read a book by the kind of man that goes round shoving his hand down strange toilets in the South of France?

But give me credit. I was pretty quick to realise that the author of this note must have been the last person to use that cubicle, and I burst out of the door in search of my criminal. In doing so, I almost knocked over Lord Crappenleigh, who was coming out of the one next door.

"Careful, dear heart. You seem in a bit of a hurry. Bit of a panic with the old automatic flush, eh?" he gurgled to me.

He seemed perfectly calm, but I now had *no* doubt. I had caught him red-handed, hot-willied, or whatever. He was the only person who could have written this note. All I had to find out now was if he and Venus were partners, or if (fingers crossed) she was completely innocent.

"Strange things, aren't they?" I said. "Gives a whole new meaning to the words a right royal crap, doesn't it. Having trouble with my one, before you moved next door, were you?"

He didn't answer, but I had made my point. I had flushed out my villain.

CHAPTER TEN

Tuesday 26th January

IT ALREADY SEEMED THAT MONDAY MORNING WAS A LIFE-time away. Before I met the Orange eyebrow, before the Vicar learnt that someone had stolen his business plan, before Venus got under my skin.

And the world was about to turn again. Although it started much the same. I showered at the unearthly hour of 7am, cursed the Vicar and his villa a million miles from Cannes, spilled my coffee down my T-shirt, and flirted with Venus and her 'butterfly tummy'. Just the same.

That was until the Vicar, who had been "doing his E" (reading his emails, not experimenting with mind-faltering drugs), suggested that I should maybe check mine.

Now, let's be honest, Punksters, my average email session

is up there competing with Boris Becker's twenty-second-insemination-in-a-restaurant-broom-cupboard-routine for some kind of sad gitfart speed record (well, I'm a sad gitfart, with no emails. He's an international superstar, who gets to fuck waitresses). I lie in bed – this how feeble I've become – dreaming of the day when I will log on to AOL and hear Joanna's sexy voice (does anyone else think that?) say 'you've got mail'.

Which explains why, unlike ordinary mortals, I had proudly ticked all the boxes requesting junk mail on my MIDEM application form.

And a good thing I did, too. Because otherwise my normally empty in-box would not have been filled with a free sample of the latest *What if?* newsletter, which, as Lord Crappenleigh might have put it, was "going to cause more than a little light precipitation to fall on our yeehah let's have a parade happiness."

"My name is Vinchennnte Sscchmaagala," I said, as I opened it. "My *Whatif?* newsletter will demystify the beeziness. Those who have no-thing to hide have no-thing to fear."

One of my better impersonations, judging by the audience reaction.

"A budding Rory Bremner." Venus gave me an approving pat on the bottom.

"Bushel hidden talents, Dear Heart." Fortunately Lord Crappenleigh did not pat my bottom.

I scrolled down the list of items on the Newsletter. The 'V''s made for interesting reading.

"WHAT IF the oh so pious Vicar, who took the moral high ground with Vincente Smagala at the MIDEM confer-

ence, met yesterday at the Café Roma with Steve Laballe to discuss their very own get rich quick internet music company?"

"WHAT IF the Vicar's plans for a TV series have been thwarted by a competitor who is proposing a similar, but better planned, idea?"

and the third, more gloriously,

"WHAT IF the Vicar's cellphone number was 44 77889 795773?"

(Don't get excited, Punksters, he has had it altered).

I was flobblegobbled. How on this dog doodah planet could they know such things?

"My, my," The Vicar exclaimed, putting his ludicrous cup of hot water with a splash of milk carefully onto a coaster. "I should be flattered. I ruffled Vincente Smegma's feathers more than I knew. His spy network would appear to be worryingly well-developed. I am sure that is the point of this 'free sample'. People all over MIDEM will be thinking, 'How on Earth does he know that?' and hurrying to pay their subscription fees."

"But how *does* he know that?" I gasped. "It's so frigging accurate".

"Language, my fine fellow. But yes, an interesting problem. Yesterday someone knew what I had written, even though I had shown it to no-one, and today someone knows what I have done, almost before I know it myself."

"Is there a connection?" I pressed. "Do you think that Smagala stole your idea? Come on, that had to be Mr Starsky and Hutchence. He went to see Bernstein straight after our meeting."

"And yet," The Vicar argued, "Luke Hutchence strikes me as family. An honourable man. Stealing my TV show is such a blatant and deliberate piece of one upmanship. I can see why Smagala might wish to do it. Why Malvolio might wish to do it." He pretended to spit over his shoulder. "But Luke? He has no desire to deliberately cross me."

"So why did he run off to see Bernstein the moment you told him about it?" I protested, as if spelling it out to a two year old.

The Vicar was already packing away his things

"We must not let this disrupt our day," he insisted. "I will bring the laptop, and we shall ride and read. If we endeavour to make our lives beyond reproach, which would include being punctual for meetings, then Smagala will have nothing for tomorrow's edition."

And so we took up our positions, with Venus and me in the front, and the Vicar and Lord Crappenleigh in the back.

And as we got to the top of the drive, I, of course, ran back to get my GoddamFuckingPisspoopingStupidArsewiping MIDEM Pass – carefully filed underneath my underpants, still inside my trousers, underneath my wet towel, all lovingly arranged into a piece of post modern sculpture in the middle of my bedroom floor.

"It is a mixture of details about high level deals, such as the fact that Stig Blomqvist is selling OSV – although I think I could have told you that – and highly personal information about named individuals. I still suspect Smegma's business is mostly a protection racket." The Vicar said as Venus piloted us along the autoroute.

His mobile phone had already rung three times. It would ring almost off the hook for the rest of the day: fans ringing to see if it was the right number, artists looking for a producer, people troubled by the *What if?* Revelations – Sorry that should have a small 'r'. The capital letter makes it look a trifle too biblical. We must keep my pathetic little tales in perspective. Even if The Vicar is inclined to think that he's God.

I was answering and taking messages. The fourth call was Harvey (Remember him? Lord Crappenleigh's son? My room-mate? Singer in my band? I assume you are concentrating here). One hundred percent reliable. Wherever there's scandal, Harvey won't be far behind. He had just ridden down on his motorbike and was afraid he was missing out. I promised him a full update that evening, in exchange for a pint and a mattress on his floor (yes yes yes. A Vicarless, Crapfree, night on the tiles in Cannes) and dumped him off the phone. "…in case," as I put it so tactfully, "someone important is trying to get through."

"The newsletter is not all bad." The Vicar was still reading his laptop. "At least it has reproduced a titbit about Wendy Airhole, who is buying OSV…"

What can I say to protect myself from an impending lawsuit? Nothing much. Print and be damned.

"Wendy's been chasing after attractive young singers again. Seems she got ensconced with a fine young man, who then asked to get out of his contract with Regina…"

He chuckled to himself.

"When she refused, he took the very sexually explicit messages that she had left on his answering machine, set them to music, and sent a copy to the Regina legal department."

He looked up at me.

"It might never have happened, of course. It just says *'What if?'* But I bet the recording is circulating as a bootleg. Perhaps I should obtain a copy." (It was, and he did. Try any of the illegal music sites I've mentioned).

Even in the space of that short conversation, I had fielded another call. They were coming thick and fast.

About half way along the drive, I got a call from Elsa (remember her? The girl on the OSV sampler). She sounded close to tears.

"Miss Sweden herself," I whispered to everyone in the car, with my hand over the receiver.

"Back page of the MIDEM news yesterday," slurred Lord Crappenleigh. "Had she been handmade by virgins in Kyoto, she could not be more lovely."

"Ask her if she would kindly hold for a few moments," The Vicar scanned his computer. "Not unimpressive! Another of Smagala's favoured targets of the day. A personal visit, perhaps." He looked at his diary. "Ask her for her address. We shall see her at ten o'clock."

"Mayhap, whilst you are there, Dear Heart, you might steal, buy or otherwise procure a ticket of the ringside variety for the filming of her video," Lord Crappenleigh drooled. "Sources close to the artist revealed yesterday that it is based on the classical tradition of snakes and scanty clothing, and is to be filmed on the morrow at a secret location."

He might want a ticket, but *I* was about to get to sit in a room with every single little delightful curve of her – as you'll find out, as soon as I write the next bit.

Elsa Pops Out

O UR MEETING WITH THE SEXOTIC ELSA IN LA BOCCA, a couple of miles out of town, at the Cannes Beach Residence, reached by parking up near the station (the underground car park was genuinely full this time), and finding a series of Cannes Beach *'Navettes'*, or shuttles, exactly as Elsa had said.

A glamour-free, self-catering beach hotel, with endless corridors, and those big round push-on electric light switches, which automatically switch themselves off. All very French (note to self: post photographs on the website).

And Elsa's room, when we finally got there, was more of the same: a small self-catering flat, with a tiled floor and white wooden furniture, made up of weird angles, so that nothing was square. A crooked bedroom and bathroom, and a crooked little sitting room, looking out onto the crooked central courtyard. A French design special. Not exactly where you would expect to meet a sex goddess.

"Do please come in. It's open," Elsa lilted in her cute Swedish accent, as we knocked on the door.

Before The Vicar gets on his high horse and lambasts me for altering the next scene, I had better come clean: OK OK, so I have changed Elsa a little. Her breasts are a bit larger (you must know me by now), her hair a bit blonder, and her English a little less good (well, a lot less good).

But remember *RULE THREE* – this is my version of events. And I fancy a cross between Lara Croft and Bridget Bardot. So stand by to be impressed, Punksters. Elsa is an absolute 24 carat babe. She was even before I remodelled her. A petite little petal, with two voluptuous fun cushions (cue the *'Dance of the Sugar Plump Titties'*) squeezed into a small white bra/T shirt thing, and a matching pair of white hot pants. She may have been walking barefoot around the room, but you just knew there was a matching pair of long white leather boots hiding somewhere. The perfect sex kitten.

The Vicar bowed to her, and took her right hand in his left hand.

"Elsa. Every bit as beautiful in the flesh as in your pictures. Shall we sit down?"

You'll have to imagine whatever bit of Chaucer he used.

We moved through to her sitting room, and she stretched herself over the sofa, leaving the Vicar and me with the white dining chairs. The Vicar placed his laptop on the table, and then stared at his immaculately polished shoes.

"A pause perhaps, before we start." He sat for the better part of a minute staring fixedly ahead of him, before thrusting his left fist into the air.

"Yes!" he shouted. "All important acts should be undertaken intentionally. So let us intentionally set forth on the path we wish to follow. Now, my dear. What do you wish from me?"

"I not know," she yodelled. "I read Punk's wonderbra story, how you helped Billy G. I want you to help me. I want to meet Punk, he's such a great writer. I want to have his babies…"

CUT. CUT. CUT.

I confess. She said nothing of the sort. Pure fantasy. But hey. A man's got to be allowed the odd wet dream now and again.

RULE TEN: At least one gratuitous sex scene in every book. Down boy. Down. Back to reality.

Alright. Alright. So Elsa made no mention of my fame or stunning good looks. She obviously suffered from severe myopia. Instead, she ignored me completely and fixed her large round baby eyes on the Vicar, muttering something totally forgettable about Smagala trying to ruin her career. Power must be sexy, what can I say. She was playing the poor, harmless, defenceless, Barbie doll to perfection.

"Well Smegma certainly dislikes you. I quote…"

The Vicar pulled his laptop round. Elsa had lain back on the sofa. Her arms were now crossed in such a way that it made her cleavage seem even larger, if that were possible.

"…What if Elsa, the hot arrival from Sweden, is not quite as hot as she claims? What if OSV have been massaging her sales figures to increase their company valuation? What if Elsa's dancing is so poor that her video shoot will use a full body stand in? What if she has been offering sexual favours to an A&R men from a rival record company to bolster her negotiations with Wendy Airhole?"

The Vicar looked up.

"They seem quite keen to put the knockers on your career."

Was that meant to be a pun?! If so it was a bit unfortunate. I thought she would burst into tears, but instead she just readjusted her pout.

"When the Lord closes the door, he always opens the window." The Vicar looked her in the eye. "How much of this is true?"

"How the fuck you dare ask me that." She wriggled on the sofa. Her legs were now tucked up underneath her, her eyes so wide, it was painful to look at. Each time she blinked, it was like watching a big pair of windscreen wipers.

"None of it," she sang. "It is all, how you say, a deck of lies".

"Come, come. I doubt that Smagala is in the habit of inventing stories. Twisting them perhaps. There must be a grain of truth."

"He lies. He lies," she chanted. "Big fat, greasy, porky lies."

"Then I am afraid there is nothing we can do to help you." The Vicar stood up. "Come along, Punk, the day is still young and we have much to do."

You know the old TV cop routine, Punksters. You pretend to get up, and when you are about to leave, she changes her mind.

"Alright. There is a grain of truth. I suspect Stig Blomqvist has had the sales figures…" she paused.

"Embellished?" The Vicar offered, sitting back down.

"Yes, imball-ished."

"And the dancing?"

"I am taking the classes. I will dance better than in the video." She adopted a proud pose, as if mere singing and dancing were below her.

"And the…" The Vicar smiled at the word, "sexual favours".

"That is not true. My boyfriend is A&R man with BGM records, but I do not be a prostitute, like he suggestions. Smagala only print those things because I not sleep with him on his fucking yacht. He is fucking pervert, offering me success if I suck his droopy little man for him."

The Vicar raised his eyebrows.

"So that explains why you are on his Christmas list. That only leaves the question of how he found out."

"No-one know that stuff. Just my boyfriend. And he don't tell Smagala. He works long nights on me. You know A&R guys. All little boys chasing the big ones. Mike make them all believe I am the big ones. I am worth it."

"I do not doubt it. Could someone have heard you and Mike talking about it?"

"No. He stay at home. They must, how you say, bugger my phone or email."

"If only you and Mike know, then Mike must be one of Smagala's paid informers," I pointed out bluntly, "or…"

"…or you yourself invented the story and told Smagala in order to get more publicity," The Vicar said.

She shot a dirty look at both of us.

"You dirty men. How dare you suggest that thing."

The Vicar held up his hand.

"I was merely completing Punk's thought process for him. He is quite correct that those are the two most likely scenarios." He paused. "But not the only ones."

He got up to leave.

"But we have already taken up too much of your time. We shall leave you in peace. Thank you for calling me. It has been most interesting. Can you make sure that Punk has your phone number here? I will let you know if I find anything. Trust the process. All will be well."

He stood up and kissed her hand. I uncrossed my legs, levered my erection back into position, and said goodbye.

Although, that should have been *'au revoir'*, as we'd both be seeing her again in a few chapters time.

WE LEFT THE SEXOTIC ELSA AND TOOK THE NAVETTE back to the centre of town.

"I rather think that I had better attend the meeting of the *Pho* group at the Lion D'Or this morning," The Vicar suggested ('Pho', for those not fluent in Vietnamese, is pronounced 'Far'). "I will show you the benefits of a proper newsletter. A group of professionals who have banded together to share their knowledge. Michael Bernstein introduced me."

It was now pissing down with rain – hardly what you expect from the South of France. The beach front was being almost washed away, as the navette turned towards the conference centre. The Vicar spotted the Lion d'Or straight ahead of us and flung the car door wide open. The driver slammed on his brakes, cursing us in his best French, and The Vicar calmly climbed out.

"Thank you, sir. Most kind. Excellent customer service," he said.

We were probably only ten yards away, but we were still drenched by the time we reached the meeting room. The Vicar paused in the doorway, before indulging in his royal walkabout, bowing to those who greeted him, and giving the few smokers a wide berth.

"Tschh. Such a filthy habit." He fanned the smoke away from his face with his hands, and made great show of his choice of a chair close to the open window. I sat opposite him, and stared out at the few brave attendees running beneath the pollarded plane trees, with coats over their heads.

Inside, all the talk was of the recent *What if?* revelations. Bernstein came over and commiserated with the Vicar over his ill fortune.

"David. Unlike you to attend one of our gatherings. I am afraid you are rather more the topic of conversation than you might wish. I wanted to assure you that I was not the source of any of the information. I was worried about the reference to our meeting, in case my secretary had let slip the contents of an email that I sent her yesterday."

"Please do not distress yourself, Michael. I am sure your house is entirely in order. Mother's the word as they say. How is '*Mutal*'?"

"Ah yes! I am pleased you picked up on my reference. I do hope it wasn't indiscrete…"

I let the conversation wash over me (like what? Like a dishwasher? A carwash? A £5.75 hairwash from the girl next door? Am I the only guy who finds hairwashes unbelievably erotic?). Several small groups rushed passed our window, in search of either coffee or lunch. I watched them absent-mindedly, until I was woken from my reveries (we're getting very French here, you notice) by the sight of a square man, whose legs didn't fit properly, with a black leather coat held flat over his head.

He turned, and looked up at the window.

Even before he did, I knew (cue Big Adrenalin Moment) that I was looking down at no less than that drum-rolling, fanfaring, heavy-on-the-Mahler, stand-up-and-God-save-the-Queen, damned accursed pimple…

…The ORANGE EYEBROW!

May seem funny now, but it wasn't then. I pulled back from the window, and told The Vicar.

"The Orange Eyebrow is down there watching us."

He was listening to the conversations about the *What if?* newsletter and did not want to be distracted.

"We do not need the Orange Eyebrow games now," he chuckled. "Let us deal with one villain at a time."

Games! The man had legs the size of tree trunks, and a spare face on the back of his head. Hardly a game.

"I'll follow him," I said. "He must be involved with Smagala, as he tried to stop you speaking at the conference."

"I should have ended this long ago. I assure you there is no connection," The Vicar insisted. "Do you not think that it is a little wet for this game of cops and robbers? You will be soaked."

"Buggery snozzle to that. This is personal. I have a score to settle," I raged, getting up out of my seat, and hurrying out of the room.

"I will meet you at one o'clock on Malvolio's boat," The Vicar barked after me. "And do not be late. We shall not be staying long. A brief show of support for the Pretty Boys."

Why does it always have to be so wet? Even when my stories are based in the South of France?!

The Orange Eyebrow was making his way along the street, going in to all the restaurants, as if looking for someone.

Following along twenty yards behind, I unfortunately had to stand outside, as otherwise I would have lost sight of him. So there I stood, getting drenched from stem to stern, as they say in Philidelphia, learning the name of every single restaurant in that sodden row: the *Pierrot 1er*, followed by the *Radeau*, followed by the very French sounding *Asian Fast Food*, followed by the...well actually I can't remember the name of the next one. But you get the idea.

At first, I held my coat over my head, but it was not long before my jeans were not just damp, they were, well, even wetter than that night on the Vicar's boat. Talk about swamp bags, I gave up trying to shield myself and took my drenching like a man – which had the advantage of freeing up my hands, so that I could get out Victoria Film'em. This was a perfect job for an undercover cameraman.

The Orange Eyebrow, T.O.E or TOE, as we could maybe call him, had dashed into a shop and came out carrying an umbrella.

"Fucking wimp," I said to myself.

He then headed away from the Palais down the Rue D'Antibes, pausing for a while outside the bizarrely named 'Old England' shop, which had a large selection of large warm Burberry overcoats in the window.

I filmed him all the way to the wonderfully named *Rue des Freres de Casanova* – only the French could come up with a name like that – where he entered the less exciting *Touring Hotel*. I waited until he wandered upstairs before presenting myself in front of an astonished receptionist.

"Mon ami qui vient d'arriver. Il a quelle chambre?"

Room *Deux Cents Dix-Sept* apparently. 217. I had found his lair, with barely seconds to spare before I was due to meet the Vicar on Malvolio's boat.

"Welcome aboard!" The Vicar greeted me.

Another large Gin Palace. I had been so intrigued in following the Orange Eyebrow, that I had not thought about the consequences of getting so damn wet. I stood in the corner of the saloon, looking like I had just been for a swim in the mediterranean, fully clothed. There was a puddle expanding outwards from me on the carpet.

"We must find Malvolio," The Vicar said, and he led me by the hand through all the distinguished worthies in search of our host. Everyone was there. Smagala, Wendy Airhole, even Breamore, who manages Billy G.

Each time someone queried my appearance, The Vicar told a different story. By the time he found Malvolio, it had become:

"I was clipping my toe nails, and one of the clippings fell in the water. Punk was good enough to retrieve it. I do like to keep these things for posterity. After all, imagine how much a toe nail clipping of Einstein's would be worth."

"Whatever," Malvolio drawled, in that slow, dark way of his. "And?"

The Vicar produced a shopping bag.

"I took the liberty of buying Punk a few new clothes. Would you perhaps have a bedroom and some towels, so that he can get changed."

He handed me the clothes.

I had to guess the sizes, and the French had nothing to match your very questionable tastes. But they will at least be dry. I assume it would be too much to ask you to leave your current clothes in the dustbin."

I doubt I have ever been in such an expensive bedroom, and I have certainly never worn such designer togs. I returned with my wet clothes stuffed in the plastic bag, ready to party.

The Vicar was, of course, ready to leave.

"Punk. Good. I think I now know everything. What do you make of this?"

He handed me a CD of The Glamour Twins' album.

"Does that not say something to you? I knew Malvolio was involved. Look. It is right there in front of you."

I looked again. Just a standard promo CD, with all the usual contact information.

"Blind as ever," he laughed. "And it would seem we have also missed this."

He pointed to a copy of the MIDEM News. Half way down the *What if?* Newsletter, it read:

"WHAT IF we asked for information about the Vicar's wife? Send to TheVicar@Whatif.com."

"I have no complaint about their attacks on me. But my wife. That is an entirely different matter, you understand. Smagala has overstepped the mark. This is where we get down and dirty."

CHAPTER ELEVEN

We are on the downhill slope now. We've moved from the "getting round to it" section to the "during" section. And that never lasts long, whatever we blokes may say. (OK. I'm speaking for myself here. I know, Sting can go on for years at a time.)

If you're reading this in a good old fashioned paper and glue book (as opposed to some new spangly computer gadget) then you can guess how near the end you are. Right now, all I have in front of me is a sea of empty pages – and Luke Hutchence wanting it finished by the day after tomorrow.

Shit, shitty, shit, shit. Maybe this plot just got a whole lot simpler.

GAL

☺

PUNK
gets that **SINKING**
Feeling

THE VICAR STRODE OFF MALVOLIO'S BOAT AND HEADED purposefully in the direction of the conference centre.

"All is becoming clear," he said. "The question is no longer who, but how. And the small matter of what to do about it."

As we reached the conference centre, someone recognized him.

"Vicar, Vicar!" he shouted.

The Vicar put his left hand up to hide his face and kept walking. The man was not giving up.

"Do you mind if I ask a question?" the man begged.

"You already have," The Vicar replied, and kept walking.

The man held out a MIDEM guide and asked him to sign it.

"Why do you wish to fetishize the relationship between the artist and his audient?" The Vicar demanded. He looked at the MIDEM guide. "And if you wish to have this guide signed, I suggest you contact John Reed, whose work it is. I would not ruin someone else's work with my signature."

We entered the conference centre, and headed to the email area. There were thirty or forty computer terminals, sponsored by *What if*, and a queue of about ten people, waiting in line.

Directly opposite was a RICARD stand, offering a free glass of RICARD in return for your business card. A more than fair exchange, I think you will agree. A great drink – mixed roughly fifty-fifty with ice cold water. Mmm. An oasis of pleasure beckoning me from less than ten yards away. I had a complete box full of over fifty business cards in my pocket. Not to mention all the ones that other people had given me. I even had one of Malvolio's that I had been handed while on his boat.

Melville Olver Spence
Melville Music Management
MMM@attbi.com

I could buy a Ricard on Malvolio.

The Vicar saw me looking at the card.

"Ah! Not so dumb. So you have spotted it." He pointed at the card. "Another five minutes and we will be able to see if we are correct."

I looked at it again, and couldn't see the significance.

I was about to ask, when the guy from outside caught up with us again. Mr Triple X from New York.

(I am sorry if Mr Triple X sounds stupid, but some wise arse on The Vicar's guestbook says you should never mention people's names unless they reappear later. And this guy certainly doesn't. Thank God).

"You ran off, Padre," Mr Triple X ranted, joining the queue behind us. "How do you manage to seem always so calm and in control? It's an art, isn't it? Have you ever thought of giving lessons?"

If anyone needed one of the Vicar's lessons, or even his massages, it was this guy.

"This is my first time abroad. I'm thinking like, why not. There's a few people I wanted to see...so I fly in from the US and arrive at Charles de Gaulle in Paris. I go to like Gate F, and then I'm sent to like Gate C, and I get on the plane, but without my luggage. I don't want to talk hygiene here, but I've lost my luggage and a man has needs. I've lost my schedule and I'm looking at these exhibitions try-ing to remember who I am going to see and when...And I'm getting so hassled. Fucking hassled. Rushing round in ever decreasing circles. My mind is all over the place. I'm trying to focus here. I'm in this space and trying to make it work, get the vibe..."

Is he annoying you? I do hope so, because he annoyed the tits of me. Yap, yap yap, just when we were about to get to the climax. And he's not finished yet.

"Do you meditate? We all get to a time in our life when we think, like, this is not working. So we need to, like, improve our inner selves...But it's difficult in this country. I mean, what are you meant to eat? All you get is bread. Bread with fucking everything. I'm off to Planet Hollywood. For some decent American food..."

He was finally calming down. The Vicar, as so often, had a surprise up his sleeve.

"Mr Goldman. Mr Fred Goldman, I believe." (Damn, so much for Mr Nameless)

"Yessir, but how?"

"I knew something of your predicament from the *What*

_if?_ Newsletter. 'What if Fred Goldman has arrived from New York without his underpants or his diary?'"

"Yeah, like, I have no fucking idea how they knew about that. I told no-one."

"But let me guess," The Vicar said. "You did email a friend?"

"Yeah, asking them to send some stuff".

"And you sent the email from here?"

"Yeah. How did you know that?"

"A common thread that appeared at the _Pho_ meeting this morning. Elsa also mentioned sending an email, and she had no laptop, so, like you, she presumably came here."

"Are you suggesting that Smagala is monitoring the email?" I said.

"It would seem a logical explanation. I notice that _What if?_ are sponsoring these terminals."

"Wouldn't that be illegal?"

"Sponsoring the terminals? Unfortunately not. Although the world might be a better place without the incessant brain washing that is thinly disguised as corporate sponsorship."

"No, reading private emails."

"I have no idea. There is probably a disclaimer somewhere here. If you use someone's computer to send an email, you may have to accept that they might be able to read it."

We were now at the front of the queue and a terminal became available.

"But all of that is for later," The Vicar said. "First, I want to find out who stole the copy of my business plan."

He sat down, and went back to Bernstein's online diary. The grey box came up again, asking for a password. He typed in _Mutal_ and clicked through the same emails that we had looked at on Monday, until he came to the one from Mmm@attbi.com.

"We discounted that as it was sent on the Friday," I muttered, feeling a knot growing in my stomach. "No one saw a copy until Monday morning."

"We did indeed," The Vicar agreed. "You recognize the email address I assume."

He tapped the business card, that was still in my hand, and I noticed Malvolio's email address on the bottom. Mmm@attbi.com.

The knot in my stomach tightened a few degrees.

"And I wonder what I will find if I open the attachment, which we so unwisely ignored last time," The Vicar continued.

I could feel two large wet patches growing under my armpits.

He double clicked on the attachment. I knew what it would be before I saw it – an exact replica of The Vicar's business plan, with a few name changes.

The knot in the pit of my stomach now took on the proportions of a large snake taking a painful stroll through my internal organs, and my mouth was so dry I couldn't swallow.

"Interesting," The Vicar noted. "So on Friday, Malvolio had a copy of a document that had been shown to no-one. It was known only to me..." he looked up from the screen "...and to *you*."

I could feel myself beginning to shake.

"I know that I did not show it to Malvolio..." The Vicar spoke very slowly, his lips thinning as he began to look ever more angry "...which makes it fairly clear who is the guilty party."

I stared across at the Ricard stand on the other side of

the walkway. My eyes were becoming blurred and it was difficult to focus. My mouth was parched, but all thoughts of a cheerful drink had vanished.

"Who?" I whispered, not able to control my voice properly.

"You, Punk!"

I abandoned all hope.

His
Hogliness's
HaLF-ARSeD
PLan

T HE VICAR LOOKED UP AT ME WAITING FOR AN ANSWER.
"You gave a copy of my business plan to Malvolio,
did you not?"

This was fast becoming a nightmare.

"N N No, I d-di-didn't," I stammered. "I wouldn't do that".

"But you did, young man," The Vicar went on calmly.
"How else did Malvolio obtain a copy? I gave you the master
copy on Friday, asking you to produce two photocopies. One
for Luke Hutchence and one for Michael Bernstein. Making
three copies in all. We have given Luke and Michael theirs,"
he continued slowly. "So where, pray tell, is the original?"

"It'll be with my things at the villa," I muttered.

"I very much doubt it," he scoffed. "Shall we wait until
later tonight for you to go though the farce of searching
in vain through that sordid pit of yours?"

I didn't know what to say.

"Now tell me. Although I already know the answer. Where,
you idiot, did you do the photocopies? You dropped in on
Vicky Cocaine at *The Place We Do Not Talk About*, did
you not?"

The awful truth sank in. I nodded, yes. Anyone who

has read the First Chronicle will recall that Vicky was Malvolio's assistant, the Uneven Struggle, whose T-shirt straining assets had attracted my attention on our visit to his office.

"And after doing the photocopies, might I suggest that you forgot to retrieve the original?"

"Perhaps so. I-I hadn't realised," I mumbled.

"*Perhaps so*?! A little less time enlarging your penis, and a bit more time concentrating on your work." The Vicar sounded very like the prosecution barrister in court. "I think that should be *Definitely so*."

I nodded. Guilty as charged. I warned you about the significance of that bloody photocopier – The Dragon Under The Stairs

Now that the prosecution was finished, he relaxed.

"There is only one mistake, and that is the failure to learn from our mistakes. Might I suggest that in future you pay a little less attention to Vicky's T-shirt, and a little more attention to the work for which you are far too handsomely paid? And please, do me a favour and pull up that fine pair of Versace socks. It is sickening how those clothes look so much better on you than they would on me."

He smiled!

"Now run along. Malvolio will be child's play. I was afraid we had encountered a real villain. Go and have that Ricard that you are craving. But be warned. Aniseed can make you go blind. But then so can masturbation, so your eyesight is doomed anyway. Especially when you are so close to the screen."

Boy, does he hit you when you're down.

He dismissed me and returned to his computer.

"One more thing," he said. "Can you please give me my

cellphone and Elsa's number. We shall be needing her help."

I handed them to him, and then went in search of my drink.

By the time I returned, The Vicar was looking smirkfully pleased with himself.

"Good," he chanted. "Everything is now in hand. I shall explain to you later how we shall deal with Malvolio – a simple plan that will let your efficiency as a studio assistant make amends for your failings as a photocopiest. We pay our own tab, and in so doing we help to pay the debt of others, to paraphrase myself."

I didn't understand, but no doubt he knew best.

"The more intriguing problem is Smagala. I have arranged for the following snippet to appear in the MIDEM News tomorrow morning."

He handed me a printed sheet, which read.

'WHAT IF Smagala's recent attacks on Elsa are due to some compromising footage of him that she has now entrusted to the safe keeping of the Vicar?'

"Well why are we arsing around?" I cried. "Use the damn footage to blackmail him into leaving you alone."

"Language," The Vicar chided. "And I would not normally, of course, approve of blackmail, but yes, in this case it would seem to be the only way." He paused.

"The only small problem is that the footage does not exist."

Why is nothing ever simple with The Vicar?

"Only a small problem?" I asked sceptically.

"Not even a problem. Only a difficulty." He smiled. "O ye of little faith. We will simply have to obtain some footage. And, as chance would have it, we have an excellent opportunity. Elsa is filming her video on the island of Marguerite tomorrow night. GC was right that she will be cavorting around in a state of undress, enveloped in a large reptile. Exactly the sort of show that Smagala and his comb-over should enjoy. We simply have to arrange to get him there, hide him in a bush, wait for him to do something indiscrete, preferably involving ejaculation of body fluids, and for you to film it."

I suspect, Punksters, that your reaction to this plan will probably be the same as mine.

"Have you completely lost the plot, your Hogliness? That is the most hairy arsed, half baked, anally retarded idea I have heard since my brother told me you can get high by smoking the stringy bits on the insides of bananas..." (Don't waste your time, Punksters, it doesn't work) "...No wait. Worse than that. Since I was four and my girlfriend at kindergarten suggested we go into the sand pit and show each other our winkies, and got us kicked off milk monitoring duty for a week. Has it not occurred to you, Mr Dumbbell, that Smagala might just have something better to do than turn up on Margherita island and go "Hello camera. I am going to unzip my flies, so that you can blackmail me."

That is what I should have said.
What I might have said.
What I didn't say.

Instead, I muttered something suitably pathetic like:
"Smart plan. Let's do it. What can I do to help?"
"Well, first we must invite Smagala to the party."
He finished typing an email:

'Come into my web said the spider to the fly.

An under dressed Elsa is filming her video on the island of Marguerite at 7.30.

The security guards have been instructed to let you come ashore.

The Vicar'

"That should do it." He pressed *send*, and got up. "And now I must confess that we are going to do something very naughty."

We crossed over the road to the Swapster stand, and the same poor assistant that he had abused the day before.

"Now, my fine fellow, how do I encode a song from this privileged pre-release copy of the Glamour Twins CD and enter it into your system?" he gushed. "Such a wonderful idea, being able to share songs with the whole world."

"And this is your great idea?" I asked frustratedly. "It may annoy Malvolio if a few fans get hold of it, but it sure won't make him give your idea back."

"Oh the fans will not be able to download it. Not unless they find it. Which will be very hard as I plan to completely mislabel the song. What shall we have? *Unknown1.* I doubt anyone will find that."

"But what is the point of putting the songs on the system if no-one can find them?!"

"Who said no-one can find them? I said the *fans* would find it difficult to find them. After all, I would not want to be guilty of piracy, now would I?"

He was keeping me in the dark about his exact intentions. After my complete fuck up with the photocopy, I could hardly blame him.

"And now most importantly," he announced. "In three

minutes time, I will have completed the seven days of decaffeination that I set myself. It is therefore time to go in search of a large sticky cake and..."

Altogether now
"...A CUP OF EARL GREY TEA".

Let's make sure we haven't lost any of the threads of my story. After all, Punksters, this is not just a simple monochrome beginner's tale. It has multiple strands, with the Orange Eyebrow, Malvolio, Smagala, Venus and Giles Crappenleigh, being weaved, sorry woven, together in a skilful multicolour tapestry.

It is unfortunately time for Luke Hutchence and Michael Bernstein to say their farewells. We never did discover what their meeting was about. I am sorely tempted to invent a scene, where I barge into a hotel room and find them in bed together. But, once you start inventing stories, where will it all end, I wonder? And I can't really go "outing" my literary agent, without good reason, can I? Not until he finds me a publisher. So strike them off your list of suspects.

Lord Crappenleigh, however, was still very much on the list, as he was definitely writing the notes from the Orange Eyebrow.

So, for an update on the Crappenleigh's, let's hop forward to five or six o'clock, when Venus joined us in the Café One Toilet – so nicknamed because of its one communal hole in the floor, shared by both men and women – but not at the same time, you understand.

"Ah Venus!" The Vicar called out, as he saw her approaching. "We should wire you and Punk to the national grid. All this electricity going to waste."

She took a seat next to me.

"Don't get too close you two, or you will short circuit. I do believe Punk is blushing.

'Thus may we see that neither wisdom nor richesse,
   May with Venus holde parity
   For she rules the world as she may please'."

"I think I like the sound of that," Venus said.

"Chaucer's Knight's tale. So you should."

He got up.

"And now, I shall leave you two love birds together, while I take a gentle stroll along La Croisette. Although I doubt I will be as successful at picking up young gay men, as Punk has been in his exciting past. Oh. I'm sorry." He put his hand to his mouth in shock horror. "I promised that I would not tell you about that."

Which is how I came to tell Venus my 'gay boy story'. Truth be told, I did that typical mating ritual thing of letting my tongue run away with me. I even told her the one about the night I spent it in Sandjus, south of Barcelona.

"I turned up in this campsite, and the owner asked me if I was staying on my own. When I said yes, he offered me a fifty percent reduction. As I walked through what proved to be a very *camp* site, there were all these men with handle bar moustaches leering and whistling at me..."

"Well, yes you are gorgeous," Venus smooched.

"Obviously," I bragged. "But I prefer to be oggled by the opposite sex. Like her, for instance," I said, eyeing up a girl as she walked past, in a pathetically feeble attempt to make Venus jealous. "Anyway, later on that night, having met up with this girl – the only straight in the village – we went skinny dipping in the sea, and we drifted down the beach away from our clothes. There was a dark mass near the shore in the darkness, and as we swam in closer we could hear this low continuous groaning sound, coming from this big, dark thing, whatever it was..."

"yes..."

"Well, we came closer and closer until we could see that the dark mass was the harbour wall,

"yes..."

"and the groaning..."

"yes..."

"I'll leave it to your imagination – all these men lined up against the wall..."

"Ugh! That's revolting," Venus squealed, almost jumping out of her chair.

"What's revolting?" asked Lord Crappenleigh, who had come to join us.

"Nothing. Punk was telling me about a great holiday he had in Sandjus in Spain. His kind of place, apparently."

"Ah yes, Sandjus!" Lord Crappenleigh drooled, sitting next to me. "So very classy. I have had some good holidays there too. I am pleased you liked it, Punk."

He put his hand on my knee.

"Woooaaah," I cried, my voice rising several octaves with the shock. "But that was some time ago, and I don't go to those sort of places any more...If you know what I mean," I added, hoping that he did.

What a nightmare. I'm in lust with his wife, and now he's trying to hit on me. Never a dull moment in my life, I tell you.

Suddenly both Venus and Lord Crappenleigh burst out laughing.

"Oh, Punk. Bless. You are so wonderfully naïve. You are priceless," Venus beamed. "I wish I could bottle you up and take you home."

And she lent over and gave me a big kiss on the lips. Having done that, she took a deep breath, putting her hands on each side of my face, before coming back for seconds. You know, a snog. With lots of moist lips and tongues, and erections in lower areas.

I was becoming actively involved, as it were, when I remembered that her husband was sitting beside me.

"You're one of a kind, too," I blushed, pushing her away and coming up for air.

"and far too much for a simple soul like me. Even if you are very gorgeous…"

I smiled at Lord Crappenleigh,

"…and happily married to a peer of the realm."

"Such a happy menage a trois!" The Vicar announced, returning from his walk. "Perhaps we should head for home, and leave Punk to his night with Harvey."

"Ah yes, Dear Hearts." Lord Crappenleigh was not ready to leave. "I had been meaning to, erm, say something on that subject. I would not wish to rock your friendly apple laden carts, but I assume you do know that, under his, erm, easy faux relaxed alabaster smile, my son Harvey is not the, ahem, angel he might appear."

He took a swig of lager, and wiped the froth from his top lip.

"This is mayhap why he is so busy sweeping the trail of our relationship with brushwood. Come on, Vicar, you know the score. He is a classic, what shall we say, Chet Baker?"

"A little cruel, I think," The Vicar said.

They had lost me long ago.

"Chet Baker?" I asked.

"A little before your time, Punk. A jazz musician from the 1950s, who claimed to be the world's best known junkie. Imagine Keith Richards on steroids. He once injected himself 40 times in 24 hours. I do not think Harvey is in that class, GC."

"I was thinking more of the strange blend of angelic looks and angelic music, with the character traits of the devil incarnate. Few people believe in evil, you know."

"Christ!" I thought . "Who needs enemies with a father like that."

Something to tell Harvey during my:

NIGHT OUT WITH HARVEY, SIOBHAN AND… SOMEONE.

And this where it gets confusing. Not the plot. That's child's play. And not Harvey, the sponger. Forget all that character assassination stuff from Lord Crappenleigh, he's a great guy, who knows how to party.

No, the problem lies in my relationship with Venus. Or lack of one. I am not making myself very clear, am I?

Come on, Punk, spit it out.

OK, so what I mean is this. Writers don't normally spend

a couple of hundred pages developing a romance with character A (in this case Venus), only to go out for a night on the town and have unabandoned sex with character B (in this case a complete stranger called...something). Or maybe they do. And maybe I didn't anyway.

You see, I told you this was difficult. I need to break this down into bits:

1. Men, or at least this man, however much they are in lust with person A, will never reject a chance for sex with person B. (Pretty obvious, but I thought I had better make it clear, in case there are any women watching, who are still mistakenly hung up on the concept of love and sex being somehow connected, other than by proximity).

2. Whenever I go out with Harvey, I drink too much (correction, I drink the right amount. It just so happens that the right amount is a very large amount).

3. There is a law of physics, which states that the fuck-ability of the woman next to you increases in direct proportion to the amount of alcohol you have drunk.

4. Whatsaname was a very attractive woman (well, a fairly attractive woman. Well, a woman), who wanted a no-questions-asked, no-sex-toy-too-exotic night of sextasy, and who, for some reason, God bless her, chose me.

That about covers it. It's a simple case of mathematics. 1+2+3+4 = me waking up stark naked in a lift in a block of flats just round the corner from the Miramar hotel.

Do you need more details than that? There's not a lot to it. Whatsaname was a friend of Siobhan's, studio goddess from Real World, now working for Diva, just as sexy as ever, but never going to give me a chance in hell, whereas whatsaname invited me up to her flat and...

Well, '...and...' nothing actually.

Which doesn't mean we didn't. And which doesn't mean we did. It means "I don't remember a fucking thing." And I think we've been here before.

CHAPTER TWELVE

Wednesday 27th January

HANGOOVVEERRR. AND NOT JUST ANY HANGOVER. THIS was *the* Hangover. The real body-shivering, inside-of-your-stomach-keen-to-be-on-the-outside McCoy. And my head...Well my head was in some parallel universe.

In fact, when I first woke up, it felt like my whole body was in a parallel universe, and that I had finally achieved the dream of all trekkies and been beamed aboard the Starfuck Enterpuss.

I was lying stark naked inside a small vibrating silver room. I knew I was on some sort of space ship, because I could hear the whirl of an engine, and was conscious of a slight sense of weightlessness. My stomach, in particular, noticed it.

And then the doors slid open, and outside my little room was the real world. Hello blinding lights. Hello nausea. Hello elderly woman, screaming and kicking me.

The doors closed again, and the space ship started to take off.

I had a lot of catching up to do. A couple of thousand years of civilisation.

First, I had to remember the whole Adam and Eve thing, and the fact that naked was not good. Next I had to remember that the fig leaf was out of fashion, and how clothes worked. The underwear was a strange triangle shape, and didn't seemed designed to accommodate the strange dangly flaps of skin between my legs, but *'Buggers can't be Schmoozers'* as the sign says round the back of the mens' toilets.

And all the while, I had to cope with the fact that every so often, the room would vibrate, the contents of my stomach would get that sense of weighlessness again, doors would fly open, and the same woman would administer a few more blows on my unprotected legs.

She still reappears in my worst nightmares.

The next time the doors opened, I literally fell out through them, carrying the few items of clothing that I had yet to master. Unfortunately, I hadn't got as far as shoes and socks.

Faced with this situation, all animals find some familiar hole to crawl into. In my case, this was the Saint Antoine bar, near the Old Port, scene of many a teenage hangover. It was still dark, and my feet were freezing from walking on the wet pavements.

"Un grand créme et deux croissants," I ordered bravely,

before throwing up in the corner.

"Well, well, look what the cat dragged in!" The Vicar greeted me, as I arrived for the planned ten o'clock meeting at Café One Toilet. "Can this be the same fine young man for whom I purchased an entire new wardrobe just yesterday?"

Only the trousers now remained. I stood before him in Whatsaname – what was her name? -'s T-shirt and knickers, and a pair of gold-plated training shoes that I had just purchased at the Monoprix supermarket. And el cheapo pair of two Euro sunglasses.

"Bless!" Venus said, taking pity on me, as I collapsed into her warm matronly bosom. Her perfume managed to be comforting, erotic and extremely nauseous, all at the same time.

Cue another visit to the toilet. Have you ever thrown up in one of those continental holes in the ground affairs? Can't recommend it.

"You have chosen a pivotal day on which to poison yourself. The Orange Eyebrow, Malvolio, Smagala. All will be resolved this very day. Fortunately your tasks are not demanding. Firstly, you will kindly give me the room number and address of the Orange Eyebrow's hotel, as I wish to pay him a visit. At midday, I trust you will offer me moral support during our encounter with Malvolio. But mostly, you must rebuild your strength, so that you are on form with the video camera, my video camera, for the entrapment of Smagala this evening."

The video camera! Shit, shitty, fuck and treble shit. Where the hell was the video camera?

"Delirium Tremens," The Vicar intoned, seeing the way

my hand was shaking as I tried to write the address for him.

His whole half-arsed plan hinged on me and the video camera, and I had no idea where it was.

As he wandered away, I let my head crash onto the table, almost breaking my nose. I lay there quite happy to be dead, until I felt Venus's fingers tickling my lower back.

More shits and fucks and double shits. The next thing, she'd be examining my latest fashion in underwear. Not something I wanted to explain.

"I've lost his camera," I murmured into the ashtray.

No response.

"I have gone and lost his fucking video camera," I shouted a bit louder.

Still nothing.

"Heeeeeelp!" I tried, my forehead still in the ashtray.

"Well?" she asked. "When did you last have it?"

Fat lot of help that was. Asking me a question. As if I was in a fit state for thinking.

"Yestewday mowning in the wain. Fwilmed the Owiinge Eyebwow," I mumbled into the table.

"Well, if you had it yesterday, you probably left it at Harvey's place last night. Is that where the rest of your clothes are?"

"Ah!" I muttered. "Didn't stay with Hawvey. Played a pwactical joke on me. Got me very dwunk, and left me naked in a lift."

"That explains a lot," she laughed. "Come on. Where is this lift? The walk will do you good."

I stood up, and turned to go

"I don't think you'll be needing this," she said, pulling off the ashtray that was still firmly planted on my forehead.

"Come on, lead the way."

Which I did, in a sort of a fashion. We were slightly hampered by the small fact that I had absolutely no idea what the outside of the building looked like. You would never guess how many lifts there are within a couple of blocks of Cafe One Toilet. Thirty two and a half to be precise.

The half is for the one I had slept in. Very small and very smelly. The sort of thing Lord Crappenleigh would describe far better than me. Definitely my lift. No camera, though. Not that I expected one. I somehow knew this wasn't going to be my day. I was beginning to run the conspiracy theories.

1. Was it a coincidence that on the three occasions I had suffered post coital amnesia, and my camera had been lost or buggered up, Siobhan was always around?
2. If so, did it have anything to do with my footage of Diva at Real World? Did Diva know that I filmed her at the Carlton?
3. Was the "naked-in-a-lift" thing related to the famous story about John Paul Jones in his Zep days waking up naked in a lift. If so, who else knew that story? Harvey certainly did.
4. Was it possible that Lord Crappenleigh's bad mouthing of Harvey was a deliberate red herring, and that they were working together to stop the Vicar from filming Smagala?
5. If so why, because even an eight year old would know that the chances of the Vicar getting Smagala to do something dodgy on film were next to nil.

Of course, it was always possible that I had just dropped my camera somewhere, in which case cancel the conspiracy theories, and pray that I had left it behind when I had changed out of my wet clothes on Malvolio's boat.

"I shall enjoy this," The Vicar said, as we walked down the gangplank for our midday meeting.

And we can all enjoy it. Once my stomach has settled down.

Malvolio's Boat. 12pm Wednesday 27th January

ACT WITH INTENTION AND ALL WILL BE WELL," THE Vicar said as he pushed open the saloon doors.

Malvolio was waiting inside.

"Ah David," he smurked. "Come to beg me to give you your project back, I suppose. Thing is, old boy, that the cat's out of the bag now. Some fool was silly enough to leave a copy of your bright ideas on my photocopier. Silly me, not *your* ideas. After all, they are *my* bright ideas now, aren't they?"

The Vicar moved to the very middle of the room, placed his feet as if there were precise markings on the carpet, bowed slightly and then stared straight at Malvolio.

"You can stand there all day, if it pleases you," Malvolio drawled. "I fear I hold the winning hand. But I shall enjoy watching you grovel. You have my attention."

Still the Vicar said nothing. Malvolio ran a hand through his thick black hair.

"Haven't you grown out of the long stare routine? Very

good on college students, but not so good with the big boys, I'm afraid. Bit of the magic powder and I could outstare anyone."

He pulled a bottle of Remy Martin out of a cupboard and took a swig straight out of the bottle.

"Help yourself, Sandleforth, if you want some," he nodded to me.

The very thought of it brought a bellyful of recycled alcohol into my mouth. The only time I've been thankful for a weak stomach.

"I'm sorry. I need to use the bathroom," I spluttered, holding a hand to my mouth, and heading down towards the cabins. I could hear Malvolio making jokes at my expense as I went passed.

"Oh come on, fuck this for a game of dominoes," he said finally. "If you've got something to say, say it, or I'm out of here, and you can wear the carpet out all you like."

I paused in the corridor to watch the stand off.

"I have bad news for you," The Vicar spoke loud and clearly. "I stand here with the power to bankrupt you. No!" he raised his finger to his mouth. "Do not say anything. One word from you, and I walk out of this door and rain down financial ruin on your head."

Malvolio raised his arms, before relaxing again.

"Think before you speak," The Vicar advised him. "I mean what I say. If I hear so much as whisper, I shall turn and leave."

Malvolio made a theatrical show of zipping his lips, and then lounged full length on a settee. "Good," The Vicar said. "We have an understanding. I shall explain my position and -"

Malvolio interrupted him by theatrically tossing one

of his shoes into the air, where it landed on a sideboard.

"Let that be your last chance," The Vicar said.

I left them to it and moved quietly into Malvolio's bedroom, where I had changed out of my soggy clothes almost exactly twenty four hours before, leaving the door open so that I could follow the action.

"I advise you to take this considerably more seriously," The Vicar was saying from just above me. "Your next interruption will be your last act as a wealthy man."

There was another lengthy pause, while I crept round to the far side of the bed.

"Finally!" he went on. "Let me explain your predicament. You may recall the radio show which I produced for the Glamour Twins. You have, after all, just released it on CD – without my permission, I might add."

Malvolio must have tried to respond. The whole boat shook with the power of The Vicar's next...

"Silence! You have been warned." And then more calmly, "You would be well advised to let me finish. You will recall that this show was a mixture, it is not for me to say whether or not it was skilful, of the music of the Pretty Boys and some Russian samples. 86 different samples to be precise..."

No camera beside the bed. It was impossible to put my head lower than my stomach, so I lay flat on the floor in effort to have a look under it.

"...Now, I have checked with the copyright societies, and I know that you have not acknowledged or paid for any of these samples..."

Nothing under the bed. I started to search the drawers in the hope that he had picked it up and put it away.

"...So let me paint the doomsday scenario for you. The owners of all 86 samples sue you. Not once, but twice. Once on behalf of the writers of the music and once on behalf of the performers. That is One hundred and Seventy Two lawsuits. Each with sizeable legal costs and accompanying damages. Many millions, I am sure..."

The wardrobe beside the door contained a rather fine looking whip, but still no camera.

"...I see fear in your eyes. You have assumed that, unlike the Pretty Boys, I actually know the name of all the samples we used. I do not. Your future lies not in my hands, but in the hands of Punk..."

At the mention of my name, I stopped for fear that their eyes would somehow turn in my direction.

"...Being an efficient assistant, he noted down the details of every sample. Which gives you two scenarios. Firstly, we could contact all the owners, and encourage them to sue you. Which has its appeal. I put some copies of the track on the rather second rate Swapster system last night, and have already had four replies..."

So that explained what he was doing.

"...Alternatively, we give you the list and you can contact them in advance to negotiate a fair rate, saving you millions in damages and legal fees..."

I went and sat back down on the bed. You had to be impressed by the Vicar. He certainly had Malvolio where he wanted him.

"...And what might we want in return? Just two things. Firstly you sign this sheet of paper, in which you acknowledge my ownership of the Vicar Chronicles, and lose any right to market any similar project. And secondly, you give Punk a production royalty. I may have agreed to work for free, but there is no reason why he should be penalized."

Well, I'll be flobblegobbled. A royalty on the Glamour

Twins album.

"...I hardly think you need time to make up your mind, as I am asking for nothing more than what is already rightfully mine. Thank you. I shall not take up more of your time."

I heard Malvolio coming down the steps towards me, unleashing an impressive string of swear words. I rolled off the bed, and lay on the floor on the far side.

"Mother-fucking, cream-pie-sucking, brown-tongued, sanctimonious, self-serving arsehole!" he shouted back up the stairs. "Who the fuck do you think you are? No wonder Smagala did a number on you." I poked my head out to see him snorting a line of coke on the dressing table.

He grabbed the copy of MIDEM News off the bed, dialled a number into his mobile, and kept going.

"You little sheep-shagger, you have not heard the last of me. Fuck me, if anyone needs knocking down by a couple of tent poles. Don't go walking down any dark alleys."

He hurled his mobile across the room and started to scream out the porthole.

"What if the Vicar was a fucking poofter? What if he shagged sheep in that mansion of his? What if one of his partners in that venture of his with nice little Steve Laballe had a huge pair of devil horns ready to gouge his pert white holier than thou back side?"

He picked up his phone again. "Better beware my inno-cent little Vicar. What if the world of vulture capital has sharks that even you can't tame? Ho ho ho! Beware Santa bearing money."

He stormed out of the room, and up the stairs.

I followed, pretending to bang the toilet door shut on my way past, and headed straight for dry land, still without Victoria Film'em, The Vicar's precious camera.

The Vicar was waiting for me, waving the signed document.

"Melville Olver Spence. Returning all rights to The Vicar," he said smugly. "That removes part of our problems. And I think your friend the Orange Eyebrow need trouble us no more. He has promised to withdraw. I have only one reservation."

"Which is?" I asked.

"Have you, by any chance, lost my video camera?"

I took a deep breath. This was obviously the time to own up. Even a complete fuckwit like me could see that.

Another deep breath.

"No," I said confidently. "I put it in the car this morning in case it rained."

"Are you sure, Punk?"

Only a fool would pass up a second chance.

"Yeah. It's fine. Safely in the boot."

"Definitely?"

"Definitely."

The Vicar sighed with relief.

"Thank Goodness," he said. "Because I noticed an identical camera sitting on the Orange Eyebrow's dressing table. I thought he might have stolen it from you." He patted me on the back.

"At least that's one thing we do not have to worry about."

Shit, shitty, shit, shit.

Shit.

SHIT!

Sex, Lies, and No VideoTape

6pm Wednesday January 27th.
On Board a launch heading out
to Marguerite Island.

Now I know quite a lot of this story is happening on boats, but I don't want to mislead anyone – maybe fooled by those exotic music videos – into thinking that this is normal for the music business. It's not. This boat out to Marguerite is the only time that my work has ever taken me onto to a moving boat. And I mean moving. Up and down, up and down. My nervous system simply wasn't ready to cope with a world that didn't stay still.

What's that film where the hero is rowed out to an island to be beheaded? I can't remember, but that was how I felt. This was the end. My body had packed up, I didn't have a camera and the Vicar's whole plan would fall apart because of me. Not that I'm fatalistic or anything.

"Spit spot, best foot forward," he chanted, as we climbed onto the jetty. "Now is the time when heroes walk the land, and great deeds will be done."

It seemed a pity to ruin his enthusiasm. We wandered down into the grove where they were filming the video. I prayed that one of the cameramen would have a spare camera.

At first it seemed that I might be lucky. There, on a silver case, was a spare camera. They had one for filming the video, and another for a 'making of' documentary. But would they let me use it?

"Ah dear sweet Elsa. Punk's sweetheart.

And prively he caught her by the quaint
and said Surely unless I have my will
for hidden love of thee my blood I spill."

The Vicar greeted Elsa, who was being made up.

"Myn be the labour, and thyn be the glorie," she replied (well, I told you she wasn't as dumb as I made out. She's the only person who has ever quoted Chaucer back at him.)

"Very good, young lady," he answered. "Very good. And now while you are preparing, perhaps Punk and I might have our own rehearsal."

He turned to me.

"Punk, you will discretely follow Smagala up from the jetty. Elsa's bodyguard has instructions to stop anyone else from coming ashore with him. Let us assume that he hides behind these bushes to watch Elsa. You could hide over there to get some good footage of him."

I obediently hid behind the tree.

"Good. You do not need to do any filming yet. Save your battery. Perhaps you can come and do your excellent impersonation of Smagala, when I come and accost him."

All of this seemed totally unnecessary.

"So Smegma," he said, putting his laptop on the floor in

front of me. "Do you not think that you should put your pecker away before you talk to me?"

I stared at him blankly.

"Come on, Punk. A little role play. It is obvious that I have caught Smagala in the act. If anyone should understand *that*, it is you."

This was going from bad to worse.

"Come on. How might Smagala react? You do an excellent impression. Let us make this real."

I was going to get sacked anyway, so I took this as my chance to vent my fury.

"I will wobble my codger as I like, you pompous old windbag."

I thought he would explode, but, no, he stayed in character.

"You may not laugh so much when you see the footage Punk has. He has filmed the whole of your pathetic little session."

"Oh pleasse. Pleasse!" I lay on the floor and begged him. "Thiss will ruin me. I will never be able to look at my friends again. I will do anything. Anything. You must help me. I have money. How much can I pay you for that footage?"

"You think you can bribe me?" The Vicar sneered. "What if I just broadcast it on the internet? What if I showed it at tomorrow's semen-ar, sorry seminar? My poor little joke, don't you know."

I was getting into now. And anyway, Smagala's shoes didn't seem so far removed from mine.

"I will do anything. Anything. I cannot afford to lose my job. I could not help myself. She is so sexy. So sexy. I will give you anything."

"Well you can start by confessing that you have been reading people's emails," The Vicar scoffed.

"Yes, yes," I said. "I deed it. I deed it all. I read your emails. But if you tell people I will be ruined. Ruined." I crawled over and clung to his legs. "I will give you anything. Money. Girls. I know many girls. But you must not tell anyone. Please. Please. You must do this for me. We all make mistakes. One little mistake. One stupid little mistake and I will be ruined. This is so unfair."

I was now genuinely in tears.

"So unfair. You've got to believe me. I did not mean to lie. I was so stupid. You must give me another chance. I beg you. I beg you. I kiss your feet. I bow down. I grovel."

The Vicar put his hand down and picked me up.

"Come, come, Punk. I do think you are getting a little carried away. But very good."

He picked up his laptop.

"And it is very important that you keep filming while I talk to Smagala. Do not come out just because I mention your name. I need to get a film of the whole confession."

I swallowed deeply, and consoled myself with the fact that it was highly unlikely that Smagala would show up.

"He's here." John taps me on the shoulder and whispers in my ear.

"Shit. Shit and double shit. You know I really thought he wouldn't show up."

"Well he's here. Standing just over there."

I rushed down to the second cameraman to beg, steal, or borrow his camera. They'd begun filming Elsa with her snake. It was bloody freezing, and they had large overhead heaters to keep her warm. From where I was, she seemed to be completely naked.

"I'm sorry," he said, predictably. "I need it. I've got to

get B roll footage. You wouldn't expect me to miss this, would you?"

Of course, I wouldn't. But where does that leave me? What the hell did I do to deserve the Orange Eyebrow?

I had no alternative but to tell the Vicar the truth. But we all know how the conversation would go.

"Smagala's here, but there's something I have to tell you…" I would begin.

"Sssh!" He would say. "You will disturb the filming. Do as we have planned. Follow him and film everything he does."

"But…"

"No buts. Do as I say."

You see. I wouldn't have a chance.

I snuck off to watch Smagala.

Things were not going according to plan. Far from hiding in the bushes, Smagala was standing out in the open, in the middle of the path. It may have been quite dark out of the glare of the spotlights, but even I could tell that he hadn't opened up his trousers. And he obviously wasn't going to.

Come on. Even I knew it was a ridiculous plan, so why was The Vicar so convinced that it would work? For the first time, I began to fear the Master was losing his touch.

THE VICAR AND I WERE ON THE ISLAND OF MARGUERITE, trying to get some compromising footage of Smagala.

"Vincent, so pleased you could make it. I thought you were a man who would not refuse a challenge."

Smagala stepped into the light, and smoothed down his hair.

"Yees. I was intreegued to come. It was good of you, Miss Elsa, to put on this show for me, but I am disappointed. Girls and snakes. This I have seen before. I own websites which show this all the time."

"I am sure Punk has visited most of them."

Another comment about me and dodgy websites. Did he know more than he ought to?

"Good for him. So long as he pays his money, and does not waste my time in visitors area. No. I was intreegued to know why you wanted to invite me. And why you put comments in MIDEM News about *'indiscrete footage'*. We both know you have nothing."

"But I did not invite you. The only email, that I sent, was from me to myself."

"Yes yes. But you knew I was monitoring everyone's email.

Let us not play games. Why else would you send an email to yourself. No-one does that. You knew I would read it."

Holy shit and Crappipuss. I suddenly realised that this was the confession the Vicar had been waiting for. And none of it was being recorded. "Think, Punk, think, you overgrown baboon," I told myself. "There must be something you can do."

"So I am right that that is how you get your information."

"Yes, yes. Do we have to waste time with this? I read the emails. But most of it is just rubbish. I filter on a few names that interest me."

"The Vicar and Elsa, for example?"

"This you know already. Actually, I find very little out this way. I have many informants, foolish enough to use their personal credit cards on some of my more exotic websites and who, how shall I put this, want their tastes to remain secret. Rock and roll and sex. They are perfect partners," he said smugly, or should that be smagly.

"Like Bribery and Blackmail. Well, at least you are honest about it. And as you are so knowledgeable about it, it may not seem so out of place if I indulge in a little blackmail of my own."

Smagala did not seem unduly worried by any of this.

"Punk, perhaps you could come out now." The Vicar waved me forward.

"I regret to inform you, Smagala, that my assistant Punk has been filming this entire meeting. Including your recent admissions."

I wasn't sure what to do. The Vicar would have to know the truth sooner or later. I stepped out of the bushes and held up both hands to show that I had no camera.

"Sorry, boss," I whispered. "I have lost the camera."

Smagala burst into laughter.

"You are so funny. This is all the sense of English humour, yes?"

Well, actually, yes. Amazingly and unbelievabubbly, it was. I, Punk Sanderson, was having a joke at Smagala's expense. Seems hard to believe, I know. A once in a lifetime achievement, but, yes, I was laughing at him, because I had a trick up my sleeve.

Don't look so shocked. You all thought that I was an utter fuckwit, didn't you?

Well you tell me. What would you have done in my place? I bet you wouldn't have come up with a solution as brilliant as mine. Let's look at the nightmare scenario:

1. I'm in the middle of nowhere
2. My career is over, if I don't record this conversation.
3. I have no recording gear of any kind.
4. I am suffering from severe alcohol poisoning.

So what do I do? I'll tell you what I fucking well did. I reached into my pocket and pulled out…wait for it…wait for it

MY MOBILE PHONE.

Still not with it? Well, we can't all play for Einstein United. Excuse me if I get a little cocky here. My team just won the cup final, and it's customary to slag off the losing fans. All will become clear.

"Excuse me, Mr Smagala," I said in my important voice. "But you may be interested in the contents of my…

V O I C E M A I L..."

(get it now?)

"...You see while you were talking, I called myself on my mobile. And I left myself a message. Or rather..."

I paused for effect, and pointed a finger at him.

"...you left me a message, because I recorded everything you said."

I let out a deep breath and looked at the Vicar. He bowed his head to me, to acknowledge my moment of triumph. I nodded to all sides of the ground, receiving applause from the trees, the bushes and the various creep crawly things that come out at night (long snakes. Three or four feet long. Not nice).

Smagala was less convinced.

"It would not record from over there," he said doubtfully.

"Oh yes, it would." I said, not letting him spoil the moment. "It's crystal clear. It wouldn't sound better with a Neumann U 87 plugged straight into a Fairchild Mic preamp with an Apogee A to D converter, 24 bit, 96 khz..." (studio talk, you know) "... I've already checked it. Listen for yourself."

I pressed 1 to play the message, and he put the phone to his ear.

There was a shadow on his face, so it was difficult to see his expression. Not that I cared. Last minute, in extra time, twenty two seconds to go, and I had scored the golden goal. The celebrations had already begun. I was stripping off my shirt down at the corner flag and practicing my victory dance (with apologies to people in the US, who have never heard of football, sorry soccer, which is only the greatest game in the world. Duh!).

"I agree," he said after he had heard it. "I geeve in. Very clever."

He held the mobile and stuck out his long stubby finger. I knew what he was doing even before he did it. Only a fool would let him get away with it. At the end of every message the same three options, '*Press 1 to replay the message, Press 2 to save it, and Press 3 to delete it.*'

I just stood and watched, as his finger jabbed into the number 3.

"Oops!" He laughed. "But now I have just deleted your message. I am sorry."

It was like falling from the top of a rollercoaster all the way to the bottom. No worse. It was like having the happiest moment of your life, your first orgasm with Angelina Jolie, and then waking up to discover it was all a dream and you've just wet the bed in a prison cell in solitary confinement on the mental wing of a hard labour camp in a country where you don't speak the language in sub zero temperatures with 25 back to back life sentences on a planet with no sun where all the food has run out and no-one has ever invented alcohol.

So it's not surprising that I sank to the ground utterly defeated. God, I hadn't felt this bad since…well, since never. This was it. My low point. No job, no girlfriend, no money, no prospects. I didn't even have any underwear, for god's sake. I was standing there in someone's else's knickers. And they itched like crazy.

Smagala looked down at me.

"Don't give yourself such a hard time. It's your boss, this Vicar, who needs his brains checking out. I thought he was smart. But no. He is more stupid than my wife, and she has no brain at all."

Was I wrong or did the Vicar's highly polished halo seem to be slipping?

"Excuse me, Mr Vicar. But did you really think that you could blackmail me with this message? That I would worry that people knew I was reading their emails? You are a, what's the word, dumbfart."

He stared dismissively at the Vicar.

"I came here to *encourage* you to tell everyone what I am doing, to put articles in MIDEM News blaming me for being such a naughty little boy."

Now he had lost me completely.

"Do you think we got much information from all those silly emails? No. Impossible to read very many. We want people to think we were doing it. You don't understand people as I do. If they think I am the guy who's reading other people's emails and rustling through their dustbins, then they are all going to pay to read my newsletter. It's good to be bad. People like that."

He looked down at the Vicar.

"You are so pathetic, so English. Compromising pictures! Only the English are so hung up about sex. Even if I had masturbated on camera, do you think I would care. I would have paid you money to give me the footage, to use on my websites…So much for your great plan, Mr Vicar. Tomorrow I have even more juicy stories about you and your wife. Mostly lies, but who cares. It is not the truth, but people's perception of the truth that matters. I think you are finished."

With that, he walked away, turning and spitting on the

ground as he left.

CHAPTER THIRTEEN

There's enough bad luck going round at the moment without having a Chapter 13.

The Vicar: *"Punk, Have you heard the story about the mysterious Chapter 13?"*

Punk: *"But I thought there was no Chapter 13."*

The Vicar: *"Yes. That's what's so mysterious about it."*

Although if there was a Chapter 13, it would be the perfect place – given my luck – to tell you about the advert the Vicar has just shown me:

'Old hatted Peer of the Realm seeks Dear Heart to drape on the arm that is playful and teasing. Be the Lady of my leisure for one hundred days.'

So, if I'm reading that right, Venus wasn't married to Crappenleigh and I had a chance all the time. And the Vicar didn't bother to tell me!

Not that I could afford her. Although I think the Vicar's wrong if he thinks she needs paying for her services, if you drift my catch.

Anyway, there is no Chapter 13, so you don't know any of this. Maybe the Vicar's luck will change and his half-baked plans will go better over the page in...

CHAPTER FOURTEEN

THE GREAT
VICTATOR

T HE RECRIMINATIONS ABOUT THE VICAR'S COMPLETE
cock-up with Smagala, began as soon as Mr Combover
started to walk away.

"But you promised me," Elsa warbled, from inside her
yellow dressing gown. "You said that he would agree to
leave us alone. What sort of a failure are you?"

"Later, later," The Vicar said in a distracted voice.

"Yeah governor. I thought you were meant to be cool.
Looked more like a first round knockout." The cameraman had a go.

"Perhaps."

"Seems your plan was pretty fucked up from the start."
The B-roll cameraman chipped in. "And Punk has worried
his arse off over that damn camera."

"Language. Language. And Punk should be worried

about that camera. It was not his to lose." The Vicar was walking along the path after Smagala. It was very dark, and as we dropped down over the side of the hill, we could see the lights of the jetty.

"Keep up, children. We must not let him get away," he said. "I need him still to be in earshot, when I get to…here."

He stopped on the top of a rock, some six feet above the rest of the path.

"Smagala!" he called.

There was no reply.

"Smagala. One moment. I have one more recording that might interest you."

He bent down and carefully removed an MP3 player from his bag. He switched on a small torch and waited for Smagala to walk back, which he did, of course, and as he reached up to take the player from the Vicar's hand, there was a bright flash from in the trees.

"That will be John, Elsa's bodyguard…"

The Vicar looked at me.

"… the official photographer…"

And then back at Smagala

"Taking a photograph of a proud and imperious Vicar staring dismissively at a scared Smagala, who is grovelling at his feet."

"This is ridiculous," Smagala shouted. "I would never grovel to you."

"But the camera never lies," The Vicar answered. "And you should listen to that recording. The quality is not great, you understand, but people will be able to make it out."

"More of your English humour. This MP3 player doesn't even have a microphone. You can't record with it. You have to download music from a computer."

"There is that," The Vicar said calmly. "Which is why, in the very best tradition of TV chefs, it contains an interview that I prepared earlier. Before you even reached the island. I am afraid it makes you seem a very weak pathetic man, who cries like a woman and grovels on his hands and knees. Pornographic images may not damage your reputation, but I fear, in your macho world, this would utterly destroy it."

"This is rubbish."

"Is it? You should listen. Most compelling. The more you deny it, the more believable it will seem. People know that I have some indiscrete photographs of you, because, as the saying goes, they read all about it in the papers. They will hear the tape recording of you grovelling before me, asking me to return the footage. We even have the photographs to prove it. What was it that you said? Ah yes, I remember. 'It is not the truth, but people's perception of the truth that matters.'

The Vicar turned to walk away. Smagala grabbed at the Vicar legs and the camera flashed again. I have seen the picture. I know he was trying to pull the Vicar off the rock, but it looks for all the world as if he was holding onto his legs trying to kiss his feet.

"The next step is up to you. You can print a full apology in your next newsletter or I will expose you as a weak and pathetic man."

He glared angrily at Smagala.

"And never, *ever* mess with my wife."

A bodyguard appeared behind Smagala.

"And therefore this proverbe is said full sooth
  He will not live well that evil dooth
  A beguiler shall himself beguiled be."

"Thank you, John. I think we can wipe this smegma off the island now. Time perhaps to crack open those fine bottles of Champagne I so skilfully snaffled on the flight over here."

OK. Not so half-baked, after all.

THE LAST SIX PAGES

"YOU CAN'T STOP THERE, PUNK." DONBLEDORE PASSED the wine list to the Vicar. "What happened next? You haven't explained all that stuff about the Orange Eyebrow."

"Ahhhh…right," I mumbled. "I was hoping to miss that bit out. It's pretty embarrassing. It was a long while ago, and look how responsible I've now become."

I held up my hands to show my napkin stylishly shoved into the collar of my T shirt, and my new trousers, which, let's face it, had 'responsible' written all over them (except for an annoying tomatoey splodge on my right thigh).

"There is only one mistake, my dear Punk. Not to learn from your mistakes," The Vicar intoned, immaculate, as ever, with his starched white collarless shirt and black leather waistcoat. "I am sure that the Orange Eyebrow taught you something."

He pulled a paper tissue out of his pocket, dipped it in his water glass, and handed it to me.

"Now are you going to tell Donbledore the end of the story or not?" He put down the wine list. "An extraordinary Woodward Canyon Cabernet awaits you once you have finished."

"Well get ordering," I said. "There's not much left to tell…"

I was interrupted by the sound of *'Roxanne'* coming from my pocket. It took a while to make the connection: Roxanne, Ringtone, Mobile phone. You know how it is. Or perhaps you don't. It was Sean Fitzpatrick (familiar to all readers of the first Chronicle as our f***ing Irish f***ing spy at f***ing Virgin f***ing Records). His language in his opening sentences was sufficiently fruity for me to guess that this was not a call that the Blue Rinse Brigade on the next table would want to hear.

"Later, Sean. I'm in a restaurant."

I rang off before he could argue. Donbledore was still waiting for his story.

"It all resolved after MIDEM," I explained "on the flight from Nice back to London. Nothing as dramatic as the Hijack announcement on the way out, but still pretty scarydelic. I had the window seat, and the Vicar was sleeping beside me on the aisle, with his neck cushion and eye mask, when I saw him coming down the aisle towards me."

"Like who?" Donbledore asked.

"The bloody Orange Eyebrow, of course."

"Language, Punk," chided the Vicar.

"Sorry. The Not so bloody Orange Eyebrow. And he was big. He almost had to turn sideways to squeeze down the aisle. You know that joke about only going through the turnstile sideways, unless you are going to Bangcock. No? Sorry, I am ruining my own dramatic tension. Picture this vast man, all tattoos and metal protrusions walking towards me, reaching inside his leather coat to take out a small bag. He held it in his hand. It was about the size of video camera…"

"I am not sure you should be mentioning video cameras, given your current success rate," The Vicar mocked.

"Maybe not," I admitted. "Anyway, I thought the bag might contain the camera he'd swiped off me. But then it could be a gun. He walked really slowly towards us, as if he was deliberately trying to scare me. I tried to warn the

Vicar, but he was impossible to wake. And he had his legs jammed in such a way that I couldn't get out of my seat. All the while the Orange Eyebrow came closer and closer."

"Yeah, yeah. I think we get that bit. What happened next." Donbledore swilled the wine around the bottom of his glass.

"Well…"

I felt my mobile phone vibrating in my crutch. The mad Irishman again.

"Not now," I hissed. "Give me five minutes." And I shoved him back between my legs. Best place for him. (That's not quite the right joke, is it? Sounds a bit homoerotic. And it's not that sort of story. At least I don't think it is).

"Where was I?"

"The Orange Eyebrow came closer and closer."

"Oh yes. Well, I just froze. He smiled at me a bit like Jaws in the Bond movies before he kills someone, walked up to me, smiled again, and dropped the bag in my lap."

"And?"

"Yeah. Well. The Vicar said something to me like 'I think you had better open it'. I slowly unzipped the bag, and it was stuffed…with paper."

"Paper?" Donbledore repeated.

"Yes. Telephone bills, and internet accounts," The Vicar explained. "Or to be more specific, my telephone bills, and my internet accounts on which Punk, my overpaid, over-sexed, and much overrated assistant, had been running up huge costs."

He looked at me.

"Although, Punk had denied it every time I asked him."

"Well, I had made a few calls," I muttered. "And The Vicar might have asked me about the bill a couple of times… Well, three or four times." I corrected myself as I saw The

Vicar's eyes flash.

"A few calls!" He exploded. "£975.43 worth of calls to be precise. And 95% were sex chat lines. Riotous Rita seems to have been a particular favourite. I asked for an itemized billing. I only hope that Punk got value for money."

"Well, you've got to give them a go," I blushed, hoping the tips of my ears were not going red. So I was rumbled by the Vicar. It's happened to people far smarter than me.

"Yeah. But I still don't get how all this stuff got into the hands of this Orange Eyebrow character," Donbledore was asking. "And what about those messages? All those mysterious rhymes?"

"Hardly Shakespeare!" The Vicar laughed. "My favourite was the one on the automatic toilet. How did it end?
'There's one more conference for the Vicar
I'll be waiting in the Tickler'."

"So who sent them?" Don asked.

"Oh come on, Don. Not you too. Me, of course," The Vicar bragged. "Check the story again. It stares you in the face. I was the only person that Punk did not suspect, and yet I was the only person who could have done it. I spied this giant of a man with an orange eyebrow wandering around MIDEM, and invented my own latter day Scarlet Pimpernel. The things I am willing to do just to keep my bumbling side kick amused."

'Bumbling side kick amused'?! 'Hard working arse licker confused' more like. I've written the whole of the story of the Orange Eyebrow, and I am still not quite sure I understand what went on.

His Vicarious Deviousness, the Lord High Confuser, was in no mood to explain further. He was eyeing up the dessert trolley.

"Now. Will either of you join me in sampling these little chocolate beasts of delight?"

My crutch vibrator went off again. This time, I got up and walked away from the table.

"Well are you going to *fucking* well talk to me or not?" Sean screamed.

"Sssh, Sean" I whispered. "I am in a fancy restaurant in Seattle".

"You've got more than fancy *fucking* restaurants to worry about," he ranted. "You'll never believe what I just heard. Am I right in thinking you're in the studio with Alex from the Glammer Twins?"

"Yeah. Well, we're only in pre-production at the moment. You know, so-ngwri-ting," I sang down the phone. "We move into the studio next week. Bob's barn."

"You'll be lucky if there is a *fucking* next week. Ever met that wanker Ruiz Rafael? Produces one *fucking* dance hit, and suddenly he's made head of A&R at Vagina *fucking* Records?"

(Oops! Perhaps I had better apologize for all these F bombs. I know they distress my great auntie. And it's 'Regina' Records not 'Vagina', obviously).

"...Well, Crapface, guess what I just *fucking* overheard," Sean went on, as if my auntie's feelings didn't matter a bit. "Ruiz *fucking* Rafael trying to get your golden boy, Alex, turfed out onto the street. Bye bye record contract. Bye bye working in studios with the Vicar. That's what! Do you know he's already fired Brad, who's only looked after Alex and the Glammer Twins for the last three *fucking* years?"

"Nope."

"Oh yes. Skewered Brad right and proper. Given him the fucking old anal sniperooni. And he was having a huge great fucking argument with Bendy Wendy saying that your boy 'Tosser Alex' ought to go too."

"Bendy Wendy?" I asked.

"Wendy Airhole? the big squeeze? Head of Regina Records? The only friend you've got? I thought they were actually going to start hitting each other. Handbags at dawn. Believe me, it's pretty fucking bleak for Alex. Although after his recent fucking sales figures. I think I'd be tempted to throw him off myself. 100 Cds! In the whole of the fucking US! That must be an all time record."

"The figures might be wrong."

"Wrong, my arse. He's just lucky that Wendy, managed to change Ruiz's mind. This time. He's hanging by a fucking thread. Although…" he paused. "Is anyone else listening to this?"

"No."

"Well, then you're lucky I'm around. Because I might just be able to help you."

"Do you want to talk to The Vicar?"

"No. no. Far too ethical for what I'm going to fucking recommend. Look, there's a rumour going round, and you didn't hear this from me, that Ruiz is leaving the label in a couple of months. This is what I would do, if I was you…"

I couldn't believe what I was hearing.

And how do you expect me to do that?" I asked.

"Do you have any imagination?" he said. "I thought you were the guy who wrote all those fucking books?"

Jesus. Here we go again.

THE VICAR
Will Return
In...

Katgirl's Ghost
and the
Disappearing Discs

The **VICAR CHRONICLES** are also available as :

VIDEOBOOKS
(yes, that's films of Punk telling the stories,
while hanging out in studios)

AUDIOBOOKS
(the same thing, but for people who need
to keep their eyes on the road.
Definitely not for sweaty people while jogging)

GRAPHIC NOVELS
Cartoons adventures of The Vicar and Punk (who becomes
a small guy in a silly hat – pretty accurate, really)

SONGBOOK#1
The first album by The Vicar.
Available at major music stores,
assuming there are any left (that's music stores, not albums).
Also available for download.
No thieving, Punksters. Big Brother's watching you.

Further details at www.thevicar.com

The printers have made me add an extra blank page.
Please feel free to use as toilet paper.